SHADOWS AND DREAMS

SHADOWS AND DREAMS

NIGHT & FOG, SANDCRABS & SUN

A novel

OR

Life Liberty and the pursuit of GAMBOLERY

OR

IT NEVER ENDS

by

Joseph Lucilla

Ninety-five percent of the following short meander through the prickly bush of torpidity was written in the spring and summer of 1974, the other five percent was written in bed.

Joseph Lucilla
February, 2011, the year of the rabbit.
And let's hope the coming year
has a somewhat stiffer back bone
than the bushy tailed, long eared rodent.

PROLOGUE

DEAR Mr. and Mrs. America, boys and girls. In this great land of tin-gods, Easter bunnies and deficient heroes with green hair, gaudy make-up and tawdry dresses, let me, but for a moment, intrude upon the darker recesses of your souls long enough to interrupt the maddening, garish dash toward the altar of mammon to impress upon you the coming cataclysmic descent into the darkening, whirling maelstrom.

Dash? Descent? Whirling? No, not another doomsayer. So you say. Nevertheless, wish as you might, verily I say unto you: It's coming; it's coming.

It has been some time now since The Iliad and the Odyssey. You remember: The Greeks? Democracy? Pericles? Socrates? The Greeks were a great people, a lot like the American Indian, great venerators of the land and such. The Acropolis still stands. And the Romans ... hardy people, they. Many accomplishments of note including a plethora of the greatest of historians. We have the National Enquirer, Barbara Walters and Suzy, menial panderers to the public's boorish voyeuristic tastes, and a Thucydides they are not.

Be that as it may, I therefore, since you are not aware, obviously, of your aboriginal habitation of a dinghy listing ten degrees to port, have taken it upon myself the dubious task of recording the "decline and fall" of the American Empire (sic), since said empire conveniently happens to parallel my own.

Having so stated forthwith, I take on this disagreeable chore through no misguided reasons of love, honor, respect, etc., since said notions have long since fallen by the wayside, but rather because of an abiding and lasting concern for justice, to wit: Every common criminal deserves a last chance. Hence, you may consider this little extravaganza your court of last resort.

It has always seemed a dubious matter at best in my thirty some odd, short years of life, why a people who talked such a good game played such a bad one, and subsequently, like the illustriously plumed and embellished hen's ass photo playing the barnyard, I was hit by the stud-cock-robin of wisdom in that nations are much the same as people in that their actual exploits are no match for their verbal acrobatics, and the greater the phonetic gymnastics, the lesser the deed. At present the "good ol' U. S. of A." is number one in the "carnival of prattle."

Given said format, it seemed only a matter of time before discovering that America is and always has been, except for a very brief period in the latter 18th and early 19th centuries, a castrated Texas longhorn steer, imposing but impotent, a tiger without fangs, a bear without claws. In other words, Mister and Madam, you are a cabal of charlatans, a complete and total sham, an orchestration of lunatics waltzing to Mozart in cement shoes. You are a miniscule, iridescent zygote flopping about in the gooey muck of a Satanic, imbecilic, malformed bolt of sperm. The occupants of a biological cesspool, the lodgers of the stink-tank of the universe.

And how, you ask, have I come by these astonishing revelations? Aye, and a good question indeed, me Bucko. But that, painfully, is my vexatious tale. A trail of ignominy bathed in festering ignorance, a veritable fools' paradise swimming in a sea of counterfeit tastes and paralytic sensibilities.

But, you say, "Who knew?" Of course, and nobody knew Hitler was rounding up Jews and Gypsies either. Maybe they thought all that frenetic movement in trucks and boxcars were the winners of "The Gong Show" being transported to idyllic fields in the Bavarian woods?

We have followed the good book only when it has suited our venial ways, so much so that we conveniently explained the enslavement of a whole race of people with the "bringing of Christianity" into their witless, benighted lives, the spirit of Christ into their flagging, empty souls.

Thus spake Zarathustra. Bravo. In one fell swoop you have obstreperously scaled the heights of degradation. You have made God an accomplice in your pathological excursions. Then with the bold effrontery of the thoroughly wicked, you, by the revered forces within the law, decreed them to be only two-thirds of a person as if the other third was squirrel, or rabbit, or possum, or a Tasmanian devil, maybe?

In two hundred short years you have participated in no less than nine wars (count them) including that hyper insanity Viet-Nam, and innumerable minor skirmishes—if they can be so called, such as race wars and labor riots. You hand out jail sentences to pot smokers and pensions to bribe takers. Put Lockheed and Chrysler on the dole, but slash Enrique Rodriquez's food stamps because he has a part-time job shoveling slop at the local landfill.

Nabob's "make money" and with the fickle peculiarities of simpletons are proclaimed civic heroes with all the attendant, meaningless paraphernalia thereof. Judges dispense nonsense clothed in legal mumbo-jumbo masquerading as justice, and are accorded respect reserved only for dead martyrs, and your civil servants have more time off than an aging prostitute. You're stockpiling H bombs faster than bon-bons, and if you fought World War II like you fought the "war on poverty" you'd all now be speaking German. And today you couldn't lick a two-cent stamp.

Washington, Jefferson, Jackson and Lincoln are dead, and so are Hitler, Goering, Goebbels and Himmler. The blackened specter of the latter, however, continues to grandly roam and plunder this terrain unmolested, while the former merely reside restfully between the dusty, curled pages of archaic history ledgers. The spirit of evil gathers strength with each passing day while the ravenous jackal tears away at filthy carrion as one eye ever scans the landscape for warm, fresh, blood-laden flesh and bone.

So, what follows is my life, which is your life. My demise, your demise. Just the average bumpkin looking to have made it as best he could, the impossibility of which equaling that of a tick-ridden water buffalo reciting the Gettysburg address … in Swahili.

So, come along on this short trip through the prickly thorns of the bramble bush. Pull up a chair and adjust the specks; read on, Buck and Bella. This kaleidoscope of tomfoolery is happening now, and to you. Hopefully you may avert the predictable calamity. If not, then your emblazoned star-spangled arse will become just another dust-covered monument in the historical parade, a fit and proper ending for your grievous ways and a suitable target for all the bloomin, feather asses of the world. Ta. Ta.

Regards,
John J. Rosko I, July, 1974, Deceased

P.S. Some time later:

As duly noted I had met my untimely demise in July of 74'. However, needing some time to become accustomed to my present domicile, I also had not begun transposing the record of my earthly carousing until 75' … 79' … 81';

actually I am not entirely sure. Actually I am not entirely sure where I am now, or even what year it is since time is of no consequence … up here … down there … wherever. Similarly, you may not be reading this until '91, or 2001, or 2101, however that last being highly unlikely since the odds of you reading, or eating, or even breathing by 2101 are longer than you can count, if you get my drift.

Have at it, my dears, have at it. Time is short, and amorphous.

* * *

The music box of life can be,
So broad and sweet and sometimes deep.
Soft, sweeping dreams wafting high;
Mud, dirt, green slime slinking through time
Dark, silent shadows flitting behind.
Tinkle over the glossy keys
Skit along the slippery scales.
Play on and on this kinky rhyme
But please to play it on the straight.
Heed not false muttering tearless squalls.
They serving only falsetto soulless strains.
The malodorous living have their daily,
Insipid graveside rituals.
All coming to rest in the drearily endless,
Satanic black hole of banality.
Roll it again but not so quick.
I need some time to learn the tricks.
And if, per chance, this song, I see,
Is but only a bag of fleas.
Be kind to me, do hear my wail.
Slam down the lid.
Pound hard the nails.

* * *

I

IN THE BEGINNING

ONCE upon a time I was born. Not a bad start really, although a traumatic do-dah. All I could mutter after the fateful event was "da" and "blah" no matter what anyone said to me.

One night when I was six or seven, I had overhead Pop say to Mom: "Well, what do you think; shall we give it another try?" To wit, Mom replied: "Why don't we give 'that ol' hole' a rest?"

In the ensuing conversation I subsequently learned it concerned begetting more offspring, wherein it eventually occurred to me that the birth of children must take place much like a tomato plant: dig a hole, place the seed, cover it up, and pray for rain. And why not? In death we are placed in the ground so, we go from whence we came. Later, to my great relief and heterosexual pleasure, I learned there was a bit more to it. It has been since, one of the myths I have delighted in debunking over and over. Because of that conversation and the following enlightenment, I have developed into an incurable iconoclast for no better reason, I am sure, than the pure joy of it all.

The first five years were comparatively uneventful. The usual happened with sickening regularity. At one, my Aunt Tillie, in her exuberance to induce sleep, flipped me backwards over the rocker and cracked my skull. She succeeded; I slept.

At eighteen months, Grams gave me a big, heaping teaspoon of peroxide thinking it was cod liver oil. Did you ever see a little, blue baby with a purple tongue, and two, big, beautiful green eyes bulging out of his head?

At three, another of my gracious aunts locked me in the cellar as a means of teaching me to behave. But I fixed her. While there, I stretched the elastic on her pretty pink panties. I giggled for a week observing her resourceful, but failing efforts, to get her drawers to stay up. She tried string and she tried scotch tape. She should have tried throwing them away. Once even, I could have sworn I saw a pair of suspenders underneath her blouse.

At four, I drove Gramps' pickup into the garage. Not bad you say for a four-year-old? But you see the door was closed at the time. Not much damage was done, a few dents here and there and a bunged-up garage door. A lot of dust, and noise, and smoke though. There was quite a commotion for a while, as you can imagine, and gruffly was I hauled out of the cockpit. I was immediately stripped of my wings and grounded indefinitely. So far as I know, I was the first who ever tried a takeoff without ever having had the benefits of flight training of even the remotest kind.

As happens to most young folk, the time comes when he must participate in the second traumatic event of his life-he is sent off to school. For a five-year-old, going to school in America is like getting hit in the face with a big, wet bag of shit. Any five-year-old, however unimaginative, can think of numerous ways to spend his time, school not being one of them. I attended a parochial school. It certainly was.

I can't remember too much of what went on that first year, and it's just as well. The second is a little clearer. Our Sister was a youngish pudgy-looking sort named Maureen, Sister Maureen. We called her Chlorine. Kids can be cruel. Come to think of it, though, she wasn't too nasty as nuns go, although I and a few other pint-sized demons in the budding, flunked. That's right, flunked. And if you're wondering, "Why flunk a six-year-old?" you got me, mate, but I think it had something to do with stupid—us, and her. Maybe we deserved it, maybe not, but it seems that whatever can be learned in the second grade can be learned eventually anywhere. As I recall those days though, it appears the human species can devise more ways of molesting the ego than one can imagine. The church is dead, the church is dead; long live the church. Nietzsche once said, "God is dead." What I want to know is: "What's in the will?"

The third grade I'd just as soon forget entirely. Nothing happened, and when I say nothing happened, that's just what happened-nothing. Nice way to spend a childhood; spent one whole stinking year in the third grade, and didn't learn a god-damn thing but Hail Mary's.

Yes Virginia, Mary, we're hailing Mary. You remember Mary, the Virgin Mary? Uh, huh, sure, and my Grandmother invented the Atomic bomb.

She claimed she talked with the angels, or, at least one that we know of, for sure, at least. And wouldn't you of had a lot of questions if one appeared and said it was a "messenger from the almighty" and you was named the designated Mother of his son, and he was going to plant a seed in you, and, an-na, an-na, an-na. And wouldn't you have asked the obvious: Why? And do you have any identification? And what precisely is my "Son" supposed to do? And at age 33, they're going to nail his unlucky hiney to a make-shift, wooden cross for all our sins? All this, and heaven too? My, my; looks like I drew the short straw.

And then, the Son. A somewhat delusional soul who took to roaming the countryside speaking in parables, and who had the uncanny ability to be able to hallucinate on cue, and who claimed he was "the King" TO THE ROMANS! TO THE ROMANS? HE WAS THE KING … TO THE ROMANS? One could veritably say, he blabbed himself right up onto that suffering, bloody cross. The seeds of our destiny. Hail Mary.

Halfway through this disaster someone got the bright idea to flunk the whole class for the fall semester. That someone was our fourth grade Sister. Is there no end to this mockery? Somehow the little darling got the perverted notion that if she failed the entire class, it would somehow act to motivate us to better things. God bless America. Little did she know we didn't give one good damn one way or the other. We were ready to flunk fall, winter, spring, summer, mid-summer, mid-fall, or any other concocted semester she cared to pencil in. What did we care? All the grades looked the same to us: catechism, spelling, geography. "Johnny be quiet." "Jimmy, put your feet down." "Mary Jane, you're late." "Peter, stop talking." "Suzy, you stink." We only went for the laughs. In time, Sister Theresa did realize her folly and indeed got rid of us quicker than the runs.

It was also in the fourth grade that my very first love affair bloomed. The object of my affection was a melon-faced, little snipe named Ginny Bingo. I don't know where she got a name like Bingo, she sure wasn't any prize.

We did the usual things kids do at that age. I carried her books home from school, and now and then knocked her in the head with geography. She didn't have a very good sense of direction, and with my child's mind thought she needed "more training." She never did improve, although after a while I noticed she began to walk with a wobble, and I used to try and grab her can now and then. What the hell, it did beat playing solitaire. I never did succeed in getting a good grip on her, and I suppose it was just as well. I don't think it would have looked right, two shitty-pants, nine-year-olds wheeling a baby down the street. When one is nine, a feel here and there suffices, fortunately.

In the fifth grade we had a banger. You know, someone who likes to take a swing upon occasion for the emotional effect it has. Uplifting, like a good belt of firewater. Well, Sister was a swinger, and she'd never even been to fun city. But in all fairness to the dear heart, there were some in that class who could draw out the ire like cow crap draws flies, and might I add, yours truly, upon occasion, could be included in that number.

There was one particularly satanic, little monster with the unlikely name of Goodson, Tommy Goodson, whom we called Blinky because of a pair of the biggest, blackest, bug-eyes you ever saw, and with hardly an eyelash, giving him the appearance of someone trying to hold his breath past the count of four hundred and thirty-seven.

Blinky was the practical joker in the class. (He later went on to become a politician.) He would do things like tie your shoelaces together, let the air out of bicycle tires, or glue the pages of your history book together. Blinky was a real joy to have around. One time he put a bunch of stones in the rear hubcaps of his Uncle Pete's 39' Chevy. Uncle kept driving up and down the street with his head stuck out the window trying to catch from where the noise was coming from. All the while, Blinky, with the look of the Angel Gabriel spread across his angelic face, was standing up the street watching innocently. Blinky always had a way of looking like a simpleton, which for him, was a dead giveaway. He must, to this day, still have the scars of a wayward childhood revealed on his scorching red bundezo.

Another time he put two stinking rotten eggs in the bottom drawer of Sister Concepta's desk. That was a rotten kid. All through catechism, spelling, and halfway through geography, the good Sister was smelling, squirming, sniffing, looking behind her, under her, over her. She even began to smell herself. When she finally "got wind" of them, her eyes, like two poison darts, went straight to "you know who."

Slowly, she rose from her chair, casually walked over to Blinky, and as cool as Daniel Boone aiming "ol' Betsy" at a fleeing deer, flung both eggs at Blinky, and Blinky, trying to appear innocent as always, was caught unawares, and so got it right smack in the puss with both barrels. Sister then calmly turned, walked back to her desk, sat down, and reported calmly, "Now class, as I was saying, Rhodesia is part of Africa." What class. I liked her best of all the nuns. She had a lot of balls for a sequestered old maid.

It was about this time that I became an altar boy. Sometimes I can't help feeling sorry for non-Catholics who have never had the benefits of such an exhilarating experience. What with the smell of the candles, the organ smothering Gregorian chants, the incense and the close proximity to the holy and near-holy, it forced one, at times, to think of things other than frogs, baseball, and bicycles, and why not? Somehow, just being around all that wax and statuary gave one a feeling for the super natural, sparked the imagination, and as long as one kept a proper perspective about it and understood it for what it was---an attempt to capture and hold the mythological and therefore the feeling of the past enshrined in a marble vault, then it was a useful experience. But if one tries to read into it God and the devil, and heaven and hell, then I'm afraid one might just as well be the flat rock the cow pissed on, for each in his turn will be equally wet.

I should also not fail to mention, that along about this time I made my first acquaintance with the good fathers. You know, priests. Ah, yes, the holy of holiest; Lord, bless us all. . . . .

Our pastor was a crusty old bird named Keroli. Now Father was an old Sicilian who smoked the stinkingest stogies west of Martha's Vineyard. They smelled like some old deadwood that a pack of wild hounds had jointly converged upon in revenge. Between his bad teeth, the cee-gars, and a decided affinity for the wild grape, his breath smelled like the dungeon of, one, Edmond Dantes. When one dallied to Father for confession, one always, at the time of receiving penance, had to fight back the urge to blurt out, "Please, Father, enough already! My penance was coming here." Long before I learned anything of the law I knew what double jeopardy was.

Father, having said fondness for the grape in a form other than that observed on the vine, liked for you when serving his mass, to empty the wine cruet to the dregs. He didn't give one, good wit about the water, only that much necessary to satisfy the laws of the church sufficed. But the red . . . ah, yes, the red. That's where the ram hit the rhubarb. And, we altar boys, being hep to the dude, well, it made for some interesting situations.

On one occasion in particular, one Franky, the pimp and myself were serving the seven o'clock mass. Franky wasn't really a pimp. We were only ten at the time and in the pre-pimp stage. We called him that because he had a mole on his left cheek which looked like a pimple, so naturally we called him "the pimp."

Anyhow, either because of the early hour, or Franky didn't get enough sleep the night before, whichever, Franky was feeling unusually brave that morning, a trait the little pimple did not ordinarily exhibit, he always being the first to run for cover at the first shot. Franky had an amazing sense of self-preservation. Frankie's a lawyer today.

When Father came over the second time near the end of the mass for his refreshment, Franky decided to "play stupid," a feat for which he was not entirely unequipped, and so lifted the jigger before emptying all of its contents.

Father naturally, immediately began to panic, and jabbed Franky in the stomach with the chalice, both as an indicator of his irritation and a warning. Franky, not paying any attention, turned as if to put the cruet down, and Father, faced with the mortifying thought of his going without breakfast, quickly grabbed Franky by his cassock, pulled him close against the chalice, and as cold as Satan himself, admonished, "Poura, you dumma kid." Franky poured, and to this day I don't think realizes how close he came to getting a holy cruet stuck up his elevated arse.

The good Father was also famous for his Sunday sermons. He would climb up on the pulpit, give the Holy Gospel as according to whomever, and immediately go into the "special collection" pitch. There was always a "special, collection," either for His Royal eminence, or the Holy Father, or the bishop, the war orphan's fund, homeless prostitutes, unwed mothers, juvenile delinquents, you name it. Funny thing, with all the help these folk were getting, how come they're all still with us? I always wondered how anything as frequent as once a week could be referred to as special. I thought what made it special was its infrequency due to its uncommon nature which was what made it infrequent in the first place. But what do I know, I'm just your basic, average, 20th century American, who happens to think our future is behind us, and the worst thing that could ever have happened was winning the Revolutionary War.

The collections had all the earmarks of a con game: take from the poor to give to the poor. The church is practicing a form of taxation. Like the state, it takes from the people to give back to the people, and like the state, those who need it the most, get it the least. I wonder if it has ever occurred to anyone that the poor are poor because there are the rich, and there are the rich because they keep taking from the poor. It's called free enterprise; of course---free for them, and what an enterprise. At the carnival it's played with three shells and a pea, and it's called a shell game. The barker should be running the country; I think he is.

Christ said, "It is easier for a camel to pass through the eye of a needle than for a rich man to enter the gates of heaven." There is something amiss. If I were a rich Christian, I would lose no time in giving away all of my goods, for I have never yet heard, or seen, a camel pass through the eye of a needle.

Wondrous things, words. Like morality, they can be adhered to, or not, depending on the convenience of the moment. By the way, every four years Father donated to himself a big, black shiny new Chrysler, by holy decree I guess. That covers all the bases. He was a hell of a guy, Father. None of that "poverty is good for the soul' crappola for him. He sure knew how to live it up. Long live the church. Hallelujah.

Our Sister in the sixth grade was a namby-pamby. Sister Cleofa cried a lot. She cried on rainy days; she cried on sunny days. Sister was the town crier. Why did she cry? Who knows? Maybe it was her glands. She sure had a set. The damn things were working overtime.

In that same class, as luck would have it, if that's what it was, were three Sisters of the lay variety---Italians, Neapolitans, I think, and only recently removed from their former place of residence by maybe . . . six-months?

These darling young ladies appeared to be only three months apart in age, and were inseparable. It was a mystery how they got into this country since we were at war with Italy at the time, such as it was, and nations don't usually accept DP's from those being called "naughty-naughty." They must have been smuggled into the country in rotting cheese crates because they smelled like old provolone. The Sisters were fond of Sister Cleofa. Sister Cleofa was fond of the Sisters. It was a regular mutual admiration society. Whenever one saw Sister, one also saw the "three stooges."

One morning, in the middle of history, I think it was the second voyage of Columbus, one, Jimmy Piccone flung an eraser at Rocky Brenda, missed, and instead hit Sister right in her "Glory Bee's to the Father." Well, you never saw such a scene after that. Sister didn't know what to do first, drop her beads or a bucket of tears. But not for long because, alas, the Sisters to the rescue. Straightaway did they rush to her and immediately begin, "Sister this," and "Sister that" until all four of them were knee-deep in the briny stuff. Such watery events occurred on a regular basis. It turned out to be the dampest nine months of my life. In that class I always felt like my pants were wet.

Within this time frame, Mom began to have ailments, and so did what people usually do when they're ailing---go to a doctor. Uh, huh. The first 'medicine man' Mom saw asked her how many children she had.

"Three," answered Mom in her innocence.

"Okay, it's nerves, Mrs. Rosko. Here, take a blue pill three times a day, a red one twice a day, and a green one if the other two make you wheezy."

"Okay, Doc," obeyed Mom, agreeably.

Well, Mom hassled with this sorcerer for a couple of months until finally realizing either he was going to put her in an early grave, or she was going to put him in one, and so decided to cut the cord.

Off she went, none too merrily, hunting for another ogre. She found one. (Eess not to deefeecult.) Same setting, same story. "Take one of these, two of these, blah, blah, blah."

"Okay, Doc, just like you say."

Same ending. The pain persisted, so off she went, again. Found another, and the mindless scene was repeated yet another time. Well, this insane business continued for twelve months until the war ended and a new "el docko" came to town.

Mom was the first in line the day he opened his doors for business. As you can imagine, by this time Mom was beside herself.

Streaking into his office, she introduced herself thusly: "Doctor so and so. my name is Rosko, and if your going to ask me how many damn kids I have and give me a bunch of tranquilizers, say it quick so I can leave, saving you time and me money, and no hard feelings. I'm tired of the dam run-around . . . please . . . . . .

He didn't. As a matter of fact, he was the only one who did a little more than thump on her back and jam a stick down her throat while she coughed. He actually gave Mom a complete physical, and guess what? Yep, that's right; the nerves were just fine, strangely enough, considering what some were about the previous year. Mom's kidneys, though, were acting as if they were out on loan from another, couldn't wait to get back to same, and so began to participate in treasonous activities. In other words they were infected, one way or another.

Doctor Billson put Mom to bed for two weeks and came every other day to give her a penicillin shot. He treated Mom like a lady, which came as no great surprise to me. It was heartwarming. As a matter of fact, Doctor Belson was one of the few of his trade who seemed to take the oath seriously. You know the one about relieving the suffering of mankind. Come to think of it, when shaking Doctor Belson's hand, his eyes didn't blink assorted fruit like the slots at Vegas.

I was only ten while all this was happening, but I never forgot the runaround Mom got, or the needless pain she was made to endure. And, it wasn't just one of those things that infrequently occur every now and then, either. Many times since, I have been, directly or indirectly, involved with like aberrations, so much so that upon retiring at night, I never fail to offer up a little prayer for the medical profession. Next to priests and politicians, I like doctors' best.

At the time I entered the sixth grade, there came to our parish a priest from the old country who treated the English language with a vengeance, had a sense of humor like a wet dishrag, and was generally infected with a sinister nature, as is usually the case among witch doctors.

Along with these sterling attributes, Father Canoli, as he was called among other things, enjoyed hearing confessions. Father looked upon confession as a kind of tea social. It was his way of keeping in touch, so to speak. I have always regretted not being a priest. All those young chicks coming to lay their lurid tales at the doorstep of the understanding Father. Talk about head starts . . . inside tracks . . . foxes in the hen house. Cripes, the sugar I could have gotten, and all for just a blessing.

Be that as it may, Father, among his more endearing qualities, also had a penchant for handing out long penances, like ten Our Fathers, and ten Hail Mary's, and even a rosary now and then during a full moon. I have always had the impression that about ninety-five percent of all people have missed their calling in life, as witness the past and present state of affairs. Father was definitely one of the ninety-five. It would have been more fitting were he a judge; naturally, the hanging kind.

No doubt his character was intrinsically wound with this inclination to punish. Language is unique in that it explains nothing. As a communicative device it ranks alongside the gurgles of a six-month-old baboon. The Japanese can say 'I' a thousand different ways. It's all foreign. If you have any doubts just sit in any courtroom. After the "where as's" and "parties of the first part" one will come away shaking like a spastic leaf in a hurricane.

There will never be another war ever if all the members of the U.N. are forever forbidden to speak while occupying that august body. Think about it. Therefore, "character" can be taken as it suits your fashion.

Father, as one can imagine, made many enemies among the "little people."

Often was the time we stayed up late trying to think of little tricks to play on the "revered one." Persistence is usually rewarded, one way or the other, and so it was with us.

One bright and sunny Saturday afternoon, ten of us little troopers, like soldiers going into battle, marched in for confession. We had no more intention of confessing than polishing statues, of which there was a considerable number, large and small. The large were reserved for those eminent personages such as the Virgin Mary, who performed the miraculous feat of giving birth without having first given ass; St. Anthony, who could find house keys in the dead of night in the bramble bush; and St. Jude, who could perform miracles, the biggest being his canonization. The smallest were set aside for those not so functional, shall we say, like Francis of Assisi, who talked to the animals, and had the bizarre notion that the church should give to the poor instead of taking from them, and Bernadette, who heard voices other than that of the bishop.

Thus did we all line up nice and proper like good, little Catholic boys outside of Father's cubicle to commence proceedings.

After the person who had been in the left-handed cell came out, a certain "crazy Mary" (We called her crazy because all during the daylight hours she could be seen cleaning the church, dusting, mopping, sweeping the steps.) The priests never asked her to, they already had a janitor. Like I said, she was just nuts. I guess maybe she thought, like the union, she was paying her dues, and like the union, in all probability, would ultimately get just as good a screwing, god or no god.

After crazy Mary left, Peter Capraro went in. Peter was elected for this little escapade. Actually he was glad he was, since there was none better for the job. You see, Peter was the type who liked to win things; it didn't matter what, he just liked winning. You could have said: Hey, Pete; how'd you like a ticket for a nice big dose of clap?" And he'd have chimed enthusiastically, "Yeah, man. Can I have two?" He was that kind of guy.

Slippery Pete entered the "inner sanctum" and shouted loud enough for all the dead saints to hear: "In the name of the Father, and of the Son, and of the Holy Ghost! Bless me, Father, for I have sinned. My last confession was two weeks ago! These are my sins! MY MOTHER'S A BUTCHER, MY FATHER'S A BAKER, AND I'M A LITTLE HOT DOG RUNNING AROUND THE STREET!!!" And with that, crashed out, whence we all made for the door.

Father Canoli also came streaking out as we ran down the cement steps, two this way, two that way, and the "holy one" right behind. He didn't know who to chase first. He'd start left, stop, then right, then left again, and all the while bellowing: "All-a-right! All-a-right! A'ma knowa whoa youa alla ara; youa noa canna foola mea, anna God'sa gonna getta youa alla, evena iff A'ma donta! A'ma tella you alla righta nowa! He'sa gonna punisha yousa boysa!"

Such are the ravings of frustration. Such also was life for little Catholic boys then. Nowadays, kids, instead of having a dope, are shooting it. I think we had all the best of it, and yes, Virginia, the price of eggs has gone up.

* * *

II

WAIT TILL THE SUN SHINES NELLIE

IN the days before credit cards, poor folk took out credit with local establishments based upon one's good word. (It's a sign of the times that the computer's reputation has replaced the persons.) These "bills," as they were commonly known, flourished, and the family Rosko did also, have such an arrangement with the neighborhood confectioner, one Angie Ruperto. Angie sold candy, ice cream, comic books, cigars-you know the usual junk. Pop used it for the cigarettes, Mom, the ice cream, and I, the comics. Angie smoked the cigars.

When I turned nine, I did what every red-blooded American boy did at nine---started smoking. But being only nine, I also had the same predicament every other wastrel at nine had---no bread.

Under the circumstances there were three alternatives available: one, I could steal, but that was quickly ruled out solely because I didn't know how. Two, I could beg, but that also was rapidly removed as a solution because of my regal bearing. Uh-huh. That left only one other: Angie's. Having the bill there I could always go in and lay a little, "My pop wants a pack of Camels," on Ang, and no one would be the wiser. The logic of little children is remarkably uncluttered.

For a few days things didn't go too badly. I kept my habit down, along with the bill. But then the word got around. "Johnny's getting it from Angie's, Johnny's getting' it from Angie's. Okay everybody, to Johnny's."

What could I do, refuse? Never. A Rosko never denies a friend in need, or a gang. Besides, everyone wants to feel needed, don't they? So, off we went marching, merrily, to Angie's every night.

Monday: "My Pop wants a pack of Camels, Ang."

"Okay, John." Tuesday: "A pack of Camels for Pop, Ang."

"Okay, John." Wednesday, likewise. Thursday, same, and Friday, and Saturday, and Sunday. Ta ra, ta ra, ta ra, until the first of the month and a settling of accounts.

Fortunately for me, I was not present when Pop caught sight of the bill, for it is said, "The heavens thundered and the earth shook." Between Pop's puffs and the gangs, the air was filled with smoke. And not a shot was fired.

Pop was cool. He never said a word . . . to me. He said a few to Ang, though. "Ang," he ordered, "when that sawed-off little twerp comes in here, he'd better have cash in hand, hear, or kick his funny, little rump out."

"Okay, Joe," replied Ang. Angie had a remarkable way with dialogue, she never used any.

Angie was pushing fifty, resembled a shriveled up old prune, smelled like stale beer, and always sat on one of those short three-legged stools. She was never known to talk, or move, unnecessarily, and to Ang, most things were unnecessary.

She lived with her mother and a hermitic brother, and the story is told that, on her eighteenth birthday she huffed and she puffed, blew out four candles, dropped her left ovary, and that was the last time Angie exerted herself so.

Gingerly did I, with the confidence born of success, stroll into Angie's one calm and tranquil evening. "Ang," said I boldly, while manfully strolling toward the cigarette rack, "gimme a pack of Camels." Ang never moved a muscle but looked me dead in the eye and brusquely shot back, "You got twenty cents?" (Those were the days.)

"Wud'ya mean?" I countered offendedly. "Put it on the bill."

"Uh, uh," she replied in turn. "No change, no cigarettes."

Ah, hah! So that's it, said I to myself, the game is up, is it. Okay, fine; who needs the damn stuff, anyway? That last was duly answered in jig time. The who of the who's, was you know who.

Did you ever see a nine-year-old go through withdrawal? Scared the hell right out of me. I didn't know what was happening, what with the shaking, and shivering, and sweating. My eyes were all bugged out, and I couldn't eat, sleep, or defecate. Lord, was I a mess.

You've heard of the man with the "golden arm?" Well, I was the sprig with the "nicotine lung." I would have done anything for just one, sweet long drag. Had Mephistopheles appeared in a puff of smoke, I'd have inhaled immediately, and propositioned: "MY SOUL! MY SOUL! A CAMEL FOR MY SOUL!" In time, I recovered; I survived. For what I have yet to learn. It seems mere survival is an end in itself.

* * *

In the east during the 40s, every neighborhood had a poolroom. They were called joints (because that's what they were) and just about everybody who was anybody, or not, hung out in one, my Pop included.

Pop was an extraordinary man and I mention it merely as a matter-of-fact because to a ten-year-old most things are very ordinary.

Honest to a fault and straight as an arrow, I can't recall ever having met anyone quite like him. There have been others with the same qualities, but not to the extent that he possessed them, and that is v-e-r-r-y unusual.

In the particular establishment Pop frequented for many years sat a high-chair, a little, old, ordinary, rickety baby's highchair. Pop, barely being five feet tall and all of one hundred and twenty pounds, fit quite nicely in that chair, and it was assumed by all that it was his province to do with as he chose. Small informal clubs of that nature form a kind of cooperative behavior for the sake of tribal unity. This was part of that behavior. The chair belonged to "little Joe" Rosko. Such was the case until "fat Charlie" Bolle came to town.

No one really knew where Charlie came from; he just kind of arrived unannounced, and made himself to home, which was all right, the boy's being of a peaceable and friendly sort.

Charlie looked like a pig. Charlie talked like a pig. Charlie acted like a pig. Charlie was a pig. As a matter of fact, one had all one could do to keep from blurting out: "Porky! Porky! Porky!" when Charlie came around. Charlie also was a bit of a bully in keeping with his outward demeanor. He stood over six feet and weighed close to two-forty, the bulk of which was fat and beer.

One day, Charlie got it in his head to flop in Pop's chair. Now it is perfectly obvious two people can't sit in a highchair, especially when one of them is "fat Charlie," so Charlie decided Pop had to give up the throne.

"Okay, Shorty," big fat said one day, "let me have it." Now Pop was a lot of things, and a lot of things he wasn't. A coward he wasn't, but he would go out of his way to keep the peace. He was a better man that way, and in keeping with his peaceful ways, gave Charlie the chair, albeit none too merrily.

Charlie, like all bullies, was buoyed by his success, and so continued to play this shoddy game, no doubt thinking he had found an 'easy mark.' Tch, tch. The 'fat Charlie's' of the world feed on that sort of thing like maggots off dead flesh. It's what makes them fat, and grow, and prosper. Charlie was living well.

Well, after a few days of this tomfoolery, Pop realized that Charlie was willing to carry on this humiliation permanently. Actually Pop knew it right from the start, but you can't shoot 'Billy the Kid' before he becomes 'Billy the Kid.' You have to give him his due. A bully's ego never becomes satiated; it's a condition of the sickness.

Charlie, one evening, came strutting in like a peacock in heat, and immediately strolled over to Pop, who was sitting comfortably in the highchair. "Okay, Shorty," commanded Charlie, "let me have it." They never change their tune, this type. The singer and the song are boringly alike. Amazing how we never wised-up to "Herr Adolf" until he <u>had us</u> by the jugular.

Pop rose calmly and asked if Charlie had ever finished high school.

"No, and what the hell you wanna know for, pee wee? You takin' a survey?" Charlie wisecracked.

"Not exactly," intoned Pop assuredly, "but I'm gonna finish your education for ya freeeee," whereupon he slowly picked up the chair as if to move it toward Mr. Sap so he could flop his flabby rump in it, but instead, quicker than a politician's lie, whipped around and flung the chair, cracking Charlie right across his witless skull. Those that were there said the thud made a sound like a rock on a hollow drum, and Charlie fell like he'd been hit with a baby grand.

There was plenty of commotion after that, as you can imagine. Someone called the ambulance, and the cops got into the act. They took Charlie to the hospital, and he was laid up in bed for two weeks with a busted cranium. For a while it was touch and go, but he made it. It's a sign of the times.

Later that night, when Pop was explaining to Mom what had happened, I, in my youthful and impetuous way, blurted out, "But Pop, why did you wait so long to crack him?"

"Son," Pop replied curtly, "manhood is not determined by how many folk you thump on the head." Maybe so, but Pop sure would have been a great teacher. Brief, clear, and to the point.

It must have been a good lesson, for Charlie never again asked Pop for anything. Charlie didn't stay much longer after that. He left like he came, suddenly, quietly, and nobody missed him. Was it so well ordered for all the slovenly of the world.

* * *

As "Our Gang" blew into the seventh grade, "Hairy Mary" was waiting for us. Mary had arms like a blacksmith, and were covered with an unusual amount of hair for a woman, hairy, and fuzzy, and white. One could only wonder what the rest of her looked like as those were the days when one rarely got to see anything but the face, and sometimes the arms of nuns, what with all the robes and stiff collars. I sometimes got the impression they were trying to hide something under all that cloth, the church being the secretive and mysterious fraternity that it is, or maybe trying to smother the sins of the world, standing there with their arms up their sleeves, and that pained expression across their brow. I could see them now: "There goes pride, Sister," wherein a little chigger comes dashing out from underneath.

"Get pride, Sister, get pride."

"There goes lust; come back here, lust. Hah! Take that! And that, you little bugger. Thought you'd get away, did you?"

"There goes greed, Sister! Quick! Quick!"

"Don't fret. I'll get him!" Squash.

Sister Mary having this unusual condition, it naturally followed that eventually we would construct a little doggerel on her behalf. I don't know who made it up. It seemed like it was kind of always there, like the fog on a Scottish moor, just hanging. It went: "Sister Mary was so hairy, her fleece was white as snow, and when she talked, she really squawked, Hairy Mary was so scary." I wonder; Keats wasn't a little Catholic boy, was he?

Sister Mary was in charge of the altar boys. Sister Mary also had a heavy hand, and she liked to use it.

One Friday afternoon after school, as was the customary practice, we had all congregated in church for choir practice. The choir was situated in back, upstairs, where the organ was. Sister usually led the choir in its pained ministrations. No specialists they. With a cross, a string of beads, and a prayer, they were ready to take on the whole world, and did. The Crusades were more than a medieval chapter of history for them.

While we were going through our motions we heard a, "psst, psst," from down below. Sister went over to the railing to see "what for." It sounded like a steam leak but instead turned out to be Benny Cardello, the paper boy. He began to speak in a bit of a shout, but Sister quickly waved him off. It's not nice to blurt so in the house of the Lord. (He sure is a touchy fellow when you think about it.)

The church, like the courts, requires absolute reverence, for how else can they get their work done? Yes, they do have a lot in common: Both the priest and the judge don robes. Both have altars from which to spread the word. Each can wave a menacing finger, when the occasion arises. And each will brook no offense to its authority. The church will burn you in hell in the hereafter; the court will burn you like a piece of toast in the here and now. I think a good hotshot lawyer can bag them all on a good case of arson.

Sister went to see about Benny. First we heard whispers, then loud talking, then roars. After the roars came, Bang! Bang! Bang! Now we knew Benny didn't carry a gun and Sister said she didn't, so it was left to our imagination what all the thunder was about. A few moments later Sister came back up, alone.

The next morning I saw Benny and his nose was rearranged. Some of it was pointing east and some west. I didn't think he boxed in his sleep so I asked him, "How come the overnight surgery?" Benny said all he did was ask Sister Mary if he could be excused from choir practice because Friday was collection day and he had to get an early start. Sister said, "God came before the dam papers." (They can be colorful. . . .) Benny said he would be glad to skip the route if God would reimburse him, and that's when Sister made like Joe Louis and rerouted his nose. Needless to say, after that, Benny retreated from the altar boy scene. Sister lost more candle-carriers that way.

Benny's a judge now, and I am told, one with a penchant for "throwing the book around." Apparently that minor skirmish in church that day dislocated more than his nose. And so it goes. With trepidation did we pass through grade seven.

In the eighth we were cursed with a mousy little thing named Christina. Sister Christina was fond of announcing how "Jesus was her first and only love." She never knew what an endless source of humor she was to us all. We wondered what it was like to be in love with a two thousand-year-old corpse. We wondered if she had something going for her nobody else had, as we figured that a dead love can be a fortune cheaper than a live one. We sure hated to miss out on something good.

Sister was short, thin, and beady-eyed, Sister was. She never laughed, or even smiled, that I recall, and always spent extra time on catechism. She reminded me of Mussolini the way she used to stand in front of the class with her feet spread and hands gripping the cord binding her waist, peering down at us like a chicken hawk with those tiny, black eyes. Nevertheless, with all that going against her, she wasn't a bad-looking broad. It often occurred to me what Sister needed most was a good screwing . . . to get her mind off the dead, and such. But, then . . . . .

Did she need help? Probably, but somehow one can come to respect a Christina much easier than a 'Jack' who instantly whirls onto an analyst's couch every time an unusual thought comes upon him. Sister was strung-out pretty good, but Sister, in her fashion, was a woman. Is it any wonder we won the Second World War? Today we couldn't beat a drum in the Rose Bowl parade.

That year, for Halloween, we wanted to do something different besides the usual nonsense. We sat around half the night trying to think of something worth the effort, and, as expected, Blinky Goodson picked a winner. "Hey, I got it." he shouted with glee. "Let's put a bag of shit in the mailbox." We all looked at each other as if to say, "Now why didn't I think of that?"

By unanimous vote we all agreed it was a stinker, and we'd do it. There was only one problem: where were we going to get the goods? It was too late for a physic, and no one was going to volunteer for an enema, not even Petey Capraro. Finally, we decided one of us was simply going to have to "come up with the stuff," so to speak, so we grabbed a bunch of old newspapers, went in the alley behind the church, dropped our pants, and began grunting and snorting.

What a sight that must have been: ten little brats all lined up mooning trying to crap on cue. "Okay, everybody, nowa, one, ana twoa, ana threeea, uhhhhhhh!" It was hopeless. We tried, but nature, and the law of averages was stacked against us. We were ready to give the whole damn thing up for another year when Franky "the pimp" shouts: "The River! The friggin' river!"

"The river?" we all chimed in unison. "What about the river? We're looking for shit, not fish."

Franky wasn't too bright, but it was his kind that would think of the river. It was the illogically, logical place. Everything, and I mean everything, was dumped in the river. It was the last place anyone looked when he couldn't find something anywhere else. If it wasn't in the river, it just wasn't around.

We snared a shovel and tramped down. I've heard of duck hunting, and deer hunting, and rabbit hunting and even grunion hunting, but never turd hunting. A thing like that could start a fad: "Hey, Sam, wud'ya gonna do this weekend?"

"Oh, I thought I'd do a little turd hunting. Caught a big one last week. Almost got away, too. Got it stuffed and mounted in the trophy room, over the mantle, right next to the moose head. The misses says it sets things off right nice, it does."

The river smelled real bad . . . what else? And our ballpark, which housed a double A minor league baseball team, was situated right next to it. The stands behind home plate were closest to the river and were known as "whiff alley." They were always empty. Everyone tried to get seats in the bleachers and work their way around from there. It must have been the only baseball park in the country with the box seats in center field. Whenever somebody struck out, the chant would go up: "El Stinko! El stinko! Stick'im in whiff alley!"

When one was planning to attend a game, the weather report was crucial, especially wind direction. If it was coming from the south you were a dead duck. Many were the time the wind was right before the game, but along about the fifth inning it shifted. When it did, there was a mad dash for the hot-dog stand . . . one had to get it down quick. You just couldn't eat a dog with that breezing your way. I saw more fights start in the hot-dog line.

As soon as we got down there we realized it wasn't going to be as easy as we thought. It was pitch dark, and we needed a net, not a shovel.

We caught a lot of things that night: shoes, sticks, weeds, cans, rubber tubes, bottles, hats, and dead fish. When we snagged a pair of drawers somebody hollered, "We're gettin' close!" And so we were.

Not long after we corralled one. It wasn't a bad specimen either. It reached eight inches and had good form and texture. It must have had good luck coming down the river, because it was all still in one piece . . . I think. We tried to gauge its age and guessed in the vicinity of twenty minutes. After inspecting our prize and admiring its worth, we scooped her up, dumped her in the bag, and headed back.

When we got down to the mailbox, Rocky Brenda, who later went on to business school, and was always cognizant of official proprieties, said we ought to address it to somebody. "Yeah," we all agreed. If you're going to mail something, you've got to have an address. We thought the governor should have it, so we wrote on the bag, "To his royal highness, the governor." Children have an exaggerated sense of fairness. We didn't know much about politics, but we did know who deserved what.

We tied the bag with some string, and we even put a stamp on it. There's always one Buck who is never without rubber bands, string, worms, stamps, marbles, and like assorted articles. I don't know why; things just are that way. I guess they'd feel naked otherwise.

All would have been for naught if we couldn't witness the pick-up, so the next morning, we all gathered across the street from the box, pretending to be waiting for the bus. We watched intently as our friendly neighborhood mailman approached the scene.

He opened the box and the little brown bag must have caught his eye because it was the first thing he went for. Picking it up like one would pick up a rabbit by its ears; he held it out in front of him, looking at it curiously. He read the address, put it down, undid the string, and suspiciously peered in. Immediately he jerked his head back and swore. As he did so, he saw us staring. We quietly eye-balled each other for a few seconds before I began to feel like a German spy in one of those World War II cloak-and-dagger movies. We had all we could do to keep our composure when suddenly he jumped up, angrily shaking a finger at us, and boomed, "You fuckin' lousy kids!" (Such language from a role model.)

We looked at each other innocently. "Who, us? He can't mean us?"

"Yes, youse, youse!"

We couldn't hold it any longer. We all burst out laughing and ran like hell. At such times the legs have a mind of their own.

In school, one of "our gang" who hadn't made the first show, asked, "Did he take it?"

"Nah," Blinky answered, as he rubbed his snotty nose, and hitched up his baggy pants.

"Why not?"

"There wasn't enough stamps on it."

In the spring, dear Sister came down with an ailment, and the principal, Sister Constance, substituted for a few days. Sister Constance was constantly a pain right in the ol' boondoggle, A-N-D she disliked children. Sister was a shining example of the Peter Principle, and belonged neither in teaching, or administration; she belonged in an asylum.

During catechism one morning, she spoke of having disowned a brother because he had the temerity, not to speak of treachery, to marry a Protestant. Sister liked to impress upon us the superiority of the Catholic religion over all others. Did it ever occur to the religious vulgarians, that the spiritual is a matter of the heart, and not the mind, wherein particular sects would be rendered obsolete?

At the time, being of a young and immature disposition, I was a bit puzzled, for I failed to see what her little story had to do with religion, or morality. I sensed something awry though, but wasn't able to make the connection until later when I got out into the big, bad world, and heard descriptively, delightful little terms like, 'nigger,' 'kike,' 'spick,' and 'wop,' and it hit me: "So, that's how the flower grows." Sister ended each class with; you guessed it, the sign of the cross.

Sister sent five of us to the blackboard one day, I being one of the five, to exhibit our algebra problems. We did, and mine was wrong. I didn't want to disappoint anyone. We were supposed to check them also. I didn't, and when Sister got to it, she said, "Master John, you didn't check your problem." She said it kind of nasty like.

At thirteen, one doesn't like to be pointed out as a dunce among his peers, and Sister had the longest pointer in town. Knowing Sister, I knew she would never be satisfied with mere identification; she was preparing to drag me through the mud, so I threw a left-hook at her and caught her off guard. I replied above my years: "What the hell I gotta check it for? If it's right, I'm wasting my time, and if it's wrong, I can't do nothing about it anyway."

Sister veritably bristled and damn near sprung clean out of her high-tops. Now we were playing the game on my grounds. "Come up here!" she screeched. If eyes could write books, her's were writing a murder mystery with you know who chained to the rack. I sauntered over to her desk, and stood stiff and straight waiting to receive the traditional slap with the black glove. "Kneel down!" Sister commanded, pointing to one side of her desk.

Now there is no better way to induce subservience in someone than to make him kneel, and the church, in all its wisdom, has known this for centuries. I have no doubt that it is one of the main reasons it has kept the flock in its fold lo these many years. All Sister needed to complete the picture were the black boots, swagger stick and armband.

I knelt, and I knelt, and I knelt. I knelt in the mornings, and I knelt in the afternoons. I knelt for three days. By the end of the second day, Sister began throwing hints like: "I know what I'd do if I were you," and "There's a way of getting out of this." I'm not sure what she was driving at, but what I had in mind brought a tail of twenty years in Attica with it. By the end of the third day I began to see Sister on a broom.

On the fourth day I strolled in casually, and took my seat as if nothing had happened. Sister was stunned. Nothing strikes fear in the heart of the church like a show of defiance, for the next step is out-and-out rebellion, and a cessation of funds.

Before launching into morning prayers, she dogmatically asserted, "I don't believe I mentioned anything about you taking your seat, Master John."

"I'm not kneeling down anymore," I countered. "I didn't kill nobody. I just answered back."

"And you still are, Mister! I think you ought to apologize." "I knelt down for three days, Sister." I pronounced the "Sister" as emphatically as I could. "I done my punishment."

That really sprung her jib. She jumped up, sputtering, "All right, you! I've had just about enough of your insolence! Go see Father Keroli!"

Well, well, well now . . . go see Father Keroli, is it? She raised the flag; one is never sent to Father, no matter what one does. In all the eight years of association with the holy folk, I never saw anyone, not anyone, sent to the Father. After all, Father is very busy, what with coaching the basketball team, and saying mass and hearing confessions, and running the bingo games, one just doesn't bother Father. So, in effect, Sister was "throwing in the towel."

Sister did have other alternatives, but for reasons known only to her, she never availed herself. She could have taken me aside and talked to me like a human being, and not Genghis Kahn, even though I was a little tike. Kids are people too. I'd have been glad to apologize, even to her. After all, I was a reasonable sort. A little nasty, but reasonable. Or, she could have ignored the whole thing, and no one would have been the wiser. That wouldn't have been such a bad deal for her; she did get her 'piece of meat.' I was three days on that hardwood floor. Besides, for all anyone would have known, we could have worked out a secret deal, or, she could have slugged me, in which case I would have slugged her back, a possibility I am certain that must have crossed her mind. So, in a fit of hysteria at the increasing likelihood of losing total face, she sent me to---the Gestapo.

As I told the Father my sad tale, he amusedly sat in his chair, swinging one leg over the other like a bishop, and puffed on his stogie. Father generally regarded the nuns as a necessary evil. Actually, he said they were a "big pain in the ass." When I finished, he said, "Nowa looka here, mya boya. Yua gotta apologize tua Sister. Yua shuda notta hava talka tu hera data way, yua knowa?"

I saw I was putting the old guy on the spot, so I agreed; yes, I would apologize to the old witch. While I was prepared to kick Sister in the shins, among other places, I knew the matter had to end right here. My involvement was with her, and with no one else. It's one of the afflictions of life; one can never tend to personal matters personally, giving rise to lawyers, cops, courts, judges; laws, politicians, bureaucrats, insurance, and a lot of corruption and unnecessary expense thereof.

I went back and apologized, but it had the stink of Galileo all over it.

Finally, we graduated, and as a present, I got a, uh, well, uh, you know, my first, uh, "stroll in the moonlight?"

I didn't know what I was doing, but it didn't stop me; she said she didn't, either. She said she was a virgin . . . and my grandmother's an Easter egg. Actually, all things being equal, and they never are, we didn't do too bad. Children have a knack of turning the most comical situations into matters of great import, and vice-versa.

It was a mild, browsy summer's eve, and when we got down to the business at hand, a cricket kept chirping in tune with our rhythm. Funny how the smallest things can have an influence. Ever since that night I've never enjoyed it without music, and "God save the Queen" by the Royal Philharmonic really tunes my Stradivarius.

Upon one occasion a few years later, while my love of the moment and I were locked in fond embrace, strains of "The Battle Hymn of the Republic," was mellifluously flowing through the breeze. I had all I could do to keep from rushing out and joining the marines, an imbecilic act ranking alongside that of voting Republican, attending church services, or marching in a "right to life" parade. You know, the 'right-to-lifers?' That's those gentle, loving, god-fearing folk what devoutly say their prayers before commencing to blow your head off for having the temerity to engage in a medically, private, and perfectly legal practice. So much for the constitution; so much for religion.

After the deed was done I felt ashamed. I wonder why? I don't feel that way after eating Rice Krispies. As for Nellie, well, she held up pretty good, but then, why not? Girls don't have any masculinity to prove. She just pulled up her pants, and walked away. I felt like shaking hands.

Nellie married at seventeen, had six kids, became fat and flabby, and in general, led the usual depressing life. An acquaintance of mine, a young lady, once said "It doesn't have to be that way."

"It doesn't," I responded. It doesn't have to snow in winter, either. And the world doesn't have to spin. And the leaves don't have to fall. And when one falls into a pit of vipers, one doesn't have to get bitten." Wait till the sun shines, Nellie.

And so ended childhood. Not a bad childhood, really. As a matter of fact, it was a bargain day at Macy's, a carnival in July, a perpetual circus. But then, youth I-S wasted on the young. I never knew what a time I was having, nor did I ever think of good and bad, or happy and sad. It was just a "ha, ha" and a "ho, ho" "look out, Joe, we got some mo." Youth is wasted on the young, and time on all the rest.

* * *

III

LITTLE MISS MUFFET
SAT ON A TUFFET
EATING HER CURDS AND WHEY
ALONG CAME A SPIDER
AND SAT DOWN BESIDE HER
AND BIT HER RIGHT ON THE LEG

I entered high school in the fourteenth year of my life. It was not for me the joyful experience it was for so many others, mainly because my mind and heart were not united, that being a major and vexing problem for a teen. I had the feelings of a fourteen-year-old, but the mind of a twenty-year-old. Very dee-fee-cult living with two people in one body. I had the desire to do all the inane little things fourteen-year-old's do, but my mind wouldn't let me. It seemed, at times, that my nerves weren't hooked up to my brain, but rather to a pickled specimen soaking in a jar in the biology lab at Duke University.

These were the early fifties, mind you, a time not especially known for exuberance, the days of Ike and Dulles; Sherman Adams and the Vicuna coat; Uncle Milty and Kukla, Fran, and Ollie; and the big hits were "Shake, Rattle and Roll" and "Blueberry Hill," just a cut above "Buttons and Bows" and "How Much is That Doggy in the Window?" It also bred Richard Nixon. Enough said?

It was the childhood of modern society---Conform! Conform! So, it was somewhat peculiar, indeed, downright abnormal for anyone to disdain a D.A. (Duck's Ass, not district attorney, although I do not doubt the likeness.) For those under forty, D.A. was a hairstyle resembling a duck's ass. I might add it looked better on the duck, primarily because it was on his ass where it belonged.

Along with this distinct aberration grew another---the flat-top. Actually, the flat-top and the D.A. were made for each other. Whoever had one had the other,

37

like a whore and V.D. Everyone was prancing around like fairies in a lilac field with the damn things. That is, everyone but a few pre-stage reactionaries who fanatically clung to the crew cut and yours truly, who still parted his hair on one side and not down the back.

At fourteen, not to conform can be traumatic. An adolescent not part of the crowd is a chili bean in a ham sandwich. Uniqueness is not a quality universally admired, and especially so among the young. And so my heart said, "Fuck it." I fucked it. I've never regretted it; rebellion is part of the liberal education.

* * *

I have loved sports all of my life. It's what probably saved me from salvation. I attended the basketball, baseball, and football games, and I always managed to find at least one other as funky as myself to associate. Only one, to be sure. Strange has a smell all its own which can become gamey at times.

I loved baseball the most because it is an art form in a world gone mad, and there weren't any bands, cheerleaders, acrobats, whistles or kazoos blaring in one's ear and generally interfering with the festivities. When I go to a football game I want to see a football game, not a circus.

As a teenager, however, he who likes his hamburger without relish is adjudged weird. To this day, on those rare occasions of masochistic self-indulgence, I'll watch a game, and when one of the participants takes off his helmet, or sits, or stands, or swigs on a drink, and the band breaks out with "Bulla, Bulla," and Mr. America flips Miss America over his shoulders, I feel like I have a bib around my neck and porridge on my face. Verily, I say unto you: We are being had! To be joyful and fun-loving is one thing. To be a live, walking doodle; a noodle and a giddy baboon, now that's something else. . . . . .

The disease must be contagious, for baseball, the game of Ty Cobb and flashing spikes, the burn ball of "The Big Train," and "Smokey Joe Wood," "Pepper Martin" and "the gashouse gang," has now become afflicted. Nowadays, when someone farts, the organist poops four bars of "I've Got Rhythm," or "Blue Monday."

Tis a fickle country we live in, Buck. It invented the Atom bomb and the hula-hoop. Played golf on the moon, and mooned on the golf course. Is it any wonder we now suffer from an advanced case of pollution of various sorts? One can always tell from the stink when the flesh is dead.

In my senior year I tried out for the baseball team. It was a terrible team and the coach was desperate for players, and if there was a worse one somewhere, he must have been hiding in Rip Van Winkle's cave. I couldn't hit, run, field, or throw. You know what they say about such guys? They say, "He's scrappy." Hell, he damn near has to be when you think about it. There's nothing else left. Actually, I wasn't too bad a fielder. I never made more than three errors a game depending on how much action came my way.

To show the depths of despair one can sink to, the coach kept me all through tryouts, even though I only got one hit, and that on the last day. I leave to your imagination what the rest of the team must have been like.

The coach was a character in his own right, so I guess it was only fitting that he have a team to match. Bill Brugger was short and thin with a pot-belly, and was pushing sixty. He wore thick glasses, and always squinted, even at night. It made him always appear to be sniffing, and when in his company, one couldn't help looking around to see if there weren't any dead rats, or such, lying around. Fortunately, the only thing that stunk was us.

Coach was never without his whistle, and when he blew it, everything had to stop instantly, because he was going to give 'instruction.' You could have been in dead center field shagging flies, but when that whistle blew you had to come racing in to gather up his 'pearls of wisdom.'

He was known as Bam Bam Brugger because during the game when we were at bat, he'd swing his fist in the air, and shout: "C'mon now, Bam it! Bam it! Bam it right out there!" Every school in the country should have a coach like the Bammer. It's what youth is all about. We didn't win very many games, but we sure had a lot of laughs.

On the last day of tryouts before final cut, I became as desperate as the Bammer. I batted left-handed, although up to that time the only thing I could do with my left had was scratch my right, and by the holy grace of God, or lousy pitching, which we had in abundance, I GOT A HIT! I quickly turned to see if Bammer had seen what miracle I had wrought. I didn't want to waste it; a starving man will clutch any old, dry bone.

He saw, standing by the bench, staring, with his hands on his hips. Seeming to be in a mild state of shock, he beheld an expression suggesting either: "Is this guy another Ted Williams in late bloom?" or "Just another balloon that bust?" The next day I found out. It was the latter. I was cut. That failure, along with the fact of having no talent, was responsible for killing any chance I might have had of going on to bigger and better things in baseball. But then, that's the way it should be. One shouldn't be given to things he can't do. The bull in the barnyard looks not to waste his wad.

* * *

Whatever degree of sanity I do possess I owe to the fortunate circumstance of having been intimate with the wild, and that as a result of my providential association with my Gramps.

You see, Gramps was a butcher, but being an enterprising sort, he also sold chickens and eggs, and one or two other odds and ends which happened to be in vogue at the time.

Now in those days, folks were accustomed to buying and selling only fresh goods as opposed to frozen. Ah, yes, those w-e-r-e the days; a live chick and a fertile egg. A whole generation has been spawned without the benefit of ever having heard a rooster crow. I knew a young twerp once who thought a Rhode Island Red was a communist living in Providence.

Two or three times a week, Gramps sauntered out into the country to do business with him of the barnyard elements. He would rise at an early hour, about five A.M., so as to be back in time to open shop, around 9:30, give or take a couple of swings of the sundial, and I, during summer vacations, was a frequent and pesky companion of Gramps on these intermittent excursions into the bush. I cannot imagine what manner of beast I would have been were it not for that adventure. It is said that music soothes the savage beast. No doubt and so does the song of a robin perched on a branch, a crow in a cornfield, and a forest breeze; the cool shade, a running brook. I know, Virginia; trite, you say? Of course, but then the basic usually is. Some things never change . . . and don't try to change the truth.

He who has spent a childhood in the city has spent a childhood in chains. The dirt, the stink, the squalor, the noise, the congestion; the monuments of cement and glass fused together squashing the spirit, mutilating it beyond repair. A child who has never had the opportunity and quiet joy of saying, "Good morning, cow," quickly learns to say instead, "Stick'um up, Bub." From, "Move along, Bossy," to "I'm the boss," is one small step indeed.

As Gramps turned seventy he began to feel like it. The life he had lived for so many years, a priceless and well spent life, was coming to an end, and he knew it. Grams had been trying for some time to get him to quit, but he was having none of it. When one had for forty years lived the life one loves, it's not easy to stop cold turkey. Gramps was indeed having a hard time "freezing the bird."

To live one's life under the heel of another is constricting. First in Sicily, a harsh land which for centuries has been sucked dry by other nations as well as its own, where almost everyone is as poor as the hot, dry dirt they try to eke out a living from, and those few who aren't, are not, because they are thieves, as is the case everywhere, plying their trade openly as highwaymen, or sneakily, like greasy-palmed politicians.

And so, like so many others before them, they removed the stones from around their necks, and with their bags filled with cheese and wine (and in their hearts the promise of opportunity), journeyed to the new land to be strangled-American style.

Not knowing the language, the laws, the culture, and hopelessly poor, they were at the mercy of those whom we now fondly refer to as the Great Industrialists, or, in those rare moments of perspicacity, the all-American blood-sucker, Mephistopheles in a vicuna coat. And so they came to labor in the fields, factories, and mines.

Gramps worked first as a section hand for the railroad, then in the coal mines of Colorado. I remember him telling how, except for Sundays, he never saw the sun, and his skin was as white as a ghost's. At the insistence of Grams, who was fearful of becoming a widow before her time, Gramps quit the mines, came east, and drifted into the butcher-boy business, and a life he could live with. Now the time had come to lay it all down . . . suddenly.

I recall the day vividly. He was sitting forlornly on the davenport on the back porch with Pop and two of his closest friends, a shoemaker and a painter, who were trying to persuade him to "give it up." He didn't need much persuading; he could see the makeshift barricades and the flashing red lights.

I was very saddened by the whole matter, being just old enough to understand. Funny thing though, about the young. Everything is experienced momentously, but briefly. Like a comet streaking through space, it burns a swift and straight path only to terminate abruptly like the truth in the halls of Congress. Yes, it hurt me deeply, but nevertheless, that night I was out playing kick the can. It is not meant for the young to dwell on sorrow. It is almost as if the gods, in all their wisdom, reserve the most grievous for a more mature age when it can be felt more profoundly. Childhood is not the stuff of great tragedies. Romeo and Juliet? Even the very greatest can have moments of terrible inadequacy.

With a heave and a shrug, Gramps relinquished. He never met a psychiatrist, but he was a close friend of manhood.

His memory grows with time. It's been over twenty years now since his death, but I remember him like it was yesterday, the round, bald head; the short, squat husky body; the high buckled shoes, and the gray denims with the blue cotton shirt tucked in underneath a pair of flat, wide red suspenders. He had the moist smell of the underside of fresh bark, and went through life with a smile and tongue-in-cheek, never taking anything, including himself, seriously. No doubt that is why he was a joy to be around, and why I loved him like a Rembrandt. Quality lingers on in the soul; his sprightly ghost dances in the attic of my mind. Gramps was a precious and sacred man. Not all the diamonds are in Africa.

* * *

Being a student in the 'roaring fifties' wasn't exactly a Beethoven concerto. Come to think of it, being anything in the fifties wasn't much to toot about. It was a somnambulistic period, although I did have my moments, and being the moribund times that they were, it did force the mind back onto itself, tugging at the imagination. If one didn't have imagination in the fifties, then one was just a whisper in a hollow shell. One was forced, by circumstance, like an only child, to fall back on his own resourcefulness and develop a mental dexterity equal to the moment.

I spent most of my school time in the trade shops. The shops were in the basement. There must be something subliminal about that; when one is having an identity crisis, one attempts at some point to become invisible, anonymous, to merge with the scenery, and so, I isolated myself in the basement amongst the lumber, the whirring machinery, and the pounding noise. An association of, by, and for dummies. As for the administration, well, a good ploy, a very good ploy, indeed. Keep their busy little hands pounding on wood and tin, and they won't be pounding on the principal's door, and then, maybe, his head. Tricky, tricky, tricky.

The instruction in the shops was usually hobbled by the personal eccentricities of the individual teacher. The woodworking instructor, in particular, was a short, bullish, hard-looking man with the air of an SS man. No matter where one was in the room, one always had the feeling Mr. Hingle had at least one eye on him, usually the green one in the middle of his forehead.

Old man Hingle had one special oddity concerning the English language which he delighted in exercising. When asking permission to use any of the various machines, one had to say, "May I" not "Can I." When first put upon with this shoddy game, one tended to take it literally, so the conversation would go something like: "Mr. Hingle, can I use the band saw?" Whereupon he would give an icy stare as if you had just stepped on his kumquat and reply caustically: "I don't know, can you?" And then you'd say "Well, I think I can." And he'd say: "Well, maybe you can, and maybe you can't." And you'd say: "I don't see why not," until finally one felt like bellowing: "AIN'T THERE NOBODY AROUND HERE WHO AIN'T WACKY?" Eventually one would catch on, and say: "M-A-Y I use the band saw?" And Hingle, with nary a flicker of a smile across his broad, flat, Anglo-Teutonic face, would reply condescendingly: "Yes, you may." Whoopee! Suffice to say, one learned neither carpentry nor grammar in that class.

During the summer of my fifteenth year I was sent to live on a farm thinking it to be a nice kind of an experience. Ah, the folly of youth. What a disaster. It was just my luck the particular hayseed in question had none of the good Puritan graces, but all of the bad, meaning, he, (I) worked from sunup to sunset. And again, and again, and again.

It was a hundred-and-fifty acre dairy farm and what could have been a useful experience turned out, instead, to be only a hot summer.

I didn't mind the work as much as I did Mr. Martin's attitude. He was an old codger who valued absolutely nothing but work, money, and religion, in that order. Logical. If one works hard he will be rewarded, in cash, and then he can thank the Lord. Religion reduced to a financial proposition. Mr. Martin's idea of a vacation was to stay up one hour later reading the Saturday Evening Post. You remember the Saturday Evening Post?

He rarely laughed, but when he did it was usually when I got kicked by a cow, or fell off the pick-up, or slipped on the cow-puckies, then he would slap his knee, ala Walter Brennan, and exclaim uproariously: "That'll learn ya!" Just what it was I was supposed to learn I never found out. Subsequently, however, it was revealed that education to Mr. Martin consisted of a series of mishaps, which stretched to its logical conclusion meant, if one did not break one's neck first, one would become a Socrates. At the rate I was going, by the time I left the farm I would receive a Ph.D. posthumously.

Except for Mr. Martin, and Mrs. Martin who was an appendage of Mr. Martin, (who said Eve wasn't taken from Adam's rib?) the life did have possibilities. As already mentioned, this was a dairy farm, and dairy farms have lots and lots of milk, right? Hah! So you say. That's what Mr. Martin said, too. Verily was I discouraged from drinking up too much of the profits. At the dinner table he would broach subtle little remarks like: "Why can't you drink coffee like everybody else?" or, "Milk is money. Eat food, save money." And: "What do you think, cows grow on trees?" I never let it deter me, though, so finally Mrs. Martin, darling little broad that she was, stopped putting the creamy stuff on the table altogether. By the way, Mr. and Mrs. Martin never missed Sunday services.

One frisky morning, Mr. Martin and I traveled out to do some wood cutting. He used the wood in the winter for fuel to make maple syrup. The trees were already felled, but we had to saw them into two-foot lengths ready to be split. The particular stump Mr. Martin picked that morning was a good one-and-a-half feet in diameter. I took one long look at it lying there nonchalantly, and immediately became a man. I also got very sick.

Mr. Martin was crowding sixty-five, but was in tip-top shape. I was only fifteen, but in excellent condition myself. Athletically built with not an ounce of fat or superfluous muscle tissue, I was ready to cut down a small forest, or so I thought. He explained as how all we had to do was, "Push, pull; push, pull. Let the saw do the work," he said. I had no quarrel with that. "Just push, pull; push, pull." And so we started. Before long things began to take on the aspect of a dark comedy. I tired in ten minutes or so, and would have liked to stop just for a bit. The old man must have sensed it as he took a quick glance my way, then speeded up. I soon got wise, and being of sound mind and body determined to keep up as long as he. I was only fifteen, I reasoned, but he was no spring chicken either. That made us just about even; it was the classic match-up: youth vs. experience.

We continued: fifteen, twenty, twenty-five minutes. By now my right arm was ready to take a long, long walk, never to return. I could feel the old man slacking off slightly on his push, and the speed of our task grew considerably slower. It was only a question now of who was going to 'drop the blade' first. It had come down to wills. We each knew in our own mind, what the other was about and were determined to win out. Mr. Martin was a bigger kid than I was.

Thirty or forty minutes passed and I was all but ready to give up the ghost. I wondered to myself, how long can the old geezer last? Maybe he's not as tired as I thought. A few more tugs and I keeled over, totally exhausted. Peering over the log, I caught the old man, also flat on his back, wheezing. Hah! It was a draw.

I rolled over and flexed my arm up and down, round and round. I could feel the blood rushing through my veins like a runaway train. Every muscle throbbed, and my bones ached. I sat up after a while and leaned against the object of our affection. The old man did likewise. He looked at me saying, "I bet you're right proud of yourself, aintcha?"

"I would rather have rested once in a while," I answered. I lied. I gained a certain morbid satisfaction out of the senseless, little bit of buffoonery, but I would much rather have been sitting in a limpid pool with six glorious lovelies giving me 'what for'.

Nevertheless, I did think for just one brief moment, I had glimpsed beyond the ordinary. I understood, vaguely, a lizard snatching a bug, a spider sucking a fly, a dolphin cutting through the gleaming, slick surface of the pacific blue in the tropic sun. But how significant is it really? How significant is any of it? I could never put it on any application as part of my education. And if I could, who'd care.

A cow is a beautiful animal. A cow is divine. I think it has to do with the aroma. Being near a cow and smelling the clean pungent smell of cow dung mixed with a little horse manure and chicken feed, and hay, and oats. I would sit in the pasture for long moments, spellbound, watching them. They are the most methodical and contented of creatures, simple but functional. There must be a God of sorts; a cow can't be an accident of time. What accident can create a fourteen-hundred pound beast with a long, swishing tail; horns which seem, on it, to be mere decoration; and a hulking milk bag with four hanging teats? It must be art, impersonal and inanimate, yet breathing with life. A patch of woods, a painting, a stone in a brook, a fungus. A big, beautiful, black Angus pissing on a flat rock. Holy cow.

September finally came, and with mixed emotions, I left. I loved the farm, but not the farmer. May he rest in peace.

He wasn't a bad sort as we usually think of it, but like practically everyone everywhere, was living for all the wrong reasons. He only cared to breathe, and then to eat so he could bring in a crop, so he could make money, so he could breathe again, and eat, and bring in a crop, and on, and on, and on, ad infinitum. Poor old Mr. Martin, he was suffocating in the geometry of life. He thought the shortest distance between two points was a straight line. How sad.

* * *

Late in the spring I met a pretty little thing in English class and we struck up a love affair. At least that's what the poets call it. It was three weeks before we became 'acclimated'. But it wasn't all my fault; I had outside interests.

Strange how one's inhibitions are wiggle-de-giggly at sixteen. It took six days before I felt comfortable saying shit to her. It was another six days before she stopped turning green when I said it, but when she stopped, she stopped. It must have really uncoiled her springs, for she became unduly fond of the word. In time, she embarrassed me; she wore it like a badge. It was always, "Oh, shit this" and "Oh shit that." I began to wonder whether she was contracting a terminal case of the brown tongue. I approached her about it once and she shot back with, "Oh, shit on you!" I never mentioned it again, but I did take pains to see that we stayed out of the public eye. A broad like that can kill a reputation before it ever got started. Now that I recall, I think it made her feel eighteen. Ridiculous; all she had to do was ask, "Johnny, make me feel eighteen." I'd have made her feel thirty-five, with a paunchy husband, a greazy lover, six kids, a dog, a broken screen door, and two Japanese putt-putts in the garage. Communication, it's all a matter of communication.

One evening, while her parents were at the local cinema, (it was Tuesday, dinnerware night), we sat watching Uncle Miltie (everyone watched Uncle Miltie in those days), and just as he got smacked with the powder puff, I hilariously reached over, laughing all the while, and grabbed Carol's leg. Carol wasn't laughing, but neither did she object, until I started 'traveling'. I always did want to see the world . . . which I eventually did.

She resisted, but only as much as she thought necessary consistent with the "nice girl" syndrome prevalent at the time. The underground movement continued. A hand slid under her skirt.

"What do you think your doing?" she inquired matter-of-factly. (There are certain questions at certain times which simply boggle the mind.)

"I lost my hand warmer," I answered.

"I have a feeling it's gone forever," she countered.

"Maybe not; I've been praying to St. Anthony. You know, old Tony? He's the patron saint of lost articles."

"Yeah, well why don't you let him scratch around for it?"

"Saints aren't supposed to do manual labor."

"Too bad; you just lost your best hand." Evidently Carol was prepared to play the game to the hilt. I was in no mood for fencing. I never am when my pistol is loaded and cocked.

"What the hell, Carol," I objected in my sternest voice, "we've been going steady now for three weeks, and we'll probably get married sooner or later, so why all the static?" (Some things never change.)

"Why all the static? Look here, John Rosko, you know as well as I, we ain't supposed to do it till we're married." They were those kinds of times.

"Who says?" I countered forcefully.

"Who says? God says, that's who."

"God? Hell, you don't mess around, do you? You go straight to the top."

"Well, it ain't right."

"It ain't?"

"No, it ain't."

"Well, neither is my left-hand, but I still use it."

"You're real funny. Hah! Hah!"

"Tell me something, Miss Moral Eyes, what if all the priests, and rabbis, and ministers, and ships captains, or whoever, all suddenly took sick and passed on. Then what?"

"We'd just have to go without until some of them were born again, that's what."

"Hah!" And in that laugh the history of man was recorded. That night, after much discussion, semi-discussion, wrestling and what not, I became satisfied. Carol became eighteen. And it doesn't mean a thing, Buck.

* * *

Somewhere in the midst of this gross irrelevancy I acquired part-time employment in a small downtown business establishment, one of those combination jewelry-toaster operations run by the father, one Abey Herskovitz, and his son, Abey Junior. My duties were simple enough: dust off the appliances and decorate the exhibits in the window. For this I was paid the exorbitant fee of fifty-cents an hour.

Abey, like all "good" businessman, had an eye for a buck. Right after New Year's he assigned me to a very delicate and crucial operation: up all the price tags in the window.

Herskovitz enterprises were having a clearing-out sale, so in keeping with the prevailing winds, I was ordered to jack-up all the prices four bucks, and Voila! What was once a waffle iron for $5.98 became, with the swipe of a little green marker, a sale item for $9.98. And, you know, in a week's time the window was cleaned out, along with the public.

Some time, thereafter, in my naive and boyish way, I implored innocently, "But it ain't right, Abe." To wit, Abe replied irritatedly: "Rrite! Rrite! Vas gott tu du vit rrite? Bisniss iss bisniss." And so it is. I had gotten my first taste of the difference between fairyland and the real world. In the real world the good fairy had sharp teeth.

The 'little business' with Abe reminded me of the story Gramps used to tell of buying a horse. The old plodder he owned had died and he needed another for those regular migrations into the hinterlands to gather up his fowl. It was 1925 and Gramps could not, as yet, afford one of those crappy assed-Fords, so he was stuck with the hay burners for a while longer.

Gramps went to a Mr. Klinger whom he had done business with before, on occasion, and who had a stable of horses, among other things. He showed Gramps a string of old nags, each of which looked to have pulled a Wells Fargo stage at one time.

"Gee, Meester Klinger," Gramps said as he scratched his bald top, "Dey donn looka so hot."

"They don't?" answered Klinger, feigning ignorance. "Well hold on a minute, Tony; I got somthin' here that was just brought in from the north just two days ago." Then he disappeared behind the barn. Momentarily he returned with a sprightly looking animal, swishing his tail vigorously, bobbing his head up and down, and looking for all the world like he was ready to run in the Kentucky Derby. Gramps bought him. He plunked down twenty-five bucks, a goodly sum in those days, for old Seabuscuit.

The next morning, bright and early, Gramps enthusiastically strolled into Swifty's stall to awaken him for their mutual labors when he had all he could do just to get him on his feet. It seems old Seabiscuit was just an old sop since good ol' Mr. Klinger had run a game on Gramps. He had sprinkled red pepper on the nag's tail close up to his rear echelon, which explained his short-lived brisk behavior, but now the pepper was "gone with the wind" along with the twenty-five sheckles, and instead of "Seabiscuit," Gramps was stuck with "Soggy Biscuits."

Mister Klinger retired at an early age and moved to Florida. He was given all kinds of awards, citations, and plaques for outstanding and meritorious service to the community. Books are written and movies made about the Mr. Klingers portraying their "clever" horse sense. My Gramps? They told him he couldn't vote because he couldn't read and write. As a matter of fact they told him he was damn lucky just to be in this wonderful country, thank you.

One Saturday morning, while I was making haste for lunch, Abey popped up, and said, "Vait! Vait! Yu can't leef now; ve're to bissy. Joost go arount da korner tu da deleekatessan ont grap a santvitch. Yu kon poot eet onk my beel."

"Okay, Abe," I agreed. "It's all right with me. I like kosher food, too."

I don't know how public it is, but prices in a deli are usually on a par with doctor's fees, meaning, when said fees are observed, one tends to lose one's appetite; however, being a guest of Mr. Herskovitz, no such happening occurred this time. Nevertheless, I only had a pastrami sandwich and a pickle, which came to $2.65, a pretty good kick in the head for a sandwich and a pickle. When I returned, Abey inquired into the precise nature of the damage. I told him. "Two-dollas-siksti-fife!" he boomed. "Vas did yuse du, fok hiss vife?"

"Don't blame me, Abe," I admonished. "I didn't know you Jews were in the habit of screwing each other, too. I thought you only stuck it to the Gentiles."

"Smart dako kit. Yuse to yunk a pup tu bee pissink lok a dok."

Not long after, I asked Abey for a dime raise. Not long after that he threw me out. The great melting pot . . . . .

Eventually, this travesty, like so many others, also ended; we graduated. The night of the ceremony I felt like a barnyard mule, what with that foolish-looking cap perched on my head like a robin's nest. With the tassel swinging back and forth, all I could think of was some great, big-assed horse scatting flies. Inside the auditorium we had to sit and listen to a big-assed horse of another kind, but much less useful, tell how fine and dandy everything and everyone was. In other words, he was a big bull-shiter.

The dude next to me was the only thing keeping me awake, and were it I could be such a wondrous success. He was cutting loose s-o-o-m-e farts; real winners if you get my drift, the kind that could make the dye run in your B.V.D's. I had no idea anyone could get so nervous over a graduation. Finally, to my great relief, both the speaker, and 'Kid Whistler' ran out of wind simultaneously. It turned out to be one of the happiest moments of my life. Thank God for little favors.

The speaker received a standing ovation. He stood there at the podium bowing and waving like the ass-licker that he was. The boob thought we were applauding his speech. Little did he know the cheer was for its ending. I applauded the 'silent one' next to me. I thought he deserved a hand, too.

Everyone kissed, and shook hands, and we all filed outside where we kissed and shook hands some more, mulling about for a half-hour, or so.

I saw a young lady of sorts, whom I was secretly and madly in love with, and she likewise. I corralled her under a tree and we fondly gazed into each other's eyes. We knew we wouldn't be seeing each other anymore, she going off to college, and me just . . . going off. One potato, two potatoes.

As I looked lovingly into her dreamy, blue eyes, I pronounced, soberly: "Millie, you'd better get your nose fixed." And so ended adolescence.

* * *

IV

Jack and Jill went up the hill
To fetch a pail of water
Jack fell down and broke his crown
And Jill came tumbling after
A likely story

AFTER graduation I joined the Navy. (It beat cleaning the tiger cage at the zoo.)

In boot camp one of the first orders of business was the physical, and in the military, one does everything by the numbers. It is all very systematic. We cruised from room to room, and in each a corpsman waited to perform a specific little task. One checked blood pressure, another checked for lice, another took blood, and another X-rayed. All very efficient. Efficiency in a success-oriented society is critical . . . and impossible, the natives being drilled to rewards with minimal effort.

While standing in one of the lines, I noticed a naked little beauty directly in front of me, who didn't look to be more than four-feet-ten to me, and one had to be at least five-feet to participate in this circus. (If Napoleon was an American he never would hare gotten off the farm. There's a lesson in there somewhere.) Casually I said to him, not wanting to offend, "Say, matey? You all don't look like you can measure up to this job." "Wud'ya mean?" he countered, offendedly.

"Well, what I mean is you don't look like no five-feet from here, unless you're standing in a hole."

"Oh, that. Yeah, I ain't, but I talked them into letting me get by at the induction. I only missed by an inch . . . what the hell."

During the course of the ensuing conversation I learned that his name was

Sprinkles, he came from Cincinnati, and most of all, he wanted to be a sailor. It looked like he was going to get his wish, for what it was worth.

Besides being short, he was pudgy, shedding his hair faster than a nervous chickadee, and wore thick glasses. All in all, the most unlikely looking prospect I ever saw, but then, Lincoln looked like the county coroner.

As we inched closer to the front of the line, I heard, "Okay, skin it back, milk it down. All right. Next." We were in the 'short-arm' line.

As Seaman Sprinkles approached the front it was discovered that his 'arm' was sucked up in his sleeve somewhere, and he couldn't seem to produce it. The two corpsmen amusedly looked at one another, then at Sprinkles' smiling at his dilemma, until one finally said, "Look, matey; why don't you come back when you locate it."

Some time later, while waiting in another room, a great roar and a burst of applause issued from the aforementioned chamber. It seems Seaman Sprinkles found a finger on that arm. Happiness is having all your tools in a naked line.

Boot camp is a lot like the suburbs: nothing much happens. You eat, sleep, go to class, and do a lot of drilling. You march during the day, you march during the night. You march to the mess hall, and back from the mess hall. You march to class and back from class. You stand watch, and you do your laundry, and that's all, brother.

There was one particularly loony watch we had to stand twenty-four hours-a-day: the fire watch. What it was, actually, was the water-cooler watch. Through the peculiar workings of the military mind, it was so called because of the remote connection between fire and water. The real purpose behind this buffoonery was to prevent anyone from getting to the water except at prescribed times. This eccentric notion supposedly had something to do with toughening us up. That was an endless source of humor, for our battalion commander was the softest, prettiest-looking lieutenant you ever saw. God, he was gorgeous. Straight out of the Ivy League and the country club. This lovely young man was directly responsible for turning a bunch of guttersnipes into terrorists. A strong wind would have tripped him. Upon such occurrences, one wonders about the 'roll-of-the-dice', and if indeed they aren't being palmed by the inveterate, smiling, slick-haired greezer.

Our first week in camp, one of the saplings decided that the military was not to his liking so dutifully began wetting the bed in an attempt to acquire a medical discharge. He watered his plants three or four nights successively, when it was decided to accommodate him before the camp turned into a marshland. In the meantime, he was put in the base hospital while his papers were being processed.

It seems the clever young man was also a bit simple, for immediately upon entering his new lodgings, he turned off the faucets. He got his discharge: a bad-conduct discharge.

After we heard of the predictable turn of events, I said to my bunk mate, Raymond Hadley, "Ray, don't that seem kind of strange what he did?"

"Wud'ya mean?" he answered.

"You know, the guy wasn't even in a week and he decides he don't like it here. Kind of quick, wasn't it?"

"So? Some folk are fast on their feet."

"Yeah, but nobody came banging on his door to drag him in. If he made a mistake why don't he take his lumps?"

"He is, sweetheart. A BCD ain't exactly a prize." Aye.

Upon leaving boot camp I was sent to electrician's mate school in Illinois. It was winter and it was cold. That's all need be said about that. Sixteen weeks of rudimentary training and reassignment to a destroyer in Newport, Rhode Island.

Unless one is rich, very rich, as some are, Newport is merely a dot on the map. But I liked it for the very simple reason most everyone else doesn't, its meager population. Upon entering my late teens I slowly began to realize that people were not holy, or sacred, or special, or any of the customary adjectives used to conveniently separate them from the lower order of the bestial world. I realized that whatever souls they had were confined to the bottoms of their feet, and upon parting from this temporal wasteland, would turn into three ounces of dust, and that life everlasting was however long three ounces of dust lasts.

That being the case, they couldn't have sent me to a better spot. It was cold, every bit as much as the windy city, but I loved every minute of it as the elements were not blocked out by skyscrapers, and the cold, and the wind, and the ocean, were made for each other. I had been dropped into a small bit of heaven.

The shrill squall of sea gulls scavenging along the shoreline is a welcome sound to ears not accustomed to the nerveless squeal of the electric guitar. A downtown minus subways, crowds, traffic jams, horns, putrid busses, and the endless wail of sirens is an upbeat downtown; a downtown with bells, a Christmas with holly, and mistletoe and snow. Windy days and snappy nights; pea coat weather, bones and blood, and flesh and grubs . . . three, bitty ounces of fly-away dust.

But, alas, it was not to be. In just two short weeks, the Bequik, a World War

II relic, sprung for a world cruise. The second week of April it steamed south heading for Panama with two-hundred gleeful swabbys, and one soon-to-be very sick dog.

Have you ever been seasick? The morning we left Newport the seas were as slick as glass, as the saying goes. I had never been on the ocean before, and I had never seen so large a body of water so calm and still. I marveled at this ponderous silent mass which seemed to be a cover for all the demons waiting below to let loose their furies. The demons never awakened, but the fiends in my belly did.

One, short, hour later I was unsuspectingly sitting on the fantail (that's the rear of the vessel) with another who had come aboard the same time as I, admiring the view, when simultaneously we began to turn green. I said, while still in the mood for conversation, "Eddie, I don't feel so hot." And Eddie said, "You don't look so hot." And I said, "You don't look so hot yourself." And he said, "I don't feel so hot."

"You think maybe we're getting sick?"

"How? I've had rougher rides in a Ford."

"Maybe it's the ocean air."

"The ocean air, shit; I've spent half my life on Jones Beach. That's ocean air."

"You could've fooled me." By this time I noticed Eddie had taken on a somewhat faded, maroon hue. I felt like he looked. "Hey, man," I blurped, "I'm really feeling it now, and I ain't too crazy about it."

"Yeah, me, too. They say there ain't no cure for the damn thing, either. You just have to 'ride it out.' Maybe if we go toward amidships we won't feel it so much."

"Feel what? This god-damn thing ain't quivered in a half hour."

"Well, what the hell we got to lose? Let's go up on the torpedo mounts."

The mounts were directly a-midship; four of them, and they were about as centered as centered can get. We went up and just laid on top of them staring blankly at the bright, cloudless sky. By now my stomach felt like an obstacle course for mad Prussians. A little later I was certain Gargantuan and Pantagruel had joined them in a wild spree Rasputin himself would have been proud of. Presently we jumped up together, ran back down to the fantail, and chucked the morning's goodies over the side.

At chow time, someone said, "Eat crackers, they'll fix youse up." We angled our way down to the mess hall, grabbed a handful of saltines, and split. Just the thought, let alone the smell of food, turned what little was left of my stomach.

We ate the crackers; it did no good whatever. Some minutes later, we, and the crackers, parted company. At regular forty-five minute intervals, or so, we heaved, but our stomachs, having long since been evacuated, just went through the motions. We were sure-shot candidates for a Polaroid, leaning over the side, gagging and choking, and showing nothing for our efforts.

It continued for two days, and, I must say, the crew, to a man, showed an unusual amount of tolerance, for no one prodded us all the while. We had certain duties to perform, but we never did them. It could have been the old work ethic in reverse. If one doesn't work, one doesn't eat, but if one doesn't eat, one doesn't have to work, either. American's certainly are a fair-minded sort. God bless America.

* * *

The sea, the sea, the beautiful sea, huge, ponderous, powerful, mysterious. What secrets lie beneath thy massive, heaving folds. Power, life, knowledge, gracefully flowing in one great eternal wave. Violence, barbarism, murder, the story of man told subliminally, abstractly, in a crush of sea and salt, seaweed, wind and rock. Danger lurking behind the mask of secrecy like a vamp concealing herself behind a black veil waiting, patiently, for the right moment to devour her victim.

One dark starless night somewhere in the China Sea, the USS Hornet lost a plane in a routine take-off. It's always the machine first, then the man. Equipment is hard to replace. Expensive too. Later, someone invariably adds, as an afterthought, "Oh, yeah, we lost a pilot, too."

He had gotten no more than a hundred feet in the air when suddenly his craft took a nose-dive. Neither he nor his machine was ever seen again. The sea, swiftly and impassionedly, nonchalantly claimed another for its own. Whoosh, glub, glub ... whoosh.

It may not be generally known except to those involved, but the officers and crew do not, as a rule, get on too well, and there are always one or two officers who are especially abominable, due, no doubt, to an overdeveloped sense of superiority ... totally unjustified. Anyone who feels himself to be superior simply on the basis of his rank or station automatically becomes disqualified. One can procure all the bright, shiny medals and uniforms he desires at the army-navy surplus.

We had one such ball-buster aboard the Bequik, and his name was Caulfield, Lieutenant George Jerome Caulfield, the gunnery officer.

Lieutenant Caulfield was one of those fellows who would stab you in the back, then return ten minutes later looking for his knife. There wasn't a man-jack on board who ever had a good word for the lieutenant; A-N-D it was justified. In other words, Lieutenant Caulfield was a gen-u-ine prick.

One morning I had gone up to the pantry, that's the officer's mess, to repair their toaster. It was around nine, and the steward who had sent in the call was waiting for me.

Jimmy Roy Jackson was leaning against the bulkhead blowing his nose like he was trying to lose it. Mr. Jackson had a cold. Ordinarily, I would not have taken notice of such a triviality, except we were in the Philippines at the time, in the dead of summer. "Jackson," I asked, "how in the hell did you ever get a cold over here?"

"I dunno, man," he answered ruefully, "it mus be dis lahf."

"Kinda late for that song, ain't it? You been in now … going on fifteen, right?"

"Yeah, ah knows, ah knows. Donn remind me. Ah ain'd so shur ah gon make de twendy. Fahv mo yeahs wid dese mutha-fuckas, an I gon be reddy fo dee funny fahm."

"That bad, huh?"

"Man, yu ain'd gots no idee."

"I can imagine." As we spoke, Caulfield came bounding up to the ward room. He was known to lift a few, now and then, and that morning he looked like he had lifted the whole barrel the night before. He slumped in a chair and bawled into the pantry. "Hey, Jackson? Mix me up a couple eggs."

"Yes, suh," Jackson hollered back, "cumin' raht up, suh."

"Yu sees dat man in deh?" Jackson whispered.

"Caulfield?" I whispered back, in keeping with the mood.

"Yah, gud ol' Leetenant Calfeeld; wunna dese days de leetenant gon cum fes-to-fes wid hiself an da worl gon be rid a wun mo cok-suk-ah."

"Oh, I don't know, man. Dudes like Caulfield seem to hang on forever."

"Man, don say tings lok dat so airly in da mawnin'."

The lieutenant must have been getting restless, because he squalled again. "Jackson, you gonna bullshit all morning, or are you gonna fix them eggs?"

"Yes, suh, yes, suh, comin raht up, Meesta Calfeeld," he announced, then leaning over into the pan, blew his nose with a vengeance in the lieutenant's eggs. I did a double take and stared at him quizzically as he smiled while swirling the double eggs in the tiny, black fry-pan. "Calfeeld gon git de 'Jackson special' dis mawnin," he stated gleefully.

He brought the eggs into Caulfield, and I watched as the lieutenant ate. He took two quick mouthfuls, sipped his coffee, scooped another forkful, and seemed to be having a jolly good time. A few minutes later, he bellowed: "Jackson, you sure do know how to fix up a batch of eggs, yes sir, you sure do."

"Yes, suh, Meesta Calfeeld," Jackson agreed amiably. "I alwass lok tu du a gud job, suh. Ah takes great pride in mah wurk, suh, yes, suh." Jackson winked in my direction, and I forced what had to be a very sick smile.

I repaired the toaster, gathered up my tools and left. On the way back to the shop, I vowed always, at all costs, to be especially considerate of the parachute rigger and the cook, whoever they may be.

When we got around to it, the Bequik passed through the Suez canal one blistering day in August. Ah, I remember it well. First because of the Mid-East situation, and secondly, the genial personality of our intrepid Commodore.

As for the situation, it was the middle part of the fifth decade in this most wonderful of centuries, and warm in more ways than one.

In the area in question resides two separate and distinct species indigenous to that part of the world. They are the Arab and the Jew. Now the Arab and the Jew have been living in that neck of the woods since time immemorial, yet cannot seem to get along. There seems to be some question as to who owned Palestine first. A simple matter, you say? Apparently you have never been in a court of law, for it is common knowledge thereof, that if an issue isn't muddled before court convenes, it will be there-after.

Be that as it may, it seems the Arab and the Jew no longer care who holds the legal rights to said property, it now having come down to: "You ain't gonna get it and I don't care who your damn great, great grandfather was. Ya dig?"

At the time, being young and stupid, I didn't mind dying for my country, but I did mind dying for someone else's, and that someone else, happened to be the Jew, the Egyptian, or any deathly combination thereof, and getting blown up in the Suez Canal was not an endearing sentiment.

So ... moving right along, as we were slowly passing through the canal, one quiet, sultry morning, a few of us, who had been casually sitting on the fantail, noticed a strange phenomenon unfolding. As you may, or may not know, destroyers usually travel in squadrons (four ships) and each squadron has a commodore. He does not have command of any one vessel, but is the captain of all four; he is the commandant, so to speak, and, as luck would have it, our great and fearless leader always acted like he wished he were somewhere else. So did we. Neither of us ever got our wish. Like Siamese twins, we were stuck with each other.

As previously mentioned, we now observed the Commodore, on the bridge of the lead ship, peering intently at, guess who? Yes, dear hearts, the rag-a-muffins on the Bequik, lackadaisically enjoying the morning sun, and attendant surroundings, were the "guess who's," and the glass seemed to be embedded over the Commodore's nose.

As I watched 'his nibs,' the image of a big, fat black crow leering down at a corn field, waiting for just the right moment to swoop down and wreak havoc came to mind. Naturally, we were curious, for the commodore never showed such an intent fascination for us before. We knew something was up, and chances were, it would be our equatorial cans. Moments later it was.

The word was passed over the squawk-box that the commodore noticed certain crewmen on the Bequik browsing about topside in dungarees, and since it was not his intention to convey to the inhabitants that the United States Navy consisted of a gang of escaped convicts from Devil's Island, he would greatly appreciate it if we would all change into our blues. I shuddered to think of what I had heard, and was hoping against hope I had not heard it. But alas, no such luck. It was repeated. The Navy repeats everything; even they can't believe their own orders. Yes, indeed, the commodore did say change into something more "appealing," and yes the big, ol', meanie was indeed commanding us to jump into our little woolies—IN THE SUEZ!! Not only was it preposterous, but such occurrences, if continued, could beget thoughts of mutiny. It seems not all the nuts were in the woods.

Somehow we survived this bit of nonsense, but not without an increasing dislike for our fearless leader. In the future, when exhibiting similar eccentricities, the phrase, "The old man's got the blues again," would float freely about. As time went on, "old Man Blue," as he came to be known, developed a case of those same blues on a regular basis, as we were continually subjected to like aberrations with little pause. And the beat goes on.

Eventually we returned home all in one piece, a remarkable event considering the "unique" qualities of our captain. Although a good enough fellow, he was, nevertheless, what is known in seaman's lingo as "a fuck-up," meaning, he meant well, but the eventual outcome was usually indistinguishable from his lordly intentions. A case in point: Once, while trading movies at sea with one of our sister ships, the Longfellow, the Bequik, under Captain Green's guidance, rammed her sideways, an altogether unusual happening considering the calm waters that day.

I happened to be in the forward engine room at the time keeping tabs on the generator, when I heard a loud, crashing noise followed by a sudden lurch. Knowing that the captain was a sportsman, of sorts, I thought at first he might be trying to bag a whale. It certainly would have made good copy, using a jolly boat to ram a fish. But when I saw the squirrel next to me, a simpleton with a goodly crop of sloppy black, porcupine hair, shoot up the ladder five rungs at a time, I knew he wasn't racing to get a ringside seat at the follies. However, also being a lad of simple qualities, I stayed at my post until officially relieved of my duties.

When I did enter the world of fresh air and sunshine, I noticed that the 40 millimeter mount on the starboard side, had become a kissing cousin to the 40 millimeter mount on the port side. Now I am not a prudish sort by any means, and ordinarily would have thought nothing of such a display of affection, but I had never heard of two grown 40s becoming amorous at sea before, unless maybe the salt air has more of a magnetic charge than previously thought.

Nevertheless, Captain Green had shot the "love arrow." Touching, and although no one was hurt, we did have fodder for conversation for many a subsequent moonlit night, thereafter.

After resting in Newport just three weeks, the Bequik pulled up anchor once again and headed for, of all places, Fall River, Massachusetts. What attraction there was exactly for Fall River I never knew. The only resemblance it had to naval matters was its watery outlet.

We tied up to the dock for six days, long enough to catch the clap, a black eye, and become the unlucky recipient in a slight game of peculation. I didn't mind so much the black eye, or even the "love-bug," for in both cases I "gave as good as I got," but I sure hated to get peculated, I really did.

When it was time to leave, a tug came alongside and offered to assist "the amazing Mr. Green" with the affairs at hand. It seems there was an undertow, and the tug captain thought it wiser to be safe than hardy. Captain Green, who's star was fast descending, chose the latter course and calamity was soon to be visited upon the Bequik once again.

On the unfortunate morning in question, I had been in the forward compartment asleep, when in the midst of my dreamy dreams, I vaguely heard over the intercom, "Ship's away, shift colors," and then, "Turn to, turn to," the standard "hog call" for resumption of regular duties.

I came up from the compartment, unsuspectingly like Samson in Delilah's tonsorial chambers, and proceeded aft to the machine shop. I had gone no more than ten feet when I looked down and, "CARAMBA! LAND! THE BEQUIK was ON LAND!" Indeed it was a peculiar sensation, to say the least. After all, this wasn't a canoe we were muscling around. The first thing that came to mind was: "Green, you old fucker; you did it again." The second and more sobering thought was, "I got to get off this god-damn deathtrap."

We had our pictures taken that time … front page, too. After things cooled a bit the story came down from the bridge that when it happened, Captain Green first turned white, then pink, looked one way, and then the other with a pleading expression on his face as if to say: "Somebody, do something!" Then, exasperatedly, he slammed his cap on the deck, and bellowed: "God-damn it, there goes my fucking career!" Naïveté, at times, can be a worldwide phenomenon. The Captain's career was over the day he took the oath.

After the latest 'adventure', a few of us began to get the impression that maybe the Bequik was not the safest place <u>to be,</u> and transfer papers started circulating in record numbers. No one wanted to be a peacetime casualty. I couldn't split because I hadn't been a member in good standing long enough. Ever since, however, I've learned to sleep with the lightness of a three-legged zebra in lion country.

After leaving Fall River, we put into the Charlestown shipyard for no important reason I could think of. We always seemed to be just going somewhere, and when we felt like stopping, we stopped. The term I believe is "keeping the peace." Were it we could all have a little, mini-destroyer in our backyards.

While in Charlestown I became constipated. On the fourth day of my condition I visited the corpsman, but the oil he gave me must have been 3-In-1, because all the squeaks stopped, but I still hadn't passed the goods. The next day I took myself over to the base hospital to see he of the finger-poking trade.

Immediately upon entering, I was overcome with gratitude for having the good fortune of contracting merely a nuisance condition rather than a serious one, or I would have been in serious trouble.

The joint looked like a small cyclone had recently paid a visit, and as for his 'royal highness', he resembled one of those seedy-looking character's in a vintage Warner Brother's movie, sixtyish, rumpled and grizzled, a cigar smoker with tobacco stains on his fingers, and coffee stains on a smock which appeared to have a life of its own. Not a personable sort, I was to find, but he sure had personality. My fondest wish was for a speedy recovery. Seeing me, he turned, and said, "Okay, what's your problem?"

"Nothing serious, Doc," I answered, thanking all the saints near and dear for that small favor. "It's just that … well, I can't shit."

He took a long drag on a Dutch-master, and said, "Are you sure? Because if it's diarrhea it's much easier to handle, pardon the expression."

"Wud'ya mean?" I countered, confusedly.

"Well, what I mean is, if your running free and loose all you have to do is nothing, because you'll shit and shit until there's no more shit to be shot, and then you'll stop. But a plug-up, now that's a little more ticklish." (I said he had personality.) A-N-D, he was putting me in the mood. "I'm gonna live, ain't I?" I joked.

"Look here, Bub, I'm the one who makes with the wisecracks around here. You just laugh on cue." He took another drag, and I coughed. "You ain't got TB, too, have ya?" he inquired sarcastically. He really thought he belonged on the stage; so did I, with a trapdoor underneath.

"No," I replied, waving my hand in front of my face to scatter the smoke, "not yet."

"Shit, Bub, a little old cigar ain't gonna hurt ya."

"Yeah, and I'd like to keep it that way."

"Hells bells, I been smoking since I was nine." I looked at him incredulously, then at the surroundings. "You-are-a-medical-doctor, aren't-you?" I enunciated clearly.

"You ain't as funny as me, Bub," he slurred. I looked him up and down. "I know," I answered. He looked at me, too. "But your gettin' there," he shot back.

"I try."

"Well try this socko: eat lots of potatoes, lots and lots of potatoes. Baked ones, fried ones, boiled ones, mashed ones, raw ones. Eat all the spuds you can get your hands on. Lots and lots of um."

"What?" I replied unbelievingly. "Why, I never heard of such a thing!"

"Well, you heard it now, and you heard it here first."

"I'll say." I stared for just a moment, expecting him to disappear in a puff of smoke. "Okay, so what's the god-damn potato bit supposed to do, if I don't win a contest first?"

"Well now, I'll tell you what it's supposed to do. You'll shit, or you'll bust, that's what."

The molting old fucker … he was right—I bust.

Eventually, after having been aboard the Bequik some twenty-eight months, I put in for a transfer, and much to my surprise, I got it—to another destroyer, on the west coast.

For some peculiar reason, the USS Gupta didn't travel much, and if tin cans do anything, they do-o-o-o get around. But not the Gupta. It just cruised up and down between San Diego and San Francisco. For a while I thought I was in the Coast Guard. Quite a contrast from the Bequik which continually acted like it was auditioning for "Around the World in Eighty Days."

Aboard the Gupta I befriended a native Oak Lander, one, Al Ruckheiser. Any time the Gupta anchored in San Fran, ol' Johnny boy got a home-cooked meal, and Al's mother was quite a cook as I became quite fond of German cuisine, even though it was usually a variation on sausage.

In the meanwhile, friend Al, became smitten by the love-bug, or, at least as much as exists in one's gonads, which at twenty, can be considerable.

The young lady in question was a conniving little smidgen who resembled olive oil of Popeye fame. She was one of those changing kind of broads; she always seemed to be changing, for the worse, and the longer one looked, the worse she looked.

I asked Al, "What do you see in her?"

"Wud'ya mean?" he answered, offendedly. "She's tough."

"Yeah," I replied, "like shoe leather."

"Very funny, Jocko, but let me tell you, Johnny boy, she kind of grows on ya."

"Uh, huh, like a scab."

"Aw, man, you don't know what the hell's goin' on. She's a real hep chick."

"More like a duck."

"Screw you. I can't explain it if you can't see it."

"Oh, I can see it, all right. That's the problem." Although it can be cruel, in such matters it is best to allow nature to take its course. It did.

One misty, autumn day, Al, myself, and a slick dude by the name of Billy Wilson went out to visit this boa constrictor who lived out in the boonys with her parents, two small brothers, and a Persian cat named Anna. Lisa (that was her name) asked us to stay for dinner. We did. We had roast beef. I'm not too crazy about roast beef. Roast beef you can get at the mission. However, in all fairness to Mrs. Brink's culinary talents, hers bore little resemblance to that served up on the Bowery.

After dinner, Mr. and Mrs. Brinks, along with the two kids, went to a drive-in. Billy and I went for a stroll. Al and Lisa went in the barn. Anna went bye-bye.

I ought to mention that Al had been trying to gorge Lisa for some three months, and I have no doubt had he been able to 'tickle her fancy' his fascination for her would have long since dwindled like a dry twig in a forest fire, as the only thing she had going for her was the little kitty in the bush. I said to Billy as they disappeared behind the barn door, "Billy, me boy, it's now or never."

"I dunno," Billy replied, uncertainly. "Love can make a guy simple."

"Yeah, but what more can a guy ask for? She's had a couple drinks, it's quiet, no interruptions, and they're up in a hayloft. She ought to be as ripe as a strawberry in June, so how simple can the guy be?"

Billy and I meandered out into the field where we browsed about for some forty-five minutes when Billy, becoming restless, announced, "C'mon, man, if he ain't got it by now, he ain't never gonna get it."

As we strolled into the yard, Al and Lisa were coming out of the barn all rumpled looking and shaking hay out of their hair and clothing. As we approached, I noticed Al looked happy, but not as happy as he should have looked. Billy must have noticed, too, because he nudged me, saying, "I'll bet the sap didn't get a god-damn thing but straw up his snotty nose." How right can one be?

For the next half hour, Billy and I kept trying to get Al's attention for some kind of acknowledgment, but Al was having none of it; he kept his distance. We hung around for another half hour then headed back.

As we climbed in the car we made sure Al was in the middle. Billy drove. We no sooner pulled out of the driveway when I immediately snapped, "Okay, Sonny, what happened?"

"Wud'ya mean, what happened?" he repeated irritably.

"What do I mean?" I turned to Billy. "He's gonna run a game on us, Billy."

"I'm hep," Billy acknowledged.

I continued with the interrogation. "You know what I mean," and playing it straight all the way, he replied, "Well, we messed around a little."

"Yeah, go on; we're listening," I responded.

"Hey, look, I ain't gotta tell you fuckers nothin', see?"

"That's right, man, you ain't got to tell us nothin'." I glanced over at Billy. "Ain't that right, Bill? He ain't got to tell us nothin'."

"So, what's to tell! Nothin' happened!" he exclaimed excitably.

"Wud I tell ya! Wud I tell ya!" boomed Billy.

"Now hold on, Bill," I said, in mock fairness. "Let's be fair; let's hear the dude out."

"Hear him out? I'd like to do him in."

"Now look," Al volunteered apologetically, "you know Lisa ain't no ordinary broad."

"You're tellin' us, but neither was the bearded lady. So what?"

"Well, she had a few, and I didn't want to do it like that."

"He's setting us up, Bill."

"You got that right," agreed Billy. I continued, "You mean to tell us, she was gonna do it, and you wouldn't let her?"

"Yeah, that's right; I had her, but I just didn't want to do it like that," he replied angrily.

"Well, what the hell were you waitin' for, confirmation from the fucking Pope?"

"I think we got a reee-al ding on our hands, John."

"And then some. I don't believe what I'm hearing."

"Believe it, believe it," admonished Billy.

"Well, it ain't right to take advantage like that. It just ain't right."

"How bout that, Billy. Here's a guy who ain't been to church since his first communion, and all of a sudden he's got religion. You fucking jerk. The snatch only had two drinks. Don't you know that's why she had them at all? That cobra needed an excuse to strike. She's been askin' for it for three months. I'll bet she did everything but grab your silly cock."

"Aw, fuck you, guys. Youse don't understand nuttin."

"Hey, John? I'll bet she's laughing her ass off right now at this gink."

"Hey, John; Hey, Billy; Hey, John; Hey, Billy," Al mimicked. "You two sound like a couple of fuckin' parrots."

"Parrot, smarrot, let's get one thing straight, Al, cause we wanna be fair, ya know? We just wanna be fair. It ain't because you think your gonna go to hell, or somethin', is it? It ain't nothing like that, right? Cause if it is, then there ain't no hope for ya. Even the priest gets a little, now and then."

"She's cherry, man! She's cherry!" he screeched. Somehow he got the weird notion that that temporary condition was going to impress us.

"So was Lucretia Borgia, once upon a time. What's that got to do with anything? It's only sex … a little candy. It ain't no big thing, cherries or plums. There ain't nobody, dead or alive, saint or sinner, who gives one good fuck, one way or the other, what went on up in that hay mow tonight. You been had, suc-kah."

"Yeah," butted in, Billy. "Now I know what a turkey in the straw looks like. Gobble, gobble, gobble."

A few days later, Billy and I were down in the engine room cleaning the generator when Al came down with one of those big 'I got the bird' grins.

"Hark!" he exclaimed. "Look what I found. The chief couldn't of picked a better spot for a couple of bilge rats."

"Hark?" Dost my ears play tricks on me, or did I hear, hark?" I derided.

"Yep, Johnny boy, you heard, hark all right," Billy joked. "It seems old 'holy balls' ain't recovered from his trip into the country yet."

"If you two bungholes will quit beatin' your gums, I'll tell you what happened last night."

"Hey man, quiet," I said to Billy. "He gonn tell us sumpin'."

"Well, when I went over last night, guess who I ran into?"

"MacArthur?" quizzed Billy.

Ignoring Al's brief attempt at levity, he replied, matter-of-factly, "Lisa."

"Whoopee! Saint Albert bumped into 'Lisa, the Immaculate' John. Wud you all do then, hold a prayer meetin'?"

"Just clam up, and perk up your fucking Bambi ears, wise ass. Now guess what that stony broad tries to lay on me … me, mind you, Oakland Al?"

"Not her sweet, little wiggly bum?" I sniggered.

Al slammed his fist angrily against the switchboard. "She tells me she wouldn't let me do it cause she's heard a lot of stories about sailors, and what not, and she thought maybe I had a disease. Imagine that scungy bitch trottin' out that fucking, mangy bird?

"It's as good as any," Billy chirped.

"That fuckin' broad, all spread out like a bald eagle on a mountaintop, tellin' me I got a disease! How's that for grass?"

"Al, baby," I said, "you sure can pick um. So wud you tell Tokyo Rose then?"

"What could I tell her? I told her to go and fuck herself. A guy's got his pride, ya know?" Oh, the wonder of it all.

* * *

V

THE BIRDS AND THE BEES

HEAVEN AND HELL

LOVE A DUCK AND GO TO JAIL

PIE IN THE SKY, PAIN IN THE PAUNCH

KEEP YOUR HEAD HIGH

WOODEN HORSES DON'T CRY

AS all things must, this too, came to an end. And so, as the world turns, so did the worm. I was discharged.

I cannot describe the feeling that came over me as I walked through the gates for the last time. Euphoric? Yes, and then some. Initially it was the shock of not having to return to 'the good ship Lollipop' for another round of inanities after one thousand-four hundred and sixty. A guy could get punchy.

The Gupta was in San Diego at the time, (I said it never went anywhere), and as I walked with my papers tucked under my arm officially designating me a civilian once again, I turned for one last look and was immediately overcome with a heightened sense of exhilaration—and I never even shot dope. It was almost as if I had wings and could fly. For a few brief moments I knew what it was to be a giant bird, soaring, soaring, soaring. Alas, but it is not to be; the days of man are numbered, and the time would come when I would look upon those dutiful days with nostalgia; aye, and even longing. The fleeting legs of time. . . . .

I boarded a bus for downtown, and as I stepped again on hard ground, the feeling remained. I wondered, if there is a heaven, could this be its fetus? I walked—no place in particular, just walked— and my feet felt like the soft, fluffy feathers of a baby albatross.

I stopped in a coffee shop and had one. As I sat there all of the little things that usually happened, matter-of-factly, seemed to be happening with great flare.

Horns weren't horns, they were HORNS! And people stepped with the pounding of a Goliath. And the red lights, and the green lights, and yellow lights all came on with a whir and a bang! A fly zoomed by. Trees were bursting through the ground, and the air was howling and swirling! The whole world was tumbling helter-skelter through space. I jumped up, overcome by the intensity of life, and shouted exultantly, "E-E-E-E-E-H-A-A-H!!!"

The young lady behind the counter dropped a cup she had been wiping, and stared at me dumbfoundedly. Ah, my dear lady, said I to myself. Don't begrudge a poor lost soul, one spurting glimpse into the embryo.

As I paid my dime, she inquired into the state of my health. "Are you all right, sailor?" she asked unsurely.

"Just fine, sweetheart, Just fine. And I'll never be the same again." Hallelujah.

* * *

I came home and found an ordinary, old, funky job, in an ordinary, old funky factory. It was the kind of job that had God said: "What would you rather do, go to hell or work in a factory?" You'd have had to think twice about it. A professor of sociology did a study about such labors once. His conclusion: It's not so bad. The extent of his expertise in the area consisted of six months on a production line while working his way through college. It's that kind of world, Virginia.

As for myself, I didn't need any sociology professor to tell me what was, or wasn't, 'so bad'. My instincts were far more developed than his education. I knew If I stayed with it too long, I would become just another labor statistic in one of those numerous and seldom read government publications. The working man's life? Dreadful, dreary, the bottom of the bottle, Buck, and if anyone tries to tell you it's glamorous, ask him what he does for a living. Chances are, he's a mogul.

As I lay on a crowded beach with the multitudes, one bright and sunny Sunday, I looked to my right, and as far as the eye could see, there was flesh. Mountains and mountains of baked, brown naked flesh like so much beef jerky drying out on a slaughterhouse platform. I looked to my left, the same; I looked toward the shoreline—more yet. I looked toward the parking lot, thousands and thousands of square feet of meat, just lying there, paralyzed in the hot sand. I lifted myself up, took one, long exaggerated look around, became nauseated, picked up my suffering blanket, and headed back to the car. As I drove away, I thought, there must be a better way, there must, even if God's a one-eyed loco. The game ain't worth the candle.

I strained at the bit for a couple of years, I know not why, then headed straight back to the coast. What I couldn't find in the east, I thought I could find in the west. Youth is under the impression that identity lies in geographical location and happiness in constant, inane activity.

One of my first steps was (you guessed it) get another old, funky job in an ordinary, old funky factory. Aha! But now I had a plan. I would work a while, long enough to save a little bread, and with my G.I. allotment, enter the collegiate ranks. The best laid plans. . . . .

I worked another two years and quit. Come September I enrolled in one of the numerous institutions of higher conditioning with no great enthusiasm. To me, it was merely the lesser of two evils, and after noting the fashion with which "higher" education was being worn, I concluded that college got the best of the deal. No matter, I endured.

I majored in business. From the frying pan into the fire. Now you know anyone who abhors crowded beaches, cities, backyard barbecues, and beer, and whose idea of a house pet is a black Angus, ain't got no business in business. You know it, and I know it … but then?

Now the nonsense that is slopped about in the guise of education is incredulous and leaves little wonder why Ivan can read and Johnny can't. A case in point, even though only indirectly related, yet relevant, let me inform you of a seemingly insignificant little matter that took place in a sales management class that I had the lucky fortune to have been a member of. If this can happen in the thirteenth grade, imagine what can happen in the third.

On the day in question, our instructor, as innocent as Little Miss Muffet, asked, "What is the primary purpose of business?" Nothing loaded there, you say? Read on. Instantly, everyone blurts out "Profit! Profit!"

"Wrong, both times!" exclaimed Mr. Klutz. "Guess again." Well, who said this, and who said that, and after finally milking this little game bone-dry, he, like a sage atop Mt. Olympus, proud fully announced, "Enterprise! To engage in Enterprise!"

We were amazed, to say the least, for that was like saying a farmer milks a cow to massage her teats. Klutz must have noticed our astonishment, as he immediately added, "you see? You must not take things for granted. Profit comes later, but first, business." It occurred to me, however, that if one did not make a profit, one couldn't do much business, and the idea that anyone would go into business to practice enterprise simply boggled the mind, unless of course, it is a large enough business, in which case one can always get subsidized by Sam.

Remember the case of the "citizen" who owned a swamp in Louisiana, and the government, in its infinite wisdom, paid said citizen not to grow strawberries in said swamp? Strawberries? Beans? Oranges? Louisiana? No matter. He couldn't have grown anything in there but alligators. As a matter of fact, he couldn't have grown anything in there BUT alligators, if it meant his life.

Mr. Klutz initiated a spiel justifying this ingenious aberration of his. He strutted about like a pregnant peacock for half an hour, and you know, by the end of class he had us believing it. Pavlov's dog? But you know, I think the sap really believed it himself. You don't need a white sheet and a haunted house to scare me witless, the Mr. Klutzes' of the world will do just fine, tha-nk y-o-u.

* * *

I lived alone for a while, about nine months; I was never one who constantly needed companionship. Mostly because I was my own best company. I enjoyed myself. And why not? I don't drink, smoke, or tune in the drug scene. I'll play a game of chance, now and then, and chase a well-turned leg occasionally, but all in all, I can be trusted. I've never voted. That's right, Buck. Never did fall for all that democratic crap; works too well here. The people's choice always wins. That's enough to gag a bull elephant. I wouldn't trust "the people" to pick out my toilet paper. I'm an elitist. Yep, that's right, an elitist. Trouble is, there ain't none. So much for politics.

In time I moved into what looked like a house with six of the sorriest looking fish west of the Mississippi, five of which were students, the sixth worked at the airport cleaning out the John's on 727's, and what not. America could never be the most 'wonderful of places,' (sic) if it weren't for the truly stupid and gullible. Poor young men struggling through life make it possible for rich young men to prance through life.

In that house, which could have been built by Poe with a quill that went berserk, certain things just naturally gravitated toward each other, and it wasn't long before those other things (Dorothy and Beverly) came in our direction. Dorothy and Beverly were what are known as 'camp followers.' Dorothy and Beverly would have followed a tent.

One afternoon, Mike, our 'housemother' and the 'pigeon sisters' were discussing particulars about a party for the coming Saturday night. Mike said, "Let's have a party." Dorothy said, "W-e-e-e!" and it was on.

Everything was well and good for a while, you know, the usual smoking, drinking, dirty jokes, and a little preliminary ass feeling. Nothing spectacular. But what was supposed to be a gathering of twenty, or so, soon turned out to be a parade. There had to be some there who came in from off the street. L.A.'s like that, you know. A couple of dude's will be walking down the street and if they hear ice clinking in a glass, they'll walk in. Some folk chase fire engines. In L.A. they chase parties. I'd swear, though, once or twice I heard a foreign accent; Bakersfield, I think.

Along about ten, the joint looked like a dump, and smelled like a brewery. I never saw so many drunks so early in the evening in my life. There were two commodes in the house and a constant flush in both of them. The front lawn also, after that night, was never the same again.

I was sitting in a corner trying to catch my breath, minding my own business, when Rudy Kruza and Lester Whitehill came over and said, "Hey, man, let's get this sofa outta here; we gotta have more room." We were joined by Bobo Bunzel. "Let's bring it upstairs in Mike's room," he says. Shows you how alcohol affects the brain. We could have more easily put it outside. It was practically a straight line all the way, and everything but the kitchen sink was out there already. I guess they thought it would mar the landscape.

Rudy and Lester grabbed one end, and I the other. As we neared the door it started to get tight like everything else in the joint because the stairs were too narrow to get around the banister. We didn't have enough trouble when Dorothy staggered over and grabbed my end. The couch, that is.

"Lemme help," she says, I think. Well, we pushed, and pulled, and tugged, and finally got one end around, but Rudy somehow, got pinned against the wall. Dorothy was pinned against the doorpost, and there we stood. I was ready to call the firehouse when Dorothy says, "I don't feel sho ... sho ... sho hot." She certainly knew what she was talking about, since she was turning into the most exquisite shade of green, when suddenly, she let go of her end. "I shink I'm gon ... gonna. . . . ."

"No! No!" Rudy bellowed, while throwing up one arm to shield his face against the upcoming onslaught. Too late. Sweet Dorothy brought forth a concoction of tender, baby, sweet peas, golden corn, hamburger, and about twelve ounces of Canadian Club, no ice. I'll say one thing for dear heart, she didn't miss much of her target. Rudy was indeed a mess. When he finally untangled himself, we threw him in the shower, clothes and all.

The little incident must have had a sobering effect on everyone, for we then put the couch on the lawn, where we should have put it in the first place. Otherwise, though, it wasn't a bad party as parties go, and this one went all night. Around four A.M., I fell asleep, or passed out, whichever, differentiation being impossible under the circumstances.

Four hours later, Beverly taps me on the shoulder. "C'mon," she says, "take us to our pad."

"Take you to your pad!" I objected vociferously. "You gotta be kidding. What the hell's so important about your pad at eight o'clock on a Sunday morning?"

"They gotta get ready for the party tonight," interjected Rudy, sarcastically, from his spot in a corner.

"C'mon, you guy's," piped in Dorothy, "this place smells."

"Hah! This broad's got a lot of balls, Rudy. First she pukes all over the joint, and then she complains about the stink." I rose slowly. "C'mon, Ruu, we might as well take them, or they're gonna take us, one way or the other. We gotta get this place cleaned up, anyway."

"What the hell's that got to do with anything? We can clean it any time."

"Okay, it's up to you. We can clean it today with ordinary soap and water, or we can clean it later with a hammer and chisel."

"All right, all right," he agreed none to cheerily, "let's take um."

You wouldn't believe what we ran into outside. It looked like the Normandy beachhead on D Day. Somebody, I don't know who, was sleeping on the sofa in his BVD's with a pair of silky, pink panties draped around his neck. This was the same item of furniture previously handled the night before.

"That must've been so-o-o-o-me piece of ass," Rudy affirmed, while shaking his head up and down enviously.

"Hey, I said, "you chicks want to check and see if you got your drawers on?"

"Smart asses," gurgled Dorothy.

The girls lived somewhere in Pasadena in one of those huge, old-fashioned, brick tenement houses where a lot of little, old ladies put-up. As we cruised up, Rudy beckoned. "C'mon, hurry up. I gotta use the head."

We all got out of the car, and you never saw two sorrier looking broads in all your life. Nylons all wrinkled and twisted, shoes unbuckled, smeared lipstick, disheveled hair, rumpled clothes; God, they were a sight.

As we staggered up the walk, two rickety, old bittys were coming out on their way to church. Dorothy looked at Beverly; Beverly looked at Dorothy. As the old ladies came alongside, Beverly declared, completely out of character, "Oh, Dorothy, wasn't that the most wonderful sermon the reverend gave this morning? I never heard such a beautiful sermon."

"It certainly was," Dorothy agreed. "It really does a body good to hear a sermon like that." Laurel and Hardy, anyone?

Well, at that little bit of fluff, them two old hens just stared at each other, all stiff-legged and bug-eyed, like they'd just been goosed. As we approached the front door, Rudy admonished our tainted companions as to the advisability, considering their somewhat stygian condition, "to having kept their damned traps shut, instead," wherein I took one, long, last look at the 'twins of enchantment,' and laconically stated: "Nah, fifty-fifty." And so began Sunday; and so ended Sunday.

* * *

I had been attending school for a year and a half when I became absolutely certain of my folly. I was approaching the insignificant age of twenty-eight, and the world was beginning to take on new shapes. More and more did it look flatter and flatter. Twenty-one seemed like such a loooong, time ago.

I was also, at this time, quickly running out of pesetas'. That, more than football, or the military, will bring on a sudden burst of 'character.' I thought I had calculated my expenses correctly, and I had; however, I had no way of accounting for the vagaries of a free economy.

I have always had trouble with that phrase, particularly in economics classes. It is believed that America is the great and wonderful nation that it is because of it. Supply and demand, the magic words. Through it the market automatically insured itself of success … sooner or later.

"But, Doctor," I decried one day in mock rebellion, "the rich demand and the poor supply." And the doctor, in a rare moment of candor, did reply, "Mr. Rosko, why do you suppose there are poor people in this world? Because they are stupid, or lazy, or uneducated? No, no, my good man; it is because there are rich people, for if riches depended upon intelligence and education, Thoreau would have been a multi-millionaire, and Gandhi would've had to been given the keys to Fort Knox. It is a socio-economic fact of life, the one, iron-clad law of human existence, the rich are rich BECAUSE THEY ARE RUTHLESS!!!"

My, my, such blatant emotion in he of the establishment. I delighted in giving him grist. "Then what we have," I alleged, "is two societies, one for the rich, and one for the poor?"

"If you like."

"But that's the case everywhere."

"Assuredly. A rich soul in a poor country is much better off than a poor one in a rich country. He who is not making it gains little solace from the knowledge that he is living in a nation with the highest standard of living. To the destitute it is merely an academic exercise, so much intellectual manure liberally spread at cocktail parties by the champagne and caviar set."

"Then, actually, the market principle only works for the indigent. The opulent can afford any price."

"Certainly, but you see, it works so well in America."

"How so?"

"The impoverished belabor under the insidious notion that if they work hard and be good little fellows, and behave themselves, someday they, too, will be among the filthy lucred. In America, Horatio Alger, the ballot box, and Madison Avenue have replaced revolution. Robespierre, to us, was never anything but a blood-thirsty, power broker, and the French revolution, with its principles of equality and fraternity, nothing more than a lower class pitch at a share of the spoils."

"I'm hep."

I saw the doctor's wife once, briefly. She appeared to be some twenty years younger, and gave the impression of being, at one time, a third-rate burlesque queen, if you get my drift, and it is said she never passed Bloomingdale's without first retrieving a bright and shapely bauble of no small heft.

Is that what it takes, as college professors do not usually speak in such bold and brassy terms; they have their reputations to think of, and to the middle-class, reputation on their list of goodies ranks next to a spotless credit rating, and an early pension.

Besides, one must at all cost, be scientific. I'm sure you've noticed, at some time, teachers on strike shouting epithets at the school board and screaming from the top of their lungs: "Unfair! Unfair!" striding in high-pitched moral indignation, and performed by half-assed, semi-educated, pill-popping, gin-guzzling, pseudo-patriots, bedecked in pin-striped shirts and tweed coats. Such a deafening clamor from a privileged class.

What an obscenity. From "Give me liberty, or give me death!" to "Smaller classes! Bigger pay!" Only in America, the last bastion of freedom, only in America. Et tu, Brute.

As time past, I thought more and more of that condensed version of modern society, and as I grew older, more and more did it make sense, simple as the concept may have been, but then, the simple always contains the kernel of truth. Yes, I thought more and more of it, and along with it a short verse I came across once, I don't remember where; but isn't that the way? Modern times are the great burial ground of the profound. It went:

> Know thy enemy.
> He does not care what color you are
> Provided you work for him.
> He does not care how much you earn
> Provided you earn more for him;
> He does not care who lives in the room at the top
> Provided he owns the building.
> He will let you say whatever you like against him,
> Provided you do not act against him.
> He sings the praises of humanity,
> But knows machines cost more than men.
> Bargain with him, he laughs, and beats you at it.
> Challenge him, and he kills.
> Sooner than lose the things he owns
> He will destroy the world.

* * *

Back at the ranch, certain developments began to make themselves known. Unbeknownst to all except one (Robert Fretwell, a boarder previously in good standing,) the landlady, a kindly, old, Prussian dowager, was kicking back ten bucks a month on the rent, provided we would keep the grass cut and make certain other small improvements from time to time, like say, getting our hands on a 'touched-up' Picasso?

Mr. Fretwell, having been designated to take care of such prosaic matters, (he volunteered) was taking better care of it than anyone knew. We each paid twenty apiece, making a grand total of one-hundred-and-forty-dollars per month, minus ten. Bobby, however, was socking away the ten for himself, which, I would imagine, for a thief, was a not too difficult accomplishment, and Mr. Fretwell W-A-S a thief.

I wondered why he was out there every week, like a clock, mowing the lawn. It was the only exercise the flabby bastard ever got. He thought he could get away with it because he always took the rent to Mrs. Spitz's place unaccompanied, but one day, she crossed him up by coming over herself, unannounced, to, "Zee vass iss goink onn here." Bobby, Rudy, Lester, and myself, were gathered in the parlor when old, Mrs. Spitz dropped the bomb.

"My, my," she complained mildly, "Bott yus fellos dun't zeem tu be duink ferry moch vit da ten I bean giffink yus bak."

I looked at Rudy, Rudy looked at Lester, Lester looked at me, and we all looked at Bobby. Ooooh, did we look at Bobby. Bobby looked at the ceiling. Maybe he was expecting rain.

We didn't let on to the old girl though, no need. There should come a time in everyone's life when one's worries get less and less with each passing day. Mrs. Spitz was about fifteen deep into those years. But we corralled the little creep as soon as she left.

"Now hold it," he pleaded, knowing how close he was to becoming 'a rocket to the moon.' I know how it looks, but that ain't the way it is."

We were set to strangle the little wimp right then and there, and the only thing stopping us was the cock-and-bull story he was going to have to conjure up. He was no dancer, but he knew he had to have quick feet for this bugaloo.

"Keep talkin'," encouraged Rudy, "We're all ears."

"Well, you guys know it costs to keep up a pad, right?"

"Sure," we all piped in together. We were anxious to get to the main event.

"Okay, I've been using it for the house."

"Like what, Bob?" asked Lester.

"Well … uh … uh … toilet paper. That's right, toilet paper."

"Toilet paper!!!" Rudy boomed.

"Yeah, yeah," replied Bobby, "toilet paper."

"Well, where the fuck is all this shit paper?"

"In the garage."

"What!" Rudy continued in amazement. "You mean to tell us we got a hundred-and-twenty-dollars worth of ass-wiping paper in the fucking garage?"

"No, not anymore; we used it." I'll say one thing for the little rat, he was right on top of things.

"We used it!" Rudy bellowed, once more in obvious astonishment.

"Yeah, we used it; there's seven of us here, you know?"

"Man, if we all had the shits for ten years we couldn't of used a hundred-and twenty-bucks worth of shit paper! That's a lot of 'ass wipin,' speaking of which, we're going to get into ve-e-e-ry shortly."

Well, we let the little chiseling weasel out of it provided he paid it back, ten at a time, each week.

A few days later, I bummed a ride to school with him. I wanted to pump him a bit to see what was really going on between his pointy ears.

"Why'd you do it, Bobby," I asked. "And don't lay any of that shit paper bit on me, will ya?"

"I'm strugglin', John," he complained, as if he was the only one in that sorry predicament. "I need the bread."

I looked at him quizzically. "Bobby," I reproached, "we all need the bread. What's that got to do with anything?"

"Yeah, but I'm thirty years old." In a twisted sort of way it made sense, but not much. It was more twisted than sensible.

"Bobby, with logic like that you're going to make a fantastic accountant. Yes, sir, you're gonna fit real fine in all that muckety-muck crapola. But do me a favor, will ya? If you're gonna steal, do it from those who got to steal from. Besides being ethical, it makes more sense.

"I wish I knew how."

I doubt if Bobby knew it, but he hit onto something. Crime or goodness, which, was merely a matter of opportunity and circumstance.

Some time later, I quit school. I stuck it out for almost two years; it was just too much to bear. On the day I quit one of the counselors said to me, "You know, John, you're giving up a good thing. You're a pretty good student, and in about five years time or so, after you graduate, you could be right up there with the best of them. There's money to be made out there."

I didn't know what to say. Here was a man supposedly devoting his life to something more than 'the big hustle,' giving me his philosophy of life in five little words: "grab the cash and run."

Ten minutes later I turned in my locker key and left. Walking toward the car, I was not overcome by a feeling to look back.

Back at the pad, Rudy was just climbing out of the sack. Tough night.

"Say, man," he inquired, "what are you doin' here? It's not even noon yet."

"Hah! Look who's talking. You ain't even left yet."

"Yeah, but I had a long conversation with Jack Daniels last night."

"Some folks don't know when to go home."

"Yeah, it's hell." He sat up and slowly began putting on his socks. I slumped on Lester's bunk.

"You sick?" he asked, "or you just had it for today?"

"I've had it for a lot of days. I quit." Startled, he straightened up, placed his hands on his knees, and growled, "You what!"

"I quit," I repeated matter-of-factly.

"Just like that?"

"Just like that."

"What's the gig, man? There's gotta be a reason, and don't tell me you just felt like it."

"You're close. Business ain't my bag."

"Business ain't anybody's bag." (Rudy was studying art, the commercial kind.) "So now what?" he continued.

"Now nothing. I gotta have a little time to think and get it all together."

"Well, you better think fast. That G.I. bill ain't gonna last forever, you know."

"Fuck it."

"Yeah, sure." He rose and slipped on his pants. "You got any ideas?"

"Nope. All I know is I couldn't hack all that marketing and PR crap anymore. I was beginning to feel like one of those little, tin soldier's banging on his drum. Every time you wind him up you get the same thump, thump, thump. I've been hearing thump, thump in my dreams."

"You'd better find yourself another thump, thump just the same, or you'll be swinging a clinkety, clink lunch pail for the rest of your musical life, and clinkety, clink ain't too different from thump, thump."

On the second thump, the door slammed. It had to be Lester. Lester was a door banger. There must be some deep, psychological meaning behind door bangers; a way of letting off frustration, getting back at a hostile world maybe? "Take that," Bang! "And that," Bang! Bang! Bang! It beats war.

Lester came up, and as soon as he saw me, quizzed, "Hey, pardner, what's all this about you quittin' school?"

"Christ, that got around fast," I answered. It's barely been an hour."

"Bright boy here just broke his drum," Rudy remarked sarcastically.

"Drum, what drum?"

"Forget he's here, Lester. The furies are getting to Rudy."

"Well, how come you cut out?" Lester asked again.

"I was wasting my time, sweetheart, that's why. The gray flannel world ain't for me."

"Oh, yeah, so what? There's bread to be made, and next to lassoing the boss's daughter, this is the quickest way. Get the ol' sheepskin, and if you play your cards right, who knows, you could be president of GM some day."

"Hold it, Lester boy, hold it. You're giving me that same crap Lundy just ran down to me."

"What's that?"

"Grab it, and scram."

"So, what's wrong with that? Who was it that said 'behind every great fortune lies a great crime?' How do you think them bloodsuckers got up there, by loving their neighbor?"

"Lester, old buddy, I ain't denying that, but you're pumping a dry well. I just ain't inclined in that direction, period. Dig?"

"Dig."

Rudy butted in again. "He wants to carry a little, black lunch bucket, Les; He likes the clinkety, clink noise it makes when you swing it."

I grabbed my groin. "Here Rudy," I said, "swing on this." That afternoon I took a walk in the park. Thank heaven for grass and trees, the birds and the bees.

As I slowly made my way, I wondered if maybe I was making a mistake. I was certain I wasn't, but that didn't mean everything would work out just the same. The world had a way of methodically grinding into little pieces the best of intentions. In any case, I wasn't going to worry about it. I made my move, and that's it. What falls, falls. If there's a God, and he is just, he'll look out for me. If not, then it doesn't make any difference, one way, or the other. I knew I'd talk myself into a positive condition. The illusions of man. . . . .

I kept walking. I thought of the rich and near rich, of how they got that way, and how they stay that way. I thought of Gandhi stating: "To the extent a man has more than he needs, to that extent he is a thief." I thought of the 'limousine liberals' and those who talked like Marx and lived like J.P. Morgan. I thought of the frowzy rich, and fat cats in Cadillac's. I wondered, after all the shouting and the hoopla, the fun and games, does it not come down simply to the takers and the taken, the lamb and the wolf? A monumental money scheme masquerading as religion, law, equality, brotherhood? After the facade is ripped away, and the clammy, bare flesh exposed, can we not then see that the world is one colossal whorehouse, a giant red light beaming out to the universe with a gigantic glittering, silver penis, and two, solid gold balls hanging over the door? The fish stinks from the head back.

On the way back to the pad, I felt I had cleared some of the cobwebs. It remained to be seen, however, if the bats were still in the belfry.

* * *

One Friday night, Lester, Rudy, and I took a little trip to Hollywood. You know, the 'land of enchantment?' We couldn't do much because we were broke, a condition outstanding for its thoroughness. We just slowly drove down Hollywood Boulevard. That was just about all we could do given that Hollywood Boulevard, on a Friday night, resembles a dead carcass crawling with maggots.

As we cruised into the rubble I admonished Lester, as this little trek was his idea, "Lester," I said, "it ain't often your bulb flickers, but when it does, it glows."

"Well, shit, I didn't know it was gonna be like this. It looks like every freak and his fucking grandmother is down here." And true enough, as far as the eye could see all was one congested mass of humanity. All kinds, all sizes, all shapes, making noises not that far removed from those customarily heard in the bush. The natives were doing their thing.

We had gone about a block, (it took some time), when in the middle of the next block stood a bike gang complete with the usual, aboriginal paraphernalia. There were about ten of them all parked at the curb with the front wheels of their Junkers stuck out toward the street. You get the picture.

They sat there like Midas, not moving, but every once in a while would gun their stinking engines. What a sight, with their black, leather jackets, black boots, black hats; insignias, crosses, medals, medallions and what not. Vroom, vroom! Vroom, vroom!

"Look at them stupid fucks up there," I commented abrasively. "Whatever in God almighty hell is the fascination for that kind of crap?"

"It's like everything else," Rudy replied, "whatever turns you on."

"Yeah, I know, but Christ, it's not like your getting a piece of ass." Rudy looked at Lester, Lester looked at me, I looked at Rudy. Were we missing something? We watched as they just sat there goosing their wheelworks, and seemingly on cue, one of them would go charging up the street to survey the landscape like royalty counting his sheep, then come charging back to take his place once again, obediently among the nondescript. Gawd, what a thrill, I thought. Were it we all could be so struck with the 'lamp of inspiration.'

"There's got to be something we're missing," Lester acknowledged feebly. "I sure don't want to miss anything."

"Yeah," Rudy huffed, "There's somethin' to it, all right. They probably get their cookies bouncin' around on them puffy seats."

We were almost upon them when Lester-complained, "These cats are beginning to get on my nerves with all that horse shittin', droom! Droom! Droom!" Whereupon sticking his head out the window, he bellowed, "Stick um in your ass!"

"Hey, you god damn shmuck!" Rudy squawked, "cut that, will ya? I ain't in no mood to be hasslin' with a bunch of loony's."

"That's right, Lester, and they each probably got a tire chain under them jackets."

"Aw, fuck um," he replied in disgust, sitting back in his seat. As we came alongside they all upped and took off. "There they go! There they go! Droom, droom, droom! Droom, droom, droom!" Lester roared, once again.

"Let's get the friggin hell out of here, John. Lester's about to come right out of his drawers."

"I'm hep," I drawled. Whereupon we left and drove toward downtown LA. As we reached Alvarado, we came upon a gang of a different type, but no less amusing—the hippie's. Hippies remind me of the Baptists, they like to congregate. I had always looked upon them with some amusement, for although they were in the main, harmless, there was nonetheless, something about them that wasn't right. Nothing all that major, mind you, but still something I just couldn't quite pin down. Looking for some kind of assistance, I asked Rudy what he thought, seeing that he was warmed to the task. "About what?" he replied so-so.

"This miscellany," I prodded, "what do you think about them?"

"Hah! What's to think? They're fucked-up like everyone else."

"Maybe so, but how?"

"How? Look at um; they look like they just been thrown up outta the sewer."

"That's the brightest thing he's said in three days," butted in, Lester.

"Could be," I added, "but something else, too."

"Well, what then?" Rudy questioned. "You gotta give me a hint."

"I'm not sure, but all this raggedy ass crap started as a symbolic gesture protesting the establishment, which is clean on the outside and dirty on the inside. This rabble reversed the process and went beyond it."

"So?"

"So, now it has transcended all that. They've made a cult out of dirt. They're ugly."

"We ain't gonna argue that, are we, Lester?" chided Rudy.

"Not me, brother."

"What's happened then, is ugliness has become a way of life, an end in itself, something to strive for, and that's perverse because there's enough natural ugliness to go around ten worlds without creating it artificially. Dirt for dirt's sake. They wear it like a badge."

"That's good, I like that," Rudy enjoined. "Dirt for dirt's sake, Yaaaaay! That would make a great slogan for some grubby politician beggin for the hippie vote."

"Shit," Lester snickered. "First they gotta stay off junk long enough to get to the polls."

"And besides," I continued, "notice how they all look alike, act alike, talk alike. I'll bet they even hold their peckers alike when they piss. All together now, thumb and forefinger, now shake it three times. Wheeeeee! The conformism, it's stifling, that's what's really depressing."

"Yeah," Rudy seconded curtly, "just like the friggin' astronauts. When you've seen one, you've seen them all."

We drove on, not speaking. Presently, Rudy pulled over and parked, saying something about a 'couple of beers.'

We just sat there watching the variety of night life making its grand little designs on life. "You know?" Rudy finally uttered. "It's not so strange really, all things considered."

"What's not?"' Lester asked uncaringly.

"The hippies. Why shouldn't they freak out? What's the big deal? There's the aborigine of Australia, a stones throw from the stone age, midgets in Africa fuckin' with poison dart blow-guns, tribes in the South Pacific shrinking heads on sticks, and natives in the West Indies still sticking pins in dolls. What the hell, it's all part of the same human race; still one, big, stinking fucking bag of shit."

"Christ" I murmured, "that's depressing. Aren't we ever going to climb out of the gue?"

"Yep," Rudy agreed, "we're still falling out of the monkey tree." The sobering thoughts of imperfection silenced us momentarily, but shortly, when the beacon of truth was thrust upon me like a whore at a political convention, I shouted exuberantly, "I got it! I got it!"

"What! What!" Rudy shouted back.

"They're their father's sons!"

Rudy's eyes glazed over. "Big deal," he responded curtly. "Hey, Lester, did you know we had a genius in our midst? Revelations like that only come from the Bible Buster. So they're their father's sons, so what?"

"So what, he says, so what. Don't you get it?" I waited for something to register. It didn't. I trudged on. "They got the same shit swimming around in their nuts as their old man! It's too close! Too close!"

"What's too close?" Lester muttered unenthusiastically.

"His god-damn eyeballs," Rudy hissed.

"The generations!" I flushed excitably. "The generations! It's too soon! Too soon! Of course they're fucked up. They're still hanging on to the old lady's pouch."

"Hey Rudy," said Lester dully, "find a gas station, will ya. I gotta piss." It WAS … those kind of times.

* * *

One day, while standing on a chair changing a light bulb, I fell off and sprained an ankle. Lester drove me to a doctor I had found in the yellow pages, and who, oddly enough, said to come right over. I should have had my suspicions, he being so eager to help so soon, but … of mice and men.

He took one short look, there not being much else he could do, then sent me to the hospital for X-rays. It was one of those run by the nuns, and before I even had a chance to say "Jack Sprat," some chick in a green uniform raced up, looked me over like a piece of meat on a hook, and satisfied that I didn't need the last rights immediately, announced emphatically, "Sir, before we can do anything I have to get some information. Would you mind coming into the office?" Being an agreeable sort, I acquiesced.

I need not bore the reader with trifling details, for as anyone who has had dealings with the 'mercy' profession can guess, what the young lady wanted to know was: WHO IS GOING TO PAY THE BILL?"

"Me."

"How?"

"Ve-e-e-e-ry slowly."

"With what?"

"Greenbacks, unless the hospital takes chickens."

"How can we be sure?"

"We can't."

"Do you have hospitalization?"

"No, but I play a great game of handball."

That taken care of, off I went back to the waiting room, to sit impatiently for two painful hours. By now my foot had swollen to twice its normal size and felt like two, giant, polar bears were playing tic-tac-toe on it. No one even had enough sense to give me a shot of somethin … anything.

When I was finally wheeled into the X-ray room, I was met by a technician who looked like Walter Matthau, but was wearing a dress, and in that impersonally trained manner they are so famous for, she ordered me to lie on my back, then proceeded, none too gently, to arrange my foot around what looked like sandbags. She took the picture, skitted around the barrier, and said, "Now, Mr. Rosko, would you lie on your right side, please?" I did, and after situating my foot on the X, she positioned it so-so around those sandbags again. Noticing I was beginning to get restless, she, like a trained seal at Water World, gave the "this won't take much longer" bit. The pain, by now, was excruciating. "Take as long as you like," I cracked, "but don't miss your coffee break." She didn't like that one bit. Her nose got all screwed up, and her eyes began to twitch, but she didn't crack back; she just continued to 'sandbag' me.

Taking that picture, she returned and said, with a definite glare in her eye, "Would you mind getting on your other side now, please?" The please was a mere formality. She rearranged my foot and started with them infernal sand bags all over again. I began to see the Marquis de Sade complete with black boots, whip and all. She finally finished me off, (not entirely descriptive), and I wobbled back into the waiting room.

"C'mon, Lester," I said, "Let's get the hell outta here before that god-damn dyke in there kills me." I hopped back up to the doc's office for the results of the X-rays.

"Well, there's no break, Mr. Rosko," he reported like a loan shark giving me an extension on my debt, "so we'll have the nurse tape you up, and I'll see you again in one week." Then, like a magician in a side show, he disappeared.

The nurse bandaged me, and I left hobbling on a stick recently acquired in the parking lot.

During the next few days the swelling subsided, but the ankle remained stiff. I had had sprains before and I knew, X-rays or no, this was more than a simple sprain. The next time I saw Houdini he noticed me hopping on crutches. "Hey, hey, what's this?" he asked surprised. You should've been rid of them by now," he said, pointing to my 'religion in wood.'

"Sure," I replied, "easy for you to say, but the damn thing still hurts like hell."

"Now that don't make sense; let's have a look," he replied as he headed over to do a little squeeze, squeeze.

He unwrapped the tape and started pushing here, and pulling there, and grabbing here, and grabbing there, and with each push, tug, squeeze, and grab, would say, "That hurt? How bout that? And this?"

And each time I would say, "Oh! Ah! Eee!"

"Hmm," he mused. "Something's not right."

"You're kidding?" I answered.

He took a quick glance my way to see whether I was kidding. I was, and I wasn't. Either way, he didn't think so, because I didn't see him smile, unless he was one of those bucks who were a barrel of laughs on the inside.

"Okay," we'd better get some more pictures." And with those menacing words, fear raced up and down my spine.

Off again I went, dancing gingerly for more X-rays. My friend, the merry bull dagger wasn't there this time. No matter, we went through that damn sandbag routine all the same.

When I returned to Houdini, he said, "Mr. Rosko, it seems now you have a slight hairline break, so we'll have to put you in a cast for a few days."

"Why me?" I pleaded. "Can't you put my foot in instead?" He snickered, then did his disappearing act again. The nurse immediately followed him in and wrapped my foot in the cast.

"See you again in one week, Mr. Rosko," she said, kindly enough. And I was off one more time in this boring sequence of events.

Five days later I received a bill from the hospital. $65.00 for the X-rays. The next day I received one from Dr. Leech: $45.00. "Jesus Christ" I screamed. "Jesus Christ! Jesus Christ!" All I could think of was that poor, delusional soul they hoisted up on that splintery cross. He should be here now. Every day is Good Friday.

Rudy, who was in the kitchen frying something that smelled like a cross between two-week old cauliflower and chicken feet, came running into the front room. "What the hell's happenin'!" he barked.

"That god-damn Leech sent me a bill for forty-five smackers, that's what's happening!" I protested.

"Well wud you expect, a corsage?"

"Not quite, but it does seem kind of steep for just a "friendly conversation.""

"I can see it's been a long time since you been sick. This is the new era, brother. Remember the Age of Enlightenment, and the Age of Reason, and all that crap they like to peddle in history classes? Well, this is the Age of the Bloodsucker."

"Do tell. But it ain't reasonable. It ain't even unreasonable. It goes beyond reason and unreason."

"I just got through tellin' you about the Age of Reason. That was two hundred years ago … at least. You got your ages mixed up."

"I feel like not payin' the noxious son-of-a-bitch."

"Hey, suit yourself."

I sat back staring at the little, pink piece of paper that said so much in just two short sentences. Revulsion welled up within me. I wished I was a maniac with a bazooka, but settled for more words instead, the plight of the impotent. "Ya know? Us poor saps ought to set-up an anti-medical union."

"Yeah, then what? We all gonna go on a sickness strike?"

"I ain't so sure the pricks ain't conspiring to keep everybody sick, anyway. How come they spend so little time in medical school studying prevention? The morbid motherfuckers are continually cuttin' up cadavers. It ain't human, it just ain't. Shit that god-damn Mengele is all over the world. He must be making clones down there in South America."

"He don't have to."

"That sucker sends me this shit paper for forty-five bucks, and all I saw him for was maybe two minutes, at the most. The bastard didn't even put the cast on. He made his flunky nurse do it. I must be paying his tuition from medical school."

"At least. . . . ."

"Yeah, well, I ain't going for the hokey-doke. I can understand a dude struggling to get through school, and burning the candle at both ends and all that, but that don't give him the right to be a thief. Why did he stop at forty-five? Why not fifty-five, or sixty-five, or a hundred? What the hell … what's so special about forty-five? Wud' he do, pick it out of a hat? You know what it amounts to? It amounts to the most devious kind of exploitation. He's getting fat off the misfortune of others. He knows you need him; he's got you right by the ass, and he's squeezin' for all it's worth. He's living in Bellaire while the rest of us are living in a tent in somebody's backyard. He wants payment for services rendered? Fine, but I don't expect him to go through my pockets with a suction hose."

"Look at it this way, there's forty-five bucks you won't have to worry about somebody stealin' from you no mo."

"Yeah, and for the next week and a half I eat hot-dogs and beans so that degenerate mother, with the conscience of a two-bit banana republic dictator, can drive around in a Mercedes. I'll bet he's got a big, fat plush camp up at Big Bear, too."

"You can put the forty-five on that."

As you may have guessed, after calming down, I decided to pay it. Wouldn't you know.

When I returned for more ministrations, the nurse removed the cast, and while she was gently swabbing my ankle, the doc came in. He looked at my foot, fingered it here and there, and said, "It looks all right. It doesn't hurt does it?"

"No," I replied as uncivilly as I could.

"Okay then, I don't think we'll have to see you anymore, Mr. Rosko, but if it bothers you, you'd better give me a ring."

"Sure. By the way, you don't mind if I pay this a little at a time, do ya? I ain't working." I emphasized the 'ain't working.' I could tell he sensed a certain hostility in my tone, and that was just fine with me. I was hoping he wouldn't like it, then we both could go down … together … 'for pictures.'

"No, no, there's no rush about it." And with that, he retreated, as always, into the inner sanctum. I was becoming very curious about the contents of that room.

A week later the good Sisters sent me another bill for sixty-five dollars. Two days after that I was blessed yet another time from Herr Leech: twenty-five more, it read succinctly. For the first time in my life arson and murder crossed my mind.

Actually, it dwelled quite a while. I understood now the meaning of mitigating circumstances and the surprised expression, "He shot somebody? My, my, but he was such a nice young man. How could he do such a thing?" Eees no so hard. Life has a way of unrelentingly pushing one, like the little, black rat, into the isolated corner to be tormented by the overgrown, simple-minded giant, wagging a hobnailed club. Lopsidedly are the scales tilted in the direction of pain, adversity, frustration and disillusion, and but rarely does happiness and joy sneak a rock on its end, and the gods, in their mysterious ways, spirit to us spasmodic glimpses of the Elysian fields, sufficient to keep us plodding, like thirteenth century peasants, on the straight and narrow.

But, it is in the numbers. At any given point in one's life a mathematical formula can be devised to determine his state. Just a simple equation: Pain minus pleasure = condition. But there is the unknown, always the unknown, and for that we have inserted organized society with all its attendant irrelevancies (religion, the law, governments, social distinctions), thereby guaranteeing our geometric regression. We have reached the brink of nuclear extinction by the iron hand of mathematical certainty, wherein Einstein was but a brief sneeze in Prometheus's nostrils, and Fermi a muffled cough. Consumed with anger I sat down and wrote the following:

Dear Dr. Leech:

I have just this minute received your fee for an additional twenty-five dollars. That brings the grand total to seventy-dollars for approximately two minutes 'work.' At this rate you are receiving precisely $2,100.00 per hour, $64,000.00 per week, and $3,328,000.00 per year. I do not have $3,328.000.00 to give to anyone, including the Queen of England. I realize this all comes under the heading of free enterprise, which I take to mean anyone has the right to charge what he will for his services. However, I also interpret that to mean anyone has the right to refuse to pay certain charges. I now exercise that right. If you think that unfair, I also think it unfair to charge $3,328,000.00.

What I am saying, dear doctor, is all you get is the $35.00 enclosed, and do what you will. According to the American way, you have recourse to the courts, and the law, having about as much to do with justice as the church has with religion, I have no doubt you will prevail should you choose this means. In any case, my involvement in the matter ends with this payment.

Yours truly, John J. Rosko I. P.S. Hang on to that nurse, no matter what.

As soon as I wrote this short note in madness, I crumpled it up and threw it in the waste-basket. I suppose just in the writing were my frustrations abated. And don't you think for one moment the bastards aren't counting on that little perversion of the human psyche to keep us all in line like obedient, little soldiers, dear hearts.

The next day I went to the hospital to pay the bill. As I was standing at the cashier's window, the customer in front of me was strenuously objecting to the charges he had been presented with. It seems his wife had had a baby and he thought $500.00 was kind of steep. So did I. The more he talked, the angrier he became.

He kept saying, "How am I gonna pay this? This is five weeks pay … when I'm working. All we had was a baby." And the cashier kept repeating in rebuttal, "Well, I don't know, Mr. so and so, but the hospital would like a little something down." They talk that way, you know. "The hospital this," and the hospital that." one would think all that brick and mortar had a life of its own.

He repeated one more time, "That's awful high for a little seven-pound, two ounce, baby." And she said, "What can you put down?"

"My foot! My foot!" came the adamant reply. Well, this sort of thing continued for a while until Mother Superior happened by. The church is fond of the word mother. So is Russia, no doubt due to its exalted position of respect. If one looks upon the church as one's mother, then one isn't likely to abuse it, unless, of course, one happens to have the lovingly instincts of a Lizzie Borden.

Sweet Mother inquired into the matter at hand. The gentleman, none too calmly, furnished Mother with the evidence sprinkled with generous bits of colorful hearsay. Mother, with arms folded across her chest, and hands jammed up her sleeves like an Egyptian mummy, subsequently declared, "Now, now, my son. Have faith, Jesus will help you."

"Oh yeah," he shot back, "we'll send him the bill." And Mother, undeterred and playing it straight all the way, replied, "Oh, I'm afraid we can't do that." And he, in turn, "Why not? Ain't you got his address?"

At that, the sweet Mother began to get a little red around the gills. She stiffened slightly, but continued in the same vein. "I don't know what to say, Mr. Blank, except the bill must be paid somehow. The church has many duties to perform in the service of the Lord, and it can't do them without the necessary funds." And, with that, she turned on her little, black heels and split, leaving Mr. Blank standing there with his sorrow in his hands.

He just stood there for a few moments staring at the bill as if somehow that would make it disappear. It didn't. Then, mumbling something under his breath, he reached in his pocket and pulled out a few dollars and some change, laying it on the counter.

"It's all I got right now, he said dejectedly. The cashier counted the bills—four-dollars—and gave back the change. "Here, you hang on to this," she said with a trace of sympathy.

"Thanks," added Mr. Blank catatonically. "It's nice to know we live in such charitable times."

When my turn came I stood there thinking while my few pesos were being rung up. All sorts of thoughts were pounding through my head, the most obvious being the manner in which the impoverished are continually being had. In war they're the first to go, in a recession the first to lose their jobs, inflation hits them the hardest, in good times the last to get hired, and in a calamity their predicament is altogether hopeless. There's no end to rolling the beggars. It seems to be the only thing that can be counted on, for good or ill, in sickness and in health, till death do they part, and even then the long, bony arm of wretchedness reaches straight down into the grave. "But Mrs. Fish, somebody has to pay for the flowers." The pigeon and the hawk. My cup runneth over.

* * *

On New Year's Eve, Rudy, Lester, and I were invited to a bash. I don't know for sure who invited who, but that's not important in good, ol', sunny Cal-i-forn-i-ay. There's always a winger somewhere, and one only has to be within close proximity to join in on the festivities. The only condition imposed: bring your own.

The gayety in question, as with all New Year's bumbles I have ever been to, resembled a dress rehearsal for a Roman orgy. There were approximately seventy-five persons squeezed in a pad never designed for more than thirty in any circumstances. I never saw so much ass-grabbin' in all my life. It seemed every chick there was trickin' and Mr. you-know-who always made sure he had one hand free. But being the kind of dude who finds such behavior satiating if satisfaction was not soon forthcoming, I then put one hand in my pocket. It made me look cool.

As the evening wore on, an extraordinary event began to unfold on the davenport, center room, front. At first I didn't take much notice—this was New Year's Eve. But after continuing for a half hour or so, it began to fascinate me in a bizarre sort of way.

A white male, early twenties, was sitting and looking very bored, while being grandly molested enthusiastically by a white female, also of early vintage.

What was so intriguing, was that he, the male, looked like the darkest day of a very bad year, while she, the female, could have been the centerfold of any month, of any year, in that Olympian standard of Shakespearian literature, Playboy, and maybe was. In other words, she was the toughest looking chick shrouded in southern California smog.

He seemed not to be concerned in the least, while she was making what can only be described as a superhuman effort to revive the corpse, and in this one-sided struggle, displayed the most ingenious means of artificial resuscitation known to man or beast, including mouth to mouth, hand to mouth, hand to groin, groin to groin, and a few others not included in the first aid manual. Eventually, however, I tired of this dual-handed pornography and searched for better things. It was not long forthcoming.

Off in a corner, placidly twirling a chunk of ice in her drink, stood a young lady. "Aha!" said I to myself. "Charge!"

Actually, she didn't look that good even with the bad lighting, but I hadn't been pleasantly enchanted by a member of the winsome and loving gender for some time now, and was beginning to get terrible headaches.

I meandered in her direction and noticed a thin frame, almost skinny, dark straight shoulder length hair, a prominent proboscis, and knobby knees. I was undeterred. Like 'Vinegar Joe' in Burma, I pushed on.

Approaching her coolly, I asked in my deepest Gablesque tone, "Are you trying to heat up the ice, or cool off the booze?"

She looked down (she was also some four or five inches taller than me) none too amused, and shot back caustically, "Are you a midget, or just a tall Oriental?"

Ordinarily, I am not averse to a quick game of twaddle, but when the other party cannot exactly trace her lineage back to Aphrodite, then I am inclined to get a little frosty myself; I got frosty. "My dear," I answered somewhat Clifton Webbishly, "I only came over because I was attracted to you like fleas to a dog, but apparently you're wearing a collar, among other things," and sauntered off.

Momentarily, she came my way, and apologized … I think. "Shall we try again?" she intoned. I just stared, so she then added brusquely, "Well, if your gonna have a fit I'll get a spoon."

"Yeah, well, you can get all the spoons you like, and a few forks, too, but you know what you can do with them?"

"It's going to be that kind of night, is it?"

"Beginning to l-o-o-k t-h-a-t w-a-y."

"By the way, just how tall are you, anyway?"

"Five-five, except when it's real hot, then I shrink down to five-four and three-quarters."

"Well, it beats four-four and three-quarters, doesn't it?" I didn't know whether she was coming on strong again, but I wasn't taking any chances. I went into my best Bogie. "Is that really your mouth below your honker, or a gravel loader?"

She seemed not to mind the latest dart, but instead replied, matter-of-factly, "You don't have much hair either. I prefer men with lots of hair."

"You should have been a cocker spaniel."

She was standing, so I said, giving her my glass, "Here, go get us a refill, and be careful, I've seen knock-kneed broads before, but a girl can hurt herself." If she took that I knew then I would be stuck with this crow for the rest of the night. She took it, but not without first throwing a left herself.

"I ought to dump this on your head," she intimated, but didn't, and off she went to get our drinks. She must have been as desperate as I was.

Upon returning we carried on with a lot of senseless little inanities, of which the mind is so commonly disposed. Her name was Gelda, and she was from Kansas City, six years removed. By day she was an attorney's aide, by night, anything she chose to be. This night she chose to be a vamp.

Eventually the clock struck twelve. "Well," I said, "I suppose now your gonna turn into a princess, you're already a pumpkin."

She sipped her drink, gazing at me indifferently, and retorted, "In the short time I've known you, Bub, I've kind of taken a shine to your subtleties. Know what I mean, bastard?" She was a tooo-ugh broad.

"Is that with a capital B, sweetheart?" Then with all the style and suavity of a Rudolph Valentino, I coolly leaned over to kiss her and spilled my drink in her paunch. Angrily, she jumped up and bawled, "Cripe's sake! If you can't handle that thing, put a string on it!"

Looking at her dress, I answered innocently, "I thought I handled it pretty well. Not a drop hit the floor."

"Quit makin' with the jokes, Shaky, and go get something to wipe this with," she ordered while shaking her dress. "This ain't no bargain basement special, ya know?"

I brought back a towel from the kitchen. She wiped herself, although it was mostly melted ice, and not enough of that to drown a footless flea. After the deed was done we sat again, a bit warily mind you, to continue once again the business at hand, and, I must say, being a legal secretary must do something to a girl because she sure was taking everything in sequence. I began to feel like a D.A. conducting an investigation rather than just a pure, simple-hearted soul trying to get a little New Year's nookie. After all, what's New Year's for if not to 'shoot-off' your gun?

After kissing her a few times, and feeling a little here and a little there, I reached down and grabbed her crotch. Darling Gelda pushed my hand away. "Just what do you think I am, anyway?" she objected. Hmm. Did I come in in the middle of this movie? "Oh, hell," I muttered, "this is New Year's, you know?"

"So, wudya want, a cigar?"

"No, I got the cigar; I'm looking for the box to put it in."

"Well, you'd better cool your 'White Owl,' Bub, "cause I don't like to be rushed."

"Shit, wud you come here for, to take notes?"

"No … to blow my kazoo."

"Blow mine, its got bubbles in it."

"Your a nasty fucker."

"Right now I'm just trying to be a fucker, any kind."

"Right now your succeeding."

"Are we talking about the same thing?"

"More or less."

"Wud'ya say we go upstairs."

"What for? What can we do up there that we can't do down here?"

"Look, sweet lips, don't be contrary. I've had a hard life. Let's just go, and after we get there maybe we'll think of something."

"Oh all right," she agreed, only partially irritated, and off we went.

I imagine she would like to be able to say she spent a pleasant New Year's like most everyone else, preferably with a hot, young stud, with a properly placed, protruding appendage, lunged appreciably up those parts usually reserved for such hardware. Truck drivers aren't the only ones who like to brag about their sexual prowess.

By now you may have guessed my intentions were entirely dishonorable, but it had gotten to the point where I was either going to have Gelda, or know the reason why. I had wasted the better part of the night with her, and it was too late to carve out new territory; it was this, or nothing. Besides, I was doing her a bigger favor than she was doing me.

Upstairs was worse than downstairs. Every nook and cranny seemed to have its occupants. "Christ," I growled, "half of L.A. County must be here tonight. Could it be this is the only bash in town?"

My companion gleefully responded with, "Quit your bitching; you met me didn't you?" I looked her way and smiled. What else could one do?

As we stood there like two lame ducks on a pond, I noticed a few feet away, a partially opened door. I reeled over and peeked in. It was an unoccupied closet just big enough for two. "Hey," I called, "over here."

She came, looked in, then motioning toward the cubicle, asked, "So what's this?"

"It's a closet," I answered flatly. I was willing to play the game … for a while.

"Well, I can see that, but what's the fascination with closets? You some kind of clothes freak?"

"Time's a-wasting, deary. It's the best I could on such short notice. Don't be such a stickler for details. Let's do what we can do when we can do it." And with that, I grabbed her insufferable ass, and gently shoved her into 'the library.' Trying to get a little poon-tang can sometimes resemble a military skirmish. It helps, when the time is right, to use a 'flank' attack.

We stood there, belly to belly, going through the customary routine with shirts, blouses, nylons, and brassieres draped over our heads. A few minutes later, after having become thoroughly entangled between Gelda and the hanging dishabille, there came a loud crash from the room directly adjoining our 'suite.' It seemed the bed, having not been designed for eight people, had therefore fallen. Naturally, being startled at the sudden change in acoustics, I jerked backwards, slipping on someone's panties, and fell against the door accidentally shoving Gelda against the wall. She just leaned there disgustedly staring at the ceiling.

"Christ," she complained, "I don't believe this night. Lem'me outta here."

Just enough light was seeping in from the bedroom to notice what a dreadful sight she was. Her pants were hanging down around her knees, and her bright, red Lana Turner sweater was partly pulled up over her head exposing one small titty, and the position she had been pushed in when falling—one knee turned out, the other in—resembled a broken-legged ostrich. Visions of Harpo Marx flashed through my head.

She jumped up, straightened herself, to a degree, and brusquely walked past me without so much as a wave and a hi-ho, and out of the den of pleasure, leaving me sitting there with my fly open, and my dreams in my hand.

No need for haste now as I watched the commotion unfolding in the bedroom and wondered if my star was crossed. Presently I rose, hastily flung the debris back on the clothes rack, and pitifully strolled downstairs. It was certain now to be a 'bumper-lifting' night.

I made my way to the kitchen, to see by chance if there might not be some very strong, black coffee. There wasn't, only dirty dishes piled uncreatively.

In the next room I recognized Rudy, among seven or eight others, attentively observing a young lady being hypnotized. Those were the days when hypnotism was all the rage, and if one didn't dabble, one wasn't of this asteroid. Little friendly gatherings of this sort, of which California has become so famous, were often used as schools for the occult. I nudged Rudy, and inquired, "How's it going?"

"I think he's got her," he answered softly. I glanced at the subject, and then at him, "That's not what I meant, chump," I retorted.

"Oh, well, uh … not so hot. It seems practically all the chicks here are spoken for, and the few that ain't should have never left the coop."

"Tell me about it. I had one of them hens. Another ten minutes with her and I'd have turned into a castrated Texas longhorn, good only for grazing. Wud,ya say we grab Lester and split? I think I've had it."

"Okay, I've just about had it myself," he agreed, and off we went searching for Lester.

After trudging through a mass of comingling hot flesh, he was located in a secluded spot on the back porch trying his best with what looked like the worst. There must have been a full moon that night because I never saw so many, shall I say, 'uncomely,' looking specimens in one place at the same time.

Rudy tapped Lester on the shoulder and said, "we're goin" and without waiting for an answer, turned and walked towards me. "If he's comin', he'll come," he stated matter-of-factly.

We waited a few feet distant for a few seconds. Lester had eyes only for the target. "Ya know?" I said to Rudy. "If he hits the bull's eye, he'll think he's in the bull's ass."

"Hmm, you're tellin' me," he replied knowingly. "Let's go, he's stayin." And so we did.

On the way pack to the pad, Rudy slid into a rare pensive mood. "John?" he asked soberly. "Do you ever wonder about all this?"

"All what?" I replied unsurely.

"You know? All this hasslin' around, this mad drive for sex, power, pleasure; you know, the whole bit?"

"What about it?"

"That's what I'm askin'. What about it?"

"Ya gotta give me some clues, matey."

"I get these sudden flashes every now and then that there's something fishy goin' on."

"You need sudden flashes for that? Can't you tell by the smell? The fucking joint veritably stinks." He paid no mind to my sagacious rejoinder, but continued on in the same vein.

"Back there at midnight, for instance, I just stood back and watched everybody, on cue, mauling each other, then after a couple minutes they all stopped dead, almost like … uh … a command was given and everything became subdued again. It's as if somebody, somewhere, is sitting at a giant switchboard with all these different keys: Pain, pleasure, laughter, joy, sex, war, anger, and when the board lights up, everybody performs accordingly."

"That's not bad."

"What?"

"God working for the telephone company." Rudy remained silent. "Yeah," I continued, "why not? I've heard dumber things, holy ghosts, virgin mothers, and what not. God running a giant switchboard. Yeah, that's hep. I like it."

"Did you ever wonder," he questioned, "what would happen if people lived a thousand years?"

"A thousand years? Why a thousand years?"

"Well, if they lived a thousand years, they'd be doing the same thing over and over again, century after century, through many generations. After a while they'd get sick of the whole god-damn thing, wouldn't they?"

"Who needs a thousand years? I feel it coming on already."

"See?"

"I dig it."

"If people had longer lives it would practically dissolve wars."

"It would?" I answered incredulously. "Now you got my attention. Anybody who can abolish war has to be listened to. Fire away."

"Think: Now war is experienced as a new thing, a novelty. It's surrounded by all that hoopla and glamour. That's what traps them, they're never been in a stinking foxhole with chiggers running up their bum, and eating k-rations, and sleeping when you can, where you can, and never seeing a naked broad's ass except on leave, and a shower is what you get when it rains.

Yeah, that's what traps them, all that crap about God, country, duty, freedom. It's the same old shit over and over, but each generation hears it only once, maybe twice, even though its happened hundreds of times. Now if people lived a thousand years, how many times do you think the noxious cocksuckers could get away with it? Three, four, five times? After a while the people would take an, 'uh, oh, here it comes again' attitude, ya dig? The fuckers just couldn't go to the public indefinitely, every twenty years with that, 'Okay, everybody, all together now. Pick up your itty, bitty gunny's, and charge,' shit. They just could never get away with it. They just couldn't. Sure, a few times maybe, but that's about it, brother. It's like being shacked up with the local love goddess for a hundred years. Somewhere along the way you'd have her ass coming out of your ears."

"What a way to go deef."

"Well, you get my meanin'. The dirty little cock-knockers would have to find other ways to jack themselves off."

"Since your on this kick, Rude, we really don't have to live a millennium to do away with war."

"We don't?"

"That's right, sweetheart. All we need is a law, a constitutional amendment, whatever, stating in effect, in the event of war, all the congressmen and senators sons have to be the first to go to the front lines, and no ifs, ands, or buts, about it. Then go the bankers, doctors, and lawyers, sons and the pampered little Fauntleroy's of big business, and all them rich asses who have something to lose in case we lost, not some poor slob whacking himself off to get it all together, and who ain't gonna be any worse off, one way or the other, and if he does gain anything, it'll be a small chunk of bronze, or silver, and a free trip home in a pine box. The bankrupt don't need wars to keep them empty-handed; they're that already. No charge, thank you, Ma'am."

"And his mother gets a flag."

"And Memorial Day becomes the biggest day of her life."

"That ain't bad, Jocko, but you just try and get something like that passed. Just try it. They'd bring back the rack just for you."

"I'm hep."

* * *

"I'm hep."

VI

CANDIDE

SADLY, the time came, when I, like the happy hooker, had to make my way in the world. In other words: I had to seek gainful employment, and it was during such sobering moments that Thoreau usually came to mind.

Ah, there was a man for all seasons. Old Henry had it all down. Work was something only to be done as a last resort, devoid of any mystique or especially deserving of devotion. Merely a means to an end, and sufficiently performed only to contain the elements. It possessed neither unique nor holy attributes, and was never elevated to the level of a religious experience.

Henry was never a candidate for a 'man of the year' award. After all, if everyone were like Henry, what would happen to progress? Initiative? That old get-up-and-go? If America is anything at all, it's ambition! Why look where all these sterling qualities have taken us? The ethic of competition is no mere trifle. It's made us what we are today, the best and the brightest, a car in every garage, a chicken in every pot, a T.V. in every home, a joint in every bedroom. What more could anyone ask? Beer on Fridays, football on Saturdays, church on Sundays, and all made possible by business on Mondays. Hell's bells, Henry, we really got it going. If we all listened to you we wouldn't have had the Mexican War … or the Revolution! Henry, gawd, how un-American can you be? America was founded on war, its lifeblood I-S shedding blood, its godhead freedom personified by tons of cold, dead cement slowly dissolving in New York harbor. Henry, Henry, no robber barons. Unthinkable. They built America. What would America be without its industrial empire? Industry is America, and without it, no Roaring Twenties, no prohibition, or racketeering. America without Al Capone, or bootlegging? Henry, Henry, where is your soul, your mystical sense, your sense of history? Without all that, Henry, then, no crash. Think, man, think. No crash! Now I ask you, Henry, can you imagine an America without the Great Depression? (Never could figure out why it has always been referred to as "Great." Never seemed to be all that great to me, classifying misery as great?) Why that's the kind of stuff that makes the old girl go, it's the pepper in her pot, the vinegar in her butt! Without the Depression, no New Deal (which implies someone must have been getting a raw deal), and if, as some contend, it wasn't all it was cracked up to be, someone still is.

Good grief, Henry, have you gone mad? What are you saying? Were you alive today you'd be the first subpoenaed. You can't tell us all you had in that old shack was a wooden table, a chair, a bunk, and a lil ol' unpretentious field mouse, you old pinko, you. Why hell, Henry, it's what made America great, I tell you, great, the defenders of freedom and democracy. Why just look what we did in Korea? Remember the Alamo, remember Pork Chop Hill, and Viet Nam. Not just anybody can do what we did in Viet Nam. If they can't have democracy, they can't have nothing. Learn or burn. And look at the black man. Just look, he can eat a hamburger anyplace he damn well pleases, and sit anywhere on the bus, and his kids can go to any old school, and grow up and learn all the dirty, little, mean old tricks, like the big, dirty old white man.

* * *

I navigated down to some little insignificant hole in the wall cabinet making shop to investigate the distasteful possibility of becoming gainfully employed. Ha! At $1.50 an hour, that was the offer, one wonders who's gaining? But then, of course, I was living in a democracy, a condition I am never allowed to forget, and therefore, free to refuse. I didn't have to take it. I could have gone across the street to the steel works and toiled for $1.55 an hour. Or I could have done nothing at all. I could have panhandled, or stole, or do what a lot of other folks do, pray a lot, and cry a lot, and the way I saw it, I was going to be shedding my fair share of tears whether I worked or not. And to think I was a part of this great experiment unfolding right before my eyes. I was a part of history; gol-ly, immortality has breathed upon me. It was just like it said in the books. God bless the President and General Motors. Only here, in this land, could I have it so good, only here. God bless America and all her little children.

The establishment in question built television cabinets. There were only ten of us, not counting the owner, who was also president, vice-president, sales manager, superintendant, foreman, chief stockholder, and chairman of the board. In other words: He had all the oranges and the juice, too.

Most of the rest of us were just ordinary laborers. We were called carpenter's apprentices, but for a buck-fifty-an-hour I was just another turd stuck in the drain. They could have called me King Midas for all I cared, and adorned me in silk robes, and fine linen, and all that glitters, but I was still a buck-and-a-half stick-in-the-mud. Such incidents taught me the big game was being played in the back behind the drawn curtains. After the show was over and everyone had gone home, the rats, with noses angled suspiciously in the night air, warily creep out and scurry about.

"A dollar-fifty, take it or leave it."

"But I can't live on that."

"Take it, or scram."

"But it ain't fair."

"You want it or not, Bub?"

"But. . . . ."

"No buts about it."

"But."

"What's the matter, you got a speech impediment?"

"But this is America."

"I know what it is, Bub, but you seem not to."

Didn't he have that right? If I had my way, for a buck-and-a-half-an-hour I wouldn't even roll out of the sack. If I had my way. . . . .

A short while later, I was sitting on a bench having lunch with one of the other suckers, an ex-alcoholic two years removed. Have you ever known an ex-drunk? Christ, they're boring. They continually rap about their miraculous recovery, and according to A.A., one must first gain humility, prostrate himself before the Lord meekly thumping his chest, and admonishing his weakness before he can be cured. Such pretensions merely serve as a veneer to pomposity, and America, being the home of gimmickry, has to skirt around and sneak up on things, and so the popularity of the 'how to' books and magicry.

The Sunday papers unabashedly inform us of inane, little ditties like: "How to hump your darling sweetheart without her knowing it," and "Six easy steps to a satisfying, guilt-free adulterous life," and "In just seven days you, too, can be a pimp." The power of routine stupidity and dead souls. Merrily we roll along. . . . .

Of course, it is only a part of the whole. Our fanatic devotion to sports marks a striking likeness to this imponderable stagnation. In the frustration of defeat (we have been taking our lumps of late), we dash to giant sport complexes (they're getting bigger and gaudier), as the Romans raced to the coliseum, to cancel our failure in the victory of the home team and cheers of the moment, the peanuts, the beer, and the foot-long dogs. In the throes of decadence we see the consequence of our unwillingness to grasp manhood, to grab the bull by the cohunes', and nail his hunker to the barnyard door.

Saddled with the usual wife and two kids, Howard, tall, stringy, and weather-beaten, was the picture of quiet desperation. I tried desperately to think of some way to get him off that "ain't I great, I stopped drinking" jag.

"Say, pardner," I said, crashing in on one of his Tarzan trips, "who you voting for?"

"Wudya mean?" he replied without breaking stride, "for governor?"

"Yeah," I continued, "for governor."

"Oh," he answered easily, "I always vote democrat. I'm a democrat right down the line. I don't believe in any of that 'vote-for-the-man' crap. Them damn republicans never did anything for the working man. I'd sooner vote for the devil before I voted republican."

"You may have," I answered soberly enough.

"Oh yeah?" he objected. "What about you. I suppose you're a republican?"

"No, nothing that oblivious to common decency. I usually don't vote at all."

"Why not?" he asked incredulously.

"Well, when they put up Stalin against Hitler, what C-A-N you do?"

"Wudya talkin' about?"

"Just what I said, Stalin and Hitler."

Not replying immediately, he merely stared, not being sure of my game, waiting to see what I was driving at, if anything, and if I were really as demented as I appeared to be.

"Ya gotta vote," he finally countered. "This is a democracy. How's a democracy gonna work if nobody voted?"

"Same as it does now, Howard. The fact that you can vote don't mean shit."

"It don't, huh?"

"Let me ask you something, Howard. Say there's this guy in Russia, he can't vote, right? Or if he can, he's told who for."

"So?"

"Well, this guy can't vote, and because of it, Genghis Kahn makes himself the leader, okay?"

"Yeah, yeah, so what?"

"Now suppose later on they decide to be democratic and have an election, and the Kahn runs against Attila the Hun, and the Hun wins. Would you say you gained anything because you voted? Could you say you were any better off?"

"Well, what are you saying, we shouldn't vote?"

"What I'm saying is democracy has no value unless it serves the people, ALL the people. In other words, it has to make a difference. To be a miserable wretch in a democracy is much the same as a cheerless soul in a dictatorship. The constitution is a worthless scrap of paper unless it applies to everyone, which it does not. You are benefited according to the size of your bank account. The form is not necessarily the essence. The nefarious, rotten rich have rights, the mendicant's a bag of salt and their memories. It must continually be asked, is democracy doing what it's supposed to do? And it is not entirely clear that it is.

There is a revolution in this country every four years. We bounce into a tiny cubicle, pull the curtain, yank on a lever, and all the frustrations of four years are wiped clean. In a banana republic, when a change is called for, or not, a few rusty rifles go off, and a new regime is installed. It makes you wonder sometimes whose ox is being gored."

I think I shot over Howard's head, but what the hell, sometimes some of the people, sooner or later, have to get interested in something deeper than the six o'clock news.

"So," he said, "what are we supposed to do, have a revolution every four years?"

"In thinking friend, in thinking. There's much talk nowadays about giving the President more power. He needs it, so the theory goes, to more efficiently run the store. Hell, what difference does it make? He couldn't run his ass through a windmill. Madison Avenue runs America."

"So now we gotta burn down Madison Avenue?"

"Like any rat infested dwelling."

"I believe you're serious."

"Serious? Serious? What the fuck am I talking to … a tree? Look, Howard, we're locked in. We cling to our illusions like barnacles on a tired, old, four-rigger. For instance, our tenacious observance of the two-party system would lead one to believe it has led us to Shangri-La, in which case such extravagant homage would be justified. But upon perusing the matter more closely we see that not only has it not led to that exalted plateau, but it hasn't even cleaned up

Pittsburgh. And while we are about it, let me ask you this: Just what the hell do you know about the guy you're voting for? Nothing, except what he wants you to know. And what preparation had he for elective office? Did he go to school somewhere, like say, an academy for statesman, like Annapolis, or West Point? Did he attend any special classes, obtain a certificate or degree of some kind? Did he serve an apprenticeship with testing and grading for knowledge and competency? And how about honesty? Did he pass a lie detector test on that score?

See Howard, it is the most arbitrary means of selecting the most important people for tasks that affect everyone mightily. And no, Howard, you have no basis whatever for selection of same---none. You vote according to your feelings, by your own admission."

"I never said no such a thing. I think about who I'm voting for; I vote on the issues."

I completely ignored that last, since I am certain his interpretation of 'the issues' was simply more pay, more vacation, more benefits; ta ra; ta ra; ta ra.

"Well, the fact is, pardner, we have no good way of determining who's who, and what's what. A political campaign can hardly be regarded as a camping ground for the truth, and did it ever occur to you that politics is the only profession elected by popular vote? Imagine, something as deadly serious as government we leave to the fickle dictates of the general public, that gregarious body of souls which has shown, time and again, that the only thing it can pick with any degree of competency, is its nose."

"Well, I. . . . ."

"And besides, how do you like knowing that that vote, of which you are so proud, is immediately canceled out by an opposite vote. What a set-up. You spend hours, days even, sifting through a lot of hogwash, thinking you're doing your patriotic duty, and some shmuck follows you in the booth and cancels out your vote on the basis of the wiggle of the opposition's, wife's bum. Terrific."

"So what the hell else is there?"

"Howard, why don't we just have a lottery, and let it go at that? And think of the millions we'd save in the elimination of campaigns, the bulk of which can be used to educate the rest of us baboons."

"Well, it's better than having a Queen." The obvious from the obvious. I ignored his specious reference to monarchical contrivances.

"It's the press, Howard, and television. It's their show, and we're their dupes. They've created the modern day politico, and they're shoving him down our throats. It's their time of year and the biggest event in their shabby little lives. The world is being run by a tiny, red eye atop a T.V. camera. They live and breathe for the campaign trail. And did you over notice the maniacal gleam in their eye at a convention, roaming the floor like a house-dick at Bloomingdales with headsets strapped about their ears? They'll shove a mike in the face of a plate of potato salad. And for all of, it they command incomes in the half-mil range, while maltreating the higher functions of the English language with benighted verbiage such as 'meaningful,' 'high-tech,' 'build-down,' and 'impacting.' 'And is it true, Mrs. Bitterlicker, that you switched your vote when Senator, Come-on promised you a bordello license on Park Ave?'

'Oh, no, that's not so, but he did give me the hot-dog concession at Yankee Stadium, and made my boy Melvin the organ player.'

'You've just heard Mrs. Bitterlicker vehemently deny any deal was made regarding the prize on Pennsylvania Avenue. Okay, George, back up to you in the booth.'

"Yes-siree, Bob. Obscenity piled upon obscenity; there's no rest for the weary."

"You're wacky." Feigning anger, I slammed my fist on the bench, exclaiming emphatically, "That's entirely irrelevant!"

Ignoring my outburst, he then said, "So now what? We got a lottery and no Madison Avenue. What next?"

"Next, my good man, the indispensable regulation: A political term, any term, anywhere, should be limited to fifteen years—that's plenty long, on any account—with no possibility whatsoever, of reelection after that time for any reason. It should be looked upon as what it is, a service to the people, and not a lifetime bed to lie on. An interim period in a person's life like military duty. You join, you serve your tour, do your duty, and split. Why shit, there's some old fuckers up in congress ninety-years-old, and up. It's become a home for them. 'And where would you like to go, Mr. Jones, when you retire?' 'Oh, I'd like to go to congress. The food's good, nice company, and what a pension. Wooppee!'

"It's the joke of the century, and the laugh's on you and me. Two ducks on a pond munching on dried-up baloney sandwiches, and slurping rot-gut Cokes while some lecherous, lard ass sits up in Washington with a license to steal. We is being had, brotha."

"Aw what the hell you bitchin' about? This is still the best country in the world."

"Sure, Howard," I replied disconsolately, "but for who?"

We sat there for a minute, Howard and me, not saying anything more, just gagging on our nitrated sandwiches. My right leg was crossed over my left, and I swung it nervously up and down. Finally, Howard blurted out, "Ya know, it wouldn't be that way if everyone supported his party. I give a hundred bucks every year to the Democratic National Committee." I dropped my baloney in the sawdust, spit out the Coke, and dumbfounded inquired, "You, what?" Howard was startled at my surprise.

"Wudya mean, I what?" he answered. "You heard me."

"Well now, let's just wait a minute. Let me see if I'm getting this right, cause I really ain't sure I heard what I heard, although I think I heard it, surely. You give one hundred good, American dollars, every year, to the Democratic, mother-fucking, National Committee. Is that right?"

"Yeah, yeah, that's right," he replied indignantly. "A hundred bucks. So what?"

I shook my head in disbelief. Truly I was at a loss for words, for what can one say at such a display of frivolity? But, no matter, I attempted. "Howard, you ain't got two cruddy dimes to rub together, and you're sending money, big money for you, to them parasites in Washington? Christ, man, you better get off the wagon, your brain's drying up."

He countered angrily, angrier than one might have thought under the trivial circumstances. "Well, I never heard of nothin' so un-American." And before I had a chance to respond, somebody dropped a hammer, and, like Petrucchio, we all returned to our little tasks. Strangely enough, or not, Howard ignored me for the rest of the afternoon. The ignorant are such boors.

Unsuspectingly did I stroll in the next morning, carrying my little brown bag, when the 'chairman of the board' called me into his office. One thing about working for these one-horse operations, one gets to deal directly with the man at the top. None of that chain of command doggy-doo.

The scurrilous reprobate didn't even ask me to sit down. I guess he thought I might stink up his chairs. The door barely closed when he announced, "Rosko, we won't be needing you anymore."

'We,' mind you. I gather the plural made him feel more powerful. I was taken aback momentarily, so just stood there staring wide-eyed, and open-mouthed, like a guppy on dry land. It wasn't that I was unduly fond of that particular mode of employment, but rather it surprised me in that I couldn't think of anything I had done to arouse the 'leader' complex.

After gathering my wits, however, I decided that he wasn't going to run a million-dollar game on me for no damn buck-fifty an hour, so I said matter-of-factly, "Gee, that's too bad. Send me my check; you got my address," and walked out, leaving Mr. America standing there with his power shoved back up his star spangled arse.

On the way back to the pad I tried to figure what it was all about, but for the life of me, I couldn't make the connection. Little did I know. . . . .

A couple of days later, merely out of curiosity, I called one of the other shmucko's to "get the message." By this time, I thought, the word should have gotten around, or at least the rumor, anyway.

Well, I got the message. I was fired because they thought I was a communist. That rocked me a bit because I wouldn't have known a communist if his card was stamped on his forehead, and was wearing red pants. Besides, in my rapidly diminishing naiveté, I insensibly thought that that kind of thing was over in America. Surprise, surprise. I didn't ask how such an opinion was perfunctorily arrived at, I knew. Howard, the suck hole, had done his duty, the god-damn snitch.

I thanked him and hung up, safe in my heart of hearts that America was overseeing the cause of freedom. God bless America.

* * *

After my latest success, I roamed through a period of apprenticeship not uncommon to those aspiring to hoboism. I was beginning to realize, for better or worse, that my nature had taken a turn toward the foot loose and fancy free, and, I liked it. I no longer had that burning desire to get ahead. I never did, actually, I was only made to think so.

Tis still a mystery, in this best of all possible worlds, why some lose the drive, and in others it gets stronger, although, about this time, I was eating a lot of prunes. It did keep me light on my feet.

As complicated as the human mechanism may be, I wonder if more isn't made of our condition than necessary. There is a theory circulating within the world of psychology which reduces the human predicament to the sex act. Accordingly, it states, that practically any problem can be alleviated by a healthy dose of 'heavy breathing.'

Now, you may have been led to believe that it is all the same, as one charming lady of the evening proud fully announced, one lazy night prior to slipping into that pulsating state of enchantment, 'pussie's, pussy.' That may be so, but there ain't an old Tom in town who wouldn't rather have a furry, stuck-up Persian, than a peed on old alley walker. And then there's that, old canard, or maybe not, that Hitler was afflicted by a particularly severe case of that western malady—constipation. What a charade. But for a good dose of castor oil the world had a war.

I sold magazines for a while, a very short while, two weeks to be exact. There's nothing like a stint at door-to-door selling to tighten up the girth. I highly recommend it as a necessary inclusion to the curriculum. Nowhere is the amplified sense of American rudeness manifestly expressed better than by the slamming door. Selling subscriptions to the general public is a lot like banging your head against a tree; it feels so good when you stop. I stopped, but quickly took on another belaboring chore----peddling vacuum cleaners. Not too dissimilar you say? Of course, but then all of life is preposterously familiar upon second glance. If nothing else, I did get a taste of the free enterprise system at its swaggering best. The full force of motivations, beliefs, raison d'être was brought home like a good, stiff punch in the mouth.

The training at Scooby was designed with an eye toward thoroughness. All the salesmen were assembled at an early hour (eight A.M.) in the back of the 'headquarters.' After the morning ritual, I always felt like a soldier going into battle. More specifically, a kamikaze pilot.

Twenty-five, or so, of us, would all gather for a briefing. The sales manager would point out, step by step, the superior features of the Scooby over all other cleaners. He was fond of saying, "You can't sell a product if you don't know the product." He was sharp as a tack. Expending thirty minutes on technical matters, he would then launch into the techniques of the sales pitch which included everything from, "Ma'am, could I trouble you for a glass of water?" to "May I use your phone to call the office, Ma'am," to, "Good afternoon, madam; how would you like a free book of stamps?"

This silliness ran some thirty minutes, whereupon the meeting would end with everyone standing, and clapping, and singing rousing Scooby cheers from the top of our lungs. It was a regular revival meeting. All that was lacking were the hallelujahs and the tambourines. By this time, we were supposed to be sufficiently aroused to attack a crazed grizzly with a rusty can opener, and with the words of our commandant ringing in our ears, the doors were flung open and our enthusiasm, armed with the zeal of a holy crusade, thrust us out into the street, ready to sell to anything that looked alive. "Remember, a home without a Scooby is a dirty home!" Suffice to say, I felt like the number one ass.

One morning after the usual festivities, I approached one of the other 'missionaries,' an elderly gentleman in his fifties who looked to be down on his luck also, and queried, "Say, Jack? You dig all this?"

"Come again?" he responded confusedly.

"You know, all this hooray, yah, yah stuff? You think it's necessary to make a babbling idiot out of a dude just to sell a damn vacuum cleaner?"

"Well, it must work, they're doing it."

"Yeah," I countered, "but there must be something arrant precisely for that reason. I'm over twenty-one, I don't need all the fucking Mickey Mouse crap, ya know? I really don't."

"John," he replied sadly, "I think there's something wrong that I have to come out here at all."

"Uh, huh."

I tolerated this foolishness for ten days, long enough to sell two Scooby's and collect one hundred and sixty bucks. On the eleventh day I rested, and many succeeding days thereafter. Also, I could feel a smoker coming on. There's nothing like a little reveling to clean out the cobwebs and loosen the wickets, to sit around listening to soft music, sipping on a whatever, and stroking 'Miss America's' buns while she whispers sweet little nothings in your ear. Fortunately, for all parties concerned, she does have the buns. Luckily for me, I never did fall for all that 'ya gotta be in love first' clap-trap. I don't have to be in love with a hot-dog to enjoy eating one, why a chick? Sex for sex's sakes.

So? And who is being hurt? Bring on the bewitching, overheated, honey sweetened, sea-nymphs.

You know, Buck. This life can get very complicated, very sticky, and I'll be the first to admit it. There's so much out there, so much, it can get overwhelming. But then again, don't dig up the garden before the harvest.

Forget philosophy, forget the church, forget the do-gooders, forget the hypocritical, psalm singing, sanctimonious reprobates. There is really only one philosophy for living, for this life, one and only one, regardless of whatever else you are, whatever else you believe, or would like to believe, rich or poor, king, president, prince or pauper, one ideal, one belief, one religion, one, one, one, and only one, in good times and bad, in sickness and in health, and that is—BE HONEST; BE SMART; BE KIND; BE FAIR.

This life is to short, its path strewn with to many sharp stones, its streets, avenues and byways littered with to many perverted, low-life blackguards.

You can't fight a pack of hyenas with a stick. Be honest, be smart, be kind, and be fair. You're not going to win; you can never win; you are outnumbered; you will always be outnumbered, but you'll make life hell for the treacherous devils; they will know you were here.

* * *

We planned the festivities for a Friday, any Friday. Finally, one came, and lo and behold, just like the loaves and the fishes, wine and woman appeared.

It wasn't a bad frolic as frolics go. There were the usual freeloaders and chiselers, the kitchen raiders, and sandwich grabbers, a few old faces, and some new. The customary conversation abounded, meaning religion, politics, marriage. You know, the same old garbage. And later on, a drifting toward sex and a few practical demonstrations. And lest I give the wrong impression, these secluded little rendezvous were not orgies, but it wasn't our fault. Like all losers, we hovered on the brink of success, but never quite made it.

At this particular congregation, one James T. Hooker found his way to our den of pleasure. I had known Mr. Hooker since college. Mr. Hooker was the most vile, rancid, repugnant, mother in a double-breasted suit. I didn't like Mr. Hooker, Mr. Hooker didn't like me.

J.T. was a native Californian, born and bred in one of the better parts of town, and never tired of letting you know it. He was the kind of chap who, upon occasion, felt obliged to defend General Motors. That's like handing Goliath a rock.

Along about twelve, Jamie boy must have hit upon the correct number of drinks, for he was really feeling his oats, meaning, he was attacking his favorite class of people—the unfortunate.

I sidled over to catch some of the mud as part of the educational process. It does well, now and then to hear the outrageous. It clears the mind and the startling contrast puts things in perspective. I suppose it could be classified as the power of negative thinking, and it has never been given its just due.

I listened awhile, and I must say, Jamie boy was in fine fettle that evening. He was ranting and raving about lazys, dummies, and no-goods, and singing the usual song that is sung by the intellectually debilitated, except in this case was shrewishly high-pitched, as James had a shrill voice which went well, or unwell, however, with his parrot face. It is not uncommon for one's physical characteristics to mirror the temperamental.

Jamie boy was on the tall side, about six feet, and thin. He was wearing a brown suit with a brown pin-stripped shirt and a brown string tie. He was, as the saying goes, Mr. 'Junior Executive' all the way. I think he even won one of those awards one year. You know, the kind they hand out for being the biggest ass-kisser in the county. No doubt, at the rate he was progressing, by forty he'd be sitting in the president's chair, and I don't think he'd mind a bit if the prez was sitting in it also.

I stood listening, building up a great resentment. I didn't hear half of what was being said, I was just wondering what it would be like to give him a good punch in the mouth, to feel my fist against his bony face, to see teeth fly, and warm, red blood trickle down upon that stiff, brown suit. He had the kind of face one just loved to touch. His nose was turned down and his lower lip turned up giving him a perpetual sneer. Eventually, noticing me standing off to one side, he thrust out a chalky, lifeless, hand in my direction, blurting: "Now there's the man we've got to get in this. C'mon over here, Rosko. We're solving the country's problems, and you're just the man we need." Of course he was being facetious, the fool.

We had had a few minor scuffles before, enough to realize we weren't exactly blood brothers. I really had no desire to join in, but what the hell, hostility breeds its own kind.

"What do you think about all this nonsense how the poor have it so tough nowadays, and all that crap?" he chided condescendingly.

There really are people who believe there is no such thing as the poor, and the like. I knew a hapless soul once who said the Holocaust never happened. According to him, it was all a Zionist plot to gain sympathy for their cause, and when I questioned him about the voluminous extent of the evidence to the contrary, including photographs of the camps, its survivors, and numerous eyewitness accounts, he never blinked an eye, but volunteered how 'money can fix anything.' Is it any wonder why some will go into a cave and never come out again?

"That kind of answers itself, don't it?" I countered.

"How's that?"

"If somebody's poor, then it's a foregone conclusion he's got it tough, and all that crap," I mocked.

"Oh, I knew I could depend on you, Johnny boy, to twist things around. You'd better lay off all that damn Marxist dung, it's messin' up your mind."

"I don't need Marx to count 1, 2, 3, for me, Hooker." Jamesie twinged and retorted. "Ha! Is that so! Well, tell us then, how do we deliver these poor unfortunates from our midst?" Like any good pseudo-intellectual, Jamie boy was suffering from a sever case of myopia.

"You created them, you get rid of them; get off their backs, that's how."

He threw up his arms, looked around at everyone, (this type always needs an audience) and barked, "Get off their backs! But I never so much as laid a hand on them," and laughed a sickly laugh. He also thought he was a comic.

"I know. You leave that to the law. It's not so messy that way. The courts clean the dirt from under your nails."

"Rosko," he replied indignantly, "you scare me. If everyone was like you, America would be another Russia." Christ, he was predictable.

"Not quite, but it wouldn't be the cannibal that it is either."

"That so? Well, what are we supposed to do, let anyone who wants to, come in our homes and take what they want?"

"Why not? That's what's being done anyway, only we dress it up in a gray suit and call it free enterprise, and a brown suit and call it the I.R.S., and if you object, we put it in a blue suit, and stick a gun in its hand to collect."

He shrugged and smirked, then replied, all knowingly, "Ain't you ever heard of hard work, incentive, that old get up and go? This is America, man. God helps those that help themselves."

"Funny, that's what John Dillinger said once when he was robbing a bank."

"Yeah, well just remember, there ain't no country like this country where a man can start from scratch and with a little application and hard work make millions." This coming from a man with nary a callous on his hand, nor a hair on his chalky, white ass.

"Hooker, ain't you ever heard of that old saying, "behind every great fortune lies a great crime?"

"So, who says you can't do the same?"

"Why should I have to?"

"Ha! Don't be naive. That's what makes this country great—ingenuity.

"Oh, is that what we're calling it now? I always thought it was stealing. Pray tell, Mr. Alger, how do you coincide that with justice?"

"Justice is for those who have the will to make it."

"I see. And where is it made, in the board room of G.M., or Madison Avenue? Or how about Hong Kong? I had an ash tray once that was made there."

"I make mine with these," he answered holding up two skinny, soft milky white fists, "and this," pointing to his head, "and this," pointing to his paunch.

"My, my; justice sure do get around. All those places, huh?"

"The trouble with people like you, Rosko, is that you're a loser, and losers are always looking for excuses." Well, at least he wasn't a complete idiot, he did get half of it right.

"You're probably right about the first part," I agreed grudgingly, "but I wouldn't confuse reasons with excuses, myself."

"What reasons?"

"Oh, how about paying somebody a buck-and-a-quarter an hour to wash dishes, two bucks to clean latrines, two and a quarter to pick up your stinking garbage, and all this while some big-assed starlet is demanding, and getting, a million bucks a flick, the president of a corporation seven hundred thousand, not counting incidentals, and a bull-shittin' senator forty-two grand for a lot of lying and graft, and guys like you are knocking down thirty grand just to sit in an air-conditioned office and think up insulting, stupid little jingles about soap and corn flakes, the nature of which I'd hesitate to show a fucking, mangy dog."

"Oh, yeah? Well, so what? That's what generates revenue. That's what makes us different."

"So was Jack the Ripper."

"We've got the highest standard of living in the world."

"Ah, yes. Give me your huddled masses; there's a big fat rat somewhere when a doctor can make a two-hundred-thou a year, and the sap who cleans his commode five-thou. How come some people can't even find a job while others have two? You can't justify a million dollars to some motley, fucking whore, sticking her dungy ass in front of a camera while paying John Q. America a buck-fifty to do your stinking dirty work. We don't need her at all. And that's one hell of a range, a million, to a buck-fifty, one hell of a range. That's reasons, friend, and the reason is, as it always is, money and power vs. the weak and the meek, today, tomorrow, forever; in America, or Russia, in Greenland, or the Congo. It speaks a universal language. The jackal roams free and the blood of the squirrel drips from his gleaming fangs.

Riddles, Hooker, riddles. Riddles and words. America; freedom; liberty. It might just as well be urf, smurf and durf; it is all the same-doublespeak, and it has no meaning whatever. The lion rules the jungle, the rat and the roach, the city.

The sick grin he wore was now replaced by a healthy, ugly laugh, but I don't believe he was in danger of being overrun by humor. "Go on," he admonished, "don't stop now; this is a free country." Amazing how the Billy club of freedom is so easily swung about.

I continued. "After the situation is analyzed and reanalyzed it comes down to one thing, finally. We are being overrun by weaklings. The survival of the fittest is a hoax. Take a look at who our fearless leaders are. Take a good look. In all walks of life, misfits, damn near every one of them, to the man. The weak hang on like a disease, like death itself. They feed off the exhausted like buzzards off a dead carcass and give the impression of strength while every trick is run out before they give up the ghost. In the meantime, the prostrate help it all along because they're too god-damned brainwashed to see they're being had, and that's all part of the game. They're the sorry victims, for they can't see the chains hanging about their necks, the iron fist squeezing their balls. Suck on that awhile, Buster."

He laughed and looked around to see who was watching. Trying desperately to think of something clever, he settled for, "So what could he do anyway, demonstrate?"

"Funny you should say that; it tells a lot. Why should he have to? Why should he have to take to the streets in an act of desperation? G.M. don't have to, or U.S. Steel, or I.T.T., or the N.A.M., or anyone else with heavy juice. I haven't seen the president of the chamber of commerce in the streets lately, have you? By having to take to the streets the system is saying, 'fuck you, Jack, and your grievances, and stick your letters in your ass. We ain't listening to nothin' till you make us.' It's saying, 'This ain't no democracy.' That's what it's saying. Those pulling the reins have their lobbies and instant justice, the rest of us are condemned to social movements, and the eternal illusion of progress."

I sat down disconsolately. What else? I do believe the Hookers of this world were specifically put here to wear the rest of us down. They are having un-be-lieve-a-ble success. He held out his arms as if to say, "That's it?" but instead blurted, "Keep goin, Rosko, keep goin; don't stop now. The case ain't closed."

Maybe not, but I was hoping he would soon be blessed with a terminal case of lockjaw. No matter, prayers are for the mentally defective. I trudged on. "My advice is apt and to the point. Wise up and get off your dead ass. The labor movement in this country, such as it is, ought to organize into one gigantic branch, wherein the impetus should be to raise the minimum wage, for everyone, no matter what the job, to five-dollars-an-hour, and a lid placed on how much any one person can make, say a hundred grand, no matter what he does. Beyond that, they should push like hell for industrial democracy, and an earnings ratio of no more than fifteen to one. The way things are now, a plumber gets six bucks an hour, and a dishwasher a buck-and-a-quarter. What kind of crap do you call that? Is there really that much difference between them? One cleans pipes, the other dishes. Besides, a guy can always crap in the woods, he don't need a john, but I'd like to see what the frig he'd do if he sat down in a restaurant after a hard day's work, and the waiter told him he had to wash his own crutty dishes before he could eat.

And how bout the migrant? What if every time you wanted a strawberry, or a potato, or a peach, you had to get in your car and drive out and pick the dam things yourself? Isn't that labor equally as important as that done by the chairman of the board sitting on his redundant ass thinking of ways to screw the public? You think that's a service we can't do without? And don't tell me about all the god-damn training one needs to run a corporation. Spare me, please. Eight dollars a day, broken plumbing, disease, no medical care, back-breaking work, flies, gnats, and child labor, to seven hundred thou a year, stock options, expenses, a five hundred-thousand-dollar home, a yacht, and a Lear jet. Man, that's one hell of a spread for a little training."

"Rosko, you're a bleedin' heart."

"No, not really. I merely object to getting shit on in the name of democracy. As a matter of fact, I don't like getting shit on in anybody's name. That's not hard to understand, is it, Hooker … even to a blank like you."

Jamie swirled his drink, scratched his face, looked this way and that. I know he was itching to think of something clever to say, but after all, he W-A-S in advertising, so instead, he blurted oafishly, "You know, Rosko, what your talking is communism?"

"It is, huh? Dragging that old cat out, are we? The government organizes strictly for its own benefit, business the same, the military likewise, but with the worker it's communism. Strange, there is no mind like the belabored mind."

"You make me laugh. There's millions of people not even working, and living like kings. Ain't you ever heard of welfare?"

"Ah, yes, cleaning out the closet tonight, I see. I was wondering when you were gonna get around to that old dog. Didn't you ever read the Bible, Hooker? And isn't there something in there about, 'you reap what you sow,' or to spruce it up a bit in modern lingo, 'you get what you deserve, and you deserve what you get?' Above and beyond that, America, contrary to popular opinion, ain't running on all eight cylinders. The solution to the welfare problem is so simple I'm ashamed I'm the only one who knows it, what with all the 'experts' running thither and fro."

"Really."

"Yeah, and I wonder sometimes how we survive at all, let alone do all the wonderful things we do."

"Okay, bright boy, so what's the solution? What's the answer that's stumped all the experts?"

"Perk up, cupcake, here it comes. Create a rotation system!" I shouted over the constant din of a juvenile, hard rock recording. "Everybody on! Everybody off!"

Anyone who was anyone stopped what they were doing, that not being much in any case, and looked in our direction. I was overcome by an immense surge of power, and the thought of Caesar embracing the throne entered my mind. A cute little blond who had been crossing and uncrossing her legs all night, was now flashing the whole bush. I wondered if it was intended for my benefit. I was determined however, to finish the job at hand first. There's a little bit of masochism in even the best of us. I continued, "Everybody works six months, and rests six months. That would eliminate the unemployment problem. Everybody works a while and everybody rests a while. Machinists trade off with machinists, assemblers with assemblers, clerks with clerks, laborers with laborers, and the time that a man's off, he is subsidized by the government at the same rate as when he was working, and everybody will be happy because everybody will be on welfare, and everybody will be working. Equal treatment right down the line. No one could complain about freeloaders then, because everybody would be one. That's democracy, brother. All for one and one for all. And another thing; everybody would be paying taxes, too. How bout that little gem?"

"What a pipe dream. You ain't really serious, are you? Who the hell's gonna go for a weirdo scheme like that?"

"Nobody, it's too simple. You don't need a battalion of economists drawing up reams of charts and graphs for it. Christ, it'd look like a foreign country to the experts."

"It would, ay?"

"If a technique can't be devised for it, it can't be done," and to myself, I murmured: simplicity went up in the mushroom cloud at Hiroshima. The ghost of Thoreau is dead, and then continued with, "In any case, somebody would eventually jump up and scream, 'Communism!' and everyone would scramble back into their scuffy holes with their bushy little tails between their legs, and that would be that."

"Hell, never mind that. What about efficiency?" Hooker, true to his nature, was asking all the wrong questions, predictably.

"What about it?" I answered unenthusiastically.

"What about it?"

"Yeah, what about it? I don't stutter."

"I'll tell you what about it. Not everyone's a good worker, and under this set-up, a company couldn't fire anyone for doing a lousy job."

"So what? Every company will have its share of deadbeats if everyone is working, so it'll all come out in the wash. It's a matter of probability. The odds that any one company getting an abundance of all the rotten workers is minimal, and even if it did, so what? All good things have their price. If you want to go to heaven, you have to fight the devil first."

"Oh, yeah? Who said that?"

"Rosko, 1968 A.D."

Banging his hand on the bar, he responded facetiously, "That's what I like about you John, you have an historical sense. Have you got any more little ditties for us? After all, this is a party, and every party has its clown." He then looked around to see if anyone had appreciated his witticism. Apparently not; James 'the stupid' was laughing incognito.

"Curious, isn't it, Jamie boy?" I said, "or is it? The well-heeled always seem to take paucity as a joke, but it's no joke for those scratching around in the dirt for a few crumbs."

"Water seeks its own level."

"To those over their heads, it's drowning."

"Well, is that it for now, or would you like to add a postscript?"

"Yeah, I got a P.S. for ya. Let's make poverty illegal. If we don't do anything else; let's do that much. I guarantee we'll wipe it out in six months."

"Now there's a twist for ya. Then we can round up all the poor and shoot them, is that it?"

He was joking, I think. With his type one can never be sure. Hooker was really a Fascist in a gray-flannel suit. If it came right down to it, I'm sure it wouldn't take much persuading to get him in a black armband. It all depended on which way the wind was blowing. It is essential to address such gimcracks in the manner to which they are accustomed; I did.

"Just keep sucking up the booze 'fish bait;' I'll tell you when to come up for air." He didn't take too kindly to 'fish bait' very much, but life is an endless series of boring misadventures, if not outright disasters, so what the hell, I've seen rat shit in tuna, but not his, so he must be defecating in the same holes as everyone else. I didn't wait for an answer; I knew he wasn't much on rapping, so I kept right on.

"Haven't you ever noticed how ape this country gets when something is illegal? Ordinary feelings are transformed into a religious fervor comparable to a Savonarola. It borders on the fanatical. Remember prohibition? One would have thought the only duty of the government was to break up bootleggin'. And the drug laws. Have you ever seen such zeal based merely on something being illegal? There are more organizations, official or otherwise, geared toward catching pot smokers, you'd think the world was going to disintegrate into one, big puff of smoke if they're not all caught, and their weeds thrashed into little, itty bitty pieces, and thrown to the four winds. And parking. Hah! The fuzz is out there working their little pads and pencils like the devil's lookin' over their shoulders. If you want to get people excited, you don't have to show them a picture of Raquel Welch, just make something illegal. It don't matter what, just anything handy that happens to be laying around; the friggin peckerheads will fall right out of their trees."

Jamie didn't look impressed. Good, when I start impressing the gross then I know I'm doing something wrong. I continued merely as a catharsis. He did make a handy punching bag, but I always felt like a bully when talking to Jamie boy; he was such a 'piece of cake.'

"If poverty was illegal, then the police could round them all up like they do now with the winos on skid row, and upon conviction, would automatically receive a fine of one-hundred-dollars—that is, from the court to the culprit---or thirty days in the Hearst Castle. That'll fix 'um."

"Ha! And just where is all this cash gonna come from, your Honor?" Pointing my finger straight at him, I replied emphatically, "From you, suc-kah, from such j-u-s-t l-i-k-e y-o-u."

"Yeah? Well, don't hold your breath waitin', Rosko."

"Oh, the day will come all right. Make no mistake about it; all things in their own time. It is my misfortune, however, that I'll never live to see it. Pity, I'm just the one who'd know how to enjoy it, too."

"I'll bet."

I dunked a cube of ice in my drink, and waited for a further reaction. I might just as well have been waiting for the second coming of Christ. I had no choice but to continue. "It can't be accomplished without outside help, that's for sure. There's too much against it. What's needed is some stinking, filthy rich bastard, to buy a pad in the middle of Beverly Hills, raze it to the ground, and build a clapboard shanty on the very spot, right in the midst of that pretentious display of luxury. That'll string out a few folks, for a while, anyway. That's the kind of spirit we need, and precisely the kind we don't have. Instead we have all kinds of jackasses running around making a big deal about elections, and candidates, and campaigns, and this, and that. It's like sweatin' whether the water shooting out of the fire hose is clean when your house is burning down."

I heard a solitary, "here, here," from somewhere back in the crowd. We had gathered a few extra faces by this time, but becoming weary, I looked to end this exercise in nothingness.

"You know, bozo, the indigent never have a New Year. Every year is 1929, every day a depression. So, have another drink. It's your kind of world, Hooker, enjoy it."

I turned and left, the reactionary, jackass bastard that he was, standing there with a drink in one hand, a pretzel in the other, and that sick grin spread across a fatuous, insensate face. It occurred to me, as I walked into another room, that cannibals and businessmen have a lot in common. Both will do practically anything to get a-head.

I was feeling down in my cups when I saw an old friend whom I hadn't seen for some time, and who I was always very fond of. Her name was Ingeborg Sonder, and yes, she was a big, beautiful, tall-assed hunk of a Swede. Every bit of six feet, blond and incredibly sensuous, she was one of those young ladies who one would do almost anything to bed down with, just once.

However, sweet Ingeborg had one, slight minor condition, which tended to mar her style somewhat; she walked kind of stiff-legged and Chaplinesque as if she had a mop-stick stuck halfway up her bum.

Ingeborg, some months earlier, had met with an unfortunate accident. On a hunting trip one day, her brother mistook her for a deer, and shot her in the rear. The blow severed the 'whatever' muscle that happens to be in that particular area, and ever since she's been, shall we say, kind of wobbly. Of course, not being able to control herself completely, her valve would leak, bit-by-bit, until she stunk like hell, which often was the case. She had an awful lot of pluck, though. It never stopped her from socializing, not for one minute. She kept the same even pace, and no one really minded, she was so damned nice.

They operated on her three times, but they just couldn't seem to plug up the leak. Eventually, it was supposed to heal itself. In the meanwhile, we all held our noses and smiled.

I walked towards her warily, hoping to 'get the drift of things.' I tested for wind direction and tried to get upstream. No such luck. What wind there was was coming from the speaker, a little pip-squeak character by the name of Rupert Gumberling, who liked to play practical jokes. Rupert, at the moment, was narrating a tale, supposedly true, concerning a former mayor of Montreal, who was a bit of a maverick in his time.

The mayor, at this particular phase of his administration, was having what is now commonly referred to as a 'communication problem' with the local populous, but being the hotshot that he was, he really didn't give a damn, one way or the other. However, his advisor's, being made of less sterner stuff, counseled him, as a means of getting closer to the public, to venture out on opening day of the Canadian football season, and kick out the first ball.

"Okay," says his honor, "why not?" So, on the aforementioned day, before some forty thousand fans, the mayor casually stepped up to the ball, it having been conveniently placed on the fifty-yard line, and dispassionately spoke into the mike: "Good afternoon ladies and gentlemen. I am very happy to be here today to kick off the first ball, and I would be very happy to come back again sometime, and kick all your balls off."

I must say, it wasn't a bad story, as stories go, and everyone else must have thought likewise as they all burst into laughter, including sweet Ingeborg, who naturally lost control of herself, and thereupon shit her pants.

Cripes, the stuff was all over the place. And you never saw a group of people move so fast in all your life leaving their drinks behind. Why there were bucks there pushing two-hundred-fifty pounds moving like Speedy Gonzales racing to the john with a challenging case of the runs.

After things settled a bit, we cautiously eased our way back, trying not to appear to conspicuous, waiting for Miss Ele-gan-tay to make her next move. No one said a word. It would have been like asking a blind person, "Can I help?" Besides, what could anyone say? "Can I get you a rag?" or, "Oh, pay no mind, I haven't vacuumed yet anyway?" So, everyone just kind of stood there, waiting and watching, as if to say, "We ain't making another move till we find out what's going on here."

Well, sweet Inga, stylish broad that she was, never said a word. Unnerved, she calmly shook a leg, and lackadaisically made her way to the john to take care of business. Man, that's class.

Someone covered the spot with a rag, the same as you'd cover a corpse with a sheet. For a minute I thought somebody was going to step up and say a few words in remembrance. Eventually, everyone, little by little, began to drift outdoors, and the party seemed to lose its zing. After all, how can one drink, and cat around, and play the role with a lump of shit sitting in the living room? A live bomb couldn't have caused more consternation. Some kind soul very adroitly told her not to worry about things, and that was that.

That night, oddly enough, I lovingly became sexually ingratiated. All through the performance I couldn't help thinking to myself, "what if this chick shits"? Then what? Do we shake hands, and go our separate ways, or do I say, "Pardon me, Miss, but I don't believe this was part of the bargain." Ah, sweet mystery of love.

✳ ✳ ✳

VII

Humpty Dumpty sat on a wall
Humpty Dumpty had a great fall
All the king's horses And all the king's
men
Dumped on Humpty again and again.

THE time had now come when my left foot was refusing to follow my right. The sociologists call it anomie, the psychologist's depression, the poets disillusion. I call it wising up.

I was in a quandary, a condition usually preceding a transformation, preceding a heightened state of awareness … or suicide.

Oddly enough, I knew who I was, but not where I was, or where I was going. I was losing faith, but then, I never had much to begin with … or hope … or charity. Faith, I suspected, was designed to make men stupid, hope, to keep them there, and charity to make them like it.

The church has never died in Russia. Is it because religion is a beacon of truth, or because people need their glittering illusions? Is this world too much for the thinking man, so, weakly he slides back into the clutches of songs sung of immortality, and infinite blissful heavens? The truth, like the elusive snail darter, whisking and dashing inches below the surface of a cooling, mountain stream, escapes our clumsy attempts to snare him. The Russian, it is widely held, is a primitive soul.

What is a man, ultimately? Someone who can live without gods, and faith, and miracles, and who can do so with style and grace, quietly and resolutely in the midst of science, and mystery, and the cackle of modern civilization. What is a man?

Having nothing to fall back on in these tense, illuminating moments of crisis

(I had not yet become resolute), frustration was gaining a hold, and despair was making itself welcome in the home of my heart. I was confused in a bright sort of way, and wandering aimlessly. Little did I know, I wasn't either.

I hadn't the vaguest notion what I desired (I knew what I didn't desire, which should have been good enough), or what I should do, or how to do it, so I did the only thing I could do … I ran.

I packed my comb and toothbrush, said my good-byes, jumped in my 1950 pile of scrap metal known as a Chevy, and headed up the coast. I had ninety bucks in my pocket.

I don't remember much about the trip, or my feelings, it was all very hazy, dreamlike. Dali, in a terribly frenzied state, kept coming to mind. In a violent rage with blood-filled eyes, and a horror-stricken face, brushes swirled convulsively this way and that, but every time the canvas was turned to see, nothing remained but a blank sheet of white. I drove and I dreamed until reaching San Francisco. I only stopped to piddle.

It was the middle of the afternoon in the middle of the week, and as I approached the 'citadel of the west,' I noticed off to the side a housing project banked on the side of a hill no more than a quarter of a mile away. It had always been there, but I never noticed it before, not like this. It was all so rational, orderly, practical, unimaginative to the nth degree, these little cubicles resembling coffins more than homes, lined up neatly all in a row. Same size, same shape, same color, equidistant apart. It made one wonder: We stormed Suribachi for THIS?

I continued on into the city, conscious of the steady drum of metropolitan life, only now it was more like a deafening roar. I thought of those innumerable B movies Hollywood flushed out like a giant printing press stuck on 'go' where the player keeps hearing a soft, whirring noise, steadily becoming louder and louder until, in a fit of panic and facial contortions, he grabs his ears hysterically, thinking he can block out the pounding noise. Unfortunately, the project disappeared no more than the noises.

I found myself cruising up Fulton Street watching, listening. I came to Golden Gate Park, turned around and backtracked. I stopped for coffee. As I sat disconsolately, observing the grease in my cup making crazy designs, I realized I had not found Atlantis. I put down my dime, and headed back from whence I came. As I passed the project I bowed in reverence, having been taught to be respectful of the dead. And the landscape, not exactly suitable for growing flowers, but if there was a spot to do so, I would have gone up and planted a few geraniums. Unfortunately, the only dirt I saw was in the street.

When I reached San Jose I knew I would be staying a while—no gas, and short on coin. Besides, all that up and down business was making me nauseous.

I came upon a rooming house with kitchen privileges. Kitchen privileges: A small room with an old wooden table, two chairs, a hot plate, and one of those ancient, tiny ice boxes with room only for a pint of milk, two eggs, and six pats of butter. I had a bunk in the cellar. California houses are not supposed to have cellars. This one did. So much for the law.

It was a large room, twenty-five by twenty-five, or so, with double bunks banked on three walls. There were only two of us at the time, myself, and a fry-cook who was partially stewed most of the time, or totally stewed part of the time. He occupied a bottom bunk next to the wall closest to the door. In the days to come I would be extremely grateful for such small, hardly noticed amenities of life without which our state would surely turn into a medley of convulsions.

I took a bunk situated on the farthest wall directly opposite from his. It wasn't a bad setup really for a hobo. Not exactly the Sattler, but what the hell, there weren't any roaches. Another one of those small amenities.

My one overriding and persistent predicament was knowing I had to, yet another time, enter the world of 'four square' and daily chores. Stealing, of course, was always in the back of my mind, and I always regretted never having learned how. I wanted so much to be a good, loyal, upstanding, patriotic American, and here I was, a grown man, and I had never learned how to steal. Damn, things just never seem to work out. That stink face Hooker was right, I W-A-S a loser.

I laid around a few days, getting acclimated, as the saying goes, and then got a job as a painter for two-dollars-an-hour. That was just about as far as I wanted my life—no big deal at any rate—to resemble the 'beast of Bavaria's.'

It was a two-man operation, him and me. 'Him' was a short, cherubic, pudgy Irishman, who looked like Santa Claus fallen on hard times. He had white hair, a red fleshy face, and a bulbous nose to match, looking like it was about to catch fire any minute.

I wasn't too thrilled about the two-dollars-an-hour, but Finnegan, that was the old boy's name, wasn't making much more himself, and I got to like him, not a small consideration within a rudderless life.

A great little man with an uncomplicated sense of purpose, Finni, while he worked, loved to sing old Irish songs, partly in Gaelic, and partly in south

Boston ethnic. It was a welcome relief from the uneven, steady twang of steel guitars, and the indistinguishable screeching lyrics of pop music. He drank, but oddly enough, rarely touched the hard stuff. It was beer mostly, three or four cans during the day, then a quart or so, at night. I never saw him drunk, and Mrs. Finnegan said it was a rare occasion when he did get plastered, usually at a funeral. I think he just liked the taste of the stuff. Like I said, Finnegan was a simple man, but not simple-minded. He liked beer, so he drank beer. For two people with as unlike a pair of backgrounds as we, Finni and I became fast friends. Life has its little treasures.

* * *

My life now was beset with the bane of mankind. Worse than pestilence, bad luck, or death, I was caught in the throes of routine. When one has no funds to speak of, and is forced to engage in the most menial of tasks, it is inevitable. Under such circumstances, tis one small step indeed to climb into the shoes of fatalism, but already wearing them, I merely suffered.

I worked during the day, and kept mostly to myself at night. Occasionally I would visit Finni, and he would tell me stories of Old Ireland, and I would tell him stories of Old Sicily as related by my Gramps. No doubt my admiration for Finni was linked to his reminding me of Gramps.

In time, I noticed a remarkable similarity between the Irish villager, and the Sicilian peasant. Both were hard, tough, and crude, and amazingly resilient. Both were eternal cynics, yet always retained a glimmer of hope no matter how hopeless things became. Both were habitual creatures with a talent for living one day at a time. Both were the recipients of great hardships and injustice taken with a certain air of fatalism. Both contained a wealth of humanity, yet were capable of the most mindless cruelty, usually directed at themselves. And beneath it all, lay a vast reservoir of humor, no doubt making all tolerable, and giving them super-human powers of endurance.

One night, after he had been telling me of the struggle between the Catholics and the Protestants, he said, "Ya know, Sonny," (he always called me Sonny) "that's why I left the old country years ago. I knew they were never going to settle the issue, peaceably or otherwise, not in my lifetime anyway, so I left. I just got tired of the whole damn thing, ya know what I mean, Sonny?"

"Yeah, I know what you mean, Fin." He rocked back and forth in an old granny rocker and seemed to be staring all the way back to Ireland with his pale, blue eyes. I sat on the top step of the porch, and tried to imagine what it must be like, brother against brother. The hatred, I thought, would have to be immense. Finally, I said, "That sure is a funny kind of thing going on over there, ya know?"

"How do you mean?" Finni replied between gulps.

"Well, there are just two factions, both Irish, bumping heads. You'd think after a while they'd get together."

"Ah, Sonny, me boy, the Irish are a contrary people." And then as an after-thought, "And the damned English ain't helpin' matters any either, you know?"

"Probably not, but there seems to be a ready-made solution for that kind of problem, and for the life of me, I can't understand why they don't get to it."

"What'er ya drivin' at, me boy?"

"Just this: Here you have on the one side, the Catholics, and on the other, the Protestants, right?"

"So?

"So why don't all the Catholics become Protestants?"

"What!" I think I rung his bell with that one.

"Why not? They can still believe what they like, if they need that kind of thing, but publicly, and officially, they'd be Protestants. What the hell's the differ-ence anyway? A prayer's a prayer, Protestant, Catholic, or whatever. It could be done. It's not like you can tell one from the other by looking at him. They're not different colors. My people did it here in the 20's and 30's."

"Did what?"

"Changed their names. You'd be surprised to know how many 'O'Rourke's' there are in the good ol' U. S. of A., and it worked like a charm. Hell, to this day, there's more god-damned Anglo, white-assed chicks what don't know they're married to a grease ball. There are ways, and there are ways, Finni."

"Hah! You threw me with that one, Sonny. Yep, I must say, that one's a larder." With each succeeding gulp, Finnie's face was becoming redder and redder. His wits, however, not being affected, he was able to ask if I would have done the same.

"As a matter of fact," I answered forthrightly," yes, I would have, but not for the same reasons them bungholes did. That first generation … they were, for the most part, a bunch of dickheads,"

"Were they now. In what way?"

"Well, they were living in two different worlds, the new and the old, and a lot of them, they just couldn't hack it. They were embarrassed of the old and its heritage. It was shameful. They wanted to be a part of the crowd so bad they were ready to disown the best part of them, so as soon as they got a little education the first thing they did was change their names, and move to the other side of the tracks, and rarely did they allow their parents to visit them. Oh, no, it was the other way around. It wouldn't have looked right, you know, these hard, brusque, careworn folk walking up to the front door on a cool, summers eve, with their salamis, provolone, and dago red tucked under their arms. What would the neighbors think?

Yeah, Finni, you can bet all the beer in Bavaria I'd have changed my name. I'd have picked one as American as American can get. Something like Quigley, or Peacock, or Macpherson. Or how about Alger? Something just reeking of turkey and gravy, and dripping with apple sauce. Then I'd have become the biggest ass-kisser and head-shaker this side of Mae West's rear end, 'yes, sir' this, and 'yes, sir' that, dotting all the I's, and crossing all the T's, until I'd worked my way right up to executive vice-president in charge of whatever at G.M., or I.T.T., whereupon would I, one unsuspecting Monday morn, nonchalantly walk into a board meeting, crap in the chairman's recliner, grab a handful of Havana's, and leave them sitting there, scratching their walnuts, and wondering what new form of madness was upon us. Yeah, my fine Irish friend, you can bet your sweet, Dubliner's hiney, I'd have changed my name."

"Hah!" he laughed unbelievingly. "Sure, you say that now, but would you have done it?"

Finni wasn't as crocked as I thought. Immediately he fingered the problem.

"I know what you mean, pardner," I answered introspectively. "If I was faced with it, would I really have done it, considering what I had to lose?" I thought for a moment, then said soberly, "Yeah, I think so. You see, Finni, my hate for the scrungy, cocksucking reprobates surpasses any other passion I may have, including that for the easy life. Yeah, I'd have done it. It would have been my duty.

* * *

Time was moving slowly now; aye, it was dragging. I had lost whatever inclination I ever had to accomplish anything in particular. The general was my bag, ambition a foreign land. The simple, never ever that distant, had returned to my bosom. I had matured.

Being an introspective sort, I wondered—how come? How come I wasn't impressed by the other? Living in a bourgeois society, I was also infused from infancy with all the usual claptrap everyone else was, school, God, church; country, business, success, the whole gamut of pressure patriotism.

I am happy to report however that my folks took it all with a grain of salt. Pop was fond of saying, "If you want money, want it for the time it can buy you, and not the things," and subsequently, never pushed me into the 'success' groove. Never hounded into 'doing good,' phrases such as, "Why can't you do it?" or "You have to be the best," and "Winning is everything," never issued from his lips. Mom, the same. They played it free and loose. Report card day was not the biggest event of the month, and a D was just another letter of the alphabet. They respected knowledge, and intellect, for its own sake and not for what it can 'get you.' Thank you, one and all.

So then, what was it? How did I escape? And for what, to be a bum? Was there a reason to this madness, and what was that all holy and revered reason? Well, rack my brain as I might, it had to be, ultimately, in the genes. There was just enough there to put a dent in the door. My life, not that different from any other, but atomically a cut above the nether, or else I was just lucky. Everyone who attends church does not become a priest.

It continued. Time went on, and on, and on. Days did not pass, but slid into one another, and the demarcations from one to the other became blurred. Things were no longer weeks or months, but clumps indistinguishable only by the change in weather. I wondered how long this slide into the abyss would continue, and I thought of the pathetically one-sided VonAshenback of Mann's 'Death in Venice,' and 'The Steppenwolf.' When reading them years ago, my identification with them was merely intellectual, devoid of any real intuitive sense. But now, with my own travels into the dark side, the wolf in me was beginning to bare its teeth. The soft cuddly puppy was growing into a full-fledged, stalking beast.

Each minute had a life of its own separated from the one before it, and the one after. Sixty compact seconds submerged in a bewildering absurdity made real only by the incessant tick-tock, tick-tock that bore no resemblance to reality, but existed simply as a separation between stages of madness, whereby the ticks ran into the tocks, and the tocks the ticks, merging into one, long whirring t-i-i-i-c-k, swirling through the brain crowding out all the little day-by-day inanities.

Mornings I would rise with no great enthusiasm, and it would begin all over again. With the sensation of a great weight bearing upon my shoulders, I would drag myself to the john and habitually tend to the usual functions now seeming more ludicrous than ever.

It often occurred to me, while standing over the bowl admiring my apparatus, why the penis grew where it did, secluded and suffocating between two lumpy folds of flesh. Why didn't it grow under the arm, or in the belly button, or on the top of the head like a spike? Why not where the nose is, or on the hand replacing the middle finger? Why? Why in just that specific spot attended by two egg-shaped slugs? And why two? Why not three, or four, or six, or an even dozen? And why are they outside and not inside like a women's, for added protection? Why men and woman, anyway? Wouldn't it have been much simpler to have constructed an hermaphroditic species, simplifying matters all around. Aberrations like rape, prostitution, and irate, jealous husbands would be unheard of. Behavior, much of which can be traced to some form of sexual conflict, would be considerably modified. Without the sex drive whole societies would be manifestly altered, invariably for the better, in a manner of speaking, for it is hoped something equally pleasurable, but far less destructive, could be substituted.

Why? Why men, and why woman? Are they not one more division in a hopelessly divided world? Are they the lower stage in the master plan for unity, oneness? A single species with the vagina on one hand and the penis on the other? Of course such an arrangement could have its complications. When attending a concert, for instance, one could never tell whether the audience was applauding the performance, or performing the sexual act. But then, the beauty of it all is, in keeping with the spirit of ambidexterity, it could be both.

Ah, humbug, it could never be. The fashion industry, as mindless an exercise in superfluity as ever existed, would drift into that eternal resting place by the Stygian shore, for clothing would then be reduced to merely a utilitarian function. A pair of pants would be slipped on because the limbs were cold and not as the first step in the preliminary stage of a primitive sex ritual, culminating in the careless shedding in a heap of those once so carefully tended garments, pursuant to the ravaging of the primordial beast in heat.

Slowly, very slowly, my body would work its way into a state of moderate efficiency sufficient to carry out its rudimentary functions, wash the face, brush the teeth, push the hair back, and sometimes shave. Minutes later, with a braced back and a half resolve to push on, I would shuffle into the kitchen, make coffee, and after two sips, step lively back into the latrine to deposit a goodly portion of the remains garnered the day before.

I could, at this point, inquire briefly into the why's and wherefore's of the location of the rectum. However, due to the impossibility of solving such dislocated matters with any degree of sophistication, I will abstain. But it should be mentioned in all fairness, that in consideration of most, justice would have better been served were said upholstery positioned where the mouth now dwells.

The substance deposited is also, to some degree, a matter of mystery. Cats cover it, dogs smell it, and humans stare at it in wonderment, disappointed no doubt, given its potency, that it doesn't have in its bag, a small repertoire of tricks, at least a half-gainer, or a somersault, or two.

But alas, the incarnate can always be, invariably, reduced to the basic. It appears that subconsciously we realize that after all the speeches and huzzahs, the prancing among the lilies', the striving and yearning, the laughing and frolicking, after all the shouting has subsided and the dust has cleared, what remains is fodder for the flies. The world will always be with flies.

* * *

Finni and I would start the mornings work; spread the canvas, hook up the ladders, mix the paints. On one such frivolous morning, after an hour or so of spreading a coat of lifeless beige on the side of a small, nondescript bungalow, I thought, painting is a mirror of life; back and forth, back and forth. So much time is wasted just going back and forth. I deliberately changed the method and began stroking up and down, then criss-cross, then swirls. But I wasn't fooling anyone; back and forth was the most efficient.

And so with life, we start out sweeping back and forth (school, work, marriage), then the ups and downs, (no job, new job, divorce, junk car, alimony), to the criss-crosses (a new religion, encounter groups, self-love), to the swirls (rediscovering sex, and a dabbling in the bohemian life). But always, and inevitably, whether one punches a clock, or is occasionally consumed by the 'fires of love,' or whiles away his days pumped full of the savory grape or the silent, ensnaring 'white dust' of death, the back and forth predominates. As a means of reminding us of our hardy attachment to the laws of moderation, ease and regularity, we are pulled, like the superstitious, to magic, back to the control and dictates of the witch-doctor.

Intruding upon my cerebral play world was a, "Lunch, Sonny," from my Irish playmate, and back to more mundane affairs.

Although Finni wasn't much of an eater as eater's go, the event took on the aspect of a battle plan. Finni carried a lunch pail. In it was a ham and cheese on white, or roast beef, or meatloaf, or whatever was left over from the night before; coffee, a small container of sliced, golden cling peaches, and a twinkie. The Twinkie was part of the midmorning break ritual.

Mr. Finnegan would sit on a stoop, place his pail beside him, stretch, gaze up at the noonday sky, rub his eyes, rest one hand on the pail, and stay so positioned for some moments, as if to say: "Well now, if I eat it, then I won't have it … anymore." To a working man, lunch is a momentous event, ranking second only to a birth, or a good hit on the numbers.

Finally, Finni would open the pail and stare at its contents, seemingly surprised to discover what he had discovered so many times before. He seemed to be wishing he could change ham into caviar, or some other equally exotic concoction, just for the sake of having something different in the middle of the day, in the middle of the week, in the middle of the month, in the middle of the year. But, alas, ham by any other name, is the meat of a dead pig, and a dead pig sandwich, after hundreds of dead pig sandwiches, remains—a dead pig sandwich.

Methodically, Finni would lay out a napkin and the sandwich. He would then pour a cup of coffee kept hot in a giant thermos, and let things settle for another few moments. Usually, he would say something in the interim like, "Quiet today, hey Bub?" then lift his head and rub the front of his neck up and down ever so slowly. By now, three or four minutes having expired, the grand moment had finally arrived, Finni would actually unwrap the sandwich cut neatly in half by Mrs. Finnegan. She had a unique touch; the sandwich always appeared to be cut from the finest Carrere marble and set on a pedestal atop the Acropolis for at least a thousand years. I would always twinge when Finni touched one, as it seemed anything so carefully perfected and tended should never feel the touch of corrupt, human flesh. He would now raise it to his mouth, and bite. Sometimes, on those days when he seemed to be stretching the ritual to nerve-wracking proportions, I would applaud at the critical moment when bread met lips. Finni was a bigger ham than the brand between the bread, for as time passed he became more and more deliberate. I think the applause got to him.

As for myself, I had an old, dry baloney sandwich on rye; a small thermos of ice cold milk, and a tangerine, or a pear, if the season permitted. I couldn't afford ham.

I could usually induce Finni to tell stories of 'Old Ireland,' stories seeming to have no beginning or end, and mystically gained a life of their own because they had happened over and over, century upon century. If Ireland, and all the Irish with it had suddenly sunk into the ocean, Ireland would not perish; blarney is imperishable. The Irish potato is not a vegetable; it is the Irish soul, and its roots, its nerves, digging deep down into the hard-rock earth, caressing and tugging and reaching for all the life it can give. For all of it … it just might be, there W-I-L-L always be an Ireland.

* * *

One quiet afternoon, as I sat lazily, vaguely mindful of Finni and watching a swallow dash around pecking for crumbs, it seemed to me that all but the past is illusion. There is no present, no future. They are merely categories of the mind, a murky, hazy mist, shapeless and transitory. The future never arrives, the present always a moment behind. Everything is past, and in the past, and it lasts forever. Life is built on it; there is no life without it, and it is why nations tenaciously cling to it, and live in it. It is why the Greeks built the greatest civilization; they were the best historians. It is why we have built no civilization. We build houses, and roads and cars, and stadiums, and then rebuild them again, and again, and again. We are the greatest builders of junk, and more junk. We build garbage dumps and slums. Yes, the slums; America, the land of billionaires, the computer, the steel guitar, and … the slums. The Thunderbird, the Empire State Building, the freeways, and … the slums. The Brooklyn Bridge, the B1 Bomber, chicken hawks, and … the slums. Funny, we can design, build, and throw away practically anything from socks, to cars, to ashtrays. You name it, Buck, but not the slums. Everything in America, sooner or later, is rendered obsolete, but not … the slums.

One time, in a fit of excessive mental flatulence, we attempted to 'reconvert' the slum; it was called 'urban renewal.' It is now called empty lots, and drive-by land fills; high rent districts for our comrade-in-arms—the rat. We talk a good game, but we do not respect the past, only the gold it can produce. I passed by a red, white, and blue fire hydrant the other day; I pissed on it.

* * *

Having now repaired back to the digs after yet another lazy day splashing about with old 'Dutch Boy,' I laid down to catch my breath and joyously muse over the day's happenings, happenings which tenaciously refused to take on any semblance of meaning; days where stinking paints were broth forth from messy cans and thrown on a motley collection of rotting clapboards, and if any sense can be made of that, then nonsense is my name, and raving is my game.

Around five, Cookie, my loose-living roommate, would usually stagger in. His name was William Gates, but he said everyone called him 'Cookie.' Christ, I thought to myself, you'd think after all the hundreds and hundreds of cooks called Cookie, a guy would avoid it like the plague, but not the Cooker, as proud fully he would exclaim: "Just call me, Cookie." I said to him once jokingly, "How about if I call you Cracker? There's a cracker named after a man, you know, Graham? Maybe after a while, they'll name another cracker, this time after you … you know—the 'Gates' cracker?" He frowned. The ship of fame and immortality sailed right by his darkened lighthouse.

He was, at the moment, between jobs, as the saying goes, as a result, one dark and dreary night of falling down the cellar stairs—a constant hazard of the inebriate state—and breaking a leg. Gracefully molded in a cast, he came hobbling in. "Hey, Matey?" he called out, "what say we go get a few later on? You look like you could use a good belt."

Cookie couldn't see across the room, and if he could, wouldn't have been able to distinguish a grimace from a grin. Cookie was talking talk I had heard so many times before, and like so many times before, was again grateful to my linguistic ancestry for that most useful of phonetic designations—no. Indeed, did I now, yet one more time, exercise that historic, monosyllabic privilege.

I never acceded to Cookie's wishes, but he never failed to ask. It wasn't that I considered myself better than him, although a tempting sentiment, but that I was never the type to just sit and drink, and by degrees become paralyzed. I also wasn't too fond of the establishments he frequented. The doorway always smelled of pee (mainly because some old wino peed in it), and always felt I should have brought a rag along to clean the 'colorful' glassware.

"No, Cook," I said, thinking that declaration of refusal sufficient, "not tonight; I ain't in the mood." I always try to be kind when I can.

However, sometimes, sufficient for one, is not sufficient for another as he replied grumpily, "Shit, since when you got to be in the mood?" As I said, Cookie was a drunk.

"Cook," I tried again, "I can't keep up with you; you're always in the mood."

He persisted. "Hell man, c'mon, let's go. I'll even spring for the first two rounds." Misery is as misery does.

"Cookie," I finally intoned in language plain enough for even the lowliest of the king's subjects to comprehend, "go fuck yourself."

"Okay, okay, I'm goin'," he growled, "but that paint must be getting to ya."

"It ain't the paint," I mournfully corrected.

After he left I rose to dine, although not very hungry. The fridge contained two dried-up dogs and an egg, neither of which drew out what little hunger I had.

I went down to the dump on the corner and grabbed a mature 'cat-burger' and a Coke. Upon being served I pulled a handful of straws from the dispenser and stuck them in the Coke. Unbelievingly, the young lady in white inquired, "If that was necessary?" To wit, I replied, "Guess so, it didn't look like anyone else was going to do it."

"What kind of creep are you, anyway?" she countered. "Who says anyone has to do it at all?"

"Quit squawking. Until I came in here you were ready to doze off. I put the salt back in your shaker."

"Don't do me no more favors, will ye, Buster? It's been a long day."

"Compared to what?"

"Right now, compared to you."

"Very good, and by the way," I added, eyeing an apron looking like the soup had made it its permanent home, "why don't you throw that in the wash too, once in a while. If it could talk it would also walk."

She stood real straight and putting her hands on her hips combatively, replied, "I got a better idea. Why don't you throw yourself in the wash? And besides, for a guy what frequents 'greasy spoons' you sure do have a lot of complaints."

"I have as much right to complain as the king of England."

"There ain't no king of England," she corrected.

"Yeah, now if we could only get rid of the damn queen, and a few dukes, and lords, and barons. . . . ."

"You got your countries mixed up a little, ain'tcha?"

"No sweetie, that's one thing I ain't got mixed up."

I finished off the coke, wiped my mouth, stretched, hitched up my britches and strutted toward the door like a Texas oil tycoon. As I did so, 'sweetie' gave me one of those 'either he's bats' or 'he's goin' bats' looks. I think she settled for the former.

Taking my time getting back, as I had no major appointments for that evening, I stopped momentarily in the front room where a few boarders, most of whom wore strange faces, were watching the evening news.

Riots and demonstrations were all the rage at the moment, and that's what was being shown—a riot. Where? Who knows. Does it matter? They are not unique events, but depressing in the knowledge that they are easily prevented if the powers that be were minimally in possession of their faculties, a condition more and more appearing altogether unlikely.

At this particular frolic, folks were dashing to and fro, throwing rocks and bottles, and everyone seemed to be having a jolly good time of it amongst a pale of smoke coming from a storm of dust and tear gas. Stores were being sacked and looted, and youngsters were practicing Dodge Ball with sticks and stones. One hardy soul was dragging a huge console through the front door of a rapidly diminishing appliance store, when another, in a frenzy of brotherhood, came rushing up, and together hauled it over to a beat up, old pickup, dumped it in the back, and in the spirit of Jesse James, made a quick getaway. All this, mind you, in the 'richest' country in the world. (Hee, hee.) When the truck left, I left.

No one was around, much to my liking, so I sat, alone, with the chair propped up against the wall, and with my hands clasped behind my head I peered out into the blazing sunset. In a subdued sort of way, I was enjoying being alone now, more and more.

I didn't think about anything, just tried to clear the head of all thought and memory … a kind of western meditation. It is not the easiest of tasks to sit quietly and allow the mind to effortlessly drift into a tranquil state of dispassionate relaxation. After a short time one inevitably finds oneself drowsing; however, now becoming quite dexterous at hypnotic indolence, it was a refreshing tonic after the usual round of drivel and empty sounds purporting to bear a notable resemblance to intelligent life.

In the midst of my molecular repose, Herb Kees wandered in and brought me back to the world of 'gruff and gripes.' I didn't like Herb. I didn't like him the first time I saw him, I didn't like him after I came to know him, and now, many months later, I still didn't like him. Herb, to put it mildly, was a thoroughly unlikable fellow.

Physically, as well as mentally, Herb had little to recommend him. Of medium height and on the thin side, he had an unnerving 'fat look' about him, and his skin hung grotesquely like a malnourished water buffalo's. He was divorced and had two teenaged children, a boy and a girl, whom he was altogether enthralled about, and given the slightest opening would launch into a longwinded spiel detailing their extraordinary qualities. Observing the father, I wondered about the offspring.

He never mentioned his ex-wife, and claimed to be forty-eight, but looked eighty-eight, and pumped gas for a living.

Herb, in keeping with the spirit of his kind, also chased ambulances, as misfortune fascinated him, and it is said, he habitually tuned into the morning news, that being the time accidents, and the like, are included in the public fare. Automobile, train, plane, shootings, stabbings, fires, any little old gore to whet the appetite. If Herb was a sample of the general population, an altogether likely and frightening possibility, then, yes Bucko, make your bones now, and to the devil the hindmost.

Herb was especially fond of plane crashes. I would imagine because they held the most drama and the greatest possibilities, although a good train wreck would put a twinkle in his eye. He just naturally seemed to relish other people's misfortune. No doubt this perversion was related somehow to his own wretched and uneventful life. Having taken a few kicks and slaps along the way, Herb couldn't accept its implications without secretly wishing everyone the same. To his distorted way of thinking, tragedy was the world's way of saying: "See, Herb, we're fair; everybody gets a little sooner or later" and life was made whole again for Herb. It was his 'good fairy' waving the magic wand.

As I sat peering through the back door, observing the natural wonders of the world, he came rushing up, declaring excitedly, "Hey, John, did you see it? Did you see it? Man, it was bad."

"See what?" I replied, not really caring one wit, although knowing all too well.

"That plane crash in Peru. One-hundred-forty killed. Worse crash in aviation history." (Everyone's an historian when it suits them.) "Man, it was bad."

Herb looked glum, but inside I know he felt like Robinson Crusoe at the first sight of a seafaring vessel. Conveniently, the soul can be the dark closet of putrescence. His eyes lit up and he began to tremble slightly with excitement. I thought he was going to pop his wad right there, standing in the doorway.

He strolled over to the hotplate and turned up the burner on an old pot of Colombia's finest. Coffee, cigarettes, happy tragedies that was Herb's bag. Noticing my lack of enthusiasm he quickly shifted gears.

"You see them 'fuckin' niggers up there causin all that commotion? Man, they're lucky I ain't a cop." Fortunately for both sides, I thought.

"Yeah, Herb," I answered nonchalantly, while rocking back and forth, and staring up at a rapidly, peeling ceiling. I knew in my heart of hearts, as the facile saying goes, that if I said anything more than "yep" and "nope" this conversation would have to end in 'disharmony.'

"Who the hell they think they are?" he continued. "Comin' off with that crap? Why don't the fuckin' black bastards go out and get a job like everybody else?" Mistakenly attempting to reason with the unreasonable, I offered what I thought was a plausible explanation, to a degree.

"Maybe nobody wants to give them a job, Herb. Ever consider that? They're not exactly high up on the 'most wanted list,' except on the post office board."

"Shit. Damn coons, the government's supportin' them with my taxes, and they're still complainin'. If the fuckers don't like it here, why don't they go back to Africa?"

"Too many nigger's there," I asserted facetiously.

"They're getting away with this shit, that's why they're doin' it. They're damn lucky this is America, that's all I got to say."

I was also hoping, that was all he had to say. No such luck; more was right behind.

"Try somethin' like this over in Russia and see how far they'd get. Hell, them damn commies'd machine-gun the whole damn bunch of um. They wouldn't do it more'n once, I can tell you that." Ah, yes, the Russian bear, he do make a handy punching bag.

"Yeah, isn't the Russian way wonderful?" I affirmed. "Stick around, Herb, they say we're becoming more like them, and they like us. Christ," I added despairingly, more to myself than Herb, "there's a double-edged sword for you."

"Say, who's side are you on anyway?" he complained. "Wud them shines ever do for you?" I knew if I said more than "yep" and "nope" it had to come to this.

"Well now, Herb, I'll tell you. It's not what they did for me, but if it comes to it, I'm with them because the alternative is too fearsome to behold."

"It is, huh," he replied antagonistically. Herb was beginning to catch on. "I get it, you're one of them damn, nigger-lovin' fuckers, is that it?"

"Let me put it this way Herb, I ain't too sure why we call black people niggers, but I am sure it's not something you'd write on a Christmas card, and since I don't think I'll ever be sending you one, let me just say therefore, in lieu of, get the fuck out of here, nigger."

Herb's face turned a kind of a faded green, and was about to blurt something I am sure he was going to regret, so being the helpful soul that I was, I headed him off at the pass with: "Hold it Herb; you're that close to getting major reconstruction done to that stupid load of horseshit you call a face."

Surprised he didn't answer, but instead put his cup back on the table, and sauntered toward the door, but before leaving leaned back in and shot back with the classiest of lines, to wit: "You're a real fucking prick, you know that."

Somewhat elated at the fact of my not having to do any more than 'match wits' with the sorry, sack of shit, I did not reply, but content to leave well enough alone, I merely waved, joyous in the hope that that just might be the last time of my ever having to lay eyes on the wretched, pile of vomit again.

Relieved, I retreated to the comparative safety of my bedside, where I flopped down uncaringly, hoping that the immediate future, at any rate, held more enchanting moments, and wondering why the gods would spend an arrow on so pitiful a mooring.

Lying stressfully some many moments, I gradually lapsed into a pensive mood allowing lightheaded thoughts to roll languidly into place. Inevitably however, the gossamer, mindful of our insatiable appetite for the ponderous, gave way to the solemn, and grave reflections were upon me once again.

Thus, like a magnetic flash streaking across the sky on a dank, summer's eve, I saw it all for one blinding moment, the crippled world, the paraplegic of the universe; the big garage can in the sky, the A-B-C's of absurdity; it was really all so very simple, yet blurred in its intimacy. Nazism, Fascism, the Ku Klux Klan, Joseph Stalin; tyranny, war, racism; poverty, pollution, broken-down Chevy's, artificially-colored hot dogs, bloody hands and squalid souls. It was not Herb, hell, no. It never is. He was in that number comprising the powerless.

No, not Herb, but his opposite, the grand and powerful. By virtue of their exalted position, they are the guilty, for they make the speeches that launch the wars, and pass the laws that keep us bored, haggard and dismayed. Statesmanship, never a child of healthful expectations, perished on the deadly end of John Wilkes Booth's pistol. The world is a printout of a haywire computer.

That evening, after a fitful introduction to midnight, succeeding the previously harried events, I lapsed into a dreamy sleep only to be rudely awakened by banging noises coming from the general direction of the pantry.

Sounding like someone who didn't know his way around, a seemingly habitual affliction nowadays, it had to be Cookie, or a burglar. I quickly discounted the burglar, reasoning if anyone thought he could find anything of value in this establishment worth breaking in for, he would not venture any further than the front door, before his folly, like a bad check at a teller's window, would soon be thrust back upon him. Therefore, it had to be Cookie.

He must have been all business that night, as he was having all he could do to get from the door to his bunk, said rookery not being more than ten feet distant.

Amusedly, I listened awhile, then dozed off again, barely conscious of the clanking and shuffling sounds. Vaguely, it seemed, Cookie was drifting further, rather than nearer his bunk. I paid no mind. In a moment I was asleep again.

While slumbering peacefully, a warm sensation slowly crept over my restful state. My, I dreamt, isn't this California air soothing? Presently however, what I, at first, thought was warmth, had now turned to wet. Opening my eyes, a darkish, hazy form appeared directly over me. Cookie, the son-of-a-bitch thought he was in the john! He was pissing on me! How do you like that! I was literarily being pissed on! Pissed on, I tell you! Pissed on! Even to a strikeout like Cookie, there must be a difference between being IN the john, and OVER the John.

Quick as a flash, I jumped up, turned him around, and let him finish undisturbed in another direction, hesitant to cut him off in the middle of his act, fearing a gala repeat performance later on. My mind, now frenziedly awake, schemed all manner of vengeful thoughts.

Angrier than a furry, little pussy who had been unceremoniously dumped into the Mississippi River at high tide, I made my way to the lavatory and showered.

Upon returning, Cookie was still groping, none too successfully, for his bunk. I watched the pathetic, malty sap, wishing for all the world to bounce a two-by-four off his witless skull. Finally reaching his cradle, he flopped down like a wet sack of potatoes, staying like he fell with one arm and one leg hanging over the side.

I cleaned the mess all the while thinking of retribution. It is not far fetched to surmise such inelegant behavior leading to all sorts of disjointed ramifications seemingly having nothing to do with the initial inartistic event. If allowed to continue it can reinforce itself, the subconscious rising to the conscious, becoming habit while at the same time taking on the aspect of fervent missionary work, and the last thing I needed was a drunken holy man, who, when overcome by the spirits, ebulliently embarked on a religious crusade in the dead of night, waving his omnipotent wand in a frantic attempt to gain souls for the Lord.

After some thought, I hit upon two equally appetizing methods of revenge, the 'prophylactic filled with cold water' trick, or the 'hand in the bucket of warm water' trick. I settled for the latter. Although less splashy, I was intrigued by its tranquil subtlety.

My opportunity was not long forthcoming. Two nights later, Cookie came dragging in. He found the head all right this time and did his business.

Having thoroughly covered one wall, the seat and attending parts, and most of the bathtub, he made his way back clumsily, and laid down thinking, if anything, that all was well with the world. And so did the passengers on the Titanic. . . . .

Knowing it wouldn't be long before, like Lazarus, he would rise again in search of relief, I dozed for the better part of an hour then rose and filled a pail with warm water. Quietly, I walked over to him and noticed he was lying on his back with his right hand, the one in need, resting on his chest. With my thumb and forefinger, I carefully lifted and placed it in the pail, then waited anxiously, like a participant at a séance, for the spirits to make their entrance. It wasn't long. In a matter of seconds a veritable Niagara Falls of beer issued forth. Cookie, like the greenhouse keeper, had indeed watered his plants.

I went into the kitchen and turned on the light. Just enough glare shined into the bedroom to judge the extent of the damage. It was heavy. Cookie, I am delighted to report, was sitting in 'the village pond.' Not yet fully conscious, he was stirring uncomfortably and would awaken before the falls dried up.

I removed his hand from the pail, and while pouring its contents down the kitchen drain, heard, a "Wha, wha? Well, for crissake! What the fuck is goin' on here!"

I rushed back in, feigning surprise. "What's wrong, Cook?" said I.

He was sitting up now, and had torn the blanket off. "I pissed on myself!" he shouted angrily.

"Well, I'll be," I replied in astonishment. "So you did."

"Jesus, man, I'm too young to be getting' senile," he complained.

"Oh, I don't know; you never can tell about these things. They come on all of a sudden like. That's the way it happens sometimes. You'd better hope this is a one-time thing, else wise you're gonna have to start wearing a rubber diaper."

"Diaper, hell! The useless fuckin' thing. I'll cut it off, that's what I'll do."

"Suit yourself. You know your needs better than I."

Cookie cleaned up as best he could all the while muttering obscenities to himself and whatever imps and goblins within earshot. I say as best he could, in as much as those of Cookie's caste only have one of anything, a supremely elevated condition no doubt lost upon the general populous, so all he could do was dab a little with a dry rag, and flip over the mattress.

As I watched amusedly from my little corner of the world, I wondered why he didn't just go over to one of the other bunks. Most likely an agitated mind is a befuddled mind. Soon things quieted down, and all the little chickies went back to dreamland, but not for long.

In minutes, stirrings were heard again in yonder direction. It seems Cookie's electrical impulses began to strike their natural cords once more, since he rose and shuffled over to one of the other cots. Cookie may have been a drunk, but he wasn't stupid. For the time being anyway.

* * *

Aloneness is not necessarily the wearisome condition one might imagine, and not to be derided. Like everything else, it depends. I had been incarcerated in the above described state for some months now, and was beginning to like it. As a matter of fact, I never didn't not like it.

Although having separated myself from all previous attachments and responsibilities, being alone in the city is to a certain degree, aberrant, considering the close physical proximity of persons gathered together in pursuit of common, demented activities.

It was distressing initially, to be sure, not being closely attached, as language was meant to be used in day-to-day combat, but as time wore on, I became remarkably gifted at conversing with myself. We became fast friends, myself and I, and thus developed a cordial relationship. Learning to respect each in trust and honor, we never argued or fought, but looked to one another for solace and comfort.

Now laboring only three days a week, a situation much to my liking, I would often, on those days not stolidly engaged in the moribund dictates of life, journey to the park, find a secluded spot, usually under a tree, and sit and think, or not think. Either way I learned to appreciate myself, given that I had no reason not to, by allowing myself a chance to be myself.

I would sit very still and listen to the hum of my brain. It did, softly, but it did. Eventually, a thought would creep in sheepishly, it having not been invited, and the hum would grow into a sweet lyrical melody, and finally, if the tune was more than misplaced jabberwocky, into a harmonious crescendo replete with flugal horns, tubas, cornets, drums and cymbals, shrieking and pounding and clanging wildly in a frenzy of jubilation. My skull would echo with the minstrelsy of cerebration. Beethoven, you old huckster, you were merely arranging thoughts to musical notes.

More and more I stayed alone, and more and more liking it. I became decidedly asocial, mingling only when necessary, and speaking only as a last resort. My loneness having evolved into a lifestyle, I found, contrary to Aristotle, that man may not be a social animal after all, but rather socializes through convenience. There is religion, and there is language, and there is sex, and there is sociability. The isolate man perched on the mountaintop screams for contact and submission. The empyrean air of the gods quickly inducing faintness, he inexorably slides back down to the heaviness of the mundane, it being the haven of the timorous. He gives up the 'will to strength' for the 'ease of weakness.' The dreary prattle of society is the cattle-call of the tremulous, the convulsive broken-down cities, and the dark jungle of the regressive, educated ape.

I had a dog once, a basenji. They're used to hunt lion in Africa. Basenji's never bark. Basenjis are good dogs. They catch lions too.

The other day I went to buy a loaf of bread. As I passed through the produce section, an uncontrollable urge to gorge a banana came upon me. I didn't want a whole bunch, just one, so I ripped one off, peeled it, and ate it. However, unbeknownst to me, one of the establishment flunkies had seen my 'foray into the bush,' and while I was deciding what to do with the peel, came over and announced waspishly, "Why don't you stick it in your ear?" and continued down the aisle, all the while looking back at me like I was some kind of foul excrement what usually is found in a sewer.

I didn't mind the wisecrack so much, what the hell, you give a few, you take a few, but the look, it suggested more than a hint of superiority. I resented intensely his assuming the posture of an occupant of Olympus while wearing a dirty apron and stacking shelves in beautiful, downtown San Jose.

I thought about it, and the more I did the angrier I became, until finally, having nothing better to do, I went hunting for the bigmouthed suck hole, taking another banana with me. I found him around the corner reloading the soup shelf. He was an average type person in all respects. The cans he was placing on the shelves were average.

I slowly walked toward him, peeling the banana deliberately, and eating it in full view of his ass-kissing mug. Stopping a few feet away, I neatly draped the peel over a soup can, Campbell's Old Fashioned Vegetable made with beef stock.

"You a wise guy?" he said self-confidently, taking a step towards me.

"As wise as necessary," I countered exactly.

"You want to get that peel off that can?" he continued brazenly.

"Now why would I want to do that?" I answered just as boldly. "I just put it there."

"Why you little fuckin' runt," he jabbered angrily. "I outta kick your goddamn ass." I didn't answer. Instead, I slowly and deliberately, swiped a few cans off the shelf and onto the floor.

He lunged toward me. "Why you," he blurted while grabbing me by the shoulder.

Instantly, I swung a wickedly, hard left into his belly. He let out an, "Oooooph," and fell back against the shelf and then the floor, amidst a crashing avalanche of Campbell's, Mrs. Grass's, and Hebrew National soup. He lay where he fell, painfully clutching his midsection and groaning.

I rushed over to the checkout stand and went into a passable act. "Hey," I shouted, pointing innocently in the fallen's direction. "You better see about him. I think he had a kind of an accident," and casually walked out.

Two steps later, I took off like the tin rabbit on the end of the stick at the dog races. The last thing I was going to allow was the satisfaction of him seeing me busted. It isn't often one gets the opportunity of aiding the good when whimsically presented, therefore, one should snatch at it with all the miserly greed of a scrooge.

I turned the corner and raced back toward the pad. By the time I reached safety, I had become giddy and lightheaded and was overcome by a heightened feeling of exhilaration. The adrenalin was flowing mightily, and my blood was shooting back and forth like poison darts from a pygmy blowgun. Gracious! I felt like I had just interpolated Venus de Milo.

A few days later I related to Finni the banana peel incident. As I did, I became more and more furious. "You know, Finni?" I said resentfully, "justice ain't got nothing to do with laws, and courts, and cops and judges, and all that raggedy-ass crappola."

"No?" he replied in character.

"No," I replied in turn. "It's competing, and winning, and still losing. I never did get the fucking bread."

* * *

After I had been a resident in good standing at the home for some three years, or so, a young man of twenty-five, and also of the lower class came to stay.

His name was Rick Van Winninger, and he worked in the cannery. Everybody who was anybody worked in the cannery. Tch. He took a bunk down in 'the hole' with Cookie and me, and seemed to be a good enough sort, an altogether unique condition, whenever.

Rick was an 'Okie,' and had come to the coast as a youth of nineteen to seek his fortune, and had since, like myself, found his bag of goodies contained a variety of sweets, but no gold. He had never married, or been to college, or prison, or the service. Rick, to put it mildly, had been leading a very sheltered life, if not carefree. The combination of my now solitary ways and his shy demeanor, it was three weeks before we said more than the rudimentary "hello" and "goodbye" to one another, even though we saw each other, each and every day, however brief.

It couldn't be helped seeing each other every day, that is, both being tapped out, where could we go, and what would we do after we got there? Feed the pigeons? I suspended that bit of nonsense long ago when a grayish, filthy bloated specimen gave me what I was certain was a "Huh, so you think I'm the pigeon, ay?" look. Now, when one of the little darlings gingerly steps my way, he gets a quick "scat" and a "shoo" for his troubles. He'll dump on my head, and priggishly flaunt his meager talents my way, but I don't have to feed his feathery rump. Let him scavenge and grovel, that's what he was made for.

Rick had only one year of high school, and a mild sense of inferiority for it, since, to me, he usually prefaced his remarks with, "You're a college dude, John, what do you think?" Little did he know, not much more than he, if that.

Rick's two predominant virtues were his kind heart, and a total lack of pretense. He only lived to munch on a burger, sip a Coke, shine his 1939 remade Plymouth coupe, grab a little tail now and then, and plunk on his 'gee-tar.' I have no doubt Rick could have continued on in this fashion for a thousand years with no complaints. I also have no doubts, if any of the aforementioned activities were removed for any length of time, he would become fertile ground for whatever convenient, cult or fad, happened to be passing.

Evil does its dirty dance indiscriminately but can spin a filthy, mean boog-a-loo among the indiscriminate. He was living proof of my dearly beloved Pop's oft said belief concerning the proper functioning of this here Union, to wit: "It ain't no big deal being a politician, all you had to do was find out what the people wanted, and make them think they're getting it, and if two conflicting groups wanted the same thing, start a war, and they will both be pissing in the same fox-hole."

Of course it doesn't say much for justice, but then a wandering, impotent Jew was crudely hung from a cross because he insisted he was the King. And the Easter Bunny is a charming, little rabbit who delivers colored eggs to the little kiddies on the same day as the above mentioned 'rise from the dead,' and if you can find a connection there, you can find a Zulu in Afghanistan.

Rick had all he wanted, or so was made to believe, which, to the powers that be, was satisfactory. Rick caused trouble for no one.

One hazy afternoon, having just returned from my promenade in the park, I came upon my fine, fish-smelling friend sitting on his bunk strumming inter-mittently on his gee tar. I had never heard Rick play anything to its conclusion. As a matter of fact, I had never heard anything that didn't sound like, 'On Top of Old Smokey.'

I sat down, loosened my shoes, looked over toward him, and asked, merely as a means to conversation, "Say, pardner, how long have you been playing that thing?"

"Nine years," he answered, while continuing to pick.

"Nine years!" I questioned in disbelief.

Astonished at the tone of my voice, he stopped and looked up. "Yeah, what's wrong?" he asked none too enthusiastically.

"Well, I'll tell you, Bub," I explicated, now being in the swing of things, "All I've heard for almost a month now is, 'On Top of Old Smokey', and I never heard all of that."

"Oh … well, I never really played steady until lately, but I'm picking it up pretty good now."

"I see. Your all not that serious about it, is that it?

"Yeah, I just kind of plunk on it for somethin' to do. It used to be my uncle's, and when he died, I took it. You play?"

"Only spoons."

"You from around here, John? Your name is John, ain't it? I ain't too good on names."

Ignoring identification, I acknowledged my whereabouts instead.

"Nobody's from around here, Rick," I reproved. "California's just someplace you come to get things out of your system, and then leave when it's done. It's that place just over the hill which after crossing you find is depressingly similar to the place you just left. It's not so much a home as a way station, and every country should have one for its outlaws, outcasts, the restless, disgruntled, and fading movie queens."

You mean we're the only one's that got a California, John?" he shot back sarcastically. It seems my newly found friend could fling a spear with some dispatch himself.

"Yeah," I replied, pretending not to notice his bite, "except for Russia, but you go east there, and they call it Siberia."

"You like it here?"

"I don't like it anywhere."

At that he looked at me kind of sadly as if to say, "Everybody likes it some-place." Rick hesitated to believe things were all that bad. He had it made, or so he thought, and he didn't wish for anyone coming around to hitch up his touched-up Plymouth and tow it away for junk. I was sorry I said it since the natural innocence of the Ricks among us, makes the world tolerable.

Speaking as I had to such as Rick was akin to banging the baby over the head with the bottle, a dastardly act given that babies, spiders, dying cockroaches, and defused electric guitars are among that vanishing number of pleasures encom-passing my enclosed circle. One shouldn't be so quick to harshness, and the benefit of a doubt should always prevail. Quickly changing the subject, I asked if he had ever been married, to wit, he replied, "No, somebody say I was?"

"No, it's just that them who wind up in these dumps are usually running from something, and that something commonly includes a depurified old squaw with long hooks, and a penchant for holding a grudge right into the grave."

"Why should she be holding a grudge?"

"Why not? When she begins to lose feeling for the old man, she simultane-ously develops an overdeveloped sense of injustice, and guess who's the cause of all her troubles?"

"The old man. . . . ."

"Give the man a cee-gar."

"But why the old man?"

"Why? Because the world is a bag of lopsided Rubik Cubes. He's the one that 'stole' the best years of her life, loaded her down with drudgery and shitty-asked kids; besides, he's handy. When he begins to resent her misplaced neurosis she begins to hate him. After all, the least he can do is quietly accept the blame for her falling star, and what was once a beautiful friendship has inexorably turned into a snarling hate. He becomes a fugitive, she a bloodless bounty hunter. He seeks relief from the stretching claws of misery until finally his only refuge is a cave deep in the bowels of beautiful, downtown San Jose."

Rick frowned quizzically. "Are broads all that bad?" he asked unsurely, hoping for a positive response.

"Rick" I responded pointedly, "does the pig oink?"

Later that evening I mused over the short chat I had had with Rick, and it conjured up memories of an old maid aunt of mine since departed from this grand isle.

Aunty was fond of running about the house naked, she was, and what a sight was this sixty-six-year-old hag bouncing joyfully about in the altogether like a nymph in a porno movie.

Aunty was underfed, undersexed, and her skin hung like dripping wax around a melting candle. I was only five, or so, at the time, but it seemed odd to me even at that tender age this grotesque woman displaying her unbecoming wares so unabashedly. After some time the only article I seemed to notice was her vagina as she seemed to be all vagina, hairy and effusive. It stuck out like the bearded lady at the carnival.

Aunty was a crotchety old bitch who seemingly delighted in anger; anger for anger's sake. She ranted at her unwed state, she ranted at the marital state. She had few pleasures, but somehow always seemed to be occupied. She liked to cook, but ate little. She cleaned constantly, yet the house always had the look of a bivouac area. She played solitaire, a game requiring only her company, and she gave regularly and generously to the church, no doubt a compensation for her lack of emotional giving. No matter what subject was broached, Aunty would have an adverse word for it, not out of any extraordinary intellectual qualities, but rather sheer spite, a trait consistent with her patently, acrimonious nature. Aunty was a nasty old bitch.

As I grew older I thought of Aunty, now and then. How could I forget her? And as could be imagined, Auntie's, sweet and loving pussy, predominated, for

Aunty was all pussy. Eventually the image of Aunty also brought thoughts of a big, red lobster with it. And why not? It lay there quietly and unassumedly, but when it clapped its prey between its pincers it devoured it in smothering fashion much as a snake a frog. Yes, it was the pincers that were so much alike those two, throbbing folds, twitching and quivering, big red lobster, black widow spiders; jellyfish, fly traps, clapping vaginas, old hermit crabs. Pinchy, pinchy, pinchy. It was fortunate Aunty passed away when she did, as I was beginning to get an uncontrollable urge to set her bush afire.

* * *

VIII

OLD MOTHER HUBBARD WENT TO THE
CUPBOARD
TO GET HER POOR DOG A BONE
BUT WHEN SHE GOT THERE THE
CUPBOARD WAS BARE
AND SO THE POOR DOG HAD MOTHER

NOW being a loner it did not prevent me from seeking female companionship upon occasion. Actually, all I wanted was the tail. The frills I could do without the price being outrageously exorbitant.

Be that as it may, I therefore, one dark and dingy evening, went-a-hunting for my quarry. It is not hard to find, if one, like a birddog in the bush, knows where to look, and no longer being a stranger to the neighboring haunts, I knew where to look, and I looked to a gin mill called the 'Four Feathers,' just another watering hole, but unique in its manner of display.

Above the door hung a neon sign shaped like a chicken's butt, just the butt with four, long feathers issuing forth from its bunghole with the rows of bulbs being so arranged along the feathers as to give the appearance of four giant fingers reaching down into the chicks behind, you know, first the top bulb would blink, then the next, and next, and next in rapid succession until reaching its destination. But, as is always the case, most of the bulbs were burned out so what was once a fondled chicken's behind became just another eyesore.

The site in question always gave me the impression of being a pirate's hangout. I really can't say why, but the trodden sawdust generously sprinkled on the floor mixed with the muffled whispers conveying the notion of secrecy, and the suspicious eyes furtively dodging to and fro, and the dark, dank atmosphere all combined to make one feel he were sitting on an ocean beach with 'one-legged

Pete,' the bartender, who wore a peg leg in the manner of Long John Silver, and who banged it up against the bar in imposing fashion when things began to get out of hand which was usually the case each and every night I am told.

I usually sat by the door at the Four Feathers, not only because I fully expected Bluebeard to come strutting in at any moment enabling me to eyeball him up close, but because the distance between me and it was the shortest possible … just in case. Besides, I didn't want to shake his hand. When knives begin to flash, and guns drawn, John J. would like to keep his options open, and one being a wicket having as one of its more useful attributes a smooth and quick swing to and fro, for when the time comes to 'draw the blanket' over J.J., it would have to be for something far more transcendent than a pick-up bar room brawl in a pirate's cove.

Why then, you might ask, would one so unassuming and modest, and with nothing but the best for everyone, locate himself so? Well, I do it for four reasons: 1, it's convenient, 2, I don't have to make silly conversation (what do you say to a pirate? Raid any good ships lately?) 3, It's cheap, and I'm-busted, and 4, the kind of gaff I'm looking for, use the Four Feathers as a watering hole.

Not in pursuit of anything more entangled but sex, I troddled in about twelve and had a beer. The place was bustling considerably for a Monday night, but included only 'three heifers in the corral,' two of which were roped, and the third not, but one look explained that. I hung around for forty-five minutes, became restless, and left.

After having driven two blocks I noticed someone standing on the corner that looked familiar. It was Rita, a local 'lady about town.'

Rita was a Spanish type, and outside of that didn't have too much going for her. She was dark, slim mish, and of medium height with a large, broad face surrounding a somewhat elongated aquiline nose, and did have a certain amount of sex appeal, but you had to work at it.

Rita was bedecked in a cheap, skin-tight, black silky skirt, a string of Navajo beads, a collar pin, a broach, four gigantic glass rings of various sizes, shapes and colors, and blue shoes. Rita knew how to do it up good. She looked like Sammy Davis in drag. If love were as easy to come by as despair the world would be one, long sweet song of felicity.

I pulled up alongside the curb, leaned over and hollered, "I'll take ya if it's within the county." She troddled over, peered in, and said matter of factly, "Ya wanna go out?"

"Not too far," I answered correctly. She straightened up, gave a little wiggle, and then leaned back in saying, "Ten bucks."

"Five," said I.

"Nine," said she.

"Six."

"Eight."

"Done."

She got in, looking at me warily and accused with more than a hint of disappointment, "You ain't exactly a rich oilman from Texas are ya, squabbling over a measly two bucks. What would you have done if I had insisted on ten?"

"You'd of had to take credit, or I'd have had to keep on driving. All I have is eight and change."

"Ha! Eight and change, eight and change. You got some nerve, sport. Ain't you ever heard of inflation? You couldn't get in the mission with eight and change."

"No lie."

"You know it. A chick could starve with dudes like you cruisin'."

We didn't go far, two blocks maybe, when I was directed to park in a fleabag hotel lot, and we checked in. As we passed the desk Rita gave the clerk, a seedy-looking gent of about fifty, a nod, and he, in turn, gave a wink. At least that's what I thought it was. Later I learned it was a nervous twitch.

We went to supposed Room 22, one of the numerals was missing, but the imprint still showed. The telltale signs of the past … if we choose to notice.

Not long upon entering, I noticed we were not alone; our performance was to have an audience. The roaches were making it known that they were not, as yet, an endangered species. It must have been a slow night as they weren't moving much, but just kind of hung there with baited breath, staring, like a sexually depleted octogenarian in the front row at the burlesque in expectation of things to come. Oh, the stories they could tell.

Rita immediately stripped and I likewise, but less hurriedly. She was down to the nub before I could say, "Gin." American industry, I thought, while gathering in the speed with which she disrobed, could very well take a lesson in production from the oldest profession in the world. Incentive and reward, it is all a matter of incentive and reward, and all with nary so much as a foreman, or supervisor, or whatever, to look over her shoulder. Amazing how the simplest things go unnoticed … or is it?

Crawling in bed, she clicked her fingers, saying, "The bread," I glanced at her, momentarily pondering over the injustice of prefabricated sex roles. She should have been paying me, but deciding not to be contrary, I handed her a five and three ones. She leaned over and shoved them in a drawer of a small bed stand. I continued undressing. In a few seconds, Rita, becoming impatient, urged caustically, "C'mon, will ya? This ain't no weekend stand."

"Hold on, sweetheart," I responded in like tone. "This ain't gonna be no 'jump on, jump off' deal, either, or you can hand back the bread, and we'll say our goodbyes now."

"Well, Christ, you could move a little faster. The night is still young and I can't afford to waste it. This is a very precarious business."

"Yeah, like driving a nitro truck. So what? That's life. You take the good with the bad and 'fuck um all but six.' And don't hustle me. There'll be opportunities after I'm gone. Your profession always has a clientele."

"Yeah, but we're like athletes, we have short careers."

"They're overpaid, too."

"Look, Jack, if everybody was like you I'd need the hot dog concession at Candlestick Park, and for eight bucks you're lucky you're getting the bun with it."

"Ain't work hell?"

I finished undressing and popped in the sack, whereby Rita immediately, like a robot on a Japanese assembly line, spread her gams, and announced, "Okay, let's go, Samson."

"Hold it!" I protested vehemently. "Let me just kind of lay here for a few seconds, will ya? I don't gulp my food, ta, ra, ta,ra. You dig it?"

"Oh, shit! You ain't one of those 'I just wanna talk' fuckers, are ya?"

"Honeybunches, for eight bucks we're gonna do more than talk, even if it's only to play with your ears."

"Well, c'mon, start playin'."

"Let me catch my breath first; I'm so enthralled I can hardly stand it."

"Smart ass. You ain't exactly no Clark Gable yourself."

"Yah, but then I ain't hawking my wares either."

As I lay there I could see, as already mentioned, Rita's somewhat imperfect structure, but she did have a certain sexual attraction, and for eight bucks that's all I wanted her to have.

We commenced with the activities, but I was struggling to keep it 'interesting.'

After chugging a while she lay there like a stump, giving a half-hearted pump, now and then, almost on cue as if someone was directing her from the ceiling. At one point, in the midst of this travesty, I stopped and said, "I ain't disturbing you, am I?"

"As a matter of fact. . . . ."

Much to my surprise, after what seemed like an eternity, I 'engorged,' I think. Rita, who by now I recognized to be a very 'sensitive' individual, announced sarcastically: "See, that wasn't so bad, after all, was it?" To wit, I replied, "Kiss my ass."

I cleaned up, to a degree, in a rundown john, came back into the bedroom and started dressing.

"Well, shit," she said. "You might as well stick around a while now. It's almost two, and I ain't in no mood to go back out on that street no more tonight." I think she was beginning to like me. Sic.

"Yeah," I answered, "nobody's exactly knocking down the door to get in here, are they?"

She sat up in bed with her legs crossed like the Maharishi, and replied as I contemplated her navel, "You sure do get in your licks, don't you?"

I put on my pants and sat in an easy chair stained with only the gods knew what, resting my feet on the edge of the bed.

"Ya know," she said thoughtfully, "at the end there, I was beginning to like it."

"Ha!!! Why, your so full of shit. . . . ."

"Yeah, honest, but I wouldn't want something like that to get around. Bad for the rep."

"Well don't sweat it. You're talking to the right guy if you're trying to keep a secret."

"I am, hey? You haven't exactly impressed me as being the silent type."

"But I got scruples.

"Is it catchy?"

"Not as far as I know."

"Oh, a philosopher, aye?"

"There's no such thing."

"What was Aristotle, a pretzel?"

"Well, how' bout that?" I replied cheerily, "I hit the jackpot … an educated whore."

"I'm not stupid, either."

"You're telling me."

"What's that supposed to mean?"

"You got my eight bucks and all I got was a dried-up muff burger. In Japan, you get soft music, sake, sweet smiles, a bath, fish heads, and a rubdown."

"They lost the war."

"In-deed."

Rita never left the bed. She laid there with her head propped up on the pillow staring into space. I shifted my weight, saying, "You know, we're not alone."

"We're not?" she replied acquiescently.

"No."

"Well, unless it's the vice squad, we're okay."

"I speak of them damn eternal night crawlers."

"Oh, yeah. Well, pay them no mind. If you don't bother them, they won't bother you."

"My, but aren't they considerate."

We had been watching the speedy, little wall streakers for some time when it eventually occurred to me that their busy movements seemed to be coupled with an unusually undemanding nature, so I mentioned it.

"Ya know, sweetheart, the little, black bastards do get around, but they seem to mind their business. Not one has come down here to bug us."

"Yeah, aren't they the cat's meow?"

"It could be worse."

"Yeah, they could be people, then the first thing they'd have said when we came through the door was, "take off your shoes.""

"Ho, ho, ho! Listen to us now. I haven't noticed anyone making any demands on you."

"Look, Buster, a while ago you gave me the story of your life."

"I did?"

"Sort of; now I'll give you mine. I can't remember a time when someone wasn't making demands on me. 'Rita, sit still.' 'Rita, play nice.' 'Rita, don't say that.' 'Rita, go to bed.' 'Rita, go to school.' 'Rita, don't spit.' 'Rita, go to work.' 'Rita, get married.' 'Rita, think like this.' 'Rita, think like that.' 'Rita, spread your legs.' 'Rita, don't spread your legs.' And it all has a purpose. This is your box, Rita, and this is what you can do in your box, and as long as you stay in your box, and be good, and do like you're told---good and told being synonymous—you'll be happy and you won't end up in the can. And when you're sixty-five we'll give you a pension. Nice, nice. The stinking pukes. You know why I'm a whore? You really want to know why? Well, I'll tell ya. It gets the respectables' ears perked up and on their tippy-toes seeing bums, tramps, whores and derelicts, and a general all-around motley breed of cat swapping spits and rubbin' elbows with their dainty, sweet smelling, sheltered, well scrubbed, white-assed kiddies. It forces them to think the unthinkable. It's the leveling factor. The eminent in their positions of high honor need to be reminded that we are living in two worlds largely of their making. In theirs, tulips grow, and green grass, and lilacs; in ours—weeds. They need to know, not for their sakes—they're beyond the limits of hope—but for ours. It does wonders for the spirit to bump into them on the street and stare into their big, baby blues, knowing all the time, and them knowing that you know. It takes the edge off their arrogance. It's my way of getting in the front door. That'll grab them every time. A whore in the foyer. It's the least I can do."

"Rita, my darling—I said in all honesty—this could be the beginning of a beautiful friendship."

We, in between catnaps, carried on random conversation for another two hours, when finally I left. As I drove along in the crisp morning air I thought to myself, Now, how bout that? Dignity, fading fast in the sunset, has a few rebellious twitches left after all. Hallelujah. And, as you can imagine, Rita and I were going to become like two scabs on a wino's ass---itchy close.

The next day, Rick, drawling in his usual, unassuming way, asked about the night before. "Hey, man, you' all sure made a night of it last night, didn't you? What's goin' on out there? Am I missin' something?"

"No, Rick," I replied casually, "you ain't missin' a thing. I was merely in the company of a 'young lady of the evening,' and we gabbed, among other things. That's all."

"What's that 'among other things' business." Pondering for a moment, I answered easily, "Come to think of it, it was business, but we fucked, too."

"Ah, so. You fucked, too. That's nice. You didn't fight?"

"As a matter of fact. . . . ."

"Jeez, I gotta get out there one of these nights and get some action. I ain't had any in so long the shock, when I do get it, will probably kill me."

"Yeah, if the shock in not getting it don't paralyze you first."

"Why don't we cruise together some night, John? You've been here a while, you ought to know a few chicks."

"No, I don't, but I know where to find them, which ought to be just as good."

"That suits me."

"Somehow I thought it would. You're gonna have to get that stinking fish smell off, though. I ain't musclin' around with no dude what smells like a pickled herring. It's all right to look like one, but you can't smell like one."

"Yeah, I can dig it. I've seen some barracudas in my time, and they do all right in or our of the water. What's wrong with tonight? You ain't doin anything special, are ya?"

"No, not tonight. It's not raining."

Rick drew a look of puzzlement. "What's that got to do with it?" he asked. "Water make um grow … like plants?"

"No, but it makes the mold on them curdle. Besides, I don't like to waste a clear day in San Jose sittin in a saloon trollin for pike."

"Is that right? Christ, I'd sit in the Sahara if I could get a piece of ass out of it."

"If you were sittin in the Sahara you'd be lookin for more than poon-tang."

"Yeah, but I'd risk it. Okay John, you say when. I'm always ready, know what I mean?"

"Yep, I believe I do."

* * *

By now I had quit with Finni and was on unemployment, where I intended to stay for each and every of the twenty-six glorious, indolent weeks. He, being the great little gent that he was, had been putting in the fund, with my help, and now graciously consented to my request for, rest and relaxation. And indeed, Virginia, was I surely up to the task at hand, was I ever.

I drew my checks, week, after week, after week, loving every minute of it, and I never once, not once, felt guilty about any of it. I deserved it. As a matter of fact, I was proud strutting right up to the window, chest out, head high, handing the perfunctory clerk my card all filled out neatly and signed in the proper place, whereupon I would be handed a check which I immediately took to the cashier, still walking tall, and receive my fifty-five dollars. It wasn't much by a magnate's standards, but sweet mother's milk just the same.

I stayed put for the twenty-six weeks, then practically on cue and eerily robot like, some hot-shot economist, sitting in a plush office in Washington all decked out in hardwood and magenta, said something about a depressed economy. I don't know what he meant by that. It's always been depressed to me (low wages or no wages, take your pick), but because of the new distinction I was back on the list for another thirteen weeks using each and every one of them also, t-h-a-n-k y-o-u.

I thought of writing the charming gentleman to express my deepest heartfelt appreciation, but didn't. What the hell I thought, his Girl Friday would, in all probability, get it, crumple it, and throw it in the basket with the rest of the incidentals. Sometimes I get this funny feeling that America's being run by pleasant, twenty-five-year-old, mini-skirted, one-hundred-dollars-a-week business school graduates who can type one-hundred-twenty words a minute, take a fast short-hand, brush off visitors with the expertise of a bartender on the strip, smile on command, and who play with the bosses balls by day, and her pre-law boyfriend's by night. I get the funniest feeling.

* * *

Over the next six weeks I saw Rita five times, always at night, always in the same bug-infested hostelry, and always after she had closed shop. Needless to say, we were becoming attached to each other for reasons other than sex, but the fruit of lust was by no means a dead issue. However, I must not fail to mention, I always made sure she gave herself a good douche; she didn't have to be told … but I wasn't taking any chances. A-N-D how I escaped catching one of the more 'exotic' love bugs is, well, more luck than mystery. A-N-D what could a body be possibly thinking, if anything, to deliberately, voluntarily, mindlessly jump into a tub of downright, stinking, filthy water where a half-a-dozen others have gone before him, A-N-D P-A-Y F-O-R I-T? And you think we're living in the twentieth-century? I wonder why I keep hearing chariots rumbling in my head.

On night number four, in the midst of disrobing, I drew out a five, and Rita immediately motioned for me to put it away. "It's gone beyond that," she intoned matter-of-factly.

"Oh," I replied in jest, "does this mean we're in love?"

"Better than being in the shitter."

"Ah, my dear, you do take the edge off of class."

"Let's just say I'm like Robin Hood. I take from the rich and give to the poor."

"Well, if you're Robin Hood, does that mean I'm Maid Marion?"

"You can be Little John if you like."

"I don't think there was any hanky-panky going on with Little John, maybe Friar Tuck, though. That funky monk wasn't around just for prayers. Robbie had to be buttin' him."

"Probably, there's not much to do in a forest. A body could get tired of huntin' and fishin' all day." I don't think Rita was much on nature.

Eventually it got to be where I was invited up to 'the big house.' I was a friend now, not just a customer. She lived in a small, one-bedroom pad nestled quietly in the slum. It was furnished, however, like the queen's chambers; antique furniture, oriental rugs, fancy art objects of all kinds and description; air conditioning, hi-fi, the works. Upon entering I declared humorously, "Well, not much to see from the outside, but I wouldn't be ashamed to bring 'her royal highness' herself here."

"Yeah," she replied, matter-of-factly, "It's not bad."

"I'm not going to ask the obvious."

"Which is?"

"Business must be booming."

"I wouldn't say that, but it's steady," and with a wink added, "and you can flim-flam the tax man, too, if you can dig it."

"Yeah, I can dig it. By the way, how much A-R-E you sending in for this anonymous penthouse?"

"One-ninety-five."

"One-ninety-five!" I screeched. "Christ, they even get you in the slum."

"Especially the slum. What do you think makes it the slum, the low curbs?"

"Jesus, people ain't got no fucking respect. They're downright disgusting."

"You're telling me, and all those ornaments you see here a-l-m-o-s-t belong to me."

"I didn't think they belonged to the cat. What is he, Siamese?" A little brown pussy was stretched out napping on one of the three, plush easy chairs.

"Yeah, and he cries, and cries, and cries. I was warned about that, but I took him anyway. He's drivin' me bats. One of these days I'm gonna screw up enough nuts to flush his cringing ass down the john, and be done with it."

"Aw, you wouldn't do that to the sandy little fucker."

"I know, I'm just a sucker at heart, but it makes me feel good to dwell on it."

We were standing in the middle of the room, me with my arms folded across my chest. I gave everything another once-over, then asked unknowingly, "What did you get all this junk for, anyway? I thought you were a working gal."

"I am a working gal. I work very hard for what I get. And wud'ya mean, junk? All this you see here is the real thing."

"Yeah, well, maybe. And it's all very nice, but-what-do-it-do?"

"Ain't you got no poetry in your blood? It's art! Art!" Pointing to the console, I replied, "And I suppose that hunk-o-junk is a Picasso?"

"Well, what do you think I work for?"

"Carramba! I hope it's not for shit like that! You'll never be able to retire." Rita gave it all a look herself, and had an agreeing expression about her. "Actually," she solemnized, "I don't really need all this."

"I gathered."

"I only bought it to see what the filthy rich feel like."

"And?"

"They're filthy all right."

"To say the least."

"Now that I know, I'm gonna start getting rid of it. Like I said, I really don't need Persian rugs, and gen-u-eine fake, Aztec v-a-ah-zes. Living from credit card to credit card ain't my style. Let those suburban saps with the working wives what don't know any better pay that interest. It's good for business cause when the old man starts to feel the pinch, and he will, he'll come lookin' for ol' Rita baby."

"Sweetheart, you're beautiful."

"Better than that, I'm a conniver."

"Yes, that do make a difference."

"In America, next to owning the store, it's everything."

"Do tell."

Rita and I, after we took our pleasure, would sit up in the rack and play a game. It was called The President's Game, and it all started casually enough with no great motivation behind it. We were just lying there one afternoon in the altogether, she smoking—that was the only bad habit she had—and me trying to escape the fumes with little success when I noticed plaster cracks in the ceiling.

"Hah!" I announced exuberantly. "A hundred-and-ninety-five a month, and you got cracks in the ceiling."

"Good, if there weren't I'd be paying twenty more a month."

"Ain't it a shame? Nobody gets their money's worth anymore. You pay through the nose and they still want to screw you. Sometimes I wish I was President, just for a week, that's all, just a week. I used to get this same kind of feeling some-times when I was in the service. After seeing how the show was being run, I got the opinion that almost anyone could be an officer. The more I thought of it, the more I was convinced. I said to a buddy of mine once, 'Buddy, I'd like to be an officer for one week.' Buddy glanced at me humorously and shot back, 'Aw, whatsa matter? Ain't little kookin's happy being a peon?' And in return, I replied, 'I'd be a lot happier if a M-A-N, now and then, got to wear a set of bars.'

"I see," he said, "a body can't argue with that, but if everybody was a man we wouldn't need a military, cause men don't need wars and we wouldn't be here"

"I'm hep, but keep it rolling. You're onto something."

"There's not much else to it. If men were men and not the fucking sheep-dip they are, they wouldn't be so god-damn afraid of everything, and if they weren't afraid, they wouldn't need no fucking armies and navies, and all that shit, and we wouldn't be bobbin' up and down like a couple of jackasses climbin' the Sierras, so be glad the world's one, big, fucking chicken coop, cause that's the only way dudes like you and me can ever get to see this world. The suckers can't have their cake and eat it too. Their fear has a price, and we're it. But if you're so inclined, what would you do that the rest of these assholes ain't doin' already?"

"Oh, nothing spectacular. It's what I wouldn't do that'd count. Like I wouldn't show my fat, Annapolis ass unless I was shittin', hey? These cocksuckers around here don't know nothin' about nothin'. Like Banfield the other day. He gave me this shit-lickin look cause I didn't have a hat on. Imagine that? We're so far from anything resembling life, I haven't seen a gull in five days, or a flying fish in two, and he was itchin' to make an issue of it. I wonder sometimes, what kind of crap runs through an asshole like that? Where they come from, what schools, what neighborhoods; what kind of jerk his old man was, the kind of funky broads that turn him on, if they do. Ya hep? It's scary when you really think about it, downright scary."

"Yeah, but what would you do?"

"Nothin', just nothin.' I'd just quit fuckin' over people, that's all. Before you can do somethin' you gotta know how to do nothin.' These block heads don't know nothin' and the little somethin' they're supposed to know they don't know nothin' about that either. You remember the time Bundy told him he didn't have the brains he was born with?"

"You mean when we were out a thousand miles into the Pacific, and he wanted to search his locker for a pint of Jim Beam?"

"Yeah, that took a genius, didn't it? Admittedly, the honcho is a drunk, but zig-zagging the way we were that time, it took us five days to get where we were. Now do you think a bonafide boozer is going to save a pint for five days? Five, mind you. He done good just getting it back to his locker."

"No lie."

"Anyhow, he was a hundred-and-eighty degrees off course. That's Banfield's problem. He H-A-S the brains he was born with, and that's A-L-L he's got."

Rita seemed impressed. "So," she butted in. "Maybe so, but you're a civvie now and we just made you Prez of the U.S., none of this small time ensign crap. What are you gonna do now? You got the juice, talking's done with. Daniel Webster's dead and things are in the saddle ridin' man. We want action."

I stretched out, twinkled my toes, eyeballed the cracks, and said authoritatively, "Okay, you got it. I'd get the sucker who owns this dump and drag him by his balls over here and confront him with this ratty quilt work he calls a ceiling. Then, in a fashion consistent with the high honor of the office, I'd slap the dogshit out of him. Moreover, still grasping him firmly by his suckled, suburban nuts, I'd drag him down to the fuzz-house and charge him."

"Charge him! For what?"

"Anything, vagrancy, loitering, pandering, who cares? Just something to get on paper. Every cocksucking criminal should have a rap sheet."

"Okay, then what?"

"Then, with my hand still steadfastly ensconced about his macaroons, I'd drag him back up here and make him an offer he can't refuse. Either he plugs up the cracks pronto, or he's going to get his bell rung. The choice is his, a cracked gong, versus a slick ceiling. Isn't democracy wonderful?"

"Aw, c'mon, be serious. What would you do? Quit with the idle chatter."

"Idle chatter, you say?" I replied offendedly. "Oh, no, but I am serious, to be sure, my dear. I am very serious. That's the problem. Folks have got the mistaken impression that the jerk in Washington does not stink after a fast game of handball, but verily I say unto you, he stinks, he stinks. And now, not surprisingly, he himself has the impression that what he smells is the fragrance of roses in June. He isolates himself in that big, white house with a steel fence ringing it, away from everybody, guarded by a whole phalanx of strong-arm boys. Christ, you'd think he was Caesar. You can always tell the biggest crooks by how many body-guards they have. What's killing me is I have to pay for it. Oh yes, sweetheart, the thing is, he don't trouble himself with cracks in the ceiling and bats in the belfry.

Yes, he is of a different stripe, and the color is mostly yellow. First, he stays in the house all week surrounded by people j-u-s-t l-i-k-e h-i-m, mistake numero uno. On weekends he goes to his retreat in the mountains, (they all got retreats; Hitler had a retreat) surrounded by a few cronies, mistake number two. Once in a while he'll come out on the lawn and pose for pictures, or play a round of golf with people j-u-s-t l-i-k-e h-i-m, mistake number three. On those rare occasions he does come out to meet the folk—he I-S their servant, isn't he?—he can't possibly know what's going on. Shit, Kansas City could disappear and he wouldn't know till he turned on the tube and saw that the football team failed to show up for its usual Sunday afternoon punctilio.

He'll issue communiqués and decrees, make a statement to the press now and then, and give a speech covering little, saying nothing, and involving nobody. Pericles must be turning over in his grave. Democracy? Shit, America's just a big, overgrown banana republic. And the cracks, what about the cracks? In Holland, what started as a tiny crack turned into a flood.

Yes, ma'am, honeybunches, you can bet your sweet bundejo I'd love to be President for just one, short, redundant week. That's all, one week. Admittedly, much can't be done in one week, but I'd plug up all the god-dam cracks."

* * *

One Monday night, a rainy, June Monday, Rick and I went visiting our friendly neighborhood boy's club, the Four Feathers.

Rick was wearing, or decked out, I should say, in what can only be described as, something or other, out of the vaudeville era, including a brand, spanking new pair of high-waters. Rick always wore high waters. I asked Rick once, "Rick, how come you always wear high waters?"

"Well," he responded seriously, "it's like this. Every time I buy a pair of pants, they shrink, even the ones that ain't supposed to. They shrink too. One time I get a bright idea. I thought I was going to beat the game. I bought a pair two inches too long, but I didn't wear them, I just washed them. Every time I did my laundry I threw in the pants. It worked like a charm. They shrunk right down to size. Trouble was though, the cheap fucking things also wore out from all the god-damn washing, so I had to throw the shitty things away before I had a chance to wear them."

I didn't bother to ask Rick why he never thought to wash them in cold water.

So much for bright ideas. So, Rick, with his little boy jeans, and I, set out for a quiet evening of 'fun and games.'

Now one who is not so disposed to this sort of thing may have the mistaken impression that it is all fun and games. That, dear heart, is decidedly not the case. If the spirit of competition has left the boardrooms of GM, and Ford, and US Steel, it certainly has not in Gin Alley.

We no more than became settled when Rick announced spiritedly, "I bet I can chugalug a Bud quicker than you."

Ah, hah! I said to myself, so this is the kind of night it's going to be, is it?

"No, Rick," I immediately rejoined. "Save yourself the trouble. First, I don't give a damn, and second, if I did, I wouldn't be making no damned contest out of it. If I want to see a race, I'll go to the track. I concede, you win. See, I picked the winner and neither one of us is any the richer for it, not to speak of wiser. Save it, pardner, save it."

"Jeez," he objected, "it ain't no fun like this."

"If you want action you should have joined the elephant act at the circus. That'll keep you on your toes."

"Okay, okay," he objected disgustedly, "but it's gonna be a dull night."

"Rick," I advised in friendship, "learn to live with the fuse capped. The best things in life are those that move about slowly and methodically like a big, old, fat broad I had once. She just kind of sat on it and rolled and grinded, r-e-a-l slow. Every cord and muscle and nerve was movin' and groovin'. Coordination, Rick, ya gotta have coordination … and harmony. You'd be surprised what grand gifts can be accrued with just a little harmony and coordination.

"How do you like that? I challenge a guy to chug and I wind up in the sack with 'two-ton Tillie.' According to your theory then, turtles must have the most fun? They ain't exactly the quickest cats around."

"Well, the analogy leaves a bit to be desired, but you're getting the picture. And look how long they live; all the more to enjoy it."

Rick called out, "Bud." I said, "Whiskey." When he heard that, his hair stood up on end and his toes curled. "Whiskey!" he exclaimed. "Whiskey! Man, you ain't even got a job and I might as well not have one for what I'm makin', and you're drinkin' whiskey. Who all here can afford it, Diamond Jim?"

"Hell, Rick, for such a young man, you sure do worry a lot. You take care of the beer and I'll cover the C.C."

"Nah, I'll cover my end. I don't want you to think I'm one of those fuckers who runs to the can when his turn comes around."

"O-o-o-k-a-y, but don't sweat it. You just take care of the malt. Things have a way of workin' out even in the worst of times."

"You're an okay dude, ya know, John?"

"Yeah, I know."

"Shit, don't let me force anything on ya."

Giving him the high sign with my middle finger, I murmured, "Here, force this sucker where it fits best."

Rick and I sat for a couple hours nonchalantly hoisting a few and speaking of all manner of things wet and dry. We spoke of growing tomatoes, killing Dutch Elm disease, fighting crabgrass, hot rods; being poor, hitchhiking, mag wheels; Christopher Columbus, the Nina, the Pinta and the Santa Maria, everything but sex, war and politics.

As we were getting into "who killed Cock Robin," two crows came strutting in and took a seat right next to Rick. One of them was enough to pop your eyeballs right out of their sockets, the other, pop them right back. She was hor-en-dous.

The 'good' one was sitting closest to Rick, and as far as I could tell in the closet darkness, had all the qualifications to make it anywhere, any time. She was, as the saying goes, stacked. Tallish and Grecian looking, and looking like she had just come out of the sauna, she was all peaches and cream. I yearned for her to just sit on, and melt, like strawberry sherbet in the noonday sun, all over me. Luscious was a lady tonight. The 'bad' one? Well, I don't like to be cruel; people can't help what they are, but I wouldn't have been surprised to hear her bark.

As soon as they came in, Rick and I stopped whatever we were discussing, and like two trappers who'd been in the woods two months past too long, stared glassy-eyed and gaped-mouthed. After they had sat down, and we had regained our composure, Rick leaned over to me, inquiring, "Well, what do you think?"

"Never mind what I think, it's what I feel."

"Okay, wud'ya feel?"

"I ain't feelin' nothing. I'm numb."

"What the hell's a chick like that doin' in a dump like this, anyway?"

"How many times have I heard that b-e—f-o-r-e?"

"I ain't leavin' here without makin' a pitch."

"Give it your best shot, Buck, but if you think I'm gonna get stuck with

Pluto over there, this friendship has just ended." I responded in the manner I did just to be convivial; I had no illusions about either Rick, or me, gaining any success with 'Aphrodite,' but we can dream.

"We'll worry about that when we come to it." Rick also was a bit of a dreamer. I, myself wasn't 'worried' about anything, because nothing was going to happen.

"We'll, here goes," he confidently asserted, and upon uttering those last words, Rick then summarily turned toward that luscious, hunk of pulchritude, and as casually as asking for a light inquired into the nature of her sex habits. In other words, "Did she fuck?"

Immediately I clutched my glass and raced down to the other end of the bar crouching there like a fawn in the woods in expectation of the worst. It wasn't that I was so shocked at my chum's behavior, but rather at that particular moment I could think of a number of places I'd rather be than in the can, and presently that distasteful event loomed as a distinct possibility.

I watched intently from my place of hiding and observed what seemed to be a conversation taking place between dumb-dumb and the 'Sweetheart of Sigma Chi.' It continued for a minute, or thereabouts, whereupon the two foxes rose and walked over to a booth. It looked like Rick's pitches fooled no-one, and least of all, the batter.

He noticed me slinking at the other end of the bar, and motioned with a grand sweep of the arm to return to the scene of the crime. My response to that was half of the victory sign.

In a matter of moments I saw ambling in what at first appeared to be a giant redwood, but turned out to be a human instead and walk straight over to 'Sweety.' All manner of fearful things raced through my mind as my life flashed before my eyes, seeing myself lying in the sawdust and grime, all bleeding and broken, ambulances screaming up, strange voices trying to be helpful, "Stand back, folks, give him some air." Traction, telegrams to unsuspecting mothers in the dead of night, quiet, choked sobs in black accoutrement. I waited in suspended horror as my brain shriveled up and became a residue of barnyard fodder. I could swear I felt a warm sensation trickle down my leg.

Words were said at the table, the girls rose, and all three left peaceably, whereupon my heart resumed its customary "thump, thump" instead of the fast dribble it had been doing. Still not completely recovered I shakily strolled back over to Rick.

"Hey, John," says Simple Simon, "you' all sure disappeared in a hurry." I eyed him warily. "Did you see the dude that came in here?" I asked clearly and emphatically.

"Yeah," he answered casually, "big ol' fucker, wasn't he?" I stared unbelievingly. "Big ol' fucker!" I shouted heatedly. "Is that all you got to say? If he ever hit you the holy fathers could have stuck you up in the steeple at Notre Dame, cause your chimes would have been ringing forever."

"Aw, hell, he wasn't gonna do nothin'."

"He wasn't, ay? I had a friend once who replied similarly in a like situation. Those were his last words before coming in contact with a very large, ten pound hambone masquerading as a fist."

"Did he hit 'im back?"

"Hit im' back! Hit im' back! Rick, my fine unawares friend, to this very day he is part of the scenery at the 'Last Stop Café' in Sasebo, Japan, which unfortunately, turned out to be h-i-i-s last stop. So much for retaliation. And being that I came so close to my own personal Pearl Harbor, I ought to know what almost started the bombing. What did you say to her, numb nuts?"

"Not much of anything. After I introduced myself, she gave me one of those "who are you?" looks, then said, "You didn't learn that at Dale Carnegie's, did you, sonny boy?"

"Then I said, 'Who's he?' and she said, "Never mind, just drink your drink and quit while you're still able, farmer." She called me farmer, John. Imagine that scruffy bitch calling me "farmer.""

"Just no damn justice in this stinking world, is there?"

"Jesus, that made me mad, but before I could answer they got up and went to the booth. And she never did say whether she fucked or not."

"Rick," I murmured softly, "I'm sure you don't know it, but that lovely Mediterranean meatball, by her silence, just might have saved your life."

"Aw, hell, it wouldn't have been much of a fight."

"You're telling me."

"He'd have hit me and I'd have refused to get up, and that's all there would have been to it." Like a big brother, I put my arm around Rick's shoulder, admonishing in a sobering tone, "Rick, if that creature ever hit you, you wouldn't have been A-B-L-E to get up, not then, not tomorrow, not ever, comprende?"

"Yeah, but I bet it would have taken more than a light jab," he rebutted proudly.

"Sure. Drink your drink and give my organs a chance to fall back into place.

I feel like Einstein's 'Theory of Relativity.' Nothing seems to be where gravity put it."

Nothing much happened after that and it's just as well. One needs time to recover from the frightfully unusual.

We stayed until close to one with Rick getting thoroughly bombed. He was drinking that damn slush like a line was attached from his mouth to the vat. I also sported a slight glow.

In his enduring friendship with the malt, Rick, after reaching a certain point, became totally placid and quiet. In his condition I wondered how he kept from falling off the stool.

There must be a mechanism akin to a boxer's, who all but knocked out, still stands flailing away instinctively. Residue of Neanderthal Man? Finally I said, "Okay, cut the line and let's get the hell out of here." No answer came forth, but he must have heard me because he emptied his glass ever so slowly, then slid off the stool like only an inebriate can without even so much as losing his balance, and stood there facing the bar rocking and weaving, and waiting patiently like a robot for the next command. I gave one. "This way, Buster," I urged simply, not wanting to unduly confuse him.

I moved toward the door watching to see in what fashion Rick was going to navigate the hundred, or so feet, to the car. He turned v-e-r-r-r-r-y slowly and stepped in the direction of the door stiff-legged ala Frankenstein. I made no attempt to help as I was curious to see if he could do it.

Shakily, he staggered toward it, and upon reaching it stopped, and peered out into the starry night making a wheezing, gasping sound as if the malt and hops were having a violent discussion somewhere in the vicinity of his severely, maltreated liver.

"Let's go, Flash," I ordered, watching curiously, and he began again a slow, lock-kneed step, slowly, slowly, slowly. Had I not known better I'd have thought he was in acute pain, but to the contrary, Ricky baby, was warbling soprano.

When finally we reached the car some minutes later, he stopped, leaned against the door with his feet spread, stared down at Mother Earth, and drawled, "I gotta pish." Not a little irritated I shot back, "Not on you tin type, Mister. I ain't dragging you all the way back there just so you can piss. Piss in your damn pants for all I care you stupid fuck. And why didn't you take care of that little matter while we were still in the damn, fucking joint?" and his witless reply, duly expected from such in his condition: "I din't hafta."

"Well, shit, in your condition I ain't about to do no backtracking. We'll be here all friggin' night."

"Wusha meen, in my cundishun? Wush rong wi-wi-wish my cucu-cundishun? I kin sta-sta-stagger wish da be-besta dem."

"Yeah, sure. Well, c'mon, take the damn thing out. And face away from the car! I don't want you fading what's left of my $29.95 special." And Rick, in his turn replied, surprisedly perceptible, "Yus go-go-gotta bee ki-ki-kiddin'."

He turned and began to fumble with his fly. For a while I thought I was going to have to lasso it for him, but finally he whisked it out, and leaning with one hand against the door, and me propping him from behind, he relieved himself, to put it mildly.

Did you ever take a beer pee? Did you ever see anyone take a beer pee? Well, all that frothy liquid comes rushing out in a torrent, and it seems it will run forever and ever. And it sprays all over, very uneven but very steady. And Rick, he sprayed, the fender, the front tire, the hood, the curb, the walk. He even managed to squirt a passing Tom some four feet away who shook his head bothersomely, and in all probability would never ever forget Rick's face, among other things.

After what seemed an eternity he finished and shoved the infernal contraption back in his pants where I wished it had never left. Of course, Rick didn't miss his shoes either, but when he made a move to get into the car I quickly collared him, ordering, "Hold it, pardner. You ain't getting in this car with them damn, stinking shoes."

He looked down at them, asking puzzledly, "Wush rong wish my sh-sh-shuz?"

"Just take them off," I stressed, "and I'll explain it to ya later."

He did, taking another five minutes for that, then slid in the front seat, and with the other worldliness only a drunk can exhibit, slammed the door like he had a grudge against it. With the shock waves reverberating through my ears I looked up at the black sky, and wondered if there was anything up there besides a quarter-moon. I turned on the key, and we were on our way. Wheee.

When we returned, guess who we ran into? His royal highness, 'the Cooker' himself. The two of them started a conversation I wouldn't have missed for a gloriously, good screwing on a balmy, Summers eve.

Both stupefied, and neither of whom speaking a word of the King's English, they just burped and blurbed incoherently, but were certainly giving it their best, nonetheless. I couldn't make a word of it, but they looked like two high-powered, world renowned ambassadors at the U.N. I wondered if they were discussing the Versailles Treaty, or Hitler's march into Czechoslovakia, or the Charge of the Light Brigade, or maybe nothing more profound than the advantage of booze over broads, or vice-versa. In fifteen minutes or so, they decided to shuffle off to bed certain in their heart of hearts that God was in his heaven, and all was right with the world.

The next morning, Rick, not once ever showing the effects of the night before, rose and troddled off to another day of meaningless labor. Not so with Cookie. He slept till noon. I got up at eight myself for a solitary stroll in the park. It wasn't as pleasant as it could have been since I was still penniless, and coin in America is directly related to freedom---the only kind that really matters---freedom from poverty.

Wisdom begins with the notion that Big Brother is dead and Big Mama strumps down Main Street with exposed vagina beckoning all her sons to come and fill of the fruits of creation. The world will self-destruct at that precise moment Big Mama 'gathers in her flock.'

Upon Rick's returning, I asked, if by chance he remembered anything of the night before. He said no, and asked what I had in mind since the whole point of getting bombed in the first place was to forget. It makes sense in a way, but then I think I would prefer to remember sometimes, what I'm trying so hard to forget. It may be worth it in the long run when one considers the "nailing down of the pine lid" is the final "remembrance of things past." Moreover, it is not the best of ideas to destroy all the evidence, unless, of course, one is a crook, a condition more and more in abundance these frightful days.

He desired to know what I had done all the live-long day. I suppose stuffing fish all day does whet the appetite for even the simplest of pleasures. "Nothing much," I responded catatonically. "Took a walk in the park and watched the squirrels gather nuts."

Eyeing me warily, he interjected caustically, "I think you're getting a little squirrelly … and a lotta nutty."

"Indeed?" I countered, not minding a little bantering, my being aware of its beneficial effects upon the vital juices.

"What the hell could be goin on in the damn park that's so all god-damn important?"

"My good man, tis' a damn sight more goin on there, than that stinking fish-hole you spend all day in."

"Yeah, but I gotta do that."

"Uh-huh. And we had to drop the bomb. We all got to do what's in our blood, Rick. Some have to lie, cheat, steal … even kill, me, I'm a simple kind of guy. I just have to stroll among the lilies of the field and the birdies by the brook. Sides, I'm broke."

"Shit, why don't you get a job?"

"I said I was broke, not stupid."

"Hell, a guy's gotta work, John."

"That's exactly what those doing the shoving would like you to think, and in your case, those shoving fish, so's they can drive around in big, fat Caddy's. 'You gotta do it.' Well, I can do without it. Those that eat um ought to stuff um. And you know where they can stuff um."

"Jeez, you're bitter, Jack."

"Yeah, well, wud you expect, Mother Theresa swaddled in rags and manila hemp? Symbolism is for those who believe in progress while standing in six tons of rat shit. I ain't had that kind of life."

"But. . . . ."

"And were it many more so inclined, it would mean wide-open eyes, and covered asses. As it is now, they're just a big, red, bull's eye."

"I don't get it."

"Hell, man, it ain't so hard. There is a natural law in the universe governing us schmucks, the same as there is in physics, or astronomy, or mathematics. You know, 'two parallel lines shall never meet,' and 'what goes up must come down?' Well, the axiom concerning schmucks is: 'They are chicken-hearted do-do's.' Not exactly a new found observation, but so just the same. Having so stated, it then follows that they'd as soon rip out your guts as assume any position of discomfort. Education, therefore, consists in realizing such as soon as possible, and although this may not keep you from getting fucked on every corner, it will keep you from catching the clap. Call it 'the law of the condom,' if you like.

Yeah, you can bet your sweet raspberries I'm bitter, just like a fucking lemon. And the average suck hole? Well, he's up there in the clouds singing the Star Spangled, mother-fucking Banner every time somebody hollers, 'Play ball'! Well, baby, as it turns out, he's playing with your balls and whacking you off, and while you're popping your wad, he's rifling your pockets. You end up with wet pants and hazy dreams, and he with loaded saddlebags."

"I kinda get it, in a way, but what the hell's The Star Spangled Banner got to do with it?"

"Ha!! Y-O-U G-O-T T-O B-E K-I-D-D-I-N-G. Everything Jocko, everything. One of the most forgetful moments of this bedraggled life was the time I stood amongst thousands at a ballgame with my hand over my heart while they played the fucking, raggy thing."

"What's so bad about that? What's so wrong about a little patriotism?"

"Patriotism my friggin' ass. You ain't heard a fucking, Anglican word I've said, Rick. It's part of their stinking, rotten game. America, god, church, democracy, free enterprise, the piss-assed Constitution; stars and stripes f-o-r-e-v-e-r. Don't you see? That's the whole, waxy ball, brother, placidity and acceptance, everybody stupid, like you. . . . ."

"Suck off."

"And all for the sake of power and control. That's their dungy bag---control. Don't waste it playing the other fool's game, cause you gonna lose, suc-kah. He made the rules, and he made them for his benefit, not yours. He gonna win, not you. They ain't no way in hell you can beat him, no way. And it's really sad, you know, when you think about it, cause the average man only lives some fourteen years, roughly, give or take a year or two, and if you're indigent, less than that, given that so much of his idle hours are taken up with guzzling beer and witnessing a constant parade of drivel slung across the video screen. Hardly a condition to be described as living.

"Fourteen years?" Rick questioned perplexedly.

"Sure. You can't consider the first eighteen as living, certainly. Childhood, at most, is a time of unconscious mobility, and the teens can best be described as semiconscious meanderings sprinkled with generous dabs of anxiety, boredom and frenetic non-happenings, so much so that the likes of Alice Cooper, Boy George, Kiss, (and a bit later Buck, a gangly, slinky, puzzling phenomenon with effeminate tendencies and dubious talents bedecked in black, silk garb, rhinestones, and a white glove), turns them on.

So much for youth, Ricky boy. From sixty onward, one is beset with encroaching, old age, and all of its debilitating paraphernalia, wherein what one likes to do, one cannot, and what one can, one doesn't like. That leaves forty-two years. Out of that, one-third is spent working, another sleeping, relinquishing the remaining third for 'living,' said grand total amounting to precisely—ta, ra, fourteen years. Ducky. And, In that miniscule fourteen, one is willing to use it derogatorily. In other words: wars, oppression, killing—the usual frolic-some behavior dominating through evolutionary history by the linear regression of homo sapiens. And in that sparsely told tale lies the inherent insanity of mankind, the willingness to spend fourteen years, a paltry fourteen, mind you, which he can reasonably call living, subtracting, and, in general, causing havoc amongst all things live and sundry. In truth, does the fox snare the hare in vain, for the trapper's steel jaws awaits him in due time. Ya hep to it?"

"Then if a dude only lives thirty-six years, that means he's really living only seven."

"Now you're catching it, but four-and-two-thirds, actually."

"Shit, that ain't even old enough to get a piece of ass."

"Aye, now you're really on to it."

"What the fuck's the point then? Seven years, fourteen, seventy-two, it's all the fucking same."

"B-I-N-G-O!! Just so many numbers at the local, fund-raising raffle, and just as pointless. You pays your buck, win your shiny, new Chevy, run out into the street in exultation, and get hit by a bus.

Hannibal froze his dumb, African ass crossing the alps with a bunch of fat elephants, only to end up in a far-away, lonely corner of Persia with a poison pellet stuck in his gullet. Caesar conquered the world, or what amounted to his share of it, to deftly receive a dagger in the back, and Hitler basked in the glory of military conquest, but ended up deep in the earth like a mole, surrounded by a phalanx of spiritual perverts, and a half-witted broad. The philosophy of life, my dear friend, consists in one, tiny, pregnant five-letter word: brief. The dust of your bones will not withstand the ravages of time."

"Christ, you're depressing."

"Only because you have been brainwashed to the power of positive thinking. You'd have done well to have been taught the power of 'live and let live' instead. We might have been able then, to have saved so seemingly insignificant a creature as the snail darter.

"Well, what the fuck's so important about a stinking little fish?"

"One small step, Buck, from that to the golden condor, to the tiger, to the hawk, to the rhino, to the Jew in Germany."

"Shit, you sure do skip around."

"Shit, I sure do."

"But what's all this got to do with … with … with accepting things? You got to accept things."

"I ain't got to accept a god-damned thing but the long, long, bony hand of death reaching for my jugular. That's inevitable, and I don't have to like it either."

"Yeah, but you got to accept it."

"In a manner of speaking. I leave to myself, however, the satisfaction of telling the powers that be that I'm wise to their shitty, bag-ged tricks, and they can all go suck off. That's the difference between acceptance and non-acceptance, letting the bastards know you're hep to them.

You see, Ricky baby, my not busting my ass is my way of telling the limp dicks to fuck off. Stuff their own smelly fish cans, the blackguard mother-fuckers."

"Yeah, man, but … but you're only hurtin yourself. Ya gotta get bread some place."

"I'm getting my checks, and I'll do so till the bitter end."

"But what are ya gonna do when that runs out? That pit has a bottom, ya know?"

"Then I'll corn hole some rich, fucking hag good enough to stand her hair on end, then maybe she'll want to marry me. Wouldn't that be the cat's meow, having the fox in the henhouse. Hallelujah, brother!"

"Flying high, now, ain'tcha?"

"More like racing to the four winds on a sea of indifference."

"I think I envy you, but I'm not sure."

"Join the crowd."

"You mean there's others who envy you, too?"

"No, others not sure."

* * *

I went to see Rita the next day. I always had to catch her before the "first act." In time, I made sure I was the matinee show. You can understand that, can't you Buck?

We must have been feeling the same that day because neither of us said much, that being unusual.

I walked in, catching her curled up on the couch reading Eric Fromm's, "The Sane Society," and exactly how many can confess to that small accomplishment? So much for 'education.' Or how about "Philip Wyllie's "A generation of vipers."

How many have even heard of Philip Wylie? No matter; The shark attacks the movement and not the substance.

"You know, sweetie," interrupting her cerebral meanderings soberly, "I really got it heavy for you."

And she, just as seriously, replied, "Yes, I know."

"You know?" I questioned. "How do you know?"

"Because I got it, too, and these things are usually mutual. But no sweat, I won't make any demands."

I really did love the girl in a quaint sort of way, and not relishing her getting down on herself because she was a whore, admittedly not the sweetest of vocations, I replied, quick enough, "Sweetheart, what you do for a living is your business, and maybe peddlin ass ain't the most respectable of occupations, but it's a lot straighter than some high society stink hole sneaking around motel rooms, with this john and that, while the old man's culturing an ulcer nine-to-five.

Besides, I'm the last guy in the world to be playing the reputation game. I lie, cheat, and steal whenever it suits me, and the only reason I haven't done so in a bigger way is because I don't know how. But I never lied, cheated, or stole from my friends, and if you're anything, you are my friend, for sure, and I do love you, and you can say anything you damn well please to me, or ask me anything, or demand anything. And don't worry about rights cause I'm telling you, you got every right in a world without rights, and you got it because you deal from the top, and that's rare, and anybody that rare can say, and do, anything they damn well please to me.

What the hell are friends for anyway? The good folk who love each other should love each other, and to love and be loved, and be kind to the distressed, and mean to the wicked, and leave the rest to the cheaters. It's only fitting. So demand; no frills needed. I'm a simple sort; a song, a dance, a smile, a jug of wine, a little lovin … what the hell, I'd give you the world if I could, and not look back once. Who cares, and what matter? Play it again, Sam, we're the only folk in the world."

I noticed my short recitation had picked her up as her eyes flashed and watered, and she stood motionless, just staring, not saying anything, then impulsively swung her arms about my neck and gave a big hug. We merely stood there in the middle of the room, not saying a word, yet becoming 'rich in time.'

Rita and I, that afternoon, built a fire in each other's soul. We enjoyed it in all its goodly abundance, allowing for a smidgen of trumpery, yet quiet and tasteful. We laid there, and pursued, and relented, slow and easy and thoughtful. It was a priceless and blessed event. We didn't play The President's Game that afternoon. He should have it so good.

Thereafter, Rita began working less and less, and cavorting more and more. It was that kind of life.

* * *

IX

JACK SPRAT COULD EAT NO FAT
HIS WIFE COULD EAT NO LEAN
JACK SPRAT GAVE UP HIS WIFE
AND NOW HE'S LEAN AND MEAN.

ONE trivial weekend, I went down to L.A. to see Rudy. It was said that he had tied the knot and was camped somewhere in Encino. (Where else?) When I saw his pad, an anxious feeling clutched my gut. It was a Saturday afternoon, and I sat for a moment, in the car, in front of the house, watching.

A typical suburban neighborhood (aren't they all) dogs barking, hordes of kids (all blond) cluttered the streets. (I never saw a black-haired kid in the suburb.) A car would cruise by, now and then, with either a teenager, or a housewife driving, and there was the inevitable putt, putt drone coming from the numerous power mowers giving the whole vicinity a nerve-wracking, muffled sound.

But the one thing that defied sanity most about the infernal environs was the lack of smells. It had no smell, none, of any kind, good, bad or otherwise. Not of leaves, trees, flowers, grass, food, or even garbage. It was almost as if it was trying to demonstrate its sterility. Correction: Sometimes there is a smell, the only one I've been able to detect. When the wind is right, a steady drift of dog-pooh will pass. I know, it's not much, but any old straw to a drowning soul.

In this twentieth century Erewhon, with a chicken in every pot and a skate on every walk, America is being overrun by scruffy, scab-backed barking dogs. And bark they do, incessantly, night and day, at kids walking, kids running, kids on bikes, kids without bikes; mailmen, birds, sirens, gnats, flies, cats, and other of the various assortment of the canine persuasion. I, when beset by this abhorrence, would sometimes get the uncontrollable urge to arm myself with a big stick, and forage through every bush in the neighborhood, and if a dog barked, bludgeon its master. Tis only fitting.

I slowly disembarked, walked up to the front door, and peering through the screen, shouted, "Anybody home?"

An auburn haired female of thirty, or thereabouts, wearing green shorts and top, boat shoes and hair curlers, came to the door. Tall and well-built, although slightly on the heavy side, she greeted me with a friendly, "Hi," and a "Can I help you?"

"I'm looking for a rat named Rudy. I'm told these are his scamping grounds. A look of confusion crossed her attractive face as she began to laugh, and not knowing how much of a joke it all was, then frowned, then smiled again, and frowned again. Finally she said, straightaway, "Yes, Rudy scamps here, but I don't think he's a rat … yet." Now it was my turn to make faces. "Okay, now that we have that settled, I'm John Rosko."

"Oh!" she exclaimed exuberantly, unlatching the screen. "Come in! Come in! Rudy's gone down to the hardware store. He'll be right back. I've heard a lot about you. I almost feel like I'm married to two people."

"Do tell."

"But I do believe that's bigamy."

"You believe correctly."

"Can I get you a drink? Have a seat. What would you like?"

"Well," I advanced, while easing myself in a rickety, antique, old granny rocker, "if I know Rudy boy, he has some good ol' 'dago red' hid away somewhere."

"Oh, yes, does he ever. I'll be right back."

That "does he ever," sounded like Rudy was socking it away pretty good. That was unlike the sport, for although he had his hang-ups, boozing wasn't one of them.

She returned with a bottle of Chianti, and a fritzey glass, handing both to me, saying, "Take as much as you like; if you don't, Rudy will."

"By the way," I inquired while pouring myself a generous helping of the grape, "how is Rudy?"

She sat on the sofa, crossed her legs, and shrugged. "Oh, I think he's starting to feel his oats."

"And he's not even a horse."

She smiled. "Yes, well, I think it'll work out, though. I'm glad you came. Maybe he'll cheer up now. He's been moping around with a long face for a couple of days now. He'll really be glad to see you."

"And surprised." Then I added helpfully, "I'll see what I can do, but no promises. I'm not Houdini, and I can't stay long."

"Oh, Rudy isn't going to like that. He'll expect you to stay a week, or two, if I know him."

"Oh, no, no," I said quickly. "That's impossible. I couldn't stay in paradise for two weeks."

"It wouldn't be any bother, you know. Not a bit. This is a three-bedroom and there's more than enough room."

"Uh, huh. Well, you know, I never did get your name?" I asked clumsily, trying to veer the talk in another direction. "No, you didn't, did you? It's Christine. Christine Kranzer up until two years ago."

"That's a nice Irish name."

"No, it's Danish, I think."

"I hear Rudy's a father."

"Yes," she answered proud fully, and getting up, announced, "Would you like to take a peak at Rudy junior? He's taking his nap."

"Where's he taking it?" I jested. Smiling, she replied, "In here," and we trooped to little Rudy's bedroom.

He was a Junior, but there wasn't much to see. Such a tiny, little tike, lying there on his belly. I could only glimpse one side of his sleeping face, and all I could really tell was that he had dark hair. This family, I could plainly see, was not long for the burb'.

"Oh," I expressed, and the 'oh' was like all the ohs' that have ever been enunciated upon seeing a baby. "Isn't he cute? He looks just like a baby, the little darlin.'"

Christine frowned, then smiled, and uttered, "You're strange, all right. I've never heard anyone refer to a baby in such precise terms before."

"It's the wine," I excused, holding up the glass. "I'm really quite normal, but I give myself plenty of leeway."

We returned to the living room and sat down. "What do you do?" she asked warmly.

"As little as possible," I responded casually.

"I see. Well, what do you do when you're doing as little as possible?"

"Oh," I countered flippantly, gearing up for the contest, "sometimes I don't even do that much."

"How much do you do when you're not doing it?"

"Actually, I don't do anything. It can be referred to … as nothing."

She cocked her head to one side, and inquired, "Are you a lawyer?" knowing full well I was not.

"That's good; I like that," I replied, noting the similarity. "It's not bad, not bad at all. They do little of note, and are also evasive," and looking straight into Christine's big blue eyes, I complimented directly, "Rudy did alright for himself," then leaned over and held out the wine bottle for her delight, inviting, "Here, have some red. Let's drink to friendship." Quickly taking the bottle, she drew two long gulps such that would have made 'Klondike Kate' herself proud.

"Good heavens!" I exclaimed, "Did you say you were a Dane?"

"Thanks," she replied, handing back the bottle. "I needed that." Shaking my head wonderingly I took back the red as I heard a car pull into the driveway. "That must be Rudy now," she acknowledged while rising and moving toward the door for confirmation.

I saw Rudy walking slowly up the walk carrying a small bag. As he came through the door, Christine greeted him with, "Look who's here, hon."

He spotted me in the rocker and immediately flushed. "Well, damn you! What the hell. . . . ." I rose, we shook hands, hugged, and in general, was very pleased to see me, as I him.

"Christ sake, John, where the hell you been? You sure don't tell anyone where you are, do you? What the hell's the big secret? For all anybody knows, you could be dead. It's been, what, five years? Get some drinks, Chris."

"I did," she answered amusedly.

"Sit down, man. You sure like to shock a guy. What the hell you been doin? You livin' in L.A. again now? You got an old lady yet?" he never waited for an answer to any of it. He kept rattling off the questions like a hotshot D.A. shooting for the governor's chair.

"Damn it all, John, I sure am glad to see ya. Christ, I don't see anybody anymore, except a few stiffs down where I work. They sure ain't nothin' like you and Lester, though. No personality, know what I mean? Just people, assembly line stuff. Whatcha been doin', brother? Tell old Rudy baby all about it."

"Ain't been doin' much of anythin', pal. Not much of anythin'."

"Well, Jesus, you had to be doin' somethin'."

Chris gave me that "oh, we're not going to go through that little bit again, are we?" look.

"What about broads?" he continued. "You hooked up with any broads?"

"Rudy?" Chris interrupted. "Do you have to be so crude?"

"Aw, hell, this is me ol' pal, John. John digs it all. Shit, I'd have married him myself if he was a chick."

"Thanks a lot," she countered sharply.

"Did you ever go back to school?" he continued.

"Ho! Ease up, Jack. You know me better than that."

"Well, what then? Where are ya workin'?"

"And you know me better than that, too."

"You ain't workin' neither? You ain't workin', you didn't finish school, and you ain't married. Christ, you're the only one that made it from that old gang."

"Oh, you're a real riot today, hot stuff," Chris complained. "You didn't know he was such a riot, did you, John?"

"Oh, yeah, I knew! I knew!"

"He's not so hilarious when he has to muck it up at six in the morning to shuffle off to work, though, are ya, Buster?" Not bothering to answer, he asked instead how I was getting along without working. I told him, which was "just fine." A huge satanic grin broadened his face, as he said, "Damn it, if anybody could do it, I knew you could," whereupon Chris butted in again. "Damn, this conversation is chafin' my thighs," and left the room somewhat bristled, to put it mildly.

"If I didn't know you better, John, I'd apologize for my old lady's bad manners, but I know you don't give one good fuck."

"You got that right, Butch."

Rudy and I talked a while about this and that, and nothing much, and finally, with a wave of the arm, invited me to see the backyard. I don't know why, it wasn't anything I was especially yearning to peruse. I suppose it's part of the regalia in the booneys.

We went through the kitchen and out the back door, and there we were, faced with the ultimate in the American dream in all its Philistine splendor: patio, barbecue pit, lawn, hedges, and two fruit trees all surrounded by a seven-foot high, red board fence. One look and my stomach tightened. Is this really, what it's all about ... this fool's paradise?

We walked out toward the middle of the yard, and it suddenly struck me that Rudy had no dog.

"Hey, slugger?" I inquired in amazement, "Where's the pooch?"

"Pooch? No pooch."

"No pooch?"

"Nah, the one you just saw in there," pointing toward the house, "is all I can handle."

"Aye, do I detect a note of discontent?"

"You sure do," he replied dejectedly while hacking at the ground like a beleaguered bull.

"What's wrong, Rude? You got what everybody else has around here."

"That's the problem. We all got everything, and nothing. It's an old song, John, all these fine houses, and lawns, and commodities, and what not. Yet it's lifeless, characterless, and I'm stranglin'. It's nothing a guy can sink his teeth into. It has no depth. It's like listening to bad music all day. You get numb after a while. You can't feel anything, distinguish anything. The world becomes one, big whitewashed barn. It's just here, like the ground and the air. It only has the capacity for staying the same, today, tomorrow, forever. It's … horrifying. It's like a disease that never dies, but only gets worse. It's the boss here; it's the master, and us folk are just here to serve I-T, maintain I-T-S existence. It's like we're just janitors, John. I go to work, I obey the law, I support my family, I pay the mortgage, and I go into debt, all so the stink hole can be kept up. I'm just a fucking janitor, John … a motherfucking custodian for a big clump of shit surrounded by a lot of crabgrass."

I had no idea Rudy was in such a condition. I tried to help, but all I could think of to say was, "I don't know what to say, Rude."

"You don't have to say anything. The fact that you don't have your foot stuck in this friggin' bear trap says it all."

"What I mean is, if you're lookin' for fifty-dollar-an-hour advice, I don't have any. I don't know what to tell you that you don't already know. Can I say desert? What kind of advice is that? Can I say leave this no-man's land? Where would you go, into the stinking city? Can I say change jobs? They're all alike, a drag, and boring to the nth degree. It's hustle country, and its got us all by the balls. I can't even say work it out. That's going to happen, one way or the other, no matter what you do. I don't know what to tell you. I look around and can't help agreeing. You got everything and nothing. And if you're lookin' for sympathy, you got it, brother, have you ever got it."

"Aw, shit. Sympathy that would be dandy if you were my creditors." Then, leaning close, whispered coyly, "You ain't, are you, John boy? They didn't send you down here to feel me out, did they? I can't help getting the feelin' sometimes that this is a war, and they have their agents sneakin' around all over the place cloak and dagger style."

"Like I said, Rude, I don't have any advice. You're drowning, and I don't have a lifesaver to throw ya. But if it's any consolation to ya, I'm not much better off, if any. I have a room in the same hell, and they shovel coal down there, too."

Rudy, now gazing at me suspiciously, answered, "You're not?"

"No, I'm not. I have it, shall we say, a bit easier, in a manner of speaking, but I'm not happy."

"You're not? But that don't make sense."

"Maybe not, but there it is. I'm poor, half-educated, disillusioned, frustrated and futureless. I'm living in a world which I know is mad, and dedicated to ripping my balls off. I know it, don't like it, and can't do a mother fucking thing about it. They tell me to write letters when they deserve the firing squad instead. They want love notes and kisses when they should be getting a bullet in their ass.

I always have that feeling you get in that dream where the big, bad monster is chasing you, and you can hardly run, yet nothing is holding you back. The only difference is, in the dream I always wake up before it catches me. In life, the awakening is death, and I wonder how long this black nightmare will continue.

Happiness is an illusion, Rudy. We're not meant for it. We think too much. Not well, but much. We always imagine, and want more no matter what our circumstance. We reach the saturation point too quickly, the dope pusher's paradise. If I have a chick I want two. If I have two, I want four, if I can get four, I want a troop, thus the harems of the East, but eventually, even they begin to bore me. If I can have my favorite meal every day I will tire of it all too soon. Yet a bird never tires of a steady diet of worms, a cow grass, or a cat fish. If I buy a new car, it's not long before I want another. The same with houses, clothes, vacations, good times, or what have you. And if I have gads of bread, in time, that also loses its gleam, although I must say, even though it doesn't bring happiness, it can, like the always endearing, sweet broads ass, brighten up a starless night. And, what the hell, getting though the night is the trick."

"And the day."

"Uh, Huh. Ultimately, Buck, we can never realize peace, or tranquility. Eastern philosophy is a perversion. Zen is death. Imagination? A curse with a kiss, the venom in the cobra's fangs. With it we can move mountains, without it, not even a house of cards. It is our very own, special limitless burden. It puts our head in the clouds, then dashes it to the ground. We imagine, but cannot achieve, for what we achieve is already there. What we know as creation is merely the revising of the existent. We shuffle a few thoughts around, and we think we have accomplished the impossible. In the meantime, the world is burning down around our ruddy, deef ears. We're like a bad band that can't put two, good notes together, but it sure can make a lot of noise. That's all we are Rudy, noise makers, pounding on tambourines and bashing cymbals, yet can't play the simplest tune.

Bubby, we're cursed to eternal struggle without victory. The best we can hope for is a draw. That's life. And the tragedy of it? Impotency in the midst of universal creation, weakness masquerading as vitality, and no better example of it all than the brute of Bavaria, Herr Adolf.

Yes, Buck, with a minimal degree of consciousness mixed with despair, hope, pain, anxiety, fear and a smattering of joy, we zigzag through it like pieces on a chess board, some powerful, some not, impatiently striving to trap the king. And if we do, what then? We start all over, and so it is with life. We're born, we live, and we die, then start all over like a game of chess. We all line up and charge. We reach a certain point, then line up and charge again, and again, and again, and again, ad infinitum, and that's this nebulous presence we call life and death, or so it seems.

And happiness, and meaning, and God, and eternity. Line up, charge! Line up, charge! Line up, charge! Motion, baby, motion. That's all there is. But motion does not necessarily imply action, or progress … and there's the rub.

Actually, Buzz, we're pests is what we are. We're the scabs on the back of the universe. It can take us, or leave us. We contribute nothing, and have no value. We can all disappear tomorrow with no great loss. A maggot has more use. So, there's my advice. Feel any better?"

Quickly he shot one of those "you gotta be kiddin' looks."

"Well," I added on the bottom line, "there's something to be said for resignation, and in your case, it'd probably help because although you ain't exactly got the world by the short hairs, you also ain't exactly rummaging through garbage, either. What you got, just about everybody's got. We're all suffering from the same malady: boredom, anxiety, and envy. What you thought you wanted, you don't want after all. So what's new? You want to be a cow? This is twentieth century America, the age of frustration, and an aimless kind of greed and imbecility, a perpetual state of menopause, and unless you're ready to cut loose from your family and start a personal renaissance, there's not a hell of a lot you can do, except get a hobby, or a mistress, or a mistress with a hobby. Spice your anxieties with a little red pepper."

"That's it?"

"What do you want, a sealed envelope from Price Waterhouse?"

"Christ, you sure are a lot of help. Except for the mistress, I could have gotten the same crap from that dumb, fucking, yo-yo priest down on the corner."

"Probably so, but the fact of the matter is, any advice is no advice. I can't climb your mountain, and you have to walk in your own shoes. I can only guess, and get a general impression, and that impression is, you're in a rut probably, but you ain't really got any problems. Troubles yes, problems no, and better you should have troubles. So, how can you solve a problem you ain't got? You've bought yourself a whole, new world, one of shiny cars, mortgages, tool sheds, screen doors, aluminum siding, bicycles, and dog shit, and now you don't like the price. Well, that's too bad, you may have to pay it just the same. You signed this lease, and are just now catching on to the fine print. You're stuck, and so is the prick that sold you this pile of rat shit, and you're both going to have to pay … each in your fashion."

"Yeah, but it's the interest I'm complainin' about."

"Hell-o-o-o-o. Stud, everybody who buys on time pays the vigorish. You'll do well just to keep out the crab grass … and have a tank full of gas, now and then. That's success in your "brave new world.""

"Aw, shit. You ain't telling me there ain't a better way?"

"No, I ain't. I'm asking: what are you willing to pay? The cost of leaving all this may be too high."

"So, how high can it be?"

"Rudy, you're the best friend I ever had, and I take you for more than one of those simple-minded, jelly-spined, non-persons who splits just because he's got a few wild oats tickling his peppers, and unless you've really got a messed-up marriage---beyond hope—then you've got to stay, for Junior's sake. Old fashioned? That's too god-damn bad. The fact of the matter is, he's better off with you than without you, and that's all you have to know. Like I said, get a hobby; golf, model airplanes, kung-fu, something to shift a few molecules around. Under the circumstances, there's not much else you can do, that is, that's fair to everybody concerned. And, in a few years, it'll A-l-l be over anyway, no matter what."

"In the meantime you're giving me that shitty, friggin clap-trap about "adjust?""

"In a manner of speaking, yeah, and like I said, unless you're ready to do something drastic, which I highly disapprove of for reasons already stated, then your options are considerably limited."

"Now you sound like the Secretary of Defense."

"Goes for him, too. Look, Jack, I know what I'm saying ain't too attractive, but life rarely is. You have to live it within your means. Get yourself hypnotized and have the bloke tell you, "You're happy! You're happy! You're happy!""

"If you were in my shoes, would you do what you're telling me to do?"

"Ah, Rudy, now you're getting away from it. I could never be in your shoes, no more than you could be in mine. It's no accident you wound up here, and I wound up nowhere. Putting me in your shoes changes the person, making the question irrelevant because then I would not be John Rosko. We have separate rooms in the same hell pal, and the temperature is the same in both."

Rudy kicked at the ground, tugged at his belt, sighed, and looked up at the sky, then disconsolately affirmed, "Yeah, I know, but I just can't help feeling sometimes that there's something better, you know, for the human race, I mean, something besides this same … deadness."

"Yeah, I'm hep; I get the s-a-m-e feeling. But do you remember that hippie, Mindy, the one that blew her brains out?"

"Yeah, the one with the scales on her eyelids, and couldn't get through a sentence without saying 'fuck' at least six times. What about her?"

"Remember how everybody used to say, 'wow, what a free spirit,' smoked pot, snorted coke, shacked up with anyone she got a yen for, and selling her beads, among other things, living from hand to mouth just like a big bird flying high above the tumult. Remember how everybody envied her, especially the dungy broads what claimed how happy she must have been, living such a carefree and gay life, a chick living a man's life in a man's world. And then they found her one day with her brains splattered all over the wall. Remember?"

"Yeah, I remember. So what?"

"Well, didn't something seem kind of strange when you heard about it? Something out of place? The way she did it, I mean."

"The way she did it?"

"Yeah, you know, with a gun. Why didn't she stick her head in the oven, or drop a handful of pills? They must've been lying all over the fucking joint. Didn't the gun bit seem … over the top? A little too violent for the circumstances? It's almost like she wanted to attack the very thing that was causing her problems---the brain, and just smash it to bits. Despair exploded in her soul, and gunshot in her skull."

"I take it then I got to shoot my prick off?"

"You'd only miss."

"Ha, ha; you're a real Bozo."

"But you see? Things are not always what they seem. Life is a booby trap of mirages. It is much to easy to become disconsolate and remain so. There is only one thing that can help us, my friend, and it's not God, or the church, or democracy, or money, or you name it. It's courage, hard courage, for that is the only virtue that feeds on itself. It is the hardest to come by, but like all rare metals, difficult to tarnish. Steel balls, brother, can weather a lot of storms."

"Okay, fine, and maybe what you say is so, but you still ain't much help."

"What the hell do you think? I'm your knight in shining armor?"

"I'm getting the feeling I'll be feeling worse after you leave, than when you came."

"Like I said, you ain't got no troubles to speak of, and what few you have, are in your head. What else can I say?" He did not answer. The conversation had ended.

Walking toward the house, he said, "C'mon, I'll show you the kid."

We went into the bedroom, and Rudy, Jr. was still lying on his belly, and I still couldn't see what he really looked like. I stood beside the crib staring a few moments when Rudy finally asked, "Well, wud'ya think?"

"Well, what am I supposed to think? It's a baby," I replied matter-of-factly.

"Oh, really?"

"Yep, it sure is."

"So, that's how Coop got his start."

"Okay, I'll go and come back in and we'll do this bit over." I walked to the door, did a few mimics, huffed and puffed, ruffled my hair, turned around and strutted back in like King Kong. When I reached the crib I looked into it, and, like 'Watson of Sherlock Holmes fame,' responded casually, "Huh, I say, Holmes, who said the banana ain't got no seed?" And Rudy, fondly gazing upon his offspring, proudly, announced, "He's a good kid, John."

"Well," I acknowledged, "I didn't think he was Jack the Ripper."

"You know, John?"

"What, pal?"

"Remind me never to go to a parade with you. You're the kind of guy who'd kick a hole in the drum."

"No?"

"Yeah, and throw stones at the majorette."

I stayed with Rudy over the weekend. His son W-A-S a damn good kid, and his wife an excellent cook, although a touch on the bland side.

Sunday afternoon, his next-door neighbor, an average-sized man with a pot-belly, flushed face, and porcupine hair, stuck his head over the fence, and invited us over for a cookout. He was wearing a dirty, white apron, and when he smiled I knew he smoked cigars.

Rudy glanced toward me and quickly said under his breath, "Let's go, man, the guy's a real wacko. We'll have some laughs."

"Laughs! Laughs!" I admonished my good friend. "The whole world's a laugh. I wake up every morning in stitches. I can hardly control myself. My stomach veritably aches from all the frolicking. The whole, damn show's a barrel of chuckles. Besides, Rudy, the world is infested with the 'average, good Joe.' I see them every day, all of my life. So how come the funky swamp is sinking in a pit of quicksand?"

We went; we laughed; and nothing changed, here … or anywhere.

It was disturbing not to be able to cheer Rudy up. The court jester is dead. Long live the court jester.

I stayed two days, they being two of the most somber days of my life. I was sorry because I had come to see a dear friend whom I hadn't seen for a good while, and we didn't have a good time. But, it couldn't be helped, the world is a rock of ancient fossils.

As I was getting in the car to leave, Rudy mentioned as how it hadn't been such a wing-ding weekend for me, and he was sorry. I told him there was nothing to be sorry about, the middle ages were behind us. He said not to let too many weekends go by before I came to see him again. I said I didn't know Tuesdays from Saturdays anymore, but I'd keep it in mind. There was a camaraderie between us, as between all good friends, and I drove away sadly, waving back. I never saw Rudy again.

On the way back I thought of the recent happenings, and as expected, wasn't feeling too well. I wondered if things were really as hopeless, in general, and in the particular, as I had painted, but then I realized that hope, in America, is a mass produced commodity like toothpaste, and sold on the open market, subject to the whims of the moment. I thought of the Marquis de Sade locked up all those years in an insane asylum. Confinement didn't cramp his style. He took some wild trips. I thought of how a conversation might have gone with him. Something like this maybe: "Hi, Marque."

"Hell-o-o-o, matey; how's it goin'?"

"Oh, you know, a slash here, a slash there."

"They treating you alright?"

"They don't treat me at all, but who needs them anyway? Just leave me a box of pencils, and I treat myself."

"But don't you miss your freedom?"

"Hah! How much freedom does a body need? Due west of here I have seven feet of the damn stuff, then a hard right, five more, straight up, ten more. Carramba! It's almost more than a body can bear. Why, whatever is one to do with all this freedom?"

"Gee, Marque, it's nice to know you're making out." The Marque scratched his head, and mused, "Making out, making out. Now where have I heard that before?"

"I'll be going then, Marque. I just stopped by to see if you needed anything."

"Hell, I don't need nothing. Wait, there is one thing you can get me."

"What's that?"

"One of them new-fangled, six-foot whips with the tassels on the tip. Technology, great thing, technology. Pretty soon they'll be making them so's they can recoil themselves."

"No doubt, and with a pair of matching boots."

As I drove I thought of how I must have sounded like Babbitt himself, complete with Rotary and Chamber of Commerce mentality. I wouldn't have wanted to hear that mush if I were in Rudy's shoes, for sure, but what the hell, there's a multitude a lot worse off than he was, in a number of ways.

So maybe there were a few displaced atoms, so what? A little time, a little wine, a little tenderness stroked in the usual, customary locations, and they'll all fall back into place, for are we not all members of the animal kingdom, subject to the same animal laws? To the mind, with its distorted capacity for imagery, sand pebbles can resemble bricks, but who knows what tiny piece of grit is clogging the gears, and in time can cause as much damage as a well-placed blow from a sledgehammer? The tongue of the barking dog can be quieted with a swift kick to the tail.

Tiring from so much thinking and driving, I stopped to rest and pulled into a small, deserted looking place, called Aunt Martha's. Wearily I hauled myself from behind the wheel, stretched my legs, and slowly made my way to the door.

I could see only one body sitting at one end of the counter reading a newspaper and sipping coffee. I walked in and as I did, the young lady behind the counter looked my way. It must be said that if the individual in question was Aunt Martha, then Uncle Martha must be worn to a frazzle. She W-A-S fortuitous!!! Immediately upon laying eyes on her, my bird stood right up on his tippy-toes, and began screeching hysterically, "Hallelujah! Hallelujah! Hallelujah!"

Reaching five-six, or so, she had close cropped, dark brown hair, chestnut eyes, a-a-a-a-n-d built? Uh huh, uh huh, uh huh. Stren-u-ous? Gawd, it can be unbearable, and when a John comes upon a Jane in that celestial condition, only one thing comes to mind and remains there until a definite solution is reached. The sex was just oozing out of her like syrup from a maple tree. Standing there staring, I forgot about Rudy, Ratty, Rutty, the brown fox, or cow corn in the meadow. The hairy canary was warbling for all it was worth.

I weakly meandered over to a stool, and sat down. Presently she came over and asked casually, "What'll you have?" Hopefully I thought I detected a gleam in her eye. "Coffee," I replied, trying to sound as cosmopolitan as a tired, run-down, busted twerp can at ten bells in the middle of the California desert.

She brought a cup over and as she laid it down, I mentioned, while motioning toward the forlorn soul at the other end, "You all sure do a bang-up business around about here, don't you?"

"Yeah, well, this ain't exactly the hottest location in town."

"Town? What town? I saw one lame dog as I came in."

"It's dark. You missed the hotel."

"It's dark, I'm glad I missed the hotel."

"It's dark, but not that dark. You found this place."

"Well, we've established one thing, it's dark."

"Buddy, in this dump, we're thankful for anything we can get, and if you stick around six more hours, we'll establish the light, and then you can see the hotel."

"You mean," I continued in the same feckless vein, "it actually gets dark and light here like everyplace else?"

"Oh, yeah! And a cock crows once in a while, too."

"But, my sweet, does it have anything to crow about?"

"What's a damn chicken know anyway?"

"You might have a point there. . . . ."

"Well, if that's it, I have to get back to work," and with that abrupt about-face, she did just that.

I sipped on the coffee while sweetie-pie, leaning thither, and bending fro, was cranking me up like one of those little, toy soldiers. I had to do something besides just sit there, my strings were becoming entwined. "By the way?" I inquired hopefully, "What's your name?"

"Maiden or married?" she answered curtly.

"Uh, oh," I said to myself, and I suppose her old man's the cook.

"Whatever suits you," I affirmed disconsolately.

"Melissa Mugwump." The way it sounded is the way it hit me, and I almost lost a mouthful of Colombia's finest. I thought, "this broad has got to be putting me on." Surely she must have noticed the bemused look on my face as she quickly added, "What's the matter? Cat crap on your tongue?" Then I did spit up. "No," I returned, smiling and wiping myself, "but how come all you farm gals have names that sound like a frozen bottle of milk popping its cork?"

"What'ya mean farm gal'?" she chided.

"Okay, so maybe you don't have one foot stuck in cowshit, but how come all them freaky names like Betty Lou Appleknocker, and Linda Mae Humpbunger, and Sally Ann Picklelicker belong to farm girls?"

"Where did you say you were from?"

"I didn't."

"It has to be New York."

"As a matter of fact, Texas."

"Hah!" she blurted, unbelievingly, "Not on your life, sonny boy. Not with that accent. Besides, you look too foreign, anyway."

Why the nerve of that furry bitch, calling me a foreigner. I'll bet she never saw the Empire State Building except on a postcard. "It don't matter where I'm from," I snapped. "And it don't matter where I'm going. It don't even matter where I am now, which by the looks of it could be the set from an episode of "The Twilight Zone."

"Well," she concurred, while wiping a greasy counter, "that don't leave too much left."

"It don't leave nothing."

"Nothing at all?"

"That's right, nothing at all."

"But something has to matter."

"Why."

"Because, that's why." Because, that's why? Sometimes I think the intellectual capacity of the average American ranks alongside that of a semi-trained, moronic baboon.

"Because nothing," I replied, merely for the sake of conversation, "name one thing."

"Well, love matters." Oh, cow cakes; now I was sure I was talking to a baboon. Norman Vincent Peale a-g-a-a-a-i-n. What an overrated, horse's ass, I thought.

"Shit," aptly, was all I could think of. It was good enough.

"Shit?" she responded, seemingly surprised. I couldn't imagine why. It fit.

"Yeah, shit." Obviously by now our conversation was in no danger of being included into the 'Who's Who' of the greatest debates of the 20th century.

"You ever been in love?" Now it had sunk to those depths reserved only for clam shit and groupers.

"Sure," I affirmed, playing along while wondering if my newfound playmate could dig a hole deeper than the blue Pacific.

"When?"

"Plenty of times. When I was nine, I had a dog. Nice dog. He came when I called, and would roll over, and even jump through a hoop, now and then. Nice dog. I loved him and when he was two he got run over by a train. So, he lived, he tricked, and died. So what? It don't matter now to nobody or nothing. It's like he was never even born. He could've been the smartest mutt in the whole world, so what? He's dead, and that's it, and it's like it never happened. I don't hardly ever think about his doggy ass anymore. He's maggot shit. So, what's the damn difference, anyway?"

"That's different."

"It is? From what?"

"People, that's what. People matter." She did it. She dug the blue Pacific.

"To whom?"

"Themselves, and, each other." Christ, is there no end to it?

"You wouldn't know it by the way they act."

"It still matters."

"Yeah, to an imbecile. Does your life matter?"

"Sure."

"Why?"

"Well, I was born, wasn't I?" By now it was also apparent that the young lady to whom I was speaking was not the greatest example of American education in action.

"So, I give birth to a great, big brown turd every morning. Does that matter?"

"You're being ridiculous." That really hurt.

"I believe the word is absurd, and who cares that you were born? Don't answer, let me. Your mother? Your father? Your sister? Your friends? Whoever. So what? Who are they? Who cares that they care? Who are you? What are you? Who is anybody? You say people matter to each other, well, so what? So let's go back to the dogs. They matter to each other too; so what. That don't mean nothing to nobody but their yelping asses. And who the hell are they? Just a bunch of scruffy, damn mutts what don't mean dog-shit, not to them, not to you, and not to anybody, or anything, in this w-h-o-o-o-l-e motley, fucking world. If the whole stinking world disintegrated this very minute, what difference would it make? None! The Christian's keep trying to blow it up on a regular basis, and, ha, ha. Irony? The religion of peace, love, brotherhood can't wait to see how fast they can send us all to perdition.

"Cripe," she injected, "for a guy whom nothing matters, you sure do get upset."

"It don't matter; I don't know any better. And what did you put in this mud water you call coffee besides that dishwater over there?"

"You're lucky you got that. It's warm, ain't it?"

"So is the piss in my radiator, but I ain't drinking that."

The sleepy-eyed character at the other end, rose slowly, and walked over to the register. The 'lady in white' took his change and rang it up. He left, and she returned, saying, "I'm closing this joint as soon as you finish."

"Closing!" I blurted, "Why, hell, it's barely ten."

"Bub, it don't make no difference what time it is. There ain't been five souls in here since six. We're closing." Seeing my opening, I jumped in. Time was of the essence. "I don't suppose there's a motel around here?"

"Oh, yes, you can suppose it, but what do you want with a motel when you can shack with me.

I couldn't believe my ears. Was I hearing right? It then occurred to me, however, that Lady Godiva could be sporting an advanced case of the 'galloping crud' or some equally exotic malady just waiting to make an unscheduled visitation upon one so unsuspecting as yours truly, for after all, it can definitely be said, "it's only this easy in the movies." It did appear, nevertheless, that I would soon, albeit very carefully, and wary, soon know, if, in due course, I would be, once again, standing in the "butt jabbing" line at the local infirmary. Life does have its little risks, but I will have my pleasure.

Ecstatically I blinked a couple of times, and with all the sophistication of a man caught farting at the altar, replied, "Okay." Then, adding as an afterthought, I inquired matter-of-factly, whether Mr. Mugwump happened to be in the near vicinity. "Funny you should ask," replied she. "Just this very week I kissed dear hubby good-bye."

"And," asked I cautiously, "just where did you kiss him off to?"

"I kissed him to Japan," she answered smartly.

"Would that, by any chance, be by way of the watery seas?"

"It would."

"And would I also be correct in assuming then, that your loved one is in the service of his country?"

"Fraid so. With the fleet."

"How nice to know patriotism isn't dead. And just where might he be 'fleeted' to right about now?"

"Oh, I'd say on or about Guam, or Midway."

"Then would it be fair to say that if he took a notion to return immediately for any reason, he could not reach these sacred shores before, say, next Tuesday?"

"Yes, I think that would be a fair assumption." Thoroughly heartened, I straightened up and announced, "Okay, how long will it take to close this dump?"

"As long as it takes to shoo out the cat, douse the lights, and slam the door."

We left shortly, and I followed Melissa close behind, feeling like one who had just been awarded a ten-year contract as the second-shift piano player at a Las Vegas whorehouse.

After about a mile-and-a-half, she pulled into the driveway of a small, red bungalow, a typical desert dwelling. I needn't remind the reader of the state of excitation I bore. Suffice to say, I was stimulated, as this whole matter was pleasantly, but entirely unexpected.

From a purely sexual standpoint, at times a stand well worth taking, Melissa had it all, the body, the face, the movements, pure delectable sex at its deliriously, filthy best. If ever there was a machine made for one thing, this was that machine, and little ol' me was going to get to grease its gears! The gods allow but the merest glimpse of paradise to make the burning sun a warming fire, kindling the dry cinders of hope resting apprehensively within our battered breasts.

Up the front walk we went, and I wondered if she was anywhere near as excited as I was. Probably not, I being to her merely the object to relieve her obviously lonely and boring state. No matter, this was no time for such mundane concerns as selfless love and emotional giving, but rather, grab the pig by the ass, and shove the apple in her mouth. The embers warming the luau, desire to shish-kebob the porker stuck from hind-hole to gullet with the stinking, greedy hands of man.

Although I knew it was only a matter of time, I had all I could do, neverthe-less, to keep my shaking little paws off her butt. She had that kind of wiggle, and for the first time in my life I seriously wondered if it might not all be too much for me. However, the night would not pass without my finding out. The sooner the better, and if it was, well, so much for that.

Melissa asked if I wanted a drink, whereby I gave the quickest 'no' ever sput-tered in the English language. She beckoned me to make myself at home as she disappeared into the bedroom.

As I sat restlessly, she began asking all that trifling, dumb crap like, "where you coming from?" "Where you headed?" and "What do you do for a living?" I took all I could, that not being much in my understandably agitated condition, and so inquired, somewhat put out, if the lady was planning on 'polite conver-sation' all night. The lady said to hold my horses, to wit, I replied: "My horses aren't what was in most need of holding."

She returned from the bedroom saying something about impetuosity, and I, about not keeping Mother Nature waiting. Subsequently, to my great hetero-sexual delight, I was 'delighted' and not to digress at length with the gaudy details, I would like to remind, in passing, that a strange bed, at times, can be very warm, very warm indeed.

I awakened at seven joyously refreshed, and glanced over at Aphrodite. She was sound asleep. Drats. I lay there momentarily watching, beauty having a beneficent effect upon my fast becoming, beleaguered soul.

Presently, I bounced into the john, and did this and that. Looking in the mirror, I admired myself at length, then returned to the boudoir scratching myself in all the usual places.

Methodically I dressed and repaired to the kitchen to perk up the black bean. As I sat comfortably, musing over the blessed event of the night before, Melissa came strolling in in her nighty, yawning. 'Good morning' seemed apt for the moment, so I said it. "Good morning."

"It'll do," she responded complacently.

Noting the fatalistic strains, I wondered nevertheless, if a more gleeful mood would have been more in keeping with the good times, the sensitive tissue in a man's fickle nuggets being easily bruised, I wished not to sandpaper said rotary playthings unnecessarily this California morn'. "I'm making coffee," I drawled, stating the obvious.

"No, you're just boiling it. It's already made."

"Okay, it you're going to get technical, we'll get technical. I'm not boiling the coffee, I'm boiling the water."

"Okay, okay, if the water's ready I could use a cup."

I went into my best W.C. Field's. "Say no more, my dear, your wish is my command," and poured her a cup. Then, continuing in the same vein, added, "two scoops, or one?"

"One."

"Black?"

"Black."

"Coming right up, my dear. A moment tarried is a moment lost." And scooping a spoonful of sugar in her cup, I placed the pot back on a small electric stove, and returned to my seat in expectation of more sterling conversation. Melissa also sat, yawned again, then asked what I did for a living. (I guess it was not to be.) "This I-S Monday morning and you don't seem to be in too much of a hurry to get to your job."

"As to the first part," I replied, "as little as possible, and as for the second, I'm not."

"As for the second, why not?"

"Because I don't have one to hurry to."

"How do you get along?"

"I'm a gigolo."

"From the looks of that heap cluttering my driveway that must be with a small g?"

"Well, I'm kind of in between jobs right now."

"Uh, huh, quite a bit so, I would say."

"You don't believe me?" I asked, feigning insult.

"Let's just say I'm inclined to take your words somewhat lightly."

"What more can a guy ask? Every bloke should have such a mate. Loving husband returning home at two-am., with lipstick smeared on a previously white collar. Loving wife: 'Dear, what's that on your shirt?' Loving husband: 'Oh, it looks like lipstick. Someone must have brushed up against me accidentally.' Loving wife: 'Oh, well, no mind, I'll clean it in the morning. Don't forget to turn out the light, dear.' Loving husband: 'I won't. Love you.' Loving wife: 'Love you too, sweet.'

"Gee, I didn't know I said all that."

"You'd be surprised. . . . ."

"Not likely."

The young lady was j-u-u-u-s-t a bit too slick to suit me, or so it seemed; I was hoping not, an arrogant broad being similar to squirreling around with hot stones in one's pants. Quickly I changed the subject, asking, "How it was?" Melissa, not yet completely awake, asked in turn, "How was what?"

"How was w-h-a-t? The screwing, sweetheart, the screwing." Nonplussed, she countered indifferently, "I've had better." And I, just as supinely rebuffed, "But not last night."

"Oh, that's cute, and where would I have gotten it, anyway?"

"Well, there you go. We gets what we can, when we can."

"Yeah, I suppose so, but it don't keep us from wanting more, does it?"

"No, and when we get it, it immediately takes the position of less, because wanting something and having it, are distinctly separate conditions, so as soon as we get it, it no longer belongs in the same category as previously, whereby wanting has changed from future to past, and what has past takes on the smell of "flowers at a wake."

"Does that include money?"

"A fitting exception."

"I would think so. I know people who have it, plenty of it, and they're grubbing around like beggars at a hobo's convention.

"Hah! Tell me about it. Life can be a motley bag of contradictions." Then taking a good hard look at her slinky torso, added, "and small delights, too."

I stayed three days with Miss stud jumper, my emotions varying between hot, spicy, and unbearable. We played, and romped, we hopped, skipped and jumped. We even spent some time out of the sack. I would have stayed longer, but I was getting v-e-e-r-r-y, tired, I, not being a machine, much as it would pay to be at times. I think she was. I needed rest, even from the best of things.

Besides, upon leaving a good thing, the memory of it does well for the disposition, and anything that tends to sweeten that unsteady apparatus is welcome upon these desolate shores.

I left early Thursday morning. As I walked to the car she called out, "Will you be back, spider?"

"Wild horses couldn't keep me away, fly!" I exclaimed. She silently watched as I climbed in and started up.

"It wasn't bad, ya know," she volunteered soberly, as I detected a glimpse of sadness in her eye.

"I know," I agreed, just as sadly, and drove away.

Upon reaching the city of Joseph, I laid down and rested … all day, awakening only when Rick returned in the late afternoon.

"Hey, man," he asked, "where you been? You said you'd be back Monday."

"Yeah, I know, I know." The best laid plans. . . . .

"How's your buddy down in L.A.?"

Laying there on my back with one arm covering my eyes, I replied drowsily, "He'll live."

"Oh, I didn't know he was sick."

"Rick, my boy, you can assume with great certainty that almost everyone is on the sad side of the tracks, at least on one count."

"Well, I see the trip didn't have much effect on your good all-a-round disposition."

"As a matter of fact. . . . ."

"What's that supposed to mean?"

"Nothing, except on the way back I got a little in Gros Lanos, and a little, and a little, and a little. . . . ."

"Really, just a little?"

"Ricky, baby, when it's that good, a little is all a body can take.

"Tell me about it. All it has to do is get hard, ya know?"

"Really. E-e-e-e-v-e-r-y-b-o-d-y-s a philosopher."

"Yeah, well, what kind of a chick was she, anyway?"

"I'm not sure. Everybody seems to be out to grab more than their fair share."

"Yeah, well, aren't they all? But wud'ya mean?"

"I mean, she's taking the old man for a ride."

"Long one?"

"Long or short, I don't think I'd ever want to get too serious about someone like her."

"No?"

"No."

"Why not?"

"Because, Ricky, me boy, the fuzzy little tarantula in question just got hooked up to some poor sucker, who is, this very minute, somewhere between Midway and Yokosuka."

"Oh, he's in the navy?"

"Either that, or an Olympic swimmer. And here she is, inviting me to spend a few nights."

"Yeah, it's hell, ain't it?"

"The poor sap. The fucking military is overrun with them. I don't know how we ever won a war."

"God's on our side."

"He better be."

"So, what about this poor sap?"

"Well, malty as they come. I can just see him now. A dullard around thirty, career man, kind of hokey, likes to drink and brawl, turns on to hillbilly, fucking music, nascar, the W.W.F., and really thinks he's got it made. And if ignorance is bliss, he has. A lot like you, Rick."

"Fuck you."

"And while he's stuck halfway out in the Pacific somewhere, scratching his itchy nuts, and dreaming of dear, sweet Melissa, she's grabbing his allotment, and I'm grabbing her ass. Terrific. Just like a Hollywood flick. Everybody gets a little in the end. The only reason I don't feel too bad is, I know the first thing he's gonna do when he sets foot on dry land."

"That's a cop-out if I ever heard one."

"Ha! You're nut so dumb, after all, but it don't change the truth."

Rick scratched his face and screwed up his nose. "Christ," he admonished in a tone betraying irritation, "I don't really know what you're complaining about. It's small potatoes."

"Sho' nough."

"So? What's the big fucking deal?"

"None. I'm just trying to walk through this shit without falling in it, you fucking nerd."

"Okay, pardon me."

"As I was saying, there was a fluke on board the dinghy I had spent some time on, to digress for just a moment in this vertiginous pit of dementia. He had married some broad, a cross between a barracuda and a shark, as I recall.

The sorry, son-of-a-bitch never had a chance. He was like a man sitting in a bathtub with a school of baby piranhas just aching to be big piranhas. Ten days after they got hooked up, we steamed out for points west, and there they were, the loving wife, and her best friend, all painted up like ten-dollar whores on a Saturday night, watching us pull out, and him, up on the bridge, gazing fondly at his true love as we slowly pulled away.

I was on the fantail watching like Walter Houston in that flop house in "The Treasure of the Sierra Madre," first Humphrey Bogart, then Tim Holt, as they solemnly swore that the stirrings of the gold bug would never taint their friendship.

And so, I watched, first those two faded rubies, standing and waving like two dead pines in the Adirondacks, then Slim on the bridge. Back to the dock, back on the bridge, and to this very day I'd swear on a stack of bibles as high as the governor's slush fund, that as they stood there, smiling and waving so tenderly, the party of the first part was saying sweetly to the party of the second part, 'Good-by, honey, good-by, you stupid son-of-a-bitch.' Yes, Rick, I can just imagine the scene between Melissa and her loved one as he left for distant shores."

"But when you think about it, it's not such a bad thing. He got what he wanted, and she got what she wanted."

"Yes, Ricky boy, but at what price? That is always the question. How much is that doggy in the window? And does he have worms?"

Soon, again, did I look to Rita, and I was happy to see her. I was always happy to see Rita. Rita had class, and a big heart. Rita was all heart. Rita was as rare as a Christian in Mongolia. Little by little she was slacking off in 'the business'. She made a little, and invested wisely, so an early retirement was her ace in the hole.

"Hi, stranger," she greeted me at the door.

"Not yet," I chuckled, "but that's why I'm here."

"How's everything down in Angel town?"

"Bad, bad. That place depresses me. Monstrous, absolutely monstrous."

"You noticed, huh?"

"Noticed? Christ, it grabs ya by the what's it."

"I'm hep. So, how's your buddy?"

"He's in tough shape, but I think he'll make it."

"What's wrong?".

"Nothing."

"Nothing?"

"Yep, nothing. That's the matter, nothing's happening. There seems to be a vacuum of intensity."

"I see."

"Did you ever read, The Decline and Fall of the Roman Empire?"

"No, I don't think so. . . . ."

"Well, anyhow, what I remember about it was the vitality the Romans had, even when they were skidding, especially when they were skidding. They went out in style, you know what I mean? They had ... well ... energy, but America ... shit, someday I think I'll pick up a paper and read somewhere on the back page: 'U.S. disappears. Sometime during the night, the United States of America, long a thorn in the world's side, packed its bags and left town. Experts today are pondering, not where it might have gone—no-one really seems to care—but why it took so long.'

Unlike times long ago and far away, America has, as can be guessed, manufactured problems. When you think about it, we have problems we shouldn't have, and that can be the biggest problem of all, and that's what's wrong with my friend Rudy. He doesn't have any problems, but he has."

We laid around that day and played the "What Would You Do?" game.

"Rita, me girl," I opened, "what would you do if you were the "you-know-who?"

"Well now, let me see," she replied, while lying restfully in the altogether.

"Why don't you. . . . ."

"No, no," she interrupted quickly, "no fair helping."

"What do you mean, helping? I was advising. The Prez has advisors."

"Yeah, sure, and I'll catch the clap if I let a sailor screw me, too."

"Okay, no helpee."

"Let me see," she repeated. "I know, I'd legalize prostitution."

"I might have known."

"What's wrong with that?" she asked offendedly.

"Nothing, but you could have waited a mite longer before you nailed that board down. The country does have more pressing problems, you know."

"Maybe so, but a person has to do what's closest to her heart. Besides, I'm an expert in the field."

"Probably."

"Probably?"

"Okay, you're an expert."

"Kiss my ass. . . . ."

"Must I?"

"Let's get on with it, and I'm surprised at you. You should have picked up on the fallout that something like this could lead to."

"Like what?"

"Well, for one thing, it would make people less hypocritical."

"Hah!" Giving me one of those sideways glances, she finished what she was about.

"And that would be a major improvement, no matter what."

"I'll drink to that."

"Then after they've loosened up about that, they can let their hair down about gambling, and drugs, and race, and religion. The shackles would be off. Freedom one and all."

"Y-a-a-a-y! All that for the price of a Jane?"

"I ain't no sociologist, but I can see what can come about. One thing leads to another, and before you know, we could have a country a poor soul could be proud of."

"What if a certain "lady" ain't doing so good? Can she get subsidized by the government?"

"Of course. Why not? The rich are subsidized by the poor, why not a poor working girl? What's fair is fair."

"Yeah, we gotta be fair. What about price controls? A think like that can get out of hand. Without controls only the affluent can get the finest goods, like they already are with everything else."

"Whatever can be worked out."

"Sure, but some people are greedy. I knew a cat once that got ripped off by a pig for thirty bucks when she wasn't worth thirty cents. But he never could do too good, you know? So he had to take whatever came along, and when he got desperate he got hog swill. Afterwards, the more he thought about the screwing he got, but didn't get, the madder he got. Finally, he got so mad, he went home and beat up his sister, and punched a hole in the dog."

"Vicious brute."

"Yeah, it was a damn nice dog.

* * *

I was getting in the mood for a bash (it comes upon me regularly, like a woman's time), but I was out of touch with things, as they say, so if I wanted it bad enough, I had to improvise. I knew I could count on Rick to go along with anything that had the scent of evil. Rick would rummage through a hornet's nest for just a hint of lechery.

I wonder sometimes what kind of world this would be without sex. We certainly would be way ahead of the game in a dreary sort of way, given the time spent by the average soul thinking about it, thinking about getting it, and getting it. Of course, related activities, such as time spent on looking presentable to the opposite sex, would also have to be included. I dare say, it's a wonder anything gets done at all.

To be specific, I was employed briefly once as a 'stamp licker' in one of the numerous, frivolous offices dotting the plaster landscape. There were three males, including myself, and thirteen females, ranging in age from eighteen to sixty. I had sex on my mind ALL THE TIME. It was unbearable, and provocation to a woman, any woman, any age (you'd be surprised the action a sixty-year-old chickee can turn on) comes naturally. Ever since that little stretch of drudgery, my feelings toward the opposite sex has been tinged with, shall we say, a goodly sprinkle of animosity? There is something decidedly snippy about a "lady" young, or otherwise, using her can, to fill her can.

It was said, that one of the studs in the office had, at one time or another, fashioned his way with eleven of the thirteen foxes, and all within the space of one year. I respected him. I ADMIRED HIM!!! And they gave the medals to Sergeant York. As if that wasn't enough, but every one of them tricks thought SHE was the only one!! Impossible, you say? Well … me too, but you should have seen him. Christ, he was smooth; he was beautiful; he was an arr--teeste.

Yeah, he was good, but he spent an awful lot of time getting it 'up and down.'

It's hard, oh, so hard, keeping one's mind on one's work with thirteen assorted hens fluttering their feathers in the breeze. I asked a lady friend of mine once, in the spirit of ignorant youth, if sex was the same with them as with men. "Oh, no," she quickly admonished, giving me that tired old line about quality vs. quantity. "Women enjoy it more for the experience." And there you have it, Buck, experience. Shit, even cats do it right the first time.

I approached Rick, one breezy Friday evening, and volunteered a little filth for filth's sake. "Rick, me boy, let's go find a basher."

"Basher?" He frowned. "Who do we know in this town who's throwing one?"

Putting my arm around his shoulder in a brotherly fashion, I answered with all the knowledge of one cohabitating this swirling, precarious dwelling some thirty-odd-plus years. "Rick, as unlikely as it may seem, it appears that that sloggy bit of education I received at the hands of the Gargantuans is going to pay off after all. You see, pardner, when one is on, or about, a college campus, one need not be invited to be invited. The whole campagna, and attending area is a standing invitation. One just kinda moseys in, western like, dig? Now all we have to do is take a little stroll down San Carlos Avenue until we come upon a reason-ably noisy settlement, and make ourselves to home. Ya hep to it?"

"Yeah, man, that's great. That's all there is to it, huh? I like it. Sounds filthy, and where there's filth, there's orgy. I'm ready."

"Ho! Not so fast. We have to wait for the moon to appear first. It's only five bells. Let's give the band a chance to work itself into a slutty frame of mind."

"Do you guarantee success on this expedition?" he asked with a trace of uncertainty.

"No," I answered in my best Bella Lugosi, "but the joy is in the expectation. Hee, hee, hee."

"You're vile."

"We all have our little virtues."

"Well, let me know when we start."

"Let you know when we start? Where the hell do you think we're going, up the Amazon? Speaking of Amazons, I knew a chick once, in Boston, who had the most prodigious rock pile you ever saw."

"I take it you mean ass."

"Well, either that or she was growing the biggest tumor you ever see."

"Here we go again."

"I mean, man, it was huge, nice, but huge. And she wasn't a big broad, either, considering the bucket she had trailing her. But for her size, it was T-O-N-D-A-L-A-Y-A! We used to call her the Boston Butt."

"Aw, man, I work with dead fish all day, and this is what I have to come back to?"

"You know what the Christians say?"

"No, what do the Christians say?"

"We all have our crossy, crossy."

* * *

I laid down for a bit. One has to work himself into the proper frame of mind before going into battle. Lying motionless for a half hour or so, I slowly, but surely, began to steel myself for the coming offensive. "I will not be defeated, I will not be defeated," I kept saying over and over. "No matter what the obstacles, I shall overcome." I repeated it until my mind and spirit were fused into an iron bond. I rose and did fifty push-ups, fifty sit-ups, and fifty deep-knee bends. Then five minutes of deep breathing, and another five of rope skipping. I went into the pantry, turned on the gas, and held my hands over the flame. Then I took a cold shower, AND NOW I WAS READY! E-E-E-E-E-H-A-A-H!!!

Like two werewolves, Rick and I sat on the front porch waiting for a full moon to appear. As we did, I expected to see hair growing out of our hands and our features change into that of "the beast." At the gong of nine, I asked, as somber as a warden to a condemned killer at the eleventh hour, "Ready?" And Rick, replying just as somberly, quipped, "Let's go," jumped up, and began walking toward the backyard.

"Where the hell you going?" I called out.

"To the car . . .?" he shot back sharply.

"No, no, no, man. We walk, we walk. How the hell can we scout with a car?"

"What the hell; even Kit Carson had a horse."

"Yeah, and Kit Carson was looking for a fight, not a fucking."

"Okay, so let's walk. Makes no difference to me, so longs we get something besides exercise."

We strolled down San Carlos Avenue and for the first time I noticed, really noticed what Rick was wearing. He had on a pair of Levis, western boots, one of those wide belts with a gigantic, silver buckle sporting a Texas longhorn's head. You know, the kind you win, at the local rodeo for bagging third prize in calf roping, and a multi-colored, purplish Hawaiian shirt. He looked like he had just stepped off a cattle car in Wichita.

Now I was never one to judge a man by his clothes. To do so one would have had to conclude that 'Old Abe' was the local mortician. (And unlucky for us he wasn't; we might have dodged a civil war?) However, Rick was walking like

a bear in heat, and it cramped my style, such as it was. Each step was accentuated and pounded hard on the pavement, and his arms were swinging like a
parading British soldier's. I just had to rein him in, and did. "Hey," I asked, in
keeping with the horsey atmosphere, "couldn't you find something else to wear?
Anything-else?" Looking at himself, he answered argumentatively, "Wud'ya
mean? What's wrong with what I'm wearing?"

"You're asking, Bub? You're really asking?"

"Sure I'm asking. What's it sound like, a bird call?"

"Yeah, well, attracting ducks is about all that horse-shit shirt's good for. This
is California, man, ya know? Not Texas."

"Oh, yeah? Well, I see lots of dudes sportin' duds like these out here."

"Sure, and they're either riding a horse, or walking a dog."

"You ain't exactly decked out like Diamond Jim Brady yourself."

"No, but I could've been his runner."

"Well, fuck um. If they don't like the way I'm dressed, I'll … I'll … I'll punch
um out."

"Why not. Just one small step from punching cows."

"Hah! What the hell do you know about it? The only cow you ever saw must
have been in a Kansas City whore house."

"Tulsa."

"And when are we gonna find what we're looking for? I didn't come out here
to stretch my legs; I'm as tall as I'm gonna get."

"Patience, patience. All things in their time."

"My time has come." I looked at him in that silly cowboy drab and was
tempted to add something like, "Your time has come and gone, buddy," but
instead I asked if he had prepared himself before coming out. He glanced at
me dumbfounded, and answered, "Man, what the hell you gadding about now,
anyway? Don't you ever get off those sidetracks? Wud'ya mean, prepare?"

"That's exactly what I mean. You just can't go out and run the four-forty
flat out without warming up first. You gots to prepare yourself … like a football
team before the big game. No booze, no broads, no cigarettes, eight hours sleep,
quiet, rest and relaxation; short walks over hill and dale, fresh air, keep cool, and
then, ten minutes before game time, you bang your noggin up against the locker
fifteen times. Training, man, you got to know how to train."

"You know, I think your brain's getting soft."

"You're working the wrong end, brotha. . . . ."

We continued walking. In time we began to detect what at first appeared to be music coming from our side of the street dead ahead. But what at a fortunate distance slightly resembled sounds pleasant to the ear, turned out to be, upon closer inspection, an electric guitar gone berserk, hooked up to a hyperactive amplifier accompanied by cymbals, bongos, a herniated drum, and a number of adolescent twits attempting to warble in the English language but instead sounding for all the world like a nest of screech owls, and in all probability also belonged in a tree.

"Hey, man," Rick jubilantly stated, "we got something here, right?"

"Wrong, man," I answered. "We got nothing here." Looking confused, he replied dejectedly, "What the hell, I thought this was what we were looking for."

"No, not by a long shot."

"Why not?"

"Listen," I advised, "and you don't have to listen too hard. Hear? Too juvenile. It's probably some funky sorority doing their weekend ritual. They're easy marks, but like a TV dinner, two bites and you're scouting for a garbage can. This is Friday night; we can do better than that."

"Well, I ain't doin' this for the music. I got a radio."

"Neither am I, but that crap in there is worse than that friggin Hawaiian music."

"So, now what's wrong with fuckin' Hawaiian music?"

"You had to ask. Well, when the man o' war I was so grievously attached to, pulled in one bright, and sunny morn at Pearl, it was met by the usual array of smiling, singing hula girls and a band, and they weren't playing and dancing to the strains of a Mozartian waltz.

All was fine and dandy for a while, very quaint, but then I realized, to my great dismay, that it was e-v-e-r-y-w-h-e-r-e. In the streets, the saloons, the restaurants, even the johns. You couldn't take a stinking crap without the shit backing up in your smelly, bung-hole. The island was virtually saturated with the bloody, fucking stuff, and like California smog, it hung like a blanket affecting your very membranes. It followed you around like the plague. Even the good ship Lollipop was afflicted.

After the first day I broke out in hives and developed a nervous twitch in my left eye. The second day I got diarrhea and the shingles, and on the third, an unaccountable limp in my right leg. By the fourth I could have easily been mistaken for one of Pavlov's dogs, spit and all. If anyone rang a bell I would have come out fightin, and if we had stayed just one more day I would have resembled a victim in the latter stages of the Chinese water torture. Rick, me boy, don't ever ask me again what's wrong with Hawaiian music. The very thought of it sends me into deep remorse. And don't make any loud noises, or sudden movements, or sneak up on me unexpectedly. I'm not completely recovered."

"You're tellin' me."

"Ricky, baby, you're beautiful."

"Yeah, sure."

We walked on and I began to hear the soft, willowy strains of modern jazz. "Hey, I think we're getting something now," I said hopefully. "That sounds like Brubeck."

"Brubeck?" said Rick innocently. "Who the hell's Brubeck?"

I stopped cold in my tracks, and threw up my hands. "Brubeck! Who's Brubeck?" I exclaimed. "What am I associating with, a fucking ostrich? You might as well ask who's MacArthur?"

"Okay, okay, so I don't know no Brubeck's. Is that a felony?"

"You know, it ain't no accident you work in a damn fish-house."

We approached cautiously like two thieves in the night, which in a manner of speaking, we were. No, I take it back. In this day and age, anything we could procure, by whatever means, could never be regarded as thievery. As a matter of fact, all things considered, it has to be regarded more as a give-away than robbery.

We tippy-toed up the walk and up four steps. The door was partly open, and I peered in. There was a mob, and that was good. That'd make us inconspicuous. And socializing, not our main objective at the moment, could be kept at a minimum to gain our "ends." It was dark, and that also worked in our favor, but unusually crowded for so early in the evening. I turned to Tex and disclosed melodramatically, "It's now or never. Check your gun belt and spread out."

"Yeah," he returned impatiently, "I only need one good shot."

I pushed open the door a bit further, and we approached our quarry warily. I was right about Brubeck, it was he. "Okay," I instructed, "let's just kind of blend in with the scenery, and if anyone questions your identity just say you're Gamma Phi Delta."

"What's that?"

"What difference does it make? Chances are you ain't gonna be talking to anybody who can speak Greek. Chances are you ain't gonna be talking to anybody who speaks English. When you see what you like, cut her out from the rest of the herd, and put your brand on her quick. These things can get v-e-e-r-y- sticky."

"Don't you worry none about that. I'll work so fast I'll be just a blur."

"And keep a sharp eye for any stray heifers not yet ripe for milking. There's usually, one or two, in a gathering of this kind, and although they can light your fire, you'll later end up sitting on it. San Quentin's not even a nice place to visit. And stay out of trouble with the studs. I think we're outnumbered."

Rick nonchalantly drifted away while I inconspicuously worked my way toward the kitchen, picked a glass from the cupboard and filled it three fingers water, then returned to center ring trying to look suave and sophisticated. I did not smile. One should never smile when one is wearing the look of gravity.

I went over to a corner and tried to size up things a bit before I made my move … you know? Who's with who, who's stag, who seems to be less well known, who seems to be the least popular. To put it bluntly, who was the easiest mark? Such bashes being what they are, one can spend practically the entire evening without ever having to speak to anyone, if he so chooses. The lights are always turned down to reasonably orgy level, and souls abound with each devoted to his own pursuits. The devil never sleeps. Soon I tired of standing, and so put into effect Play Number forty-seven—grab a seat.

Noticing at the bar a row of stools, the ones with the long legs, I decided to take one. However, as is usually the case in this mortal sphere, a small hitch is usually present. The seats in question were all being occupied by someone else's bum. Being the shy type I hesitated to ask any of them outright for their seat, and if "the one" happened to be a lady, such phrasing might easily seem "indelicate?" But having been a student of the Machiavellian ethic, I was also sneaky, so I waited, a rogue having the advantage of foreknowledge.

Two minutes passed, then three, then five. Nothing. They seemed to be set for the night. Deliberate action was needed. Sauntering into the backyard, I found a bushel basket and filled it with some old papers, twigs and dried leaves. I then snuck around to the front, gently placed it on the porch, and set it ablaze. Immediately upon setting the torch I returned to the sitting room, and took my customary position in the corner, waiting patiently for nature to take its course. In a matter of moments someone hollered, "Fire!" and three of the four sitting at the bar jumped up like they'd been goosed by the great hairy ape. A bit of commotion ensued, and in the disarray I snatched one of the seats, and took it over to my domain where I amusedly watched the proceedings taking place.

When the matter at hand was seen to be only a bushel basket fire, a few expected comments were made, such as: "why the hell would anyone set a bushel on fire?" and "I don't get it," and "There's one in every crowd." Then everyone began filing back in to take their places again.

The young lady whose seat I had taken look puzzled for a moment, standing and staring, looking here and there, and in general, taken aback. However, in the midst of her confusion some Bronco Billy strolled up, and began doing his thing, and she, from the looks she was giving him, forgot about her seat and began thinking about his.

From my vantage point I tried to determine how long I would have to sit like King Midas before the North Pole attracted the South Pole. I gauged from the hustle and bustle, about ten to twenty minutes. When one is a stranger at such happenings it is always best to be approached rather than approach. It's safer. It may take longer, but it's safer. Of course, there's always the risk of attracting the "also rans." If one is forced onto the offensive, one's chances of bagging a second-runner-up increases immensely, but at great risk, for one can never be sure what kind of tail she's dragging, or how big he is.

Some slob changed the Brubeck and replaced it with some funky, rock group. I can't say which one; does it matter? They're all the same.

I sat and suffered in silence. It played, and it played, and it played. Is there no end to it? I could endure no longer. My mind wandered, and weaved, and boggled. My body tensed by the moment and I began to panic. Uncontrollably, I rose and walked over to the player, and zombie-like, began to sort the trash. There were about twenty discs, all told, and in that number, five tolerable. I waited until the garbage that was playing finished, whereupon I immediately changed it to a Ramsey Lewis. I looked about to check the reaction. Nothing. Everyone was busy "puttin on the dog." It seems the great significance of music to the young lies not in its pleasant sounds, but merely sound. No doubt had I pulled the plug instead, I would have been met first by the fiercest stares since those dispensed by the Mongol hordes, and then outright attack.

I took the rest out back, found a trash can in a shanty snuggled cozily amongst a clump of tall weeds, a dead grapevine, and a lot of all-around general refuse, turned an old orange crate on end, and sat. Then, calmly and methodically, one by one, I smashed each and every disc, and tossed it in the can. It was cruel, but it was also just.

There's something to be said for poetic destruction, and I couldn't help noticing that the sounds issuing from the breaking platters, seemed to be infinitely more pleasant than those coming from same, when placed on a turntable, and a diamond needle made to run its grooves. Music, poetry, art, civilization— so close, and yet so far.

After having done it up right, I continued to sit there on the crate, and smash the pieces into smaller pieces. Ping! Pang! Pow! they clanged. I was having such a jolly good time, and when the pieces got too small to break I put my foot in the can, and stomped on them like an air hammer pounding up the street. After thoroughly smashing them all into the tiniest, itsy bits, I looked down into the black hole, and at that moment all the insane perversions and injustices of the world flashed before my eyes: the inquisition, and Conquistadores, the Crusades, slavery, serfdom, racism; the holocaust, the defiling of nature, the bomb. It was more than I could bear. Angrily I kicked the can like a frustrated revolutionary kicking the body of a dead dictator.

I went into the yard and walked about slowly waiting for the adrenalin to slacken. I looked up at the moonlit sky, I looked down at the sod, pawed at it with one foot, spat, heaved a sigh, and returned to the digs.

Stopping in the kitchen, I poured a heaping glass of water, dunked in a couple of chunks of ice, and moseyed back into the front room, where, oddly enough, there was the stool, still standing in the corner, unoccupado. I walked over suspiciously, sat down, and waited. I knew that night, that whatever furry, little feline would smother and bathe me in "love" that night, it could not top the previous events just recently transpired in "the Garden of Eden." It has yet to be demonstrated that subtlety does not carry with it its own fruitful fervor.

Having not seen Rick for a while, I began to wonder, and was tempted, out of curiosity, to hunt him down, when to my left I heard a soft, velvety voice purr, "I don't think I remember seeing you here before."

I turned and what I saw, at least as much of it that I could see in the dark, wasn't bad, not bad at all; little was I to learn. . . . .

The hair was red, or brown, I couldn't be sure, and she was breathless, absolutely breathless. (Yes, Virginia, I know you've heard all this before. Hear it again; that's all there is.)

I sensed a certain uniqueness about her, and although she was stunning, she was not glamorous, and somewhat unusual in that I immediately felt at ease with her, and I didn't even know her—yet. Also, she wore a dress. You remember dresses? They come down to the knees, or thereabouts roughly, and they're slipped on over the head, and not up the legs. Well, she had one of them on. I knew I had found what I had come four bloody blocks for and was determined to control what by this time had become a natural growl in my nature, so put my best all-round-good-guy side on. Opportunities, the delicious kind at any rate, are not so abundant that one can be cavalier when one presents itself.

"I've never been here before," I answered with a jumping heart.

"You with someone?"

"Yes," I replied, my eyes glued to her superbly, splendorous face. I would have given up the winning lottery ticket just to know what she was thinking.

"You don't look like you belong with this crowd," she declared matter-of-factly.

"No, I'm not. Just passing through, so to speak."

"I see. Then you're not a student?"

"Of what?"

"Of anything?"

"Close enough."

"What do you do for a living?"

"I'm an engineer." In a manner of speaking, I was, for what I had in mind was going to take quite a bit of figuring. Good things never come easy, and I was fast getting the feeling that I was looking at the best.

"Oh," she said, "an engineer. How do you like it?" She seemed impressed. I don't know why; engineers ain't nobody. "The pay's not bad, but it gets awfully tiresome juggling bridges, and dams, and what not. What do you do? You're not a student either, right?"

"Right. I teach elementary school."

"That's not bad."

"It depends."

"How so?"

"Well, if one likes teaching, and kids, it's good; if not, it's bad."

This chick was talking my kind of talk, and I knew it was going to take more than a cock-eyed, college jock to chase me out of her camp. I gave the joint a quick once-over, and thought: man, if this is the competition, I'm in. Am I ever.

She had class, and more and more am I inclined to place that small trait at the top of the pedestal. In this world of the nasty, brutish, and intolerable, class becomes a rare and precious commodity, and practically a necessity. She had brains, too, and that's crucial, and she had sex appeal, also not to be laughed at, and, she didn't stink, and that was gratifying. And she didn't have a big mouth, and that was v-e-e-e-r-y heartening. My God, I loved her ALREADY!

After gathering my wits about myself, I answered, "You know, I'm inclined to agree with you. What's your name?"

"Roberta Higgins."

"Oh, you're a colleen, are ye?"

"In a way. I'm quite mixed actually. A little of this, a little of that. You know."

"Yes, I know. I had a little mongrel dog once. Damn best dog you ever saw." The smile left her face as she quickly announced as never having thought of herself as a dog, mongrel, or otherwise, an opinion to which I heartedly concurred. All I could think of was, 'you're blowing it, you fucking sop. This ain't no 'Olive Oil,' you know.

Immediately, trying to recover, I replied just as quickly, "Oh, no! No! I'm sorry, I truly am. I didn't mean anything like that! I wasn't thinking, an affliction, at times, which strikes suddenly and without warning. It's just that I was so fond of that dog, I never really thought of him as a dog. Ya know what I mean? He was like, well, one of the family. Hell, we called him son."

The smile returned, and she asked quietly, "Did you treat him well?"

"Not like a dog. I slept on the floor and he in the bed." She smiled. Word by word, sentence by sentence, I felt myself liking Miss Higgins more and more.

"How often do you get: Miss Higgins didn't look like you when I went to school?"

"A-L-L the time."

"I can imagine. But it's true, you know. Miss Higgins didn't look like you. She looked more like Miss Jones, who looked more like Mr. Jones, who looked more like Quasimodo."

Again a smile crossed her face as she inquired into the whereabouts of that same schooling of which I spoke. To wit I replied, "Somewheres in New York."

"Somewhere in New York?" she repeated puzzledly.

"Yeah," I answered assuredly, "as opposed to somewhere in Pennsylvania, or New Jersey, or Delaware."

"I see."

"Where are you from?"

"North Carolina."

"North Carolina! Well, you sure could've fooled me."

"Oh, it's been quite a while, though. My folks moved out here when I was nine."

"To my great joy and benefit, I hope."

"Oh?"

"Well, what I mean is, well, you know you kind of get me right in the ol' pantalooney."

"You're an odd one."

"More or less."

"More, I would say."

"You were asking," I switched abruptly, "something about school?"

"Yes, I believe that was it. Okay, let's try this again. Did you like school?"

"Only grade school."

"That's all?"

"That's all."

"How come?"

"Because I am in this world, but not of it, and because of it, I liked the nuns and priests, in a left-handed sort of way, said personages obviously being dimwitted dolts, and even more so now, I am told."

"Really?"

"To be sure."

"Well, I wouldn't know, being Methodist myself."

"It's all the same."

"Maybe that's the problem."

"No, I think the problem is that we have them at all. There are no holy men, only rogues adorned in priestly raiment.

"How D-I-D we get onto this?"

"It happens." I was about to ask if, and who, she might be with, when a tall, blond, mod dressed, young stud came over and asked straight-away, "Shall we go?" Not answering the question, Roberta turned to him, saying, "Larry, I'd like you to meet," and then turning to me, laughingly asserted, "I never did get your name."

"Rosko, John Rosko, the First," I enunciated, and we shook hands as he in turn said, "Larry Bordner. Good to meet you, Mr. Rosko," and abruptly turned back to Roberta and asked a second time, "Well, how bout it?"

"Let's stay a while longer," she requested, much to my liking.

"Okay," he acknowledged, somewhat perturbed. "Let me know when you're ready," and toddled away.

"Fiancée?" I inquired unhappily. "Yes," she affirmed.

"God damn it," I blurted, taking her aback.

"You speak your mind, don't you?"

"I'll tell you something, Miss Higgins. . . . ."

"Call me Bobi, John."

"Bobi John? That's a funny name for a girl."

"No, I'm Bobi, you're John."

"Thank goodness for that." I wasn't laughing. I wasn't in the laughing mood. Bad news can be very unsettling. She noticed, and immediately turned somber also, as she quietly sipped her drink.

"As I was saying, Bob." I was beginning to feel nasty, more and more, an easily retrieved condition, and didn't give a damn if I blew it, having now got the impression it was a blowout anyway, no matter what I said now, given the circumstances. "I do not believe in love at first sight, and I don't love you now I am sure, but if I did believe, you'd be it. And I will tell you straight out, I like you an awful lot for someone I've only known six minutes. I have never met anyone that I liked so much after six minutes, or ten minutes for that matter, or fifteen, or an hour and a half, or a day and a half, or a year and a half, and I am not the fickle sort, either. I despise fickle people. I despise non fickle people. I despise a whole lotta people … more and more these days. But there it is, and I am getting very angry. Truly, faith hath dealt me a cruel blow."

She stood a moment rolling her drink between her hands, then answered seriously, "I don't know what to say."

"There's nothing t-o-o-o say. Look, I'm not much for that "can't we be friends" kind of jazz, so I'll say my good-byes now, and dream of what might have been." Upon uttering those fateful words I then gave her the surprise of her life by bussing her squarely upon her luscious red lips, and walked away leaving her standing with the look of "Ah hah!" on her exquisite face. I felt like wiring the world end to end with a time bomb on a short fuse.

In a mood that can best be described as acrimonious, I strolled, bumping from person to person, looking for Rick, not really caring whether I found him or not, but wondering if the fates were rubbing his face in it also. Not being downstairs, I then looked upstairs. Logic or habit, but just the finest of lines separating the monkeys from the baboons.

In a small room off to the left I found him plopped on a loveseat with a rumpled-looking college Jane gabbing up a blue streak. Making my way toward them, I announced curtly, "Introduce me, sweetheart," and glancing at her quickly, added, "him, not you."

"Who's the wiseass?" was the bright response from 'little miss what's it' while noticing what could have been a maybe beautiful chick if she wasn't trying so hard to look like Calamity Jane after a month on the Kansas prairie roughing it with Buffalo Bill.

She had long, dirty-blond scraggly hair, a tie-dyed shirt of unknown gender four sizes too large, a baggy set of cruddy fatigues, and a pair of combat boots, and if she was eighteen it wasn't my much. All in all, as sorry a looking case of crabs this side of the Embarcadero. Also, there was a strange odor coming from her direction. The closest I could make it out to be was a cross between horse manure, and two-dollar perfume.

I turned to Miss "Cow Shit" and asked her age. She stared open-mouthed momentarily, expecting anything but that, but recovered as her kind does, not having experienced too much of anything in depth, and shot back sarcastically, "Who wants to know, and why?"

"Rick's friend wants to know," I affirmed, "and because I'd hate to see him get into the kind of trouble he will forever be sorry for, and I get the distinct impression he will be v-e-r-y sorry, v-e-r-y soon, whether you're eighteen, or not. So I'm asking, dig?"

"Yeah, I dig. And I'm eighteen, and who the fuck are you? And go screw yourself."

Nice girl. I turned to him and admonished, "Rick, if you're planning to shack up with this tonight, you'd better take a penicillin pill first, hear? And needless to say, I hope you have a rubber, too."

As you might have guessed, I did not favor the party to which I was speaking, I just didn't. Not her looks, her manner, her speech, her smell. I had come on a bit strong, it's true, but what the hell, if my opening remark could not be taken as a joke, which was its intent, then she could kiss off. I was prepared to be my most obnoxious best. I was certainly pressed into the mood.

"You know," she went on, "I didn't come looking for you, you came here, and you could get into trouble for it."

"Oh, I don't think so. I'm not planning on fucking you. And would you like to know why? Well, let me tell you why: because I don't like you. Have you noticed? And I don't like you because you're a big asshole, so it follows that I would not want to fuck a gigantic butt-hole. I'd sooner slam the buggy toilet seat on it. Whack off on that a while, Miss Sigma Chi."

By this time, Rick had turned forty different shades of green, and his eyes betrayed grievous irritation at my decidedly linear behavior, so I thought I'd best reassure him.

"Rick," I consoled, "years from now you'll thank me for this." He didn't appear overwhelmed with gratitude. He asked that I 'please not be so helpful.' Love pie, by this time, had two smoldering coals for eyes. "How would you like to get your ass kicked?" she snapped. I looked about while positing boldly, "I don't see anyone around here that can do it."

"We'll see about that," she stated sharply, and bolted from the room.

"Jesus Christ!" Rick protested excitedly. "What the fuck are you doin'?"

"Aw, hell, brother, don't worry about a thing."

"Worry! Worry! I ain't, not about you, anyway. I don't care if you get your ass kicked all the way to San Bernardino, but you're screwin' me out of a good piece!"

"Aw, shit. Wash your mouth out with soap."

"Jesus H. Fucking Christ! And I wasn't in no mood for nothin' tonight but fuckin' either."

"You just stand aside and watch out for dirty tricks, okay?"

"And what the fuck am I gonna do if some show? Blow a bugle like Gunga Din?"

"Nothing quite so flashy."

"You were the one who said something about 'being outnumbered,' remember?"

"Damn if I didn't. Well, I was right, wasn't I?"

"You ain't gonna be takin' this so light if you get your head busted."

"Huh, do tell. But keep your eye on me, Ricky boy, and see how a dude gets his money's worth."

Rick, no doubt, thought I meant that I was going to give whoever it was a good tumble, but I was not about anything so foolish as you will readily discover, Buck.

"Now look," I said to him, "I'm going over to the other side of the room. You get by the door, and as soon as this thing goes, flick the light switch. And don't wait all god-damn night about it. There's an army here, and if we pull this off just right, we can come out smelling like a rose."

"WE!!"

"Sorry, Jack, but it looks like you're going in the crapper, too, if that's where we're headed." The look of disillusionment, among other things, was written all over my chalky-faced friend.

I saw three jocks stride in, and I knew instantly what their business was since "bad mouth" was trailing right behind. I whispered to Rick, "Okay, get by the door, and stay alive. I can whip one of them, but not all three. Not without a club anyway." And with a definitely mournful expression mirroring his face, Rick, sullenly, made his way to the door.

"Wicket tongue" pointed in my general direction and I heard her say, in what seemed to me an unusually cheerful voice, "That's him," and the conch in the middle, who I sized up as not much, or else wouldn't have dragged his two gunsel buddies with him, said, as he approached, "The young lady tells me you're rousting her. Is that right?"

He was a lot taller than me, but not much heavier, and he appeared to be trying like hell to put on a little muscle. You know, with the iron, and such, but wasn't having much success. He also was kind of gangly.

"Lady! Hah!" I laughed. "And the word is roast, not roust. I'd like to roast her funky ass … like a pig on a spit." He didn't smile, but merely continued with the interrogation. "She claims you called her some dirty names. Did you?"

"More or less."

"Why?"

"Seemed fitting enough. And I don't like her."

"You don't like her?"

"Yep, that's close enough."

"You don't even know her."

"I didn't know Hitler either."

"She says you're a smart-ass, and by the size of you, which don't seem to be much from here, you could be playing a dangerous game."

The "ain't much" part didn't strike a love chord in my heart, and determined that if I let him talk too much longer, I was going to get to dislike him almost as much as "stink mouth," and not desiring to give her the satisfaction of arousing any more emotion in me than she already had, I decided therefore to get on with the festivities, so instead of answering him I turned to her and said, "You know, a pig like you shouldn't be allowed out of the pen too often. You could stink up the whole fucking barnyard. Also, you should not be allowed to get away clean. You've got to get yours, too, one way or the other. After all, you are a co-conspirator. Ya hep to it, squirrel face?" And with that brief but succinct summation of cow-town justice, I gave her but the slightest of a backhand, not really wanting to hurt her, then pushed her backwards, readying myself as best I could for the upcoming onslaught. Instantly, the three studs jumped me as we all started swinging wildly.

The room was too crowded for anyone to do any real damage to anybody, but I did get a right, of sorts, to the mouthpiece's belly because I heard an "Ooph!" come from his general direction. At least I hope it was him. I'd hate to think I whacked the second trumpet player in the middle of his harmony.

Of course I expected Rick to hit the switch as soon as they made like the 'galloping frogs of Calaveras County,' but instead he was just standing by it, open-mouthed like the simpleton I was beginning to think he was.

"Hit it! Hit it!" I bellowed while frantically trying to fend off my assailants as best I could. He finally, and none too soon, withdrew from his trance, and cut the lights. By this time, everybody was pushing and yelling and carrying on. It looked like the last minutes of the last day of an emergency session of Congress in the dead of summer.

I squirmed out, and quickly made my way to the door, dictating, "Let's go," and to prevent successful chase, hollered as we leaped down the stairs, "Fire! Fire! Fire in the bedroom!"

"Again!" somebody squalled, disgustedly, and everybody, up and down, raced toward the doors front and back.

Rick and I shot out the back way, over the fence, through someone's yard, and out the next street. We ran a couple of blocks when Rick stopped, breathlessly, announcing, "Hold it, I'm pooped. There ain't nobody following us." I looked back, and sure enough we had made a clean getaway.

For the first time I noticed blood on my shirt, and found it was coming from a small cut on my lip. I retrieved a wrinkled hanky from a back pocket, and methodically dabbed at it.

"So," Rick uttered with a hint of pleasure, "they got your mother-fuckin' ass."

"You stupid cocksucker. What the fuck was you waiting for, the second coming of Christ?"

"Aw, hell, we got away, didn't we?"

"W-E got away, didn't we?" I mocked. "I'm the one with the fat lip, and if you had cut that switch as soon as I smacked 'pork face,' I wouldn't even have that."

"Well, shit, I didn't ask for this, you know? I got screwed out of a good piece of ass. I'm the big loser. You're lucky I hit those lights at all!"

"You're telling me."

We got back to the pad where I tended to my wounds as Rick wearily strolled into the bedroom. I followed, pressing my lip with a wad of tissue paper, and sat on my bunk. Rick was sitting on his, face in hands, looking like the little boy who had lost his dog.

"Now what?" he asked dismally. "It's barely ten-thirty, and here we are, sitting like two fucking, wooden ducks in a shootin' gallery, wasting what at first started out as a night with possibilities. You had to pick tonight to impersonate John Wayne.

"I ain't bitching."

"Yeah, sure! But you're weird. You talk to squirrels, but I'm the one who's high and dry."

"I did my best and it didn't work out. So? I didn't tell you to get hooked up with some smelly Nellie."

"She smelled alright to me!"

"What the hell do you know? You were born in a shithouse." I lay back, placing my hanky over my eyes, and placed my arms across my chest. I wasn't feeling too bad.

"What do I know, hey!" Rick responded. "A good piece beats a punch in the mouth any day, that's what I know. I could've gotten it."

"Yeah, and you would have gotten a lot more than just ass."

"That so?"

"That so? Hell, man, I thought I was going to catch something just standing next to her, and nothing too exotic. . . . . ."

"Well, we were getting along just fine. She was an old farm gal from Wyoming, and. . . . . ."

"Hah!" I interrupted. "An old farm gal from Wyoming? So that W-A-S shit I smelled on her."

"What's wrong with farmers?"

"Nothing, but there are farmers, and there are farmers, and I think she be one of the farmer, farmer's. Anyway, what are you croaking about? Go back if you love the bitch so much. Nobody's looking for you."

"What the fuck are you talking about? You must've got a bigger punch than you think. They know we were together; how friggin dumb do you think they are, like you?"

"Well, what can I tell ya, that's life. Things have a way of bunging up, even for winners, and you ain't talking to no winner."

"Hah! You got that right!"

"We gotta be honest."

"Okay, if we're being honest, tell me, what the hell did you do it for? I don't understand what the hell it was all about. Explain it, will ya? If it makes sense, I might not be so ticked off."

"Okay, sweetheart, I'll run it down to ya, but it ain't gonna make no sense just like you expect."

"I'm game."

"Okay, then, get set for a load of buckshot. It has to do with intuition, really, more than anything. It's a feeling sometimes that speaks louder than words."

"You lost me already."

"Rick, me boy, you need a compass." He shrugged. I continued, "First of all, I didn't say anything to that stinking bitch sufficient to put a bug up her ass, of which no doubt, she has a number. I made a joke, that's all. Big deal. Folks are going to have to learn to act adult if they claim to be such. She said she was eighteen, or whatever the hell it was, so I behaved likewise. She came off the wall like I was trying to plant a bomb in her ass.

This world, there's five billion people in it, and not everybody's going to spit the way you like all the time, or even half the time. As a matter of fact, you'd do good to get a tenth, maybe. Tolerance fits in there somewhere. Secondly, the ungodly spectacle of a scungy, little teenage bitch coming on like a forty-year-old petticoat, grabs me right by the nuts. And why not? I can take it from that forty-year-old, she's paid her dues, but not no snot-nosed twerp who thinks Pisa is something you eat. There's something to be said for experience. So … and yes, the longer I live, the more I believe the Puritans were right on one score: The young should be seen, and not heard. Anyway, that's it. It may not be much, but nothing ever is. That's what makes these trying times. 1776 was no orphan.

Be that as it may, therefore, I had to do what I did. I couldn't let her get away with that. Her kind thrives on getting away. A few escapes like the one tonight, and they'll begin to think they own the world. It's bad enough they're renting the back room. Before long they'll want the penthouse. Yeah, buddy, they'll shit all over you, then hate you for it. They'll become spiteful, and arrogant, and think they're doing you a favor. Slap the child, and save the man."

"Shit! You don't think you 'delivered' her with that little 'du-wa-ditty,' do ya?

"No, but it delivered me."

Rick was not pacified. "I was in!" he expounded. "I could just feel it. Damn!"

"Ah, but it wouldn't have felt any better than the slap she got. Justice is a wonderful thing."

That night I had a wet dream. Wet dreams are like strawberry shortcake without the strawberries. I always wondered why nature would devise such fractional means of expressing itself. If it were so important for the natives to have periodic ejaculations, why not arrange matters directly, instead of clandestinely in amorphous dreams? Enough of trickery. Deception is not becoming to nature. The real thing, all silky, and peachy, and perfume, is so much more fulfilling than a brain wave shot in the dark.

"How do you do, Madam?"

"Fine, thank you."

"I'd like to fondle your what's it, among other things."

"How sweet. I have a minute."

"Terrific. Your place or mine?"

"Anyplace?"

But then Westerner's have always had an exaggerated capacity for mangling the simple, and strangling the innate. It's called Christianity, but there's hope. It has, of late, been called many things. It is now being called dead. Let us hope its resurrection, in keeping with all great spiritual events, receives only poetic consideration as part of mythological lore. And let us also hope that Christ, who never dreamed that his name would be the standard bearer of the longest journey into the land of the walking dead, will be buried, finally, and for good. May he rest in peace.

* * *

X

THE COCK DOTH CROW
TO LET YOU KNOW
IF YOU BE WISE
YOU WIN THE PRIZE

FIVE days later, I received an unexpected but welcome visitor, Roberta Higgins.

Sitting on the front porch enjoying the benefits of my unemployed state, a green, late model Ford slowly pulled up. Upon seeing who it was the shock could have been likened to that visited upon the unwary gentleman who discovered he had contracted a communicable disease from his fond and loving wife.

I sat there dumbfounded with my mouth hanging open like a walleyed pike on the gaff, while she parked and gently removed her splendid torso, and gracefully glided up the walk, saying, "So close, and yet so far. You're a hard guy to find. You on the lam?"

"If I knew you were looking I would have raced through the streets as naked as the wind on wing-ed roller skates, wildly waving a red, white and blue banner."

I noticed in the light of day what I had suspected in the dark, three nights ago: She was, literally, a knockout. Brimming with sex, provocative and unassuming all at the same time, she was wearing a bright-print, mini-skirt, and a Lana Turner sweater. Lana never looked so good. Altogether an incredible young lady, my fly was hysterically fluttering its wings with barely controllable, spasmodic splendor.

She climbed the stairs, and leaned against the railing, while I inquired into her method of detection. "Oh, it wasn't too difficult. I knew your name and guessed you might be living in this neighborhood. The rest was plain old-fashioned footwork." And taking a quick glance at the meager surroundings, added, "However, I had no idea engineers lived so frugally."

"They may, and then again, they may not," I answered coolly, belying an agitated heart. "But I really can't say."

"I see. Then you're not really an engineer?"

"Hell, no. I wouldn't be caught dead with a slide rule in my shaky paws."

"What's wrong with engineering?"

"Nothing, except I can think of better ways of spending my time than playing with blocks. Somehow algebraic equations don't exactly set me afire." She smiled. "They never did me either, to be honest," she agreed. Changing the subject, she affirmed her knowledge of my being the cause of all the commotion three nights past. "And is it true?" she asked, "What I'm hearing concerning the details?"

"Probably not, but what are you hearing?"

"That you called some young girl names, and slapped her, and fought briefly with some of her friends."

"Hah! Briefly, I like that. Well, I must say, it didn't lose much in the telling, but as per usual, there's a certain flair lacking."

"Then it didn't happen like I heard?"

"Oh, it happened like you heard, alright, but the whys' and wherefores' are, shall we say, conspicuously absent, and without them the show's not worth the price of admission."

"Well, what did happen then?" and realizing she might have been too forward, quickly added, "Of course, this is really none of my business, and you don't have to tell me a thing."

"Don't sweat it," I promptly assured. "I'm impressed by your interest, and so glad to see you I'd give away the plans to the neutron bomb, and never look back."

A look of satisfaction crossed her enchanting face. "It seemed all kind of strange," she mused, "the way it happened. I mean, at least as far as I could gather. That's why I came looking for you. I wanted to find out for myself, and you didn't exactly impress me as being the lying type. That is, if you were going to talk at all."

"Oh, I'll lie, alright, if it suits me. I'll lie in a flash."

"And does it suit you now?" I gave her my dreamy, soft Valentino look, and remarked, "No, but I don't think you came scouting for me just out of curiosity, yes?"

"Yes. I broke it off with my … my fiancée."

I almost swallowed my tongue. "You broke it off with the blond Adonis?" I blurted out in astonished glee.

"Yes."

"And it's not even my birthday."

"Well. . . . ."

"And Christ isn't going to rise again shortly, is he?"

"Not that I know of."

"Then how come I feel like St. Peter at the pearly gates?" She smiled, retorting, "You're not one for hiding your feelings, are you? Maybe that's why I didn't feel too embarrassed about coming here. Your frankness is becoming, it not being a common characteristic." She stopped, and gazing softly with those delicately contoured green eyes, asked pleasantly, "Now what?"

"We ... we ... well," I stuttered, still somewhat stunned. "How sudden was the break-up? I mean, how much did I have to do with it?"

"Oh, that's hard to say, exactly. It was coming, though, that was certain. It was just a question of when. We weren't really the same types. Larry was a little too, too ... how shall I say? Conservative? Gray? I didn't feel comfortable with him. There was always a certain distance. I don't know, it just didn't have that whatever, you know? It never had a chance. But I'm here, though. That says something, doesn't it?"

"Enough and I couldn't be happier if I had just fallen into a harem of sex-starved, Turkish, belly dancers with an uncontrollable penchant for hobos.

You know, I'm very ... unusually affected by your presence, for what reasons I can only surmise. Your beauty, striking as it is, is only a part of it, since I have been with a beauty or two, before, and was not so affected. Your speech, your dress, your mood, the sound of your voice, the way you carry yourself, your manner. It's difficult to pin down, but, very impressive. I'm really impressed, and I'm getting redundant. . . . ."

"Get redundant; I don't mind."

"You're making it v-e-r-r-y hard for me not to flip for you."

"You're not going to hurt yourself?"

"I hope not. You know, the greatest mystery of life is not God, and death, and infinity, or whatever. The greatest mystery is the unexplainable composite intangibles composing the human bond. I don't have the faintest idea why I'm so moved by whatever it is you have, but I knew a quack once---it's not hard in these times---who belonged to some freaky religion that believed electricity was God, literally.

Upon expressing my amazement at such a ludicrous thought, he replied that God was everywhere, powerful, invisible, and infinite. That, he enjoined, was electricity. Now the God part, may be, is, a lot of crap, but electrical currents we know are definitely a part of the human makeup. I wouldn't doubt for a moment that when two people hit it off it's probably because they're hooked up to the same channel. You know, like a TV station, and when observing the same program can converse together about that program even though they may be half-wits. Of course, that last does do something to the quality of the conversation."

"Well, I've heard stranger things," she admitted, "but don't ask me when."

"Yes," I admitted, looking straight into her deep, limpid-green winkers, "you're the one."

Roberta, having an agreeably, reserved manner, I thought I'd tell her so, it being an attribute I greatly admired.

"Maybe that's it," she responded. "You don't like types who come on too strong."

"Oh, that's it, alright, as far as it goes. But you see I have liked types who did come on strong, also. Not too often, mind you, but it has happened. The thing is it doesn't explain everything."

"What does?"

"Yes, well, nevertheless, there's more to it, a lot more. And damn, I wish I knew what it was; I don't shun the dark, it being an invaluable aid to sleep, but I dislike keeping my mind in it. By the way, you still haven't said why you brought out the search party for me."

"Do I have to in so many words?"

"Miss Higgins. . . . ."

"Bobi."

"Bobi, you don't have to say a word, not one. Just sit there like you are. Just looking at you is the biggest thrill I've had in weeks." She crossed her legs; I made the sign of the cross. "Somehow," she affirmed, "I don't mind a bit admitting that I came here merely to see you again. Is that being too forward?"

"I don't give a damn what it is, and if it doesn't have a name we'll give it one."

"Well, I suppose this is as good a time as any to say, I like you too. I guess I'm not a great believer in tradition when it interferes with the import of the moment. Pride has its place, but like most things, should be restrained for its own good."

"Ho, ho, ho! Keep on, sweetheart, you've got my attention."

"What else is there to say except, now what?"

"Indeed." We caught our breaths momentarily. She continued, "Okay, from square one, if you're not an engineer, then what?"

"I'm a handyman, and right now I'm in between handys, or handily in between. Either way, it suits me."

"Well, what do you do when you're actively handy?" More and more, I liked this chick.

"Would you be terribly disappointed to learn I were not a man about town, am nobody in particular, have no trade, or profession to speak of, and don't care one damn wit?"

"I wouldn't."

"Then you've got it. I'm going nowhere at a pretty good clip, and I couldn't be happier. You could say I'm the last of the big-time bums, if it can be so stated. By the way, how come you're not teaching today? It's not Saturday."

"I'm 'sick' today."

"Really?" I questioned, looking up and down at that gorgeously chiseled torso, "you could've fooled me."

"I don't think too much gets by you."

"How bouts a walk in the park? Would you like that? It's not very exciting, I know, but then again, it's where you find it. Sides, there's not many bodies lingering about during the week, and that makes it just dandy."

"Okay," she agreed amiably, and off we went.

She parked by a tree where we got out, and began walking slowly.

"You like the outdoors?" I asked.

"Oh, yes, very much so, but I don't get much chance to rough it, what with the work I do."

"Too bad."

"Oh, I don't mind it that much. I feel I'm doing a useful thing, and I like to think my presence in the classroom makes a difference in at least one or two youngsters' lives."

"I hope so, and I hope you're a good teacher. We need good teachers, and from what I've seen of modern education, it's nothing to write home about. In fact, it's a wonder anyone can write at all. And if that weren't enough, everyone thinks he knows the answers to our dilemma. Hah!"

"Hah?"

"Of course. What do most people complain about? I'll tell you: discipline, their bratty, little shity snipes ain't learning … and prayers. As for discipline, they're right, there's none, and the reason there's none is because the little rat knows they've broken your stick. Now, I'm not too crazy about thumping folks, especially kids and winos, but when you raise a tiger in the jungle for nine or ten years, one does need a whip and a chair to control him. Aside from that, a little probability theory goes a long way."

"Probability?"

"Yes, the probability of every kid being like every other kid is mi-nute, therefore the disciplinary procedures used must vary. If you can't reach a toad with your tongue, a three foot stick usually can."

"That flies in the face of all conventional educational theory."

"I know. Isn't it wonderful? Right off then, you know you can't be far off the mark."

"It is said that if a teacher has to resort to physical means, then he's a failure."

"And a cobra isn't poisonous until he sticks you."

"Meaning?"

"Meaning—one can be obstinate to the point of mindlessness. You don't have to get bitten to know the consequences. The obvious, in modern societies, is the most complex. We have learned the secrets of the atom, but not of the human heart. Ironic, isn't it? You can go to the moon, but you can't go to Cuba."

"So, how does one handle the situation?"

"I hope you won't think ill of me for saying it, but at the high school level, ninety percent of the teachers should be male, and I do mean it with a capital M. I say that because the next step is to introduce a 'freedom of the classroom' law for the teacher, including any means he sees fit to: (1) control the class, and (2) see to it that some learning takes place. At this stage of the game, equality notwithstanding, women cannot fulfill rule number one, and without that you cannot have rule number two. I have, upon occasion, sat in classrooms where eleven and twelve-year-olds would take a swing at a nun. I have also sat in a classroom where the teacher, being a former wrestler, and looking every hairy bit of it, and no one, and I mean no one, ever looked like he were about to raise even a little pinky, let alone a whole hand, and, might I add, there were some pretty tough hombres in that class, too, you know? Guys who walked around with shivs in their boots, and not for adornment either, and even, one or two, who ended up in the pen with longer stretches than Wilt Chamberlain."

"But what kind of teacher was he?"

"Who knew, but he had our un-di-vi-ded attention."

Bobi laughed and rebutted, "It all sounds very reactionary to me."

"If you want to put a label on it, make it 'pragmatic.' It is impossible to teach in a classroom where two or three misfits think their mission in life is to disrupt it. I'm a great believer in the 'lose one to save ten theory,' so if you have to tap him, do so, and if you have to kick him out, kick him out. It may be that some kids, for whatever the reason, are not made for school, or life, for that matter. By the time they're fifteen, or sixteen, it's hopeless. If that is the case, then kick him out. Be kind, but kick him out. Don't beat a wild horse, and don't be senseless either; keep him fenced in. Universal education is a bad trip. No one should be forced to stay in school anymore than force him to roll under a Sherman tank."

"But that doesn't make sense. Why should anyone be forced to roll under a Sherman tank?"

"Precisely and why keep a dolt in school?"

"But then a lot of people, who ordinarily would have at least a high school education won't have it."

"I had a simple-minded aunt once. She could not learn anything beyond the level of grade three, so in a time of more sense and less 'caring,' they took her out of school. It may be that some others are also incapable of learning, for other reasons, but just as intransigent. Let us be just as sensible about them. If they can't cut the mustard at grade nine, then grade nine it is, or ten or eleven, or whatever. Life's too short to be torturing its inhabitants. The Inquisition is behind us. And besides, you equate schooling with education. IT—IS—NOT—NECESSARILY—SO. It is, in these surroundings, at any rate, merely training, and no one need sit in a dull-assed classroom reciting 'The Rhyme of the Ancient Mariner' for that."

"But all this discipline doesn't guarantee education."

"It certainly doesn't, and it's not supposed to. It is only a means to an end. The more receptive the student is to learning, the less discipline will be necessary, the less receptive, the more discipline. The problem as it always is because it's the easy way out is we insist on treating the effects always the effects. We handcuff ourselves with the effects."

"Specifically?"

"O-kay, first a kid is born into a negative environment, to put it mildly. We call it America, and cover it with sugar and spice and everything nice. There's two strikes against him right there, because here, the person, contrary to what we are made to believe, is worth less than a ham sandwich. The nobility of a nation is determined by how it treats the less fortunate in its midst. For that we have only to look about; our efforts are geared to accumulating goods, and status, and guns, and tanks, and only incidentally are we dedicated to more enlightened pursuits.

Now this poor sap of a kid, of which we speak, he's born into all of this, and from that time immediately picks up on it, picking, picking, picking. And don't think for one minute he's missing anything. He-don't-miss-a-trick, babe. The family, starting with his diet, feeds him crap. It's called baby food, sugar and starch, and everything nice. I wouldn't feed it to Fido. Then they're either paying too much attention to him, or not enough. By the time he's ripe for schooling, he'll get stuck with some doe-doe broad, rapping on the board with a stick, singing 'A-B-C-D-E-F-G,' while outside the classroom everyone is lying, cheating, stealing and killing, off-times in broad daylight, the state included, especially the state. Additionally, he belongs to a church, which in the name of Christ, (there's a switch for ya) steals from the poor to buy silk robes and marble statues, while preaching the virtues of goodness, love and charity, so by the time he's fifteen you wonder why he's incorrigible? But wondering is done with. The stick that was once used for rapping out the A-B-C's, must now be used to rap on his scruffy head."

"Oh, I can't believe that. There must be a better way."

"Oh, most certainly! There always is, but at what cost? You can waste half your time on one kid hoping to reach him, eventually. He may straighten out; you never know. But you've neglected the rest to do it, and is it worth it? Is he worth it? What makes him so special? Sacrificing the many for the few?

I don't know, but I think somehow there's a perversion of logic there, to say the least. The point is, we can't depend on someone, here and there, making the right moves. It's too wasteful, for lack of a better word, and it's no way to run a store. It just doesn't effect enough people, and in the long run we condemn ourselves to a hit-and-miss game of chance, and I don't appreciate my bread being spent on the 'rehabilitation' of a few isolated dullards scattered all over creation at the expense of everyone else.

It's a lot like prison, in a way. I'm not for spending one, lousy stinking dime for rehabilitating anyone. If a guy's too damn dangerous to be allowed to mingle with the rest of the natives, put him away. But don't torture him; don't bug him with therapy, and counseling, and this and that. Get off his back. That's what got him there in the first place, everybody climbing on his back. You want to help him? Leave him be. Let him do his time unhindered by the daily, little irrelevancies that can drive one mad, and when his time is up, rip up the rap sheet. That's the best rehabilitation he can get. Take the god-dam anchor off his back. And so it is with school. You try to reach a bad sort. If you can't, cut him loose. Just cut him loose. Let's spend a lot more time being honest with ourselves, and find out how come a fifteen-year-old kid turned out to be a little rat in the first place, rather than feed him cheese. And that's where discipline comes in. When you come across a punk, you grab him by his crutty, little neck, slam him up against the wall, and recite the A-B-C's to him, clearly, concisely, and in the King's English. If he gets it, fine; if not, give him something to remember you by, then kick his stinking rear right out into the street where it belongs, and for that it takes a man, and not a skirt, or a dippity-do counselor, or whatever, but a man.

Have you seen any around lately? I've seen lots of lettuce, and carrots, and a few peas in a pod, but men?" I drummed my index finger lightly on my lower lip and looked wonderingly toward the heavens. "Men, men." I looked at Bobi, saying, "Give me a hint. What do they look like?"

"You got me," she responded, playing along.

"I certainly hope so." She smiled. "You don't play hard to get, do you?" she answered.

"Honey, there's a lot of games I don't play, and in the few I do, I try to make my own rules."

"You can hardly lose that way."

"Oh, you can lose, alright, but you don't feel so bad about it when you know you've had a good run at it, dig? Getting screwed all the time, that's what's hard to take. I figure I was put on this tumbling, ball of dementia besides something other than getting foozled by my fellow man at every crick and turn."

"I'll drink to that. So now that we have discipline all straightened out, then what?"

"Well now, back up a ways. I think I may have misled you a bit."

"I guess so ... if we're backing up. . . . ."

"Up to now we have merely disposed of the sediment what contaminates any ol' river bottom ... two-percent, maybe."

"Uh, huh."

"Now we get to the good part. In that number, say fifteen, twenty-per-cent maybe, what thinks at 14, 15, 16, years he has all the mysteries of the universe solved, we don't kick H-I-M out."

"We don't."

"We don't; we 'save' him. To him we give the choice—behave, learn, wise-up, or you will behave, learn, and wise-up in reform school."

"I don't get it."

"It's really very simple; give him the choice. Let him decide. He's not going to get sentenced; he's going to get 'reinspired.' It's up to him. Get with it, or get without it. You go to reform school until you decide to cooperate to at least a reasonably monstrous degree."

"And for how long is he going to get "reinspired.""

"Three months, six months, nine months; one year, two years, three years, whatever, and when he reaches nineteen, if he still has his head in his ass, then off to San Quentin … and again, no sentence; when he decides to quit acting like a little prick—bingo, back he goes into the prison without bars to co-mingle with the rest of us monkey-fuckers."

"I see."

"Do you really?"

"So far."

"And make no mistake about it; when I say reform school, I mean just that. Same teachers, same accreditation, same everything, the only difference … the little rat will be confined, as he should be, until he makes up his mind which way he wants to blow his nose.

He's going to 'toe the line,' no bunkum, and no putting up with the least of his bull-shit. He can live out his life in this swamp we all so lovingly call America, or he can live it out in a friggin dungeon we call prison. It's his call, RIGHT DOWN THE LINE; at every step of the way—HIS call.

I'll spend for his time in school, but not one stinking, red cent for his time in prison. He goes to school, however far he can go, and then out into the world of work, no unemployment, no welfare, none of that mindless 'we'll pay you to sit on your ass' crap. Shit, I've seen guys big enough to pick up a house, just lolling around picking up beer bottles, if you get my drift.

Work, however small, however meaningless, shall be forthwith commenced, whatever he can handle, and for it all he receives all the benefits and privileges society can throw at him, and everybody gets treated the same, kings and paupers alike. And that, my dear is America … not this hog swill capitalism where we've traded demented, dissolute kings, nefarious dukes, and rapacious barons of the middle-ages, said poisonous assemblage freely and cheerfully blessed by that human pile of excrement and villainy—the degenerate, mother-fucking catholic church---for putrefying, satanic, corrupt politicians, scum-sucking, slime ball ceo's, and two dimensional, one-track, simple minded, military men, where the only thing that has changed are the names, and the places, and that's all brother."

"I see."

"I hope so. Yes, Bobi, I'll pay him to go to school, but I won't pay him to go to prison. Or let me be even more succinct: when you hit eighteen, you go to school, you go to work, or you go in the army. You will N-O-T be allowed to do nothing. No society has ever survived, or flourished with its citizens do-ing, noth-ing."

"Okay, I like that. And then what."

"Then back to grade one and on with the business of teaching. We instill a little curiosity in the young mind, and it doesn't make a twit how dull a kid is, if he learns to love to learn, and want to know about things, to be curious, to have a sense of wonderment, then it's done, and the rest will surely follow as night follows day."

"That's not bad, as far as it goes."

"It goes far enough."

"What about the alphabet?"

"What about it?"

"When will they learn that?"

"At age five."

"Oh, I get it. If their curiosity is peeked at five, then the alphabet. . . . ."

"As night follows day." A squirrel scampered by and ran up a tree. "You know, a squirrel learns what it has to very well without a frustrated old maid laying down the law to him. He knows what he has to do to get on. He knows that if he lets a fox, a hawk, or a speedy legged beagle get close enough to kiss him, it's kiss him good-bye. He knows he's safe up in a tree, usually, and he knows he has to store nuts for the winter. And you know? The bushy little bugger has done just fine for millions of years without having to have to sit in a chair and pay attention to teacher, his teacher being his own good sense untrammeled by the dictates of the Mongol hordes. He survives, and he does it without destroying everything in sight, and apparently these days that is no mean feat.

"To be sure."

We walked on, slowly and silently. I picked up a stone and flung it at a migrating bird knowing full well I'd miss.

"Not a very good picture is it?" she eventually declared.

"No, Bobi, it's really all very, very bleak? I honestly feel sometimes that the devils have more of the rudimentary juices than the gods. Why else this seeming conspiracy against the progress of man? Hell, we aren't any further now than when they built the pyramids."

"And maybe less."

"Less?" I replied, somewhat confused.

"With all our supposed know how, I don't think we could do it any faster or better, what with cost over-runs, strikes, and what not. One of the seven wonders it wouldn't be."

"Oh, I'm getting to like you, more and more."

"T-h-a-n-k y-o-u. "

"Not at all. A rain cloud was doing its best to block out the midday sun. I took quick aim with an imaginary rifle and fired. "Pow! Pow! Pow!"

"What was that all about?" she inquired in obvious bewilderment.

"Just trying to see if I could do a little magic."

"And?"

"No magic. That little ditty is reserved to the rotten rich to perform on the rest of us."

"It is?"

"Did you ever wonder why we have the rich at all?"

"You make it sound like it's a disease."

"Hah! Close enough, but the fact remains, we dullards accept the status quo as God-given law, an eleventh commandment maybe? Why do we have to have rich and poor, anyway? Is it because of some inherent, biological law? Is it a law of nature? Well, in a manner of speaking, yes, it's the law of the jungle, where it may surprise you to know the lion is not the king of beasts, but just a lazy, fawning, overgrown pussycat, wiling away most of his time slouching, lying about, and yawning. The jungle is ruled by the snake, the maggot, and the buzzard, and the snake in Portland, and Pittsburgh, and Denver needs to have his little someone to look down on and be able to say, "Look, I'm better than you, and to prove it, just look at what I have that you don't." They justify injustice and inequality by saying it was gotten by hard work, and that anyone can do it if they have what it takes, then they immediately proceed to devise laws, and organize matters so no one can do it. The fancy words for it are: ambition, drive, industry, and that magical pronouncement of all time, 'democracy.' But it's the cobra of class structure slinking in the high weeds, and we've come to accept it as part of life, so much so, that Americans think it's a fifth grade game, and this really is a democracy. Shit, no wonder the Greeks have a military dictatorship.

So, the game goes on. Children are taught from grade one to value nothing unless they get paid---gold stars—unless there's something in it for them. They're so deadened by the time they reach twenty-one, they see nothing perverted about living in a nation with a gross national product of one trillion while attending church on Sundays, singing, 'Glory be Jesus,' and giving to the collection in order to provide for the poor, a poor they've created in the first place. They notice nothing unusual about having all this loose change floating around, yet folks are having a hard time buying a bag of beans. All I can say is it couldn't happen to a nicer bunch. The older I get, the harder I find it to dispute the saying, 'people get what they deserve and they deserve what they get.' There's an awful lot of justice there, an awful lot. It may be all there is, and more important, all that's necessary."

"You don't pull any punches, do you?"

"I haven't had that kind of life." I laid against a tree and stared out across the green landscape. "Bobi, I said dispassionately, "did you ever try to grow a daisy in a sewer?"

"Grow a daisy in a sewer?" she repeated incredulously. "Yeah, grow a daisy in a sewer, in the stench and darkness, amongst the disease, and filth, and vermin? Did you ever try it?"

"No, I haven't. I don't know why I'd want to."

"Exactly. What purpose is there to sticking a bright sunflower down in a sewer, than command, 'Grow!' Yet, we do it all the time, don't we? To ourselves? How can a delicate, complicated, precise instrument like a child grow in a sewer? How can it spring up straight and tall amongst the slime and waste, the decayed and stagnant? That's what this society is, you know, what with all the back-biting and gnashing of teeth, the money-grubbing, the hypocrisy, the trenchant injustice and inequalities; the cowardice, the stupidity born of generations of stupidity. Poor kid; poor daisy. It has a better chance of straightening up after being stepped on by Goliath, than being stuck in that damn sewer."

"Is it really that bad?"

"Not to the punks in suits on Capital Hill, or Wall Street, or Palm Springs, but we're talking about life, human life, being destroyed at will. That's not pretty, or exciting, or something to be played down, or glossed over. Human lives being destroyed, over and over, and over again, week after week, month after month, year after year. And where is the sensitivity to all of it? Where are our heads? They're at football games reciting prayers in bowed heads, and singing the Star Spangled, frigging Banner, parading giant flags across the field at halftime while singing 'God Bless America,' and glinty-assed majorettes flipping their batons to the tune of 'America the Beautiful.'

Flighty minded fuckers; you want to know what's happening to America? Go to a football game. It's birth, life, and death is wrapped up in the pseudo pageantry of the pigskin gladiators. In the face of the obvious we keep telling ourselves, 'We're great! We're great!' But it won't wash, so, like all cowards, we hide, behind speeches, games, parades, clichés and slogans. We oogle the tube, guzzle beer, fart, scratch our ass, and secretly covet the little, teenage slut's ass next door. The world is sinking in a pit of nuclear waste and imbecility, while we patiently await the next rendition of that all-time video obscenity 'BO-NAN-ZA!'

"Where's Hoss, little Joe?"

"Up on the north fork, Paw."

"And where's Adam?'"

"Down on the south fork corralling strays."

"And where you been, Joe?"

"On the east fork squirrel hunting, Paw. And we sure do have a mite lot o' forks on this here land, Paw."

"Yeah, and I could sure use one now to stick in this here script."

"Sho nough, Paw."

And if that don't get you, then how about 'Father knows best.' Uh, huh, he sure does; then how come all our kids are nuts? Convinced yet? No? Then wrap your arms around this obscenity: 'L-O-V-E S-T-O-R-Y.' 'Hey, preppy.' 'Hey, preppy.' 'Hey, preppy.' Preppy, my ass. The only movie I both fell asleep in A-N-D walked out on. I was tempted to go right back in, so I could walk right back out again on that nauseating piece of shit. And now I save the best for last."

"That wasn't it?"

"Actually, it's a tie; I really couldn't decide, they both being a gigantic load of horse puckeys. ARE YOU READY!!!"

"I guess. . . . ."

"Okay; buck up cause it's gonna slop right to ya. "C-H-A-R-L-E-Y-S A-N-G-E-L-S.

Three, dumb, skungy ass-crackers flipping 250 pound kloppers over car hoods. It makes you just want to reach right into the screen and slap the crap out of anything and anyone having anything to do with such a prodigious heap of snake shit."

"Oh, I'm kind of with you there."

"The will is dead, and the flesh will surely follow, and it didn't have to be this way, you say? But then it did. America is a brute caught in quicksand, and unable to extricate himself, calls for the band to play in the despairing, unreal hope that somehow the blaring of bugles, and the banging of drums will miraculously lift him out of the goo." I glanced at Bobi as she gave a shrug. I could see she was more than half-agreeing, albeit, none too enthusiastically. I continued nevertheless.

"You know, practically all things have some kind of connection with everything else. A tree, for instance, doesn't grow and exist in isolation. It depends, first of all, upon the seed of another tree. That seed must fall in the right place at the right time for it to grow. If it falls on a rock, or in a pond, that's the end of it. If a bird snatches it before it has a chance to sprout, that also makes a quick end for it. And if by chance it does survive the numerous ways it can be crushed, mangled, eaten, or otherwise destroyed, it is then faced with the problem of continuance. It needs sunlight and water. An inopportune hailstorm can snuff it in the bud. It needs a certain kind of weather and it needs it continually. After that, it's worms, insects, hurricanes, tornados, ax-swinging woodcutters, and high-legged dogs. To see one standing high and dry, one would think it an easy life.

And so it is with people, so touchy, so brittle, so frail, so susceptible to the slightest breeze, a draft, wet feet, or a bad word. If it can survive nine months in a damp cave and an unwelcome smack on its rump ... I wonder about the slap. I mean, it seems such an onerous way to begin a life, you know? A bitch dog licks her newborn. There's a message in there somewhere. Most dogs are even-tempered and gentle ... for dogs. Do you think it has anything to do with the licks? Maybe if we licked our babies instead of slapping them, they would grow taller and straighter?

In any case, after being unceremoniously draped onto this cold rock, it is tugged at, mauled, jostled, punched, kicked, hassled by practically all things human, right down from the doctors, nurses, mothers, fathers, siblings; the school, the church, the law, his peers, public opinion, Madison Avenue, and a general, all-around demented brand of civilization. He is taught to be a dud, a 'yes sir,' 'no sir,' conforming, team playing jackass. A dutiful, law-abiding, God-fearing eggshell. And there you have it, my sweet—the average Joe, apple pie patriotism to the nth degree, and, they're aren't any surprises. The scene is played over and over with sickening regularity:"Bobo, I don't like what so-and-so said about me. Shoot him."

"Yes, my President, but what shall I say I shot him for?"

"National security. I'm a national, and my insecurity's at stake."

"Yes, my President." Bang! Bang! "Done, my President."

"I thought I saw a twitch. Give him a kick, Bobo."

"Yes, my President." Thump. "He's dead now, my President."

"Good. Give me a shine, Bobo."

"Yes, my President." Slick, slick, slappety, slap.

"You know, Bobo, this is such a tough job."

"Yes, my President." Slick, slick, slappety, slap.

"And how do we remove ourselves from this quagmire when Christmas is celebrated but one day of the year?"

"Yes; but what has all this to do with discipline?"

"What has it to do with discipline, you say? Well, as with all things, every-thing, and nothing. It doesn't make any difference, that's the rock in the baby's cradle. You think it really makes a difference who's elected President?"

"Doesn't it?"

"Does it make a difference if I live sixty, or eighty years?"

"I don't follow you."

"Would it have made a difference if I were ever born?"

"To whom?"

"Well … to anyone. It makes no difference that Christ was ever born."

"But then, we would not have had Christianity," to wit, I could only give one of those, "So what?" looks.

"I see. Then nothing makes a difference."

"Exactly. Things are going to happen the way they're going to happen, and nothing and nobody can change that. They will only happen sooner or later, and that sooner or later we call history. The little, petty minds of people are cluttered with the pebbles of arrogance. They think the gods look down with favor upon them, when in fact their concern for us is equal to that of a tick scratching his way up a bull elephant's ass. As for discipline, well, there's one infallible yardstick we can use to measure our progress."

"Which is?"

"The need for it indicates the extent of our error. It's like sickness; it tells us we haven't been living right. I remember reading once about Tolstoy. Early on in the 1860's he ran a school of sorts, a very unconventional type school with time spent mostly outdoors, and no specific curriculum to speak of except whatever fancied them at the moment, teacher and pupil, and no accreditation. It lasted about three years before he went on to bigger things, and in all that time, he never had a discipline problem, none, of any kind. Isn't that something? That's incredible, absolutely incredible. Three years! Christ, you'd think some fuzzy headed educator somewhere—cripes, the landscapes full of them like maggots on dead flesh—would pick up on it, try to find out how come? How come? Not one little monster in three years? But no, the plodders plod issuing forth perfunctory doctoral theses such that in a more perspicacious time would not suffice to garner a fake degree from the local backroom print mill. Would it be that, by chance sometime, you might have come across a ditty or two?"

"No, I haven't."

"Pity, you don't know what charming little exercises of the mind you missed out on."

"Somehow, though, I get the feeling you're going to tell me."

"Ah, my dear sweet Roberta, the whole world should be so pleasantly helpful."

"Would it were so?"

"Moving right along, one bright young lady surmounting the heights of asininity, composed one-hundred–and-forty-seven pages of buffoonery concerning 'the effects of classroom shapes, and certain types of furniture,' have upon the learning process. Another ninny on 'the significance of football equipment intruding upon the immature mind,' and yet another on 'the effects of posture and voice inflection of the teacher upon the mental equilibrium of the student.' What a fantastic mouthful of dogshit. Learning? How can they with dippity-do's like that leading the pack? And for all of it, they're crying to the high heavens for more pay! More pay? Why the malty assed sons-of-bitches, they're lucky they're getting paid at all. They ought to be paying us! But wait, we haven't come to the good part yet. All this is mere balderdash compared to the grand finale. Merely the preliminaries to the main event. You ready for this?"

"As much as I'll ever be, I guess," she responded in good humor.

"Prayers! How's that grab ya? Prayers! Long live George Orwell. The population is exceedingly upset, to say the least, because their drag tailed, little half-wit off-springs can't pray in school. If you can swallow that, you can swallow anything, and truly are we going 'the way of all flesh.' Little fuzzo can't pray no mo' in school. The suck holes. They probably think if he's not praying he must be fucking, a pursuit whose benefits far exceeds any irksome, dim-witted prayer might have on any account. It's hard to believe. Instead of demanding superior teaching, and a high-class curriculum, we want to know first how come Johnny didn't say any Hail Mary's today. Well grab my ass and call it the sunshine pumpkin.

Consistency is supposed to be the hobgoblin of small minds, but I think we'd be ahead of the game if we now demanded that math be taught in the churches.

Prayers?" I shook my head in disbelief. "Terrific. It's like I'm having a bad dream, and time's been turned back three thousand years. I keep getting the feeling I'd like to build a pyramid. Yes, Virginia, there is no Santa Claus, and you can't grow a daisy in a sewer."

Bobi did not reply for a moment, but presently flung a half-hearted admonishment. "I kind of get a depressed feeling listening to your version of things."

"Good. It's not exactly a Marx brother's flick, although it does resemble a three-ring circus, at times."

"It's all so very pessimistic."

"Yes, but that's not the point. The point is, is it so? Optimism, pessimism, a piece of bunko designed to trick the unsuspecting, and like a duck call in the blind, does its job. For no small reason is a duck called a duck. Indeed does he fall prey to any simple little trick, and consequently winds up with his end up in the cooker. Likewise with humans, and just as easily, if we insist upon acting like quacks."

I pulled a blade of grass and chewed on it, then continued. "I remember one time at a baseball game---great game, baseball—one of the combatants made the sign of the cross as he stepped into the batter's box. The catcher, who must have had a unique sense of humor, did likewise. It must have put God into quite a quandary for the batter fouled-off innumerable pitches before finally striking out. You know, it's a kind of an insult, don't you think? To the catcher, I mean."

"How so?"

"Well, the batter is asking for God to heap misfortune upon the catcher and his team. What right has he to do that, the bastard? Who the hell is he, anyway? Besides, you'd think a guy would have a better sense of priorities. What makes him think with all the problems facing God, he really cares one wit who wins a friggin' ballgame? He probably ain't even a fan. It makes you wonder sometimes what the hell's going through a bloke's head, not to be able to take a game for what it is—a game—and not a matter of life and death. But there it is. A game taking on the importance of an arms race … and you wonder why the arms race can look like a stinking ball game.

Oh, what the hell, it's all so very hopeless. Why else would grown men depend so much on something they never saw, can't talk to, can't hear, can't touch, can't even get on the phone. It's depressing, and very embarrassing. Sometimes I get an uncontrollable urge to go racing through the streets screaming from the top of my lungs, 'Wise up! Wise up! Wise up'! You know what stops me?"

"What?"

"Everyone would think I-i-i-i was crazy. This world, Bobi, it's a dragon's feast."

"We have to make the best of it." Bobi, poor dear, was now slinking into the pool of mediocrity.

"We do?" I remarked solemnly. "Ever been to the dog races?"

"No, can't say that I have."

"It takes the ingenious mind of man, no less, to think of innumerable ways to trick any of God's creatures that may be so foolish as to cross its path, in this case the witless hound. Yet greed, lurking on the high ground, has outwitted man in his quest for the gold bullion, as the hunt, strewn end to end with a litter of land mines, waits silently in ambush for man to stumble once again upon one of his numerous weaknesses—this time the gambling bug—will blast his dreams with a handful of losing tickets.

And the iron bunny, he's plunked out there on the stick just far enough ahead so the running dogs can't catch him, race, after race, after race. You'd think after a while the mutts would get smart, but they never do. And when, on that rare occasion one does finally catch the mechanical hare, all he gets for his trouble is a mouthful of springs and metal hinges. Can't win for losing.

So, iron rabbits, stupid hounds, wily people; does it really make a difference? Is the lowly, night-crawler any less divine than the King of Siam? Is this earth any more hallowed ground than the rocks on the moon, or the red dust on Mars? Is the Bible a sacred book written by inspired holy minds, and 'The Valley of the Dolls' a litany of filth inspired only by the gaudy love of the unholy, filthy dollar? Does it really matter?"

"Now I am depressed."

Never having it in my heart to depress such a glorious creature, I quickly consoled. "Well, what the hell, if it does, or it doesn't, why waste such a beautiful day pondering the unexplainable? Let's enjoy it; I have a feeling if we don't nobody's really going to care, but us two."

"Ditto."

I put my arm around Bobi's shoulder and declared in earnest, "I think I love you." She turned a faint crimson while replying half-jokingly, "Now you're going to have me blushing and I haven't done that since I was a little girl. And by the way, you never did say why you slapped that girl, or am I being presumptuous?"

"Sweetheart, with me, you can be anything you like."

"Oh?"

"And I slapped her because she had it coming; a fitting reason I should think."

"What did she do?"

"It wasn't so much what she did, but what she was."

"That being?"

"A smart-ass displaying an overbearing and repugnant manner, which I though necessary to nip in the bud."

"Really, now. Well, you certainly made your mark, I must say. And they say Bogie's dead."

"Bogie never died, he just kind of sailed off into the sunset. Never quite thought of myself as a Bogart, though. Cagney maybe."

"Do tell. But that 'tough guy' style is out of date nowadays, what with women's lib and all."

"Women's lib! Come now, you can do better than that."

"I take it then, given that exuberant outburst of scorn, you're not in complete agreement with the movement?"

"My dear young lady, I hope you won't think me totally unhinged, but I am not in complete agreement with practically anything that is going down nowadays."

"I should have guessed. And how come in regards to the above mentioned?"

"Because, quite frankly, it is all very senseless, baseless, irrelevant, and stems from a deep-seated sense of frustration, hate, and envy, sprinkled with a goodly amount of impotence, that last having the unfortunate ability to kill off a herd of horny toads."

"You wouldn't categorize the women's movement as irrelevant, would you?"

"No, not initially, but it certainly reached that plateau in zip time."

"How so?"

"Well, like all mass movements, they degenerate in direct proportion to their multiplying numbers, the masses being their own worst enemy. What started out with great hopes and expectations, diminished into just another power-grabbing, ego-tripping, hooray for me, screw you jag. They were right onto some hep things, and had it all together, for a while. But now, what the hell, they want equality and alimony, too. The right to usurp my rights, and the rights to my privacy. Hell, I can't even sit in on a poker game without being invaded by a bunch of sign-swinging, fire-eating hermaphrodites. I don't invade their damn tea parties and sewing circles, and why should I? people ought to be able to work out their own messy, little lives unencumbered by other's beliefs, and without that other sticking a damn sign in one's face and continually being accused of domination, because his style is not their style.

Yet, in these most trying of times, there's still something to be said for not being a big pain in the ass. They're dealers now at Vegas. Yeah, dealers. And in all fairness to fairness, you might say, why not? And on the face of it, why not? Well, I'll tell you why."

"I thought you would." Bobi was the perfect Abbot to my Costello.

"All things, however seemingly insignificant have their price and carry within them the seeds, if not for their own destruction, then at least, their own evolution, and not necessarily upward. Today Vegas, tomorrow the world. And yet another small incident blurring the distinctions between the sexes. What we gain in sticking to the exact letter of the law, we lose in those little joys that make this life tolerable and without which we can all, in one lethargic display of boredom, slide into the river of uniformity. Isn't it exciting? And you wonder why there's all this unemployment?"

"Why?

"Both the dumb-assed honkey shmuck, A-N-D his stupid bitch wife are out there in the market. Where before it was one-to-one, now it's two-to-one. Shit, we can't even add anymore. And where are the kids, you say?"

"I didn't, but I can guess."

"Anybody can guess. This ain't rocket science, honey.

"Do tell"

"In the stinking street learning about all that good shit America has to offer, FIRST HAND! DUC—KY."

"If I keep listening to you, I'm moving to Russia."

"You keep listening to me and you'll begin to realize there is no such place as America, and there are no good guys, and bad guys, only bad and badder."

"Hmnn . . . . ."

"And unisex. How can anybody get turned-on by ugliness?"

"Beauty is in the eye of the beholder."

"Beauty is in the soul of the beholder, which explains its diminishing tendencies nowadays."

"We have Warhol."

"Warhol has Warhol."

"Is beauty an absolute, then?"

"Beauty is clean air, clean water, imagination, intelligence, and virtue."

"Come again?"

"If you have that, you have it all."

"Might you not be stretching things a bit?"

"If we all, every single five billion of us, had clean air, and water, and imagination, intelligence, and virtue, can you not see the unclouded beauty in that? Do not all things follow from their intrinsic natures? Evil is as evil does; so much so that a fat pig like Goering can at one minute appreciate a Rembrandt, or so it is said, and the next order the bombing of London. The filth in the human soul runs deeper than the sewers of Paris.

I saw a chick the other day wearing a grey, pin-striped suit, tie and all, and a hairstyle that would have made 'Boy George drool.' She looked like a cross between the undertaker, and the lead singer in an all-female punk, rock group. Of course, her man, who I might add, also defied the best that Webster could offer, had eyes only for her. Beauty? Beholder? Language, my dear, has within it all the sly tricks of a Houdini. The footwork can be dazzling, but keep your eye on the bouncing ball.

Yes, sweetheart, I'd let them have it all—football, baseball, coal digging, even boxing. I'd let them climb in the ring with Joe Frazier, but while she's flexing her du-wa-ditty, I'd whisper in his ear, "Joe, baby, don't pull no punches. Kick her swishing ass right out into the third row."

"That's cruel."

"The sharply, barbed arrow, never to be wildly shot about in all directions, is well spent deftly aimed at a worthy target."

"They are getting ridiculous, aren't they?"

"Ridiculous? You're being kind. Just the other day I read an article where a female philosophy professor, philosophy, mind you, a Ms. something or other, had advised all her sweet sisters to shoot to kill any stud who tries to rape them.

Now your first reaction might be: 'sure, why not? Shoot the bastard' but think about it. A philosophy professor, a skirt with a Ph.D., a doctorate. She's supposed to be educated, and this is the best advice she can give? This is her answer? Hell, we can get that from any old Jane. We don't need her, with her eighteen years of schooling, for that brilliant piece of speculation. It's frightening. 'Shoot him' goes out the call in strident fashion. That same broad has probably marched against the war in Viet Nam, and in Civil Rights demonstrations, preaches the philosophy of pacifism, and the dignity of love and brotherhood, is against capital punishment, and for the humane treatment of criminals—excepting those convicted of rape---but when it comes right down to the nitty gritty, when it's her ass that's on the line, the real she, comes firing back with fire and blood in her eyes swinging a .38, foaming at the mouth, and shouting, 'Kill! Kill! Kill!' And for what? And against whom? Some poor sap, a pigeon like all of us, struggling, trying to make it but beat down so bad he's gotten to the point of total desperation and senselessness, he's willing to destroy his life in one sick, fitful moment of pleasure, if that's what it is. To this we get the rational, educated response of 'Kill! Kill!' There isn't even a mild attempt at understanding whereby a whistle and a can of mace would be entirely sufficient, and well within the province of sanity. But no, it's 'Kill! Kill!' as if what was being taken is all that holy.

Them suck hole canaries, they sure have a high opinion of themselves. It seems we're raising a generation of Calamity Jane's with one slight difference: I don't think Calamity was aiming at old Wild Bill's balls. Betty Boop, in all consciousness, is giving a very subliminal, primitive response. If we were to insert in place of kill, 'castrate' we would be more to the mark."

"All this shooting and balling has got me confused."

"I like you; you know how to keep it light."

"I'd better."

"Anyhow, castration, that's their bag. They've been stepped on and repressed for so long they cannot now control their rage. Their sense of revenge is total. They want to strip away the one thing men prize most, their studularity." I paused; Bobi sighed.

"Bobi," I continued in the same vein, "mass movements must be a part of the food family. No matter how delicious, nourishing and healthful they start out, invariably they always turn to shit."

"And all this was going through your mind when you slapped that girl?"

"One small slap for brotherhood, one giant kick for mankind."

We walked on quietly. For my part, I needn't have speech as a companion; I enjoyed just being near this heavenly creature. I yearned to press my sensitive palms against her round, formful cheeks which seemed to cry out for caressing.

Gusts suddenly began to swirl all about, and Bobi commented something to the effect of 'hating to break up such a wonderful day,' but she had to be getting along. We started back toward the car and I asked if I would be seeing her again.

"Would you like?" she expressed, to my great pleasure; and looking for absolute confirmation, I asked if she would really like to.

"Yes, I think so," was her reply.

"My, but that certainly is a relief to hear. It makes everything so simple. I'm so happy I met Thoreau."

"You're a lover of simplicity?"

"Especially these days."

"These days?"

"What else?"

"Can you give me a hint?"

"Words."

"Words?"

"Words … language; I saw an interview the other day on the six o'clock news—a practice I am happy to say I rarely engage in any more—where the interviewee, a gross-looking creature of the female gender, who happened to be the school superintendent for some two-bit, cow town down the coast a-ways, used the following baggage at least once in a two minute conversation: relevant, meaningful, impacting, team-play, parenting and situational."

"G-o-o-d Lord and you stayed?"

"Aye, but not without throwing up first."

"I can imagine."

"It's all a game, Bobi, and most of us are water boys and bench warmers, and if we get near a bat at all, it's the kind with wings and fangs.

"Just gets worse and worse, does it?"

"And that's the crab in your craw."

"That hurts."

"Oh, yes. I'm gonna like you."

"We all liked to be liked."

"Yes … well … but have you ever wondered about honesty?"

"Honesty?"

"Yeah. What a completely different world this would be if everything else stayed the same except honesty? Talk about difference, now there's something a bloke can sink his teeth into."

"Honesty?"

"Sure. Imagine if everyone were honest instead of the sniveling pansies they are now. Change, change, change. Wouldn't we have it? For instance, what's the lowest form of life you can think of?"

"The lowest form of life?"

"Yeah."

"A dope pusher? Sex fiend?"

"C'mon, now, stay with me."

"A Nazi?"

"That's better, but how about a political campaign?"

"Damn, why didn't I think of that?" As I have previously stated, Bobi knew how to play the game. I continued. "Imagine the fresh air blown through that tunnel. Enough, I suspect to keep the city of Pittsburgh smelling like a field of clover for a thousand years. Think of it, a politician rising up and actually speaking the truth, a highly unlikely proposition, you must admit."

"I do."

Citizen: "Mr. Blob, why do you want to be a congressman?"

Mr. Blob: "Well, it seems like the easiest way to go at the moment, given the short hours, and the opportunity to mess around, combined with a comparatively high salary, and the favorable conditions for graft. And what a pension plan, whoopee."

Citizen: "How do you feel about Civil Rights?"

Mr. Blob: "We ought to stick every nigger back in chains."

Citizen: "What about the poor?"

Mr. Blob: "Castrate 'em."

Citizen: "How 'bout the old and infirm?"

Mr. Blob: "Gas 'em!"

Citizen: "Thank you, Mr. Blob. You got my vote."

"If that don't grab you, how 'bout a war? Try to conduct the festive hostilities under these circumstances: General Fat: "How many troops have you got?"

General Stupid: "Two divisions."

General Fat: "Where are they deployed?"

General Stupid: "Just over yonder hill."

General Fat: "When are you planning to attack?"

General Stupid: "Sunup."

General Fat: "From what direction?"

General Stupid: "From over same mentioned hill."

"This could get almost as insane as war itself."

"Hmmn, you're telling me."

General Stupid: "And what will you do if I do come from over that thar hill at sunup?"

General Fat: "I'm not waiting. I'll attack you just before sunup while you're still bivouacked."

General Stupid: "In that case, I'm going to move my troops from that thar dang hill."

General Fat: "Well, so am I, then."

General Stupid: "Hell, there ain't no point in us being here at all then if we're gonna keep moving our pawns around."

General Fat: "Well, then, let's scram."

General Stupid: "Yeah, let's. I never wanted to come out here in the first place. I left a thriving, black market commissary for this hokey doke."

General Fat: "You're complaining? I left a million dollar dope operation."

"Ridiculous, isn't it?"

"Isn't it."

"If things were so, there might not necessarily be any more sanity in the world, but life would be infinitely more tolerable, for then it would come down to honesty, and hard times vs. dishonesty, and hard times, and the choice there is obvious. Honesty can be fought with, accommodated, wrestled, faced up to, and for all of its hardness, a help, and not a club over the head, because it is straight, and comes at you head on. Dishonesty, on the other hand, is slimy, a wiggly, belly crawler, a cowardly bushwhacker. It sneaks up on you like a thief in the night, and leaves a bad taste in the mouth."

Upon reaching the pad, Bobi stayed in the car, informing me of her departing.

"Okay," I replied agreeably, but did not move. A smile crossed her kind face as she asked if she could give me a lift somewhere. Brusquely, I replied that I wasn't leaving till I got a 'preview of coming attractions.'

"Oh, okay, what did you have in mind?" she answered unhesitatingly.

"Name it."

"Tomorrow night?"

"Done." I got out, closed the door, and then leaned into the window, asking if I were rushing the young lady into anything.

"No," she intoned, much to my satisfaction.

"Fine. I'll see you tomorrow then? What time?"

"Seven?"

"Seven it is. And watch out for falling trees," I advised.

"And the apes in them," she countered, still smiling, and off she scooted.

I repaired to my bunk to snatch twenty winks. No one was about, so I just lay there savoring the moment. To paraphrase an old saying, 'I hadn't felt this good in years. Whatever Bobi had, she had it in spades, and I had just been dealt a royal flush.

Lying there peacefully, our small chat unwittingly began to creep through my mind, specifically the women's bit. I wondered why. I had said all I wished about it, but nevertheless, it kept slogging about. All right, Ratzo, I'll play the game. So with my eyes half closed I rehashed the conversation.

Nothing changed. It kept coming out the same. What did change was my disposition as I was becoming increasingly disturbed at my inability to slam the door on the unwanted guest. I pounded the pillow, hoping somehow that might drive the relentless visitor away, but, like a bad dream, it lingered.

But then suddenly, and without warning, the poison dart shot out of the bush, and into the fleshy rump of the Christian trooper. It wasn't a matter of equality, freedom, brotherhood, justice. No, that was the front, the ploy. It was power! They wanted what men had simply because they had it, and this seemed like a good time to grab it, what with everybody demanding something or other. They wanted to sit in the boardroom, and run the shops, and drive the busses, and kick the football. Yeah, they sure did. Lifebuoy was for their sweaty bodies too, after a hard day at the races.

What is it when someone wants to wear the jock? Equality? Dignity? Freedom from oppression? Not on your tin-type, just a head trip yearning to swing the customary set of hairy balls. They want to screech into the mike also, spread their fuzzy, brazen cheeks, and do their thing, and they would prefer the whole world to watch.

It is often likened to the black movement. Witless lunacy abounds. They own fifty-two percent of the wealth in the richest country in the world, and they're comparing themselves to ex-slaves. Somehow I get the impression there's a distinct difference between Gloria Vanderbilt and Shanika Babutti.

Let us square the circle. A man works to support his wife, gives her a house, car, clothes, food and security, lives in and under the same circumstances as she, and is then, in an epileptic display of ingratitude, accused of oppression. Their fondness of comparing themselves to blacks surpasses insult. No exploited people ever willingly slept with their honky masters. "Darling, am I oppressing you?"

"Yeah! Keep pumping, tiger!" Gloria Steinem, I love you … whoever you are.

Freud was right. Mankind is a cluster of sickly, sexual fantasies disguised as moral indignation. Scratch a monk, and you'll find a pervert.

I was still lying there when Rick returned from a hard day's work at the fish house. He flung his jacket on a nearby chair and flopped on his bunk, complaining, "Jesus, I'm beginning to think you're right. Here I am busting my ass and I ain't any better off than you are."

"Well now, Rick, me boy, that all depends where one's sitting. To the poor, Robin Hood was Robin Hood, but to the rich he was Robin, "the Hood.""

"Hah! Yeah! Good. That may be so, but I'm beginning to get the feeling the closest I'm ever going to get to the castle is the moat."

"So what? There's nothing there but dungeons, half-witted jesters, and bald headed queens. And besides, somebody's got to do the dirty work. Just think, because of guys like you, others can buy yachts and Lear jets. You're a patriot, man, a patriot. You belong on Bunker Hill, or a hill of beans, take your pick. Sing out, brother: Hallelujah, I'm a bum!!""

"You're hilarious. You belong on the stage. And you'd make a better target up there."

"Aw, hell, Rick, don't take it so hard. Some day you might become T-H-E big fish."

Rick sat up on his bunk and began removing his clothes in preparation of a much needed bathing. "John," he said reflectively, "tell me something."

"Fire away, sweet cakes."

"Have you got any ambition at all? I mean any? Any at all? What do you really want to do with your life? Isn't there something besides just, just, nothing? You know, don't you ever yearn for something better, to be somebody?"

"Hell, yes, jelly bun."

"What?"

"What?"

"Yeah, what?" I thought for a moment, stretched out, folded my hands behind my head, stared up at the ceiling thinking, and then with all the solemnity of a Muslim bowing to the east, answered: "The bank, Rick."

"The bank?"

"Yeah, I want to break the bank. That's my big dream, my one overwhelming, consuming passion. Break the bank … or rob it." Rick grabbed a towel, slipped into a pair of thongs, and responded thusly: "You're fucking hopeless," then took to separate himself from 'Charlie the Tuna.'

It rained the next day, so I went to Rita's.

"Hi, stranger," she greeted. "Long time, no see."

"Eh, you know. Over here, over there. A little of this, a little of that."

"I'll bet. Found yourself a little chippy, hey?"

"And you think this is my swan song?"

"Quack, quack."

"Hah! You're funny. And when the love-bug bites you'll be the first to know."

"Yeah, there's some things you just can't keep from your best friends."

The hi-fi was blurting out a cacophony of grating guitar music. Sounding, more and more, like a belch from Moby Dick, I had to put a stop to it. "Say, love," I said kindly enough, "ain't you got anything but that screechy, screechy crap? You're making a reactionary out of me."

"Oh, I thought you were a music lover."

I gave a disheartening look. "Go wash your mouth out with soap. You call that music? You're ready then, to call the church holy."

"All right, all right, I'm changing, I'm changing," thereupon replacing the cardboard crocodiles with an Errol Garner.

"Why, you son-of-a-gun!" I exclaimed happily. "I didn't know you knew."

"What do you think I am a hermit or something? He's not all that anonymous."

"But only to the chosen few."

We sat around for an hour talking, laughing, joking; doing those little things life was meant for, then we moseyed on into the bedroom. To some, that's the biggest joke of all.

Rita kept getting better and better. I wondered if it had anything to do with rhythm. No, it couldn't have. It must be a love, of sorts. I was good for Rita, Rita was good for me. Isn't life grand?

She and I wrestled mightily that afternoon. She climbed on me awhile, then I on her. We did a few things which fail description. Actually it's not so much description, but there are some positions humorous to the touch, whereby sex ceases to be sex, and drifts instead into theater, vaudeville, a comic opera.

We hit the high C's that day. Yes, it was a real curtain-raiser. As I lay there vacillating between the joyful and the sublime, "the play" kept intruding upon my delights as visions of "Hamlet" kept dancing through my head, and when, in all its rhapsodic abundance the great climactic moment arrived, I expeditiously rolled on top of my paramour, and briskly announced, "Rita! Rita!" To wit she ecstatically replied, "Yes! Yes!"

"Tis a far, far, better thing I do now, than I have ever done." Boom!!!

* * *

X

THERE ONCE WAS A DUMB LITTLE CROW
WHO SAT ATOP A BIG TREE.
HE CHIRPED, AND HE CHIRPED, AND HE CHIRPED
WHEN A WICKED OLD BOY WITH A BOW
CAME BY AND BLEW HIM AWAY.

NOT so very long ago, Richard Nixon was elected President … for the second time. "Impossible, you say, Richard Nixon?"

Yes Virginia, Tricky Dick. But then, this is America. America? Yes, America. Only in America.

He said he had a plan to end the war. Now we know what that plan was—bomb Cambodia. Some plan. Some engineer. I wonder, if he was Lincoln's Grant would this now be called the United States of the Confederacy and would Jefferson Davis be sitting in the Lincoln memorial and Lee in Grants tomb.

Kissinger is the Secretary of State. My God. From Bundy, and Rostow, and McNamara, to Nixon and Kissinger. In no other profession does the peter principal work so well. One can only wonder what things will be like in another fifty, short years, or so. The world has truly gone mad.

The other day, the Supreme Court legalized abortion. The next day, the so-called 'Right to Lifers' began planning protests and demonstrations. Such misguided morality. I have yet to see any of them protesting child poverty. Such concern for the fetus, and none for the living, breathing born.

Ah, my dear, nothing is as sickening as the feigned, fatuous morality of the immoral, not to mention the overwhelming stupidity. They liken a ten-second-old fetus to a born person. They say it is a human being. And my grandmother's a cantaloupe.

Imagine, you can't see it without a microscope, and they're calling it a human being, so therefore, abortion is murder. Murder, mind you. Equating a micro-scopic, wiggly zygote swooshing up the 'love canal' to a human being.

Did you ever grow tomatoes? When the buds first start to appear, try putting them in a basket, and carting them off to market to be sold as tomatoes. The boys in the white suits would cart you off in that same basket. So much for the logic of Christian morality, or the morality of Christian logic. Same, same. It never ends.

There also came to live in this establishment, a student, one, Martin Q. Wellington. I had a short conversation with him once. In a fit of conviviality, I asked if he was related to the duke. "What duke?" he replied. Like I said, we had a very short conversation once. So much for higher learning, and in that same vein, I mentioned as how I thought it stunk, and it could very well be a wasted four years. He said, "Everybody has to get an education." I said, "You mean degree?" He said, "It seems like such a small price to pay." I said, "That's what Judas might have said upon being handed the thirty pieces of silver." Martin and me, we had a very short conversation, once.

I rarely ever saw him again. America, in her redundant quest for the 'good life,' has become a nation of 'brief encounters.'

Africa. Have you noticed lately? On a continent of four hundred million, black inhabitants, Tarzan is white. As a matter of fact, the only brown fellow in this frolicking, super foursome is---the monkey.

* * *

Bobi, true to her word, showed up at seven. I was putting on the finishing touches when I heard pleasant, lilting sounds wafting in the breeze.

"Anybody home?"

"Down here," I called out, my heart skipping a beat.

She came in wearing a powder blue, mini, and a green, silky blouse. It was times like these that I became awed of the supernatural. Truly, I believe, she was sent by the gods. Miraculously can it make the cynical humble, for amidst all the stupid, nonsensical and insensate hoopla, arrives an angel, an impossible poem of beauty direct from the heavens. The blood alternates ecstatically between wild gushes, and total repose. I took a deep breath and skipped the next as my heart paused tranquilly for a brief, enchanting moment. I looked straight into her beautifully expressive almond-shaped eyes and cooed, "If beauty can kill I don't think I have long to live."

"You like pretty girls?" she asked coyly.

"It sure beats wilting rose petals."

"Don't tell it to the bees."

"The bees? Hell, I'd trample through a whole damn nest of the bungy stingers just to get one, small glimpse of you. And I do believe I'm making a fool of myself."

"That's all right; I like it."

"So, I should say up front that I have one incurable weakness I think you should be aware of, one thing that tugs, and pushes, and runs me on, and drags me about like a dog in heat, and it is, my pet—B-E-A-U-T-Y. When it is in the neighborhood I drift in a perpetual state of excitation, become very tense, and cannot be said to be myself. And be advised, when is said condition, am good for nothing."

"Nothing?"

"Let's not be literate."

"Good enough, for the time being," she acknowledged.

"C'mon over here," I requested easily. "I want you to meet the "chicken of the sea.""

"I heard that," Rick drawled. He was lying on his bunk 'reading' a Playboy. How anybody can be so relaxed around such radiant magnificence behooves me, but there it is. The world is not a precision instrument.

In exaggerated formality, I said, "Bobi, this blond Adonis, lying on his wherewithal, is none other than his eminence, Rick Van Winninger, the baron of East Tulsa. Your highness, this is Roberta Higgins, and a finer piece of machinery the Swiss never built."

Rick raised up, saying, "Pleased to meet you, ma'am." Bobi, playing it for all it was worth, extended a well manicured hand, and replied, "Likewise, Mr. Rick."

Glancing first at her, then him, then her again, I proudly announced with the ring of the Marseille in my voice, "Casablanca will never die."

"Miss Higgins," Rick advised, "I believe I must warn you, as a friend, before it gets to the point of no return, Mr. Jack does not believe in gainful employment, to put it mildly."

"Rick," I informed brazenly, "you need a bath. You're beginning to stink." And Bobi added as how she knew all about my idiosyncrasies. "You do?" he answered surprisedly. "It's gone that far already, has it? It's only been four days."

"John is an honest sort."

"And poor."

"Rick, lie down and finish your 'reading,' and I hope you gag on 'Miss April.' Let's go, Bob." As we turned to leave, she, in her pleasant way, said something about how nice it was to meet Rick, and I countered with, "You haven't set long enough, or you wouldn't be advancing such silly notions for all the world to see." Rick put forth a distinctly audible raspberry, and on that high note, we departed.

As we strolled toward the car, it occurred to me that I did not know where my newly found friend resided, so I asked.

"On Maple," was her reply.

"Maple!" I exclaimed incredulously.

"Yes, but I had no idea the word affected you so, or is it the tree?"

"Word. Tree. Hell, I didn't know teachers made that kind of swag. That area veritably stinks of aristocracy. Those pads must run about four-fifty and up."

"No and yes."

"Come again?"

"No, we don't make that kind of swag, and yes, they do run about four-fifty, but I have a rich father."

"A-hah! I knew there was a trap door in this castle."

"What did I say?"

"Your compadre has pesos, lots of pesos."

"What's wrong with that?"

"You led me to believe you were just a poor, little ol', ordinary middle-class working stiff."

"I never did," she rebutted, a bit miffed. And in my best Stan Laurel, countered, "You certainly did, uu, uu, uu."

As we drove, I asked, as a matter of conversation, where we were headed, or was our destination 'a secret.'

"You're being kidnapped," she answered, "but you may ask."

"And you don't even have a gun, and where are we going?"

"Have you eaten?"

"When?"

"Recently?"

"How recent?"

"Within the last four or five hours?"

"No."

"Did you plan it that way?"

"When one is tapped out plans are what engineers use to build bridges."

"You don't mind dutching it, do you?"

"If I did, we'd have to settle for a Big Mac and fries."

"Good, then. I know a quaint little place where we can get a good meal."

"And then what?"

"Then we pay the bill, or wash dishes."

I looked at her affectionately, not believing I was really sitting next to this marvelous creation from the heavens, and said, "You're beautiful; you are really and truly beautiful. How old are you? How come you're not married? There isn't something wrong with you, is there?"

"My, my, but don't we have the questions tonight. Yes, I am truly beautiful. I am twenty-seven years old. I'm not married, because I haven't met a man yet. And it seems to me there's something wrong with everybody."

"Oh, oh, I think I'm riding with a radical. You're not a fire breathing radical, are you?"

"No, but I'm getting close. I can feel myself slipping e-e-e-ver so slowly. I like to think all that's not necessary in this day, but I'm not so sure anymore."

"Well, well, well, I struck gold; a thinking woman. And I know what you mean. I get the feeling sometimes the world is the cesspool of the universe, and America's a giant commode."

We stopped for a light and I leaned back, asking, "Well, what do we do after eats?"

"I'm a democratic person. You tell me. What do you want to do?"

"What do you want to do?"

"What do you want to do?"

"Uh, huh. Do you think we can get on Laugh-In with this routine?"

"I think we'd be laughed out of Laugh-in with this routine."

"I think you're right. So, how do we break the impasse?"

"Do you like movies?"

"Well, the last piece of crap I saw was the aforementioned 'Love Story,' and not much of that, thankfully. So, I haven't seen one in quite a while. Trash belongs in the dump, not up on the big screen. And I can't stand to see people getting rich because the public has the herd instinct."

"Herd instinct?"

"Yeah, they flock to all things new and blue, like the lemmings rushing out to sea. The movie folk get some young tramp with the brain of a bed bug, flash her scungy rump across the screen a couple times, pop her in the sack with her legs spread, and say, 'Look, folks, this is art. Two bucks, please.' Such explicit goings on have absolutely no relation to art, and art, if it is anything, is the exercise of the imagination. There is nothing left to imagine when I can count the hairs. All that remains are the oogles."

"But what if it is part of the story?"

"It is not necessary for the camera to zoom in on the 'he' wrapped about the 'she' with her hump flashing in the breeze. It is not necessary to record, each and every mole on her derriere, and it is not necessary to drag it out like a bad play trying to hit Broadway. I am not an ignoramus. I can appreciate a good performance as well as anyone, but I don't like my intelligence insulted, and I don't like to be put upon. When I feel myself getting nauseated I know something's wrong, and what sickens me most is the shoddy game the moguls are playing. I'll not stand in line to see garbage so some half-assed director and a soft-assed producer can live in Beverly Hills. They can kiss my ass. If the faggoty bastards want to live like kings, let them make war like kings."

"Well, if that's the case, we may have a hard time finding something to see."

"I'd just as soon gaze at you all night."

"Let's see if we can find a flick first." Slumping in my seat, I feigned disappointment. "Drats." I moaned. "Foiled again."

We drove a short while silently when Bobi asked what kind of movies I DID like, anything in particular, or so.

"Good ones," I replied curtly.

"Can you expound on that a little?" she requested. I drummed the forefinger of my left hand on my lip, and remarked, "Okay, let me see … oh yeah, 'The Train.' How bout that one? Did you ever see "The Train?"

"You mean the one with Burt Lancaster?"

"Yeah, that's the one."

"Yes, come to think of it; I did like it."

"But didn't you think there was something special about it? I mean, well, I thought it was kind of a little masterpiece."

"Oh? How so?"

"Well, the acting, for one. Burt played a good part, and he usually does if he can keep the toothy grin and the acrobatics to a minimum. And Paul Scofield, great, great, just a magnificent talent. But you know, there was someone else, I forget his name. He played the German major who kept trying to tell Paul Scofield it was hopeless. It wasn't much of a part, as parts go, but I thought he kind of did a splendid job, just splendid; could even say he stole the show."

"I don't think I remember."

"Anyway, the secret of the whole thing was simplicity, a straight-forward clarity in the midst of ordered insanity and disintegration. You hep to it?"

"I'm not sure. Can you explain a bit more?"

"Okay. It was a simple story, simply told. Singular, literate, and believable, therefore honest. No B.S.; it held your attention because events followed smoothly and logically. It was well put together, and it made sense, and the key to it all was the pace. It didn't drag. It moved straight to the conclusion. There wasn't any real deep significance to it, as simplicity has its own significance, but it was well done, very well done, and when you left the theater you got the feeling you weren't ripped off, you know? Everything fit, everything, the acting, the direction, the plot, the mood it conveyed, and all done in black and white. It took a small bit of genius to throw in that little ditty what with it taking place in grimy, railroad yards and all. It lent itself to realism, and give it a sort of quaint nostalgic kind of quality. And, like Zapata, everything just kind of fit in place.

And the editing, that's where it's really at, the editing. If you don't know how to splice the damn thing, then you ain't got nothing but Buster Crabbe swinging on a vine. Yeah, I'd say I got my two-bits worth."

"That's a big thing, is it? Not getting ripped off?"

"Indubitably. If a body can't make it in this dreary bog, he ought to have the decency to cap it with a quick bullet to the head, or a neat slice at the wrists. One shouldn't have to involve others with their diseased constitution. Another's malady shouldn't have to be mine. Let us all decline and fall of our own. 'Labiche, do you know what you've done? This very minute can you tell me why you did it? Have you any idea? Of course not. These paintings mean as much to you as a string of pearls to an ape. You don't know a Rembrandt from a doodle. You're nothing, a lump of clay, a piece of flesh. You've won, but you don't know what.' Rat, tat, tat, tat, tat! Beautiful; magnificent. And what else is there?"

"Good point."

"Yes, Bobi, one should learn to appreciate art wherever he can find it. It's the song that makes the day."

"I'll drink to that."

"And yet there's so little of it."

"Well I already know you're not one of those 'beauty is in the eye of the beholder' kind of guys."

"Hardly, and because, my sweet, it is an impassable stream. A cop out. The forerunner of lazy thinking and maudlin feelings. Life is too short to waste it wallowing in easy lies, which is why I liked 'The Train.' It looked me in the eye and said, 'Not Shakespeare, but an honest effort.' Escapist? Not really; but enjoyable, you know? As from afar? It didn't demand much in the way of analysis, but life is not a compilation of mathematical computations anyway. There's something to be said for having a good time, and the bad guy got it in the end. It was so damned adult in a frigging world of witless juveniles.

"You're right. People don't have good times like they used to. It seems there's just too much to worry about."

"Not really. Except for the bomb, things aren't all that different, just a little more hectic. People still live lives of quiet desperation, only now there's a band playing in the background. Of course, though, communication being what it is today, a tramp can't hardly pee in an alley anymore without it being televised coast to coast. Fifty years ago some old hag would have doused him with cold water, or hot, depending on her particular inclination, and that would have been the end of it.

"But you must admit the complexities of the times has changed things."

"Yes, and invariably for the worse. Too much, too soon. The species has no time to adjust. We're a mixed bag in the best of times, but now? Hell, our neck is in the noose."

"All that bad?"

"What we've done in thirty years, no one has done in one-thousand-thirty years, no one."

"So, who's to blame?"

"A moot point; no one and everyone. We are a cloth coat that has seen a better day, and until we can strengthen the cord that binds we will always be 'brother ape,' the beast in the black dinner jacket, the near-miss of all time."

"Eee gads, where does it all end?"

"It doesn't. Take the war, for instance. Any one will do, but this one is such a handy hook, so recent, and it has all the earmarks of a Mongol creation. The Thirteenth Century revisited. Genghis Kahn in combat boots and khaki brown.

And what do we see beyond the rudimentary, the little black box with the numbered balls? With the vision of two-hundred years hence, we see … a war? No, that was the least of it, merely the battleground of infirmity, the weakness of the monkey jungle. Then why? Why this travesty of paranoia; this vertiginous exercise into the darkest recesses of the bestial soul? Invade a country most people know absolutely nothing about? And methodically, with malice afore-thought, proceed to burn, decimate, totally destroy and level a land that has stood for centuries? As a matter of fact, most people didn't even know there was such a place. Ten years ago, if you had stopped someone in the street, anyone, and asked, 'Sir, where is Viet Nam?' the reply would probably have been, 'near Philadelphia?' Yet we can mobilize millions toward the destruction of that same nation merely by uttering one word: Communism, and they come right out of their trees. Were it they so 'patriotic' against the forces of ignorance, prejudice, poverty, and disease."

"Were it."

"And the peculiar thing is, what the folk know about that obdurate little ideology, they know from the newspapers and the oogle tube—so much for education---yet they're ready to kill all the 'little, brown bastards' if the man in the big white house says so.

Sad? That's a start. Also downright depressing, grown men and women rushing to mass slaughter at the sound of a hoop and a holler. Grownups, mind you, not children, but grown men and women, big boys and girls, ready, willing, and able to kill because someone, a stranger really, has said, 'It's your duty!' Horrifying. Adults, having no more sense, or critical faculty, than a colony of coo, coo ants.

Embarrassing. Somebody says to me, 'Kill!' I say, 'Why?' He says, pointing, 'Red, red,' and I, with no more thought about it than going down to the corner store to get a ten-cent cigar, say, 'Da, da.' Talk about brainwashing. Christ, it must have been invented on Pennsylvania Avenue. That's manipulation, grown men and women thinking no more about killing than, 'Oh well, he told me.' Grown-ups, adults. It's diabolical. I wonder, if the word 'communist' was absent, would we have lacked our enthusiasm? Can people fight without labels to moti-vate them to hate? What could we have done, call them the 'other guys?' The 'bad guys?' The 'foreign guys?' No, that's too common. We need something like 'communism!' it has a ring to it. All ism's have a certain flare. Communism! Eyah! Kill! Kill! Kill! Uga, bungs, bunga.

Ah, it's straight out of the bush. A word; for a small, simple word, a country went to war. Sweet Jesus, you fool. Did you really think you could save the world with the ritual of death? Not only did you fail to save it, you failed to identify it. All good men die in vain; all bad, too late. Words, language. We're fighting a war for a word."

"Not a very pretty picture."

"You won't find it hanging in the Louvre. And before that it was freedom, and before that the Kaiser, and before that Napoleon, and before that George III, and before that, and before that, and before. We fight wars on a whim and a word. We live and die with the word. There'd never be a war, were we a world of mutes."

"Mutes?"

"It's the clamor in war that holds its fascination."

"I don't believe the linguists consider themselves the cause of war."

"Somehow, through a flaw in evolution, we have learned to speak before learning to see. Have you noticed we are the only animal that has constructed a highly complex set of communicable symbols? That has escaped us. An ape like Goebbels could have taught a communications course at Harvard. And Herr Adolf. Can you think of anyone who could master the varied uses of language any better?"

"The Nazis fascinate you?"

"In a ghoulish sort of way. They are, and remain, our linchpin to the dinosaur."

"A chain, I take it, minus any broken links."

"Not even a rust spot."

"It is safe to assume then, an absence of meaning … of any kind."

"Safe? As a wrinkly, old, naked, skinny nun in a sissy, French monastery.

"I see. And any special reason why?"

"For the same reason I can't believe in Superman."

"Some people do."

"And you ask about meaning?"

We drove on slowly, quietly, for two blocks when I interrupted the soothing silence with, "Did you ever shoot craps?"

"No," she replied quizzically, no doubt wondering where this new excursion into the briar patch would lead.

"The odds on the deuce is thirty-six to one, exactly. You don't see too many shooters laying on the deuce, or box-cars for that matter, which is the same, not all that high, yet they lay off like its leprosy. They don't like the odds. Yet the odds of their being some purpose, any purpose, could be say, thirty-six million to one, or so, conservatively speaking. So, I won't bet a thirty-six to one shot, and you're saying bet a thirty-six million to one shot?"

"There is the one."

"Bobi, Bobi, Bobi, now you sound like the cracker playing the lottery."

"What's he say?"

"Somebody has to win."

"Isn't it so?"

"Sure."

"So?"

"BUT NOT HIM!"

"You got me."

"A carwash," I mumbled to myself.

"I didn't hear that," she stated curtly.

"A car wash," I repeated, this time more clearly. "Yeah, that's it."

"What is?"

"I'm convinced there's a giant, invisible, brainwashing machine somewhere in … in … in Kansas City, that everyone, very early in life, passes through like a carwash. That's it, by God, a carwash, a colossal, mind-cleaning machine."

Eventually we reached our destination, a little hideaway place called "The Roaring Fifties." The owner must have had a quaint, sense of humor. One could laugh himself into quite an appetite at "The Roaring Fifties." It could have been called many things, 'roaring' was not one of them.

As we entered I was happy to find it smelled like food cooking, and not Pine-Sol. Candles, also, were missing from the tables. Already I liked the joint.

A short, paunchy little fellow sauntered over and in a somewhat effeminate French accent greeted himself to Bobi. Apparently she was a steady customer. She smiled, nodded, and the little man showed us to a table in a corner. As we sat I asked quizzically if he was really French.

"Yes, he really is," she replied.

"My, my, how 'bout that; a real, live French waiter. I like foreigners. They're so un-American. It must be filthy not to be an American"

"Wha-a-a-t?"

"Sure. What's the point in having a carwash if you're not going to use it? Remember? Big giant? Kansas City? Do you think we're the cleanest folk on earth?"

"I don't know. We'd have to see who has the biggest carwash."

"I may be mistaken, but I think we invented the carwash."

"Didn't we invent everything?"

Yes, sir, buck, Bobi knew how to play the game. "I think we invented the Russian's," I retorted whimsically. "They seem like such a handy bunch to push around; so foreign, so eastern, so primitive. But the double-dealing Cossacks had the audacity to go and invent or steal the bomb themselves. Can't even trust your own inventions, as Dr. Frankenstein proved."

"I do believe that was fiction."

"Yeah?" I questioned.

"You don't think so?"

"Maybe the name, but not the game. Someday we shall own the world, as the worms the soil, and the fishes the ocean, but to own something is not necessarily to control it, as Dr. Frankenstein tragically learned. We shall own it, and we will use it, and abuse it, molest it and trample it, and it will devour us."

Never one to sit down to a heavy meal with a heavy heart, I attempted to strike a path to levity, and so asked in the lightest of veins if my companion of the evening knew how to eat a frog.

"Okay," she played along, "how do you eat a frog?" And with the spirit of the Marquis de Sade floating listlessly overhead, I replied, "put one leg over each ear."

"For heaven's sake."

"I don't believe heaven had anything to do with it."

"No wonder."

"I promise that will be the last of those for the night."

"Let's hope." Frenchy arrived with a salad, and a warm loaf of French bread.

"I don't believe I heard anyone order," I blurted.

"Well, it's like this," Bobi clarified. "We have signals. Do you prefer wine with your meal?"

"Why not?"

"Red, white?"

"Cabernet," I intoned, and turning to Frenchy, added, "California goods. Don't bring none of that damn, French swill. They can't be trusted. I've been hearing nasty stories about them lately. They've never been the same since they burned Joan, you know? Great people, the French. Built a World War I defense, pushed it into World War II, asked America to defend it, and now hate us for doing so. Who was it that said, "Lend a man a buck, and lose a friend?"

"I haven't the faintest."

"No matter; okay?" I didn't know our friendly waiter's name, so I asked Bobi.

"Francois," she informed.

"Okay, Francois, bring us a bottle of your best California Cabernet."

"Oui, Monsieur. Ze wein here ees da best."

"Really? Just bring us something that wasn't made on a tanker."

"Oh, no, Monsieur, no tank sere." And off he pranced gingerly to the pantry.

"He's such a sweet man," Bobi intimated.

"I'll let you know how sweet when he brings the wine."

"By the way, do you think we can find one tonight?"

"Find what?"

"A decent flick."

"We'll see."

"Seen any lately worth two bits?"

"Not in quite a while. How 'bout you?"

"Oh, I find one, now and then, but I'm like you, I get very angry when it turns out to be a bummer. Not so much for the two bits, but simply because I've wasted my time, and disappointment was an added attraction."

"That's a rich gal's attitude if I ever saw one."

"What?"

"The 'I don't mind the two bits' part. What's two bits to a Jane who has a million?"

"I'm not that affluent."

"Just how rich are you? For the record."

"Oh, just plain rich."

"There's no such thing, darling. Scratch is never plain."

"Ordinary rich?"

"That covers a lot of territory, and if you feel uncomfortable about it we can drop it, but I'm not with the I.R.S. if you're wondering."

"I didn't think so. It's just that I … I never really think about it."

"I see. It was always there like mud and cooties in a long war."

"You have a way of turning everything to the negative."

"I've had the best teachers."

"Have you now?"

"Bet on it. Poverty, chicanery, and bad luck."

"Bad luck? Where have you had bad luck?" she questioned, a bit unbelieving.

"My dear sweetheart, I have had the grievous misfortune of being born into a nation of wicked millionaires after the decline and fall of that all-time super fake, Horatio Alger, of whose bastardly spirit has never crossed the path of this weary buck."

"Ahhh, Horatio Alger. You're not a fan, I take it?"

"Fans are what's used for cooling on a hot summer's eve."

"Isn't there anything you believe in?"

"Give me a minute," I requested, and after a momentary pause, she beckoned once again.

"Well?"

"Give me an hour."

"I see."

"Can you give me a day?"

"Take all the time you need. You've answered the question."

"No fair," I objected.

"Now we're talking your game."

"I believe in filthy, drowning wet rats, succulent quails in the roaster, insect sucking spiders, the Easter Bunny, and Mother Goose.

"In other words, nothing."

"In other words, close—but not quite."

"A nihilist. Isn't it a hard way to go?"

"Yes, but would you rather be a pig?"

"A pig? Well, no, I suppose not."

"So, you see? It comes down to hardy, or piggy."

"I hadn't realized the choices were so limited."

"No one ever does until the cataracts are removed. We, all of us, are suffering from the advanced stages of catarractitis."

"Are we now?"

"Look around. Who do you know with two good eyes in his head who would tolerate, but for a moment, twenty-eight years, and counting, of missile buildup, as just a 'minor' case in point?"

"Apparently everyone."

"Ah hah! But I said, 'With two good eyes in his head.' Beware of the burrs in the saddlebags. We build bombs so as not to use bombs. Hel-loooo. 1984? We grow weeds to control weeds when in fact they cannot be controlled any more than a horde of locusts in a wheat field."

"It's worked so far."

"Very good; so far. And how long can you point a loaded gun without firing, even accidentally? I have a thirty, do I hear thirty-five?"

"This is killing my appetite."

"Were it we all so fortunate to lose only an appetite." Again Bobi was right. More and more these days do I tramp about uninvited into the hazy bog of the dark end of men's souls.

"Well," I attempted lightheartedly, "you were saying about rich?"

"Yes, well, my father is a senior vice president for a very large electronics firm up the road a piece."

"Hastings-Brooke?"

"Yes."

"Ho! You are loaded, aren't you. Oo-ee! Are you ever."

"You sound like you just struck oil."

"My apologies, ma'am. Nothing quite so spectacular. It's just that I've never been this close to a fortune before."

"If I didn't know better, I'd think you were after my money." I leaned close, to what I was hoping soon to be my paramour, and whispered, "You don't know yet."

"I think I do."

"It can be awfully tempting, especially to someone like me."

"Someone like you?"

"Oh, yes. I'm capable."

"Somehow, you just don't strike me as the type."

"I wouldn't hesitate for a moment to hook up with someone just for her bread, and not lose one night's sleep over it, either. As a matter of fact, it would probably help it. Of course, the young lady in question would have to be 'tolerable.' I wouldn't want to sacrifice too much for financial security."

"Of course. And you wouldn't feel like you were cheating?"

"Cheating? You've got to be kidding. It's irrelevant, isn't it?"

"Is it?"

"Here, look at it this way. If the mouse in question desires to marry a pauper like me, it would have to be love, obviously. Therefore, she's not losing a bank account, she's gaining a lover, confidante, husband and friend. Now I ask you, in all fairness, is she, or is she not getting her money's worth?"

"Well, aren't you generous?"

"We all have our 'wonderful' side."

"Do we now; and while we're on it, this sounds more like a business deal."

"W-e-e-l-l-l-?"

"That's cynical."

"Oh, my; let's not go down that road again."

"By all means," she agreed with a sigh of relief.

Frenchy returned with the wine, and stood staring with a white towel draped over his arm just like in the movies while I tasted it.

Not paying attention, I put down the beaker, and was about to resume the conversation, when Bobi, more in tune with the proprieties of life as can be expected with one of her upbringing, motioned toward him.

"Oh yeah, sure, great stuff. Fantastic. I can hardly taste the DDT."

"Weech?" he asked puzzledly.

"Don't fret. It's very good," I consoled. He shook his head approvingly, and smiled. "Wud Monsieur like to order now, yes?"

"Wonderful," I agreed. We did, and 'Chevalier' was on his way again. "As I was saying, what kind of flicks do you like?"

"I like the old ones. Bogart's my favorite," she confessed.

"Isn't he everyone's? He wa-a-a-s truly great. Time does tell, doesn't it? Now we know how good he really was, and how good those movies were, you know? Key Largo, The Maltese Falcon, Casablanca, The Treasure of the Sierra Madre, The African Queen, The Caine Mutiny. Those flicks had a certain exquisite professionalism about them approaching immortality. I suppose that's what quality is. Christ, I enjoyed them. I saw The Maltese Falcon nineteen times, and you know who my, favorite of favorites, was?"

"Who?"

"Sydney Greenstreet. I thought he was marvelous, absolutely marvelous. And what a laugh. There's a bird who parlayed a beer-barrel belly, and a staccato laugh into a tidy sum I would imagine. Lo-o-o-ved that laugh. Unique individual. Such a magnificent character, just magnificent."

"I don't recall him that well." Bobi, now, was displaying her youth, if not her charm.

"And how about Basil Rathbone? Never got much of a play, but he was a master, the ideal villain. Ruthless, deceitful, thoroughly corrupt, and with the looks and demeanor to go with it. Totally Machiavellian. He should have gotten some kind of an award for 'Zorro.' That should tell you something about awards. I don't think he even got a nomination. I never miss a Sherlock Holmes. If ever there had been a Holmes, he most certainly would have carried on like 'old Basil.' It's too bad. One never realizes how good they really were until they're gone and one starts comparing them with what's dancing about now, in and out of bedrooms."

"You don't think there are any good actors around today?"

"Oh, yeah, there are some good actors, real good, but there's something missing, a certain … I don't know … a certain flair. For all their talent they remind me of hollow drums. One could never accuse Sydney of being a hollow drum, could one?"

"No, one surely couldn't."

"And how 'bout Edward G.? Never really got the recognition he deserved, either, I don't think."

"He was about as famous as one can get."

"Yeah, true enough, and the bread was there, but recognition, that's a bit different. For instance, one of the best acting jobs I ever saw was his performance in 'The Sea Wolf.' I thought I W-A-S watching 'Wolf Larsen,' know what I mean? It was done so damn well, and yet, what the hell, not so much as a sniff. That's downright conniving. And Key Largo. For God's sake, that's acting. Can you think of anybody at all playing that part just like that? Perfection, just damned perfect. He, by his professional and artistic presence, C-R-E-A-T-E-D Johnny Rocco. Ya hep to it?"

"Well, I can't really say. I don't believe I've had the pleasure."

"Are you putting me on? Everybody's seen 'Key Largo' even Jose Feliciano."

"Well, I'm sorry to disappoint you."

Frenchy brought our goodies, prime rib, and we ate quietly for the most part, I, thinking what it must have been like in Neanderthal times for no special reason.

Bobi paid the damage. I left the tip, four bucks. I know Buck; kind of steep for the times, but, when somebody waits' on you, and cleans your house, and your clothes, and your car, and your dirty-assed crappy kids, respect it, always respect those doing the 'dirty work.' There's a reason it's called dirty.

The film we finally decided upon was "Who's Afraid of Virginia Woolf." As it turned out, no one, but we had a good time. The spectacle of a somewhat rotund Elizabeth Taylor 'bronco riding' Richard Burton was a throwback to Roman times. Our two bucks was well spent.

We bought a bag of popcorn (Bobi bought a bag of popcorn), and we munched greasy-fingered like two poverty stricken urchins on a Saturday afternoon spree.

As we sat there impatiently watching some inane, short subject concerning the opulent cavorting in Bermuda, I thought of the cheap trick the business community had once tried to play on the public, and for a time succeeded, said trick involving subliminal advertising. The word "popcorn" and "candy" would flash across the screen faster than the human eye could detect, but not so fast as to prevent it from being recorded in the mind nevertheless. At opportune moments, like say, in between flicks, the management would run its shoddy game on the unsuspecting audience, and before you knew it, voila, like a herd of enraged bull elephants, everyone would immediately jump up and charge the goody counter.

And they say we're free? Eventually, the California Supreme Court got around to outlawing such trickery, I think, and as I recall, there were some rumblings about prohibiting freedom, but not much. Even the best of the 'pocket' lawyers would have had to wear masks to plead the first amendment on that one.

After the theatrics, we stopped for a drink or two, again at the pleasure of Miss Higgins. I sat twirling my ice, gazing fascinated at the most exquisite face I had ever seen.

"You're staring," she said.

"I sure am," I answered, "and don't care one bit. I was just thinking. Right now the cruelest thing in this world I can think of is to be blind. There really is something to beauty besides beauty."

"There really is something to beauty besides beauty," she repeated. "Please to explain."

"Well, there is beauty, you know, the ordinary kind, the kind any one-eyed Jack can spot, and which loll about the landscape like hot lava around a volcano, and then there's the kind that transcends sight, hauntingly spectacular, and which seems to thrive on itself, like you."

"Uh, oh."

"Oh, no, this ain't no line, believe me. It would be too corny, even for Nashville."

"But nobody's that good."

"Hah, you say. I am extraordinarily taken by great beauty. It whips me around like a dog a rag doll. It is very hard to explain, but am, nevertheless, compulsively attracted to it. I sense a certain pattern of perfection, a sleek maturity ripened to an unblemished standard of refined harmony. Not of this world, yet in it. It is the apparition of the supernatural: celestial, hollowed and divine. That's it. You, my lovely cake of inspiration, are divine." I raised my glass and toasted: "To divinity; may she reign supreme, and never taint." Bobi flushed ever so slightly. She had an inimitable earthiness hard for me to identify with riches.

"You know," she said, changing the subject, "you laughed all through that movie. As a matter of fact, you were the only one laughing. It wasn't supposed to be a comedy, I don't think."

"Yeah, I guess, but what the hell, I find it hard to take such folk serious. After all, if you take a good hard look, they've got the world by the whatsa. I can't get all choked up over their kinds of problems. I haven't had that kind of life."

"Money and position isn't everything."

"No doubt, but give me twenty yards in the hundred-yard dash and you couldn't catch me with a greyhound."

"Twenty yards is a pretty good spot."

"Tell me about it. Actually, I didn't really know what the hell was going on right up until the end, but it sure was funny."

"I enjoyed it, too, in a way. I suppose interesting is the word."

"I guess you could say that. And again, isn't it the way?"

"What?"

"Like gold dust, it's the little things in life that count."

"I'd like to have a brick or two."

"From you! Now that sure brings me back down to earth."

We stayed a while listening to a small combo playing something that can best be described as a strange combination of calypso, progressive jazz, and high western, then left.

I knew Bobi had to toil the next day, so I instructed as we got in the car,

"Take me back. You're a working girl, and we'll do this again sometime, very soon. Yes?" She smiled, and to my great pleasure and relief, said the one little word I wished to hear more than any other: "Okay."

I lay back in my seat saying to that almighty being of beings, "Oh, great God of gods, your smile, every now and then, lights upon even this dreary soul. Thank you for sending this angel to me. I will ask not again. My cup runneth over. Henceforth, I will doubt only occasionally, and even then somewhat grudgingly."

Bobi, no doubt, never hearing a prayer quite so dissentient, asked if I customarily spoke to the Almighty in such 'glowing' terms.

"Yeah," I affirmed, "you have to humor him sometimes. He's insecure, and insecurity breeds disaffection, and such a contrary dolt is liable to do most anything if you don't scratch him just so, and I don't wish to offend him any more than I have to."

"But aren't you afraid he'll cast you to the demons?" (Old thinking dies hard).

"Hardly. You see, He knows I'm quite miserable where I am, and he'd never chance the possibility of my getting along with any devils. He courts a spiteful streak, and would never give them, or me, that satisfaction. Yes, he's quite content to let the relationship dangle, as is. I'm sufficiently discontented, and he obtains equally sufficient joy from it. We feed each other's sickness."

"I don't believe I've heard quite a … a, secular interpretation of the Almighty before."

"Yeah, well … it's all a lot of nothing, really. We're so far from knowing the unknowable it's … it's … just so far, far, away. Light years, light years; and yet we persist in our sick, sick, mindless, cowardly superstitions. We'll go to war for God, but never learned to live in peace with the guy next door."

"Are you an atheist?"

"I don't know. All I do know is that it's not what the Christians, or the Muslims, or the Jews, or the whoever's say it is; they're not even close. No organization what carried on a 'holy' war for 200 years, killing some 200,000 people in the twelfth and thirteenth centuries, is going to tell me what 'moral' is, NOT IN THIS WORLD, or that I can go to hell because I don't believe in the same bigoted crap he does, or who put Galileo in a dungeon for 19 years for expressing what turned out to be the truth all along, is certainly not going to tell me what God is. Hah; not on a bet. Or some stupid friggin broad on the boob tube, who rakes in millions preaching 'the Christian life,' while living like the Queen of England, is not exactly where I'd go for philosophical discussion."

"Well, then, if you're not an atheist. . . . ."

"I didn't exactly say that, either."

"You're going to have to make up your mind."

"Who says?"

"You're dithering. And I think you're awful close, and if you are, then why, exactly?"

"It's not so much that I'm an atheist, as such; it's just that I don't believe in him."

"And why not?"

"Why not? Well to be serious; what's He done lately? I can't even prove he had a hand in sending you to the same party, on the same night, in the same place, a place among millions of places. It would take a million dollar trial with the ten best lawyers and a jury of legal, religious, and philosophical geniuses, all with ESP, and still end up with a hung jury. Now I'm not saying he's not there, I'm just saying I don't believe in him no more than I believe in the President of the United States. He's there, too, but I damn sure don't believe in him, if you get my drift. He also gives me little reason to. C-A-N you? Do Y-O-U believe in that rats-ass, Nixon?"

Bobi seemed interested and willing to continue. "All right," she said, "can I play devil's advocate for a moment?"

"Honey, if you're little devilee's helper, I'm volunteering for hell raht now even being of the opinion it could be a mite crowded down there, disliking as I do, crowded places."

"You do have a set of opinions."

"Ah, my sweet, opinions are like assholes. Everyone has one, and they all stink."

"O-h-h-h, good lord."

"Let's get on with it. I believe it is all a matter of question, yes? That is always the problem. Either we don't know it, or we forget it all too soon, and when we remember it, we care not to, and when we do care, we can't answer it, and when we can answer it, it is the wrong one, and when it is the right one, it matters not."

"The question then becomes, how can one believe, yet not believe?"

"Very good. Much like the first shall be last, and the last shall be first. Everyone walks in arrears."

"Arrears?"

"Or backwards, if you will."

"Backwards?"

"Yes, backwards. One has to be backward to fall for such hog swill. As for part A of the question, how can one believe yet not have faith, as with the President, the Congress, the church, the law, the schools, the whole shmear, ad infinitum, ad nauseum. They're all there, all right, or nearly so anyway, but they all function terribly, to give them their best. As for God, well, God, for me, is a 'head scratcher.' It's out there sure, but crazy as hell to think one can make any sense of it. Accept it for what it is---a mystery, and think as hard as you damn well please about it, but be honest; be honest; B-E H-O-N-E-S-T!!

Can you tell me what things will be like a thousand years from now? Two-thousand? Two-million? You'd have more luck with those wild excursions into 'the land of universal nullity,' than you'd have trying to get within a gazillion light-years of the "god illusion."

"So, you don't believe in him at all then?"

"I believe we're going in circles, which is exactly the point."

"I think I'm beginning to catch on to your way of thinking; to be redundant, to be pointless, is not necessary pointless."

"Bravisimo. I couldn't have said it better." I paused momentarily, then continued. "My dear, I'm afraid Ziggy was right. Civilizations are judged by the quality of their illusions, and if that be so, then sadly, we remain somewhere in the vicinity of 4000 BC, give or take a century, or two.

Did you ever wonder what ancient times would have been like with all the gadgets of today? Not too different. Pain, disease, ignorance, and death remain intact, and depravity, as always, would run amuck. Throughout the years, the yesterdays, today's, and tomorrows, it is the one ever-present, changeless cargo. We have even become fond of it, and having turned the world upside down with it, we praise God for it. Hallelujah!

You see, Bobi … for sure, God, if anything at all, is most certainly not some kind of super human person with the same faults and attributes of men. That w-o-u-l-d be the worst of all possible worlds; and for one of such little faith, I have faith where it counts, so I don't have to get on my knees like some witless moron and mutter incoherently to the four winds. God is not a person, super or otherwise; that much I do know."

"Could be."

"And it's going to be a long, long, long time before we know any more than that."

"Could be."

"I think you're stuck in neutral."

"Could be."

"You a-r-r-r-e a funny girl."

"Could be."

"You know? I'm positive I love you … AND DON'T SAY IT.

"I'm all out of "could be's."

"Thank you, Lord. And you know what just came to mind?

"I couldn't even begin. . . . ."

"Tortures."

"Tortures?"

"Yeah, tortures. Maybe it was the "could be's?"

"Could be. Okay, I'll play; what about tortures?"

" It just occurred to me how ingeniously creative we can be with the subject of pain and suffering."

"You won't get an argument there."

"And it's not confined to any particular corner of the globe, either. Just about everyone has had a finger in the soup at one time or another."

"Do tell."

"I shall. And it can be a real bloody Mary; a religious experience.

"It can? And would you include it in the curriculum?"

"Right after prayers."

"And are there any you are especially fond of?"

"But of course. Everyone has their little favorites, you know. They should be on bubble-gum cards."

"Which … which pain you the most? If you'll pardon the expression."

"Getting in the mood, are ya? Okay, try on this little ditty cooked up by the venerable of the east, the Chinese, and particularly gruesome and captivating.

"It is?"

"Yeah, they would take a tin box, so big (spreading my hands six inches, or so), and cut out one side and then go and find themselves a huge, voracious, starving, sharp-toothed sewer rat, and place him in the box. Said box would then be tied snugly to the victim's belly with the open side of the box against him. The charming little devils would then heat the outside of the box v-e-e-r-y s-l-o-o-o-w-l-y, eventually turning it into a miniature furnace, and voila! There was only one place for the furry little hunger-bunger to go, ay? South."

"Oh, how awful."

"Of course. That's the whole point. Besides, is that any kind of gratitude? Just think of all the heavy thinking that went into the creation of the 'little black box.' Das not nice."

Bobi, who by now you may have noticed to be the possessor of a very quick mind, was enjoying the conversation, albeit with reservations.

"And the Nazis," I continued, "Let's not forget our jolly Teuton-merry-makers. They certainly could spritz up a slow night."

"I'll bet."

"So, now that your curiosity's peaked. . . . ."

"I can hardly wait."

"I thought so; anyhow, they would take the poor unfortunate, and strap him down so the only appendage he could move was his head; take your pick."

"Must I?"

"Whereupon a strand of piano wire would then be snugly tied about his pistollero, after which the most gorgeous, sultry, voluptuous, stark naked Fraulein, in all her filthy and devastating best, would be paraded in front of the hapless soul.

Of course, nature being cold-bloodedly impartial in all matters human, or otherwise, immediately began doing its thing without regard to race, sex, color, creed, or national origin. It doesn't take much, a bump here, a grind there, and the blood begins to flow then roar with certain anatomical parts responding to the treatment and before long---el zippo—what was once pe-nis er-ect-i becomes pe-nis-de-lect-i." Bobi winched. "Oh, how ghoulish." She grimaced.

I stared out into the black night as we rumbled along. "You know?" I continued, "I have oft times wondered what kind of man would remain silent under such circumstances."

"Apparently one with not much to lose." I could plainly see by now, Bobi was definitely my kind of gal. Smilingly, I retorted, "I see we are warming to the task."

"How much more of this is there? We are reaching the end, aren't we?"

"Not without the grand finale."

"We're not going to play 'can you top this,' are we?"

"Sweetheart, I've got one that couldn't be topped with peaches and cream."

"You a chef, too?"

"You're not going to believe what's about to get cooked up here."

"You wanna bet?"

"May I proceed, then?"

"Well, I don't think I could stop you, and I must say, you do have quite a range, from Bogart, to Virginia Woolf, to subliminal advertising; to God, to tortures. If at the beginning of this diverse, and sundry evening---I'd have said, 'surprise me,' I would not have been disappointed."

"Well, what the hell. If you can't be interesting, then you might as well build houses."

"You really do have a topper, do ya?"

"I do, but I'm merely the clerk, and out of the S file---Carramba! This one, however, cannot be attributed to any particular group, race, nation, or culture. It seems to have inspired all peoples everywhere."

"A sort of a worldly gem?"

"In a high-minded sort of way," I replied facetiously.

"Okay, let er rip."

"Hmmm, well, as you will shortly note, not an entirely inappropriate phrase. You see, our dupe this time would be given a hearty meal of his choice, he being unaware of the coming events, shortly followed by a prodigious dose of castor oil, the likes of which would enable a full-grown horse to spread enough manure to fertilize the state of Nebraska. It can readily be seen that no other action need be taken. The ends, alas, would be left to time, and nature."

"Of course."

"When the grand moment arrived, the torturee would frantically race for the john, whereby in a matter of seconds, a great explosion would be heard to take place. Breathlessly, the torturers would also dash into the cubicle, only to find, to their great surprise and dismay, that except for liberal amounts of brownish spatterings upon the four walls, the poor unfortunate had disappeared altogether. It certainly is a method designed to warm the cockles of a Torquemada's heart, but it wasn't very efficient, to say nothing of messy. They always lost their man."

"Too bad. Well, I must admit, that was a topper. I wasn't thinking anywhere in that direction, thank heavens."

"But think, the next time you're at one of those high-society bashes, and you're trying to impress the unimpressionable, you can drag out, one or two, of these little ditties. That'll grab em."

"No; if it's all the same to you, let's leave it be. I'm a quaint, sentimental sort. This can be our special, little secret."

"Why you son-of-a-gun. And I thought you were the hard-boiled type."

We reached the digs, and Bobi pulled over to the curb. "Are you going to see me to the door?" I asked humorously. "I'll let you kiss me." She laughed. Shivers ran up and down my spine. Love can turn a man into a simp.

We walked slowly and quietly around toward the back. "Well this is it?" she announced, suredly.

"Yep, it sure is." I looked about in the dark, then asked abruptly, "What is?"

After which I was immediately seized upon with the fearful notion that she would have to hoof it back to the car alone. America, you may have noticed, Buck, is no longer a place for such bravado. "You know," I interrupted soberly, "this wasn't such a good idea after all."

"What?"

"You escorting me back here." She looked puzzled for a moment before reality overtook her senses also.

"No," she answered, agreeing, "it wasn't, was it?"

"C'mon," I said, taking her by the arm. "Back we go. Wheeee!"

"Oh," she admonished weakly, "I feel kind of silly."

"Better silly than sorry … for both of us."

We reached the car. I opened the door, and she slid in. Leaning in, I kissed her, wet and flush on her warm, delicious mouth. Neither of us spoke. Mere words would have been a gratuitous intrusion.

"I'll get in touch," I said, "very soon. What's your number?"

"748-7708," she answered unhesitantly.

"Good night, and don't rescue any hitchhikers. Let the suckers walk."

"Okay," she replied as she started the car and drove off waving in the calm, warming breezes. Thus ended the most pleasant of evenings.

Never having been a late sleeper, I rose at seven the next morning. Rick was eating breakfast—two burnt eggs as I strolled into the pantry. Greeting me with an inaudible grunt, he then asked how it went the previous night.

"What do you mean?" I questioned, as I poured myself a cup of hot, black water.

"Oh, I see, we' all gonna play dummy games again today, hey?"

"Hey, babe's; we play the games we know best."

"Okay, okay, forget I asked. I'm just a poor working stiff sitting here sluggin' down my breakfast. I don't know nothing. I'm just a nobody; nobody has to care." He sipped his coffee. "Just make believe I ain't here. I . . . . ."

"Shut the fuck up."

"Say," he said, shifting gears in midstream, "did you hear that damn Cookie last night?"

"What do you mean?"

"What do I mean? Man, you didn't hear all that racket?"

"What racket?"

"What racket?"

"Say, what the fuck are you? A simple-minded parrot?"

He paid no mind. "All that damn snoring. It sounded like a lumber mill in there."

"Maybe somebody was cutting wood around here."

"Yeah, sure, and my daddy's a gigolo."

"Well, you know your folks better than me."

"Then you didn't hear him?" he asked again, incredulously.

"No, I didn't, my fine, pickled friend."

"Jesus Christ, man. Nobody sleeps that heavy."

"I do, sunshine. And why not? I ain't got no worries."

"You're tellin' me, but what the hell, it ain't human. You're supposed to be asleep, not dead."

"Well, what is sleep anyway, but brief intermittent slips into the land of the dearly departed?"

"It's a wonder you woke at all."

"Yeah, I feel the same about a lot of folk."

"Well," he said as he got up, "I gotta go. I'm a working Joe. One of these days I'm gonna learn how to get along without bustin' my ass."

"You know what they say, Ricky, baby?"

"No, what dood they say, Johnsy boy?"

"They say the learning's in the doin'. You got to do it sweetheart to know it."

"And what happens if I cain't, starve?"

"You pays your buck, and you'se takes your chances. Guarantees are what comes with one of them shitty lemons from Detroit what can't go thirty feet without a recall. But look at it this way, your death is someone else's good fortune."

"Yeah, the mortician's."

"Him, too, but I was thinking of something along more elemental lines, like the ants, and worms, and maggots. They'll recycle you, and you'll become part of the w-h-o-o-o-l-e universe. You'll fuse together. It will become you, and you, it. You'll be everything and everywhere. The sun, the trees, the stars, the good earth underfoot. You'll be the laundry of the world all cleaned, and bleached, and hung out to dry pure and everlasting."

A horn sounded. It was Rick's ride. He grabbed his lunch and mumbled as he left, "Two-hundred-million mother-fuckers in this country and I had to bump into a friggin', half-baked, poverty stricken philosopher. There's no justice, no justice."

"Now you're cooking, Ricky, baby!" I hollered after him as he left. "And how about me, S-U-C—K-A-H!"

Upon Huckleberry's leaving, I sat awhile sipping my brew, early morning always being a good time for reflection.

Quietly peering out through the back door, I noticed a sparrow perched on a limb, chirping. I wondered what it would be like to be a bird. I wondered if their wings ever tired after a heavy day's flapping in the breeze. I wondered what a blackbird would evolve into in a hundred million years. How much bigger would he be? Would he have two sets of wings, four feet, a bigger brain, maybe? Would he be able to speak? I wondered the same about humans. Would they have bigger brains? And better ones? And when they spoke, would they say something or are we forever doomed to mindless prattle chained to the political code of "speak, but say nothing?"

Slowly my mind was beginning to drift into the calming sea of repose when another strange happening occurred---Cookie staggered in.

Cookie, as previously mentioned, was a night person, and a drunk, characteristics not usually associated with early rising. But then, what is life, if not contradictory? He immediately went to the 'little black pot.'

"I hope you got somethin' in here," he drawled.

"I ain't, but Pepe the 'lil ol' Colombian coffee picker has."

"Well, you, him, who cares? I need something. My head's killing me."

"Yep, that'll do it quicker'n a bullet. What the hell you doing up to begin with?" I asked, not really caring.

"What am I doin' up?" he mocked. "Can't you hear that god-damn bird out there?" Funny, the birds never complain about us humans. "Sure," I said, "I can hear him. So what? Ain't you ever heard a squawky bird chirp before?"

He sat down and blew on the steaming brew. "Rosko," he answered disagreeably, "did anyone ever say what a fucking beauty you were?"

"A real pickle, huh?"

"Vinegar an' all."

"Yeah, lots of folk. But never a cook. You want to be the first, is that it? Cook, I mean?"

He gazed toward the heavens. "Five billion people in this world, five billion, and I had to hook up with 'Mister Cordiality.' (A day of premonitions, is <u>it?</u>) "What have I done, Lord," he added, continuing to stare at the ceiling. I was hoping that bird would fly in and introduce himself as only a bird knows how. "I'm a good fella. I don't hurt no one. Oh, it's true I gits behind onct in a while in my alimony. . . . ." (Hah! Chalk one up for ol' peg leg. It was the one, good quality I thought he had, and he was apologizing for it. Ah, but for the Ides of March.) "But I send a little when I kin', and I obeys the law, winced I know it."

"Sure," I added sarcastically.

"I'm really not a bad sort, Lord, really I ain't, so why, Lord? Why me?"

"Why not?" I countered, sipping my brew.

"There's no justice in the world," he concluded, despondently. I was beginning to think this was more than mere coincidence. Could it be Cookie and Rick were once related in another time? Siamese twins, maybe? Stranger things. . . . .

Flopped there with his legs crossed, staring out the door solemnly, he was a frightful sight. In what was once, I suppose, a white T-shirt, but now gunmetal gray, liberally splattered with egg stains, bacon grease, coffee, ketchup, and what not, he sat, his exploding beer-belly hanging over his belt. At least, I think he had on a belt. I couldn't see for all the fat. A belt, or rope, or string. Cookie was no magician. Something was holding up his pants besides good will.

"You know what the bastards did to me last night?" he complained while staring hypnotically.

"No, what did the baddies dood to you last night, sweetie?"

"They stole my coat."

"Stole your coat!" I exclaimed, somewhat surprised, since 'coat stealin' wasn't exactly No 1 in the hierarchy of modern theft these days. I thought that would have been more in line with Dickensonian, 'merry old England' times. Actually, Cookie always brought to mind the depression, and that old sorrowful tune 'brother can you spare a dime.' I waited for him to continue. He did.

"That's right, I don't stutter. Stole my coat. Stole, as in grab, take, cop, steal."

Ah, I knew there was a special reason for his being up so airrr-ly, for Cookie was a creature of habit, and early rising was not one of them. I egged him on. The sappy are such delicious morsels.

"You mean that long, tan, pretty one with the big wooden buttons?"

"Yeah," he mocked, "the long, tan, pretty one with the big wooden buttons."

"Huh, that was a hell of a frock, pilgrim."

"You're tellin' me. Cost a hundred smackers, a hundred, and it was brand new."

"Well, what the hell were you wearing it for, anyway? This is April. And besides, that bearskin was too warm for the Kodiak, even."

"Oh, don't you worry. It gets pretty thin around midnight still."

With as much alcohol as Cookie was slogging around, I didn't see as it mattered much … in December even. "How'd they snatch it?" I asked, always being one to learn more about the behavior of the species in its natural habitat.

"They took it from the kitchen. Right out from under my nose."

"You keep saying they. What was this, a gangland heist?"

"They, he, them, what the hell's the difference? It's gone, and I hope the rat bastard what has it get the cooties from it." That, I thought, was not an unlikely possibility.

"God-damn country," he continued dejectedly. "It's goin' to the dogs. A guy can't trust nobody no more. There ain't no damn law and order. Never was."

"Oh, I wouldn't say that. Somebody just made off with a coat in an orderly fashion. And the law's still there, it always is. It protects us all, while we're asleep, or awake, or working, or at play. We can't see it, but it's there, doing its duty. Thank God for the law."

"You ain't shittin' we can't see it, unless you go down to Freddy's Donuts. There's a god-damn squad car parked there day and night. Two, in fact. Freddy gets round-the-clock protection. Fuckin' cops … sure must love donuts."

"Or Freddy."

"Shit, for what it costs to put the crooked fucks out on the street, I'd just as soon take my chances without them."

"Then who'd protect you?"

"Who's doin' it now?"

"But then everything would be one big jungle."

"What's it now?"

"A marsh? How bout swamp? I'm partial to sewer, myself."

"You know how much crime there is, Jocko?"

"No, how much crime is there, fry cakes?"

"Well, I'll tell ya. . . . ."

"I was afraid of that."

"I'm scairt to go out nights, and I ain't even an old lady!"

"Yeah, old ladies and winos, they're always the first to get it."

"Who's a wino?" he objected strenuously. Of course, pride, the DT's of human nature. Just one more hot coal in the path of evolution. The curse of Eden. What we have the most of, we need the least. On the world stage it is called nationalism, and has its roots in endless insecurities. There never has been a war that wasn't fought for "national pride."

My, but the weak and debilitating can be so fatiguing. Is history to be forever mobilized by the fatuous? Nations perpetually governed by the inadequate? Is it any wonder the world is a spinning globe? Are we but a perilous, whirling merry-go-round of neuroses? It's no wonder we're all 'dizzy.'

"Hell," he want on, "it's gettin' so I'm gonna hafta start carryin' a gun."

Here we go again … the species, as a species, will never live beyond another century until we relieve ourselves of the hammer of tedium. Old age is the natural progression of the tiresome.

"I thought you did," I countered.

"Don't worry. If things keep goin' the way they are, I'm gonna get one, by God. Fuck these god-damn people."

"You might as well. If it's good enough for a politician, it's good enough for you."

"I can't get over it. I just can't get over it."

"Legs too short?" He ignored my pitiable attempt at slight levity. The Cooker was in no mood for jokery.

"Things are so lousy, a guy can't be happy anymore. I'm not happy. I used to be happy, onct upon a time, even when I was broke … but I enjoyed myself. Now everything is crime, crime, demonstrations, complaints. Everybody's mad about something. Nobody laughs any more."

Well, now. Here's a bloke who's never sober long enough to flip over the dates on a calendar, and H-E can tell. Things M-U-U-U-S-T be getting tough.

"It's just too damn hard to be happy nowadays," he repeated as he gulped down the muddy, black liquid.

"Yeah," I agreed, "a guy has to really work at it. It don't come easy any more, if it ever did. You know, Cook? Everybody should be gifted with two separate lives in two different times. That way he can compare, you know? The way it is now, a shmuck can't tell anything. He has to rely on historians, and how reliable are they, I ask you?" I tapped the spoon rhythmically on the table. "When would you like to have lived, Cook? Ever think about living in another time?"

"Naw, can't say as I have. I'm havin' enough trouble with this one."

It seems folks have to be forced into the bright lights of honesty. Only grudgingly do they unconsciously cough up the little translucent pearls of veracity.

"Yes," I certified, nodding my head up and down ala Laurel and Hardy, "I know just what you mean, uh, uh, uh."

"Why? When would you like to have lived?"

I needn't have pondered that one much, having been brought up on the Natty Bumpo series. So, what else? Frontier days, Buck. "During the eighteenth century," I affirmed straight-away. "Around the time of the French and Indian War and the flintlock bazoo. I always hankered after books and flicks about those days, even the bad ones."

"Hell," he laughingly answered, "those weren't such hot times. A guy couldn't even take a bath in those days."

Hah! There's one for you! He didn't take one N-O-W! Why would that be the first thing to come to his clueless mind? His only contact with the saline solution came with beer suds and coffee.

It all comes down to choice, apparently. One would, at least, like to have the option even though one rarely avails himself of it, urban renewal being a recent and grievous example of that lamentable condition.

Slum residents were offered, upon occasion, two and three times the value of their property, and yet, in a pique of pigheaded and misplaced defiance, refused. Some, even, had to be dragged out bodily from the vermin-laden structures.

Remember Chavez ravine? Dodger Stadium? Imagine someone, anyone, having to be forced to leave the slum? You do know the type of dwellings of which I speak? Climbing up on the porch can be a hazardous experience, one flight of stairs, and one best take out accident insurance first. Two flights, and the odds of a bold, fat rat beating you to the top are four-to-one. Three flights and one is awarded the Bronze Star. I saw a brawl, one time, in a hallway, between a rat and a roach. Damn good fight for a while, but then the roach began to wear the rat down. Finally, the roach won. He was bigger.

I rose to soak my cup. The sink, as usual, was filled to overflowing with dirty dishes. When I first came to this establishment, I naively used to wash them when I found them. I think the word got around because, I'd swear, the occupants on the second and third floors began to bring theirs down and dump them in the sink knowing I was an easy mark. I have since learned better. Now when I need a dish, I wash it, use it, then stick it back in the sink dirty like everybody else. It's so much easier to get by when the rules are the same for everyone.

"Where you goin'?" Cookie asked.

"To bed," I answered laconically.

"To bed?"

"Yeah, to bed. Something wrong with that?"

"You just got up."

"And I'm going right back." I did, but before lying restfully, I made up my bunk neatly. I was the only one who ever did. Tis just a little bit of art.

* * *

XI

LOVE

WHEN next I saw Bobi, we decided to spend a quiet evening at her pad, a small, quaint, two-bedroom dig complete with electronic buzzers and steel gates. What with the "who's it?" "It's me" routine, the warning lights, double locks and sliding doors, I felt like double-0-seven, at his surreptitious best.

Bobi roomed with an airline stewardess. Upon arriving, I could see her packing through a partially opened bedroom door.

"Hi," I was friendlily greeted.

"Did you find it alright?"

"Was there any reason I shouldn't have?" I airily questioned.

"I suppose not. What, no coat?" she expressed with an upturned brow, as she noticed my one-hundred-per-cent, flimsy, cotton sweater.

"No coat," I remarked indifferently.

Bobi was wearing a red T shirt that fit like a poured casting, and black slacks, also of the snuggly variety. Red and black was always a favorite combination of mine. I wondered how she knew. Reconnoitering her marvelous torso, I enunciated as how it was going to be both 'a pleasant and difficult evening,' all at the same time.

Playing it straight all the way, she queried: What do you mean?" Again I perused her wondrously chiseled lines, and retorted: "Don't be cruel."

She smiled coyly, while taking my arm and leading me to the bedroom remarking, "I want you to meet someone."

"The vice squad?" I joked.

"That's what I like about you—the unexpected. It keeps me on my toes."

"Me too."

We meandered into the bedroom where a tall, willowy, light haired young lady, was busily preparing for a trip. She was wearing a stewardesses outfit, part of which was almost a skirt. (Those were the days.)

"John, this is Adrienne Collette. Adi, meet John." She gracefully stuck-out a well manicured hand saying, "Please to meet you, John." I took it while answering informatively, "Don't be so hasty." She glanced at Bobi, commenting with an upturned brow, "I see what you mean."

"Uh, oh," I blurted. "Already have I made my mark?"

"Of a sorts," Bobi interjected mischievously. "And don't you know people often talk about the things they like?"

Hmnn. My granny, dear heart, always talked about the things she didn't like. Are times all that different?

"Adrienne Colette. Is that your real name?" I quizzed. A look of wonderment crossed her pretty face as she glanced first at me, and then Bobi. "Of course it's my real name. Why? Shouldn't it be?" she responded.

"Oh, yeah; I suppose so. It's just that I know how celebrities like to change their names. They never feel like the one they have is good enough, when in fact, oft times, it's too good. Funny isn't it? If they were born with the one they changed to, they would change to the one they were born with. To tell you the truth, I really prefer Archibald McLeish to Cary Grant."

"How about George Dorsey?" Adi added, in keeping with the mood.

"Who is?" I queried.

"Englebert Humperdinck." she laughingly exclaimed.

"For sure?"

"Yes, it do get ludicrous."

"It's called Hollywood," added Bobi."

"I got a better name for it." And Bobi, mindful of my penchant for the 'indelicate' pleaded, "No, please; not now."

"You going like that?" I asked 'tongue in cheek.' She stepped back looking at herself. "Yes, I'm going like this. Why? Doesn't it meet with your approval?" she snapped raspishly, but in good humor.

"Sure," I said, but I thought you were going to put on a dress."

"Ooooh, this dress too 'brief' for you?"

"Uh, oh; not me. I'm not complaining a bit."

"You got something against girl's legs, then?"

"Ah-hah! You don't really expect me to touch that line, do you? But I do try to stay on top of things." Adi looked at Bobi. Bobi looked at Adi. I looked at, well, you get the picture.

Adi admonished obliquely, "I think you've got a winner here. Be advised it's not just a turkey."

"Miss Colette," I jokingly added. The thing is, not to be a chicken."

"The thing is—stay out of the pot, Mr. Rosko."

"Aw, yus dusn't hasta call me Mr. Rosko. Yus can call me John, or yus can call me John, John, or yus can call me J.J., or yus can call me John J., or yus can call me John R., or yus can call me big John, or yus can call me Johnny, or yus can call me Johnny R., but yus dusn't hasta call me, Mistah Rosko."

They both smiled, and why not? No Nazis in this party. Pity she had to leave; we were just warming to the task.

"J.J., you have no idea what I'd like to call you."

"Ah, so you've settled on J.J., have you? How quaint."

"So long, Bub."

"Bub? Bub? I don't believe I included Bub in my repertoire, but if you like Bub, then Bub it is, or how bout Bubba John? Or Johnna Bub? Or, or, or. . . . ."

"Let me outta here."

"Outta here? Is that a name?"

"You know? If you were a train, you'd never be able to stay on the track."

"Wasn't there a song that went something like that?"

"Like what?"

"If I were a train?"

"I believe it was hammer, and couldn't I use one now. How do you talk with a guy like this, Bob?"

"Hand signals."

"Honey, I think you're going to need more than hand signals, and I won't be surprised if I poured the scotch in the egg salad tonight."

"Hmnn, scotch in the egg salad. I gots to try that sometime."

"I thought you already have." And with that last rejoinder, we all traipsed back into the front room. Adi 'straightened' herself, gave a last approving look in a full length, wall mirror and saluted, "Well, I'll be seeing you all next week."

"Next week!" I replied in amazement. "What are you flying, the "Spirit of St. Louis?"

"Not quite, but I have a few days vacation coming, and I'm going to take them … in Japan. I was undecided till now, but not anymore. I'll take them; I'll need them. Toodle loo."

"And a 'Hi, Ho." I added, as we parted friends. Afterwards I commented to Bobi on what a nice person she seemed to be.

"Yes," she agreed, "you have no idea how nice. There isn't a bad bone in her whole body. She really is terrific."

"And highly unusual in this era of the 'big hustle.' Suddenly and quite unexpectedly, I jerked forward and kissed her abruptly. "Well, what was that for?" she asked.

"Does it have to be for anything? I thought it explained itself quite nicely."

"Well it did that, and I have noticed … you sure do kiss a lot."

"Sweetheart, with you, I'm not even gonna count. In any case, I don't believe in depriving myself of the simple pleasures of life when most everything else has a price tag, one way or the other. I was overcome by an overwhelming urge to kiss you, so I did. I hope you're not offended."

"No. "

"Thank God." Bobi lowered her eyes and smiled as only she knew how, then reciprocated: "You're quite right, you know, quite." We stood staring, savoring the moment, moments far and few between, enjoying the look of the other.

"You know?" I finally stated, matter-of-factly. "People are often embarrassed at displays of affection. Why is that, you suppose? Just another little trick of the gods?"

"Who can say?"

"Yeah, who can say? But you know what I'd like to see some day?"

"What?"

"I'd like to see a man and a woman, bare-asked naked, screwing for all their worth at high-noon on the corner of sunset and vine."

"Why?" she queried, although half-suspecting my drift, I was sure.

"Why not? We see killing every day on the big bubble, and that doesn't embarrass a naked nun on the church steps. We have a war brought to us every day in our living rooms; we calmly watch, we accept submissively while folks are killing each other all over the god-damn joint, in their homes, on the street, in bars, at work and play. Not too much is thought of it. You can buy a toy gun for your kid as easily as a stick of gum. But sex, the high-powered engine of life, 'distresses' us, confounds our conventional notions of morality. To put it simply my dear: Bach is not usually found in a bawdy house."

"I wouldn't know."

"I'm glad you said that."

"Hmmm. . . . ."

"So, how come eating in public doesn't phase anyone in the least? If I see someone chomping on a dog at a ballgame, I take no notice whatever. But what if I saw a pair screwing to their hearts content during the seventh-inning stretch? Funny, if I get the bun, I can do without the relish. The bun I-S the relish"

"Where i-i-i-s this all leading?"

Ignoring her last remark, I continued. "As I was saying, I'm supposed to be shocked, why? Food is a basic drive, so is sex. Why should the one shock, and not the other? Why must I do one in private, but not the other? What is it about sex that so mortifies people? It doesn't hurt, it won't blind you no matter what the church claims, and it doesn't kill. As a matter of fact, it is now said to be one of the better exercises—depending on how dedicated one is—and is supposed to do wonders for the heart. But then the poets always knew that. So why all the fuss? Why?

"I really don't think we're going to start doing it in public, if I may say so."

"This world, tis more than a little strange, my dear. If I screw on main street, I can get busted for 'public lewdness' or 'public coagulating' or 'conjugating in public' or any number of contrived variations thereof, but if I shoot someone it's just plain murder, not 'murder in public.' Ya hep to it?"

"I never did notice."

"Think about it. A distinction is actually made concerning certain sexual derivations performed on the publics behalf, but murder?—hell, what's so friggin special about a life among many? Terrific. I contend, my sweet, that the 'average' American---there's a winner for you who put Richard Nixon in the white house twice—becomes infinitely more upset at pornography than that maniacal war in Viet Nam. That ought to swiggle your brains about a bit. He'd rather see his dumb-assed kid in a crappy brown uniform packing an MI in a far off land where he has absolutely nothing in common, and in general running amok, than sitting in a porn house minding his own, and fingering himself mightily. God, It's frightening. As a matter of fact, if junior can learn to kill with a certain modicum of assembly line precision, he'll get a whole string of beads for his trouble, and they'll stick him in a parade down main street, after which he will shortly go bonkers, but in a porn house, depending on the mood of the moment of the powers that be, he can get thrown out on his ass, as one of the less disagreeable alternatives. Yet, if he refuses to kill---not an inhuman sentiment mightn't you say—he's labeled a draft-dodger, or deserter, whichever." Bobi remained silent. We looked at each other and that was enough for me ... for the moment.

It was such a pleasure talking with Bobi. She understood so well. She knew how to listen, and had that uncommon quality of always seeming to be interested even at something so innocuous as a reciting of the alphabet. In a sense she reminded me of Will Rogers, he of 'I never met a man I didn't like' fame, which in turn reminded me of the tune, 'I don't get around much anymore.'

"Well," I finally said, "are we going to eat, sometime soon, and what ... or what?"

"Well, being Italian. . . . ."

"To be honest," I interrupted, "my great, great grandmother on my Mother's side was half German."

"German?"

"So what's so astounding about that? They not on this planet?" Ignoring my inquiries, she declared, "And all this time I thought you were a 'dyed-in-the-wool' Latino."

"I hardly think that a half-breed nanny kraut some 150 years ago, qualifies me for membership in the far-haired, Celtic superman club."

"Maybe not. Well, then, if this is going to be a night for surprises, you're not in the Mafia to, are you?"

"Not quite. But I did have a second cousin who was in the employ of that great American and humanitarian of the midway, one 'Al-phon-se Ca-po-ne' who on election day of 1928, in a perspicacious burst of inspiration, heralded: "Remember now, vote early, and vote often."

"A cousin? Really?"

"Or was it for the "Purple Gang?"

"The 'Purple Gang?' Who were they?"

"Well I'll tell you, my dear ... a bunch of crazy Jews out of Detroit who, if Hitler had them to contend with, would have had a buzz bomb, or two, shoved up his mangy, Nazi rump, and that would have been that, and a very short history of World War II in the bargain."

"Why were they called "purple?"

"I don't know. I guess if they didn't like you they made you purple."

"You're not joshing me?"

"Joshing you? Well now let me enlighten you about a few things my little cream-filled cupcake. You ought to read up on Al, and Dion O'Banion, and

Hymie Weiss, and Bugs Moran, and Charlie Lucky, and the Bugs and Meyer gang, and the 'Mustache's Pete's.' You'll learn more about the 'real' America from one short reading of such, than from a whole library of Whitman's, Hemingway's and Fitzgerald's, infinitely more. As a matter of fact, it should be required reading, without which no one can ever hope to obtain a degree … of a-n-y kind."

"You are serious?"

"As a ravenous hawk eye-balling a lame field-mouse. But then, you see; your surprised reaction indicates the extent of our educational failure, our trampling among the thorns of irrelevancies, and flighty excursions into the dark of malarkey. You think by studying a bunch of pigeons in a cage you'll learn about the pigeon in man? You want to know what it's like in hell, you have to go to hell."

"But it helps … about the pigeons, I mean."

"Honey, it's the battery that starts the car, but not the gas that makes it go."

"Okay."

"Okay? I get the feeling if everyone in the U.N. were like you, we'd never have a war, and we wouldn't need a U.N."

"Let's see about dinner."

"Which is?"

"Chicken cacciatore. You do like chicken, don't you?"

"Does the hog squeal?"

We moseyed on into the kitchen. Bobi opened the oven door and an aroma fit only for the bulbous nose of Epicurus wafted by. "Not bad," I admitted grudgingly. "We never had this fancy at home though. Latin's are a wonderfully simple folk. A piece of cheese, a hunk of bread, a goblet of wine; this slickity, bald nakedness is for the rich on holidays." I leaned over and took in a deep breath. "However," I added, "after tonight I may have to change my ways." Suddenly, I wondered where Bobi had learned to cook in such grand fashion, so I asked.

"Oh," was the casual reply, "around; it's always been kind of a hobby with me. I like to experiment with different things. You'd be surprised at some of the outcomes."

"Ho, you say. Not after smelling this bird."

"My chow mein would tempt the palette of the commonest Chinaman, and my chili is fit only for the taste buds of a Mexican angel. I made eggplant parmagian last week."

"You didn't? And you didn't call me? For shame. I could eat a whole field of eggplant."

"I didn't know you then."

"To both our misfortunes."

"Sometimes I think I ought to open a restaurant."

"You got my vote." I sat down. A pot of coffee was brewing on the back-burner. "Would you like a cup?" she asked motioning toward it. "Dinner won't be ready for a while yet."

"Sure," I stated agreeably. "Why not? I'm easy to get along with. Actually, I'm just a pussy-cat at heart," and was I given what can only be described as a suspicious glance. "Well," I corrected, "maybe a well mannered Puma?"

"That's a little closer," she intimated while pouring out two cups of the steaming black liquid. "Shall we sit here?" she asked.

"Yeah," I quickly assented. "I don't want to stray to far from the golden bird."

We did so, not saying anything more for a brief moment, then out of the blue, she asked what I would have done had I been drafted. "Well, you sure can make a sharp left whenever, but strange as it may seem," I opined, "I would have gone."

"You would!" she exclaimed, obviously taken aback considering what she already knew of me.

"Of course. You see, my sweet," I retorted as I leaned across the table giving my Groucho impression replete with Havana Tampa and twitching eyebrows, "and you are my sweet. There are ways, and there are ways, this being one of the more ingenious."

"I'm afraid you're going to have to ride that bike by me again."

"Okay, try this suit on: The great folly of mankind is its innate capacity to descend into the boggy marsh, and dwell everlasting in its murky depths rendering it virtually impossible to extricate itself without the use of hook-and-ladder, giant cranes and crowbars."

"What?"

"To be hornswaggled; add to that a deficient imagination and you have, ta, ra---the anti-war movement.

"We do?"

"We do. Very predictably they went about unshaven, unkempt, in general, slovenly and downright filthy, doing every little nasty thing to antagonize that great mass of mush known insipidly as middle America. The movement suffered from a colossal case of egotism, it being more concerned with its dingy image of peace-loving brothers, than they were with stopping this stinking, slop-mop war. Each fought for ascendancy to the throne of tree-hugging humanitarians, using as stepping-stones the corpses of millions of Vietnamese, and forty thousand fellow Americans, and still counting.

The war is proving to be a convenient vehicle for the movements more vaudevillian instincts. As they soft-shoe their way through New York, Chicago, Berkeley, Boston, L.A., etc., the war goes on, and on, and on. Terrific; as long as this war is lasting, one could almost say they're feeding it."

"Well how else could it be done?"

"What is the opposite of the obvious?"

"What?"

"They should have all gotten together, the whole damned smelly bunch, and the very first thing they should have done was BURN THEIR CLOTHES AND TAKE A BATH, then shave and haircuts—preferably crew cuts---then go find the most conservative grey suit they could, AND—POOT—EET—ON. And instead of love-beads it should have been rosaries draped about their scruffy necks, and bibles neatly tucked under their well-scrubbed arms, and when they assembled it should have been quietly and peacefully without all the hoopla and fanfare, and with all the 'praise be Jesus' and 'hallelujahs' it could have handled without dropping their monastic piety. IT'S THE NUMBERS THAT COUNT; OVERWHELM THEM WITH THE NUMBERS.

Now I ask you: How could the hard-hat in Cleveland, or the bible thumper in South Carolina, or the flag-waver in Nebraska have objected to all that stinking holiness? They would have become THEIR children, they WERE their children. And how could they have clubbed their own children? God, it could have been beautiful, beating the bastards at their own game. Hosanna this and Hosanna that ... Christ, the boat sailed and they were left hanging at the pier."

"Really."

"They could have gone on the tube and at the slightest hint of objection could have shot back with all that 'Christ is love, Christ is peace' shit, all the while clutching the official St. James version in full view of all the world to see. 'Love' 'peace' 'brotherhood;' 'praise to god' 'peace be with you.' Christ, the air would have veritably stunk with righteous virtue. The suck-hole public would have been so faked out; they would have begun marching themselves. Indeed did the ferry depart without their fuzzy rears.

It appears this life is too simple for us. We see the trees but not the leaves.

The running brook has no legs, but is perpetually in motion. It does not bode well for them what claim to hold such a preeminent position among the terrestrial."

"We are pretty much lost then. . . . ."

"The soul is but a cavernous housing for the incidental cavorting through the fairy-tale world of rubber crocodiles and plastic bears; the fun-house with crooked mirrors, and the shooting gallery of impossible dreams. Disneyland is for real."

"I'm not unsympathetic."

"Is it any wonder we have merry-go-rounds and rolley coasters?"

"But you never said why you'd have willingly submitted if called upon."

"Willingly submitted? Willingly submitted? Well let me put it this way: In the hopeful event that I may not have been shot dead first, the advantages of allowing myself to be 'duped' far outweigh those usually associated with taking a hurried trip to parts unknown. Remember now, we're talking about a chap what hates and despises this vile, bastard war like nothing he ever came up against yet, along with all the mindless, horse's ass theories given for this fabricated ruse into the darkly, murky terrain of insanity; the lies, the cowardice, the hypocrisy and what not, hates the whole shebang, top to bottom, right to left, in and out, through and through, right?"

"I suppose."

"I'd still go."

"You would."

"Absolutely. I'll not give the low-life slime the satisfaction of hounding me half way across the globe to Sweden, or wherever. No siree, Bob. I will not allow them to be the cause of my ruination; it will come soon enough without their invidious help. I say, by the profligate, nefarious, heinous bastards that they are---find another pigeon. I'll go, and attain all the rights and privileges' thereof; the pay, the rank, the medals, and upon discharge, I'd have gone to college whether I liked it or not, using up every last damn buffalo head nickel, and schemed for more. I'd have run up the tally on my G.I. bill, applied for food stamps and Medicaid, register for unemployment compensation, claimed to be an alcoholic, drug addict, and the unlucky recipient of every conceivable medical condition known to man or beast all as the result of my unfortunate participation in that blood-sucking montage of evil, and proudly grab every stinking, dirty, last red cent in the fucking, black-hearted bargain, and if the opportunity arose---rob the bursar.

Yeah, I'd have gone, I sure would, but I'd have been behind the biggest, friggin tank I could find, not move one inch forward unless specifically ordered, hit the ground at the crack of a twig, and 'reassess' my position at the first unfriendly sneeze, which, no doubt, would have been the first one I heard. The reprobate, lawless motherfuckers, would've needed a whole dam battalion just to keep their crossed, fucking eyes on me. Go? Would I ever, but they damn sure wouldn't win any war with me out there. Too bad the poor saps that did get suckered in didn't have better sense. Think of the lives we could have saved, on both sides, the billions of dollars, and a badly scourged reputation, all of it deserved. Just a bloody, stinking horror show all the way around.

And let's not forget, 'freedom.' Freedom? Freedom, my ass. You neither gain or defend it by burning babies and blowing up villages in a far-off, poverty stricken land, who's bedraggled and destitute inhabitants never so much as threw a stinking spit-ball your way.

La; de, da; de, da. And the beat goes on. Six thousand years, and it continues. Where will it end, you say? It doesn't. It's a condition of the illness, the acting out of evil of the sick-souled degenerate."

"I take it then, this war has really upset you?"

"Does the monkey swing on the vine? Is water wet? Is fire hot? It has made me feel, where otherwise it would not have, that I'd rather be living in any other era but this one. I try to think what it was like before 65'. That has gotten to be the 'good old days.' How's that for a crock?"

Hesitating momentarily, I rubbed my forehead searching for the right meaning, and then continued despondently. "What makes it so tough is our willingness to participate, with malice aforethought, the annihilation of a nation with zest, and the continuity of the four seasons. That was the thing, the monstrosity surrounding the whole damnable business, our enthusiasm to pursue villainy indefinitely. It has become our policy to continue war for war's sake, and when you think about it, that's what Hitler did, didn't he? Great company, huh? It has become our policy, the policy of the Nazi. Caught up in the war psychology, no degree of counseling can cure the patient. We have become the prototype of the 'will to evil.'

Yeah, I guess you could say it has at least one casualty. It's left me with a perpetual gloom, and no matter how good things may get, there will always remain a pale of blackness before me, like a dark cloud that refuses to rain, and stays, embedded in the sky like a rock on a stick. It has succeeded in doing what all the lying politician's and propagandist's failed to do—give us the ability to live in dishonor without remorse, without really caring. So what if a few Joe's got doused with a 'little' agent orange; some crutty 'Gooks' got incinerated; that's war, isn't it? Sides, they could have surrendered? And why don't you take your head out of your ass?

We've lost our conscience; the pendulum has swung to the far side of decadence."

"If that is so, then we're no better than anyone else."

"You d-o-o-o- catch on quick. Not only are we no better, but this 'little waltz in the jungle' has shown that for all our faked idealism and twisted dreams, that America is not an eagle after all, but a vulture."

"But this experience might teach us something, don't you think? I mean experience has its lesson."

"I know education is expensive, but who can pay this price?" Looking into my cup, I attempted a shift into a more lighter mood, asking brightly, "who made the coffee, Mrs. Olson?"

"Not in this house," was the quick reply.

"Bravo!" I happily exclaimed, and then remained quiet for a moment, staring. She, in turn, always being a wares caught my eye.

"You're staring again," she calmly stated.

"I certainly am," I admitted shamelessly. "And do you find me as gorgeous as I find you? I mean, does that irresistible feeling come over you where the only thing entering the mind is the 'object of your affection? Do you?"

"Yes," was the lackadaisical reply. I was startled, and more than a little pleased, as you can imagine, by her frankness. Leaning back in my chair, I replied soberly, "You're making it difficult."

She was about to answer, but I hurriedly broke in with, "But it's alright. I'll get used to it. Adjust, that's the big thing nowadays. I'll force myself."

She rose to check dinner. Breathlessly I watched every muscle, every limb, every bead of flesh, as they, in blessed unison, glided smoothly in undulating waves, heaving and rolling brilliantly in elegant magnificence. I thought what a marvelous invention, what an incomparable act of creation was the perfect female torso, (or even the not so perfect.) I envied the belt surrounding her trim, sleek waist.

"Well," she announced, peering into the pot, "anytime now." To wit—having my mind on a naked bird of a different stripe---I did not reply.

Giving me one of those all-knowing sideways glances, she smiled, placed the lid back on the unlucky fowl, and shut the gas. "Whenever you're ready," she coyly announced.

"How come everything you say seems to have a sexual connotation?" Pointing directly at me, she indicated rightfully, "It's you."

"Me! Me!" I cried out in mocked offense. "I never said a word."

"You don't have to. And the biggest crooks never carry a gun either." More and more was I liking this girl . . . more and more.

I wondered what it would be like to be a-sexual, but not for long. Sex, sex, sex. Gawd it's hell, Buck. A Jack can't even have a chicken dinner without visions of lechery dancing through his head. No wonder everyone has a sour stomach; invest in the drug companies, a winning bet for all times.

And then a bizarre thought occurred to me----at least bizarre in these times. I wondered if Bobi was still a virgin. She was no child, and had had sufficient time by now, to have had all of that taken care of, still, I wondered, and . . . secretly hoped.

The puritan instinct, it dies hard. And with a prize like Bobi, one always likes to be the first one, the only one, and then drag her off to a far-off cave shielding her from the rest of the lust-crazed, oogling world. Ah! The primal urge. It does no good to reason with it; it has its own logic.

"More coffee?" she asked.

"No thanks. I'm just swilling down this stuff to be sociable. Ever since that instant coka-a-rocka it seems coffee never tastes like coffee anymore."

"Hey," she objected. "That's not instant, and thanks a lot."

"Oh, keep your feathers dry. I didn't mean it personally. Look." I raised the cup and took a gulp. "See, I love it, I love it." I then wet my fingers and dabbed my shirt. "See, gutt, gutt. Tarzan like."

"Yeah, Bozo."

"Bobi, I love ya, I surely do."

"Thank you, sir."

"Much ado about nothing. It's been happening for ages." I paused, and in a few moments, I wondered out loud. "Yeah, Bobi, the elementary; it baffles us.

That's the 'crab in the cradle.' We're shooting rockets through space like fire-crackers in July, yet can't ride the New York subway without an armed guard. Elementary Watson, elementary."

"I like the way you dress, Mr. Rosko. Not too loud, not too dry." Bobi did not hesitate to make a hard change of course when she so wished. I liked her for it, apparently not feeling she needed to apologize for every move and nuance. I, just as easily, swung into the same groove. Life can be so easy when it's easy.

"See here Miss," I replied. "You've never seen me dress."

"That's not what I meant."

"I know what you meant, unfortunately." No response; just a look. In frustration I pounded my fists on the table. "Okay," I bawled, "let's eat."

"I think that would be the best thing," she agreed. And then clearing the table of the prevailing debris, she then set down a decorous orange and red flowery, table cloth conveying visions of night time in old Na-po-li. In the meanwhile I scampered to the powder room and puffed.

Upon returning I noticed she was now wearing a multi-colored apron, and resembled an angel sent by a loving god for loving things, or a hateful one for spite, and she seemed to know what she was about.

I so admire those who move with a delicate proficiency. It gives the world an aura of perfection inspiring confidence and ranks alongside trust as a virtue to be greatly admired.

I stood by the table with my hands folded behind me swaying back and forth in controlled, quiet expectation of the forthcoming proceedings. "Just about set, are we?" I asked just making small talk.

"Impatient, Mr. Rosko?"

"Starved, Miss Higgins," I replied watching pleasurably as she glided thither and fro from cupboard to table. It was impossible to think that anything so elegant would someday turn to dust. And she could cook too. It's enough to weaken the faith. "Well," she said, standing by the table with hands on hips, "I guess that's it. Shall we?"

"By all means." And removing her apron, we sat.

As she prepared our plates I reported like a messenger in the front lines: "Miss Higgins, I have a confession to make."

"This is not a confessional, and I have not taken the 'oath of silence' so anything you say may be used against you." This was, I thought, definitely going to be a beautiful friendship.

"Some of the glamour, for me, is removed when I dip into ribs and chicken all that sticky-wicky stuff, you know? It can get to be a real fright. And the table … I cannot guarantee the mood of, or physical distribution of anything now residing on it. It may all become totally unrecognizable. Might I request a finger bowl?"

"Coming right up." she replied, and rose to fetch one.

"On second thought," I reconsidered, "You'd better not. All that finger-dipping makes me feel like one of them fairy-kings of the frilly, French variety."

"Oh," she replied, not paying one wit to my remark, "that reminds me—the wine."°

"Good god. All this and the grape too?" She retreated to the fridge and returned with a bottle of Chianti vintage 69.

"It's only been on ice for 45 minutes, so it shouldn't be too cold. Wine shouldn't be served too cold, should it?"

"Hah! You're asking me, Sweet? You're the hoi-polloi around here."

"Well I like that."

"I thought you would."

"Okay then; I guess we can't go wrong, can we? We have it all." Indeed.

She poured a taste into the fanciest beaker I ever saw. I swear Virginia, it must have come right out of 'Louie-the-Sixteenths' pantry. Even if one didn't appreciate the wine, one had to imbibe merely to make use of the finery. Art should be respected, if not understood, and excellent craftsmanship utilized.

I sipped daintily grasping the glass lightly, my little pinky pointing towards the heavens. "Is this," I cracked, "the way it's done by sissy kings and effeminate dukes?"

"I wouldn't know," she rebutted smiling. "Is it any good? She asked warily. "It cost me fourteen-ninety-five."

"Fourteen-ninety-five!" I bellowed obstreperously. "The last time I was this close to a bottle of wine costing fourteen-ninety-five, it was empty … and lying in a ditch."

"Well then, it appears this dinner is going to be a success."

"I would say so. Was there some reason for doubt?"

"I suppose not, but when you plan everything so meticulously sometimes it has a way of turning out shabbily."

"I know the feeling. But remember, friendship means a lot. I would think of this meal as one of my finest, even if three, sopping wet St. Bernard's slogged across my plate."

"Oh, I don't think it'll be that bad."

We ate, we enjoyed, and true to my word, was I a fright." After tearing the last tasty morsel from its bone I noticed my gluttonous appearance. "See," I commented soberly. "What did I tell you?" I looked like a one-year-old who had been playing patty-cake with the porridge. Apparently Bobi noticed too.

"Yes, I see now why you asked for a finger-bowl, but you should have said-bath-tub."

"Oh, really? Maybe I could use the bath-tub now?" She laughed, and why not? The 'three stooges' live.

* * *

The bedroom fortunately, is not far from the kitchen, and cooking of sorts, occurs in there also.

Ecstatically, in due time, I was led straight-a-way to said chamber, and it was not long before the sheets were turned down, and the lights low. My blood began to surge like the Mississippi river at high tide.

Bobi, subsequently, began removing her clothing, slowly and methodically, piece by piece, ala 'Gypsy Rose Lee.' She had no idea, I am sure, what she was about, that of course, being the beauty of it all.

I sat and watched unspeakably enthralled. She took pride in her success as I gaped open-mouthed, my eyes glued to her resplendent torso, my nerves slowly turning into a twisted mass of soft spaghetti, while two pints of steaming, hot blood welled up in my bird forcing its head to 'reach for the sky.'

After removing every stitch and piece, she nimbly glided over to the bed, and gracefully sat on one edge with crossed legs, and leaned back with her hands supporting her on either side.

"Well," she said, with just the right touch of innocence, "Do you like it?"

Really, did I like it? With all due respect, but woman, at times, can be such dolts.

I twitched and fumbled looking for a word besides "yeah" "sure" or "uh, huh." Finally I settled for a prosy "fann-ta-stic." I know, not much either, but my piccolo was 'screaming' for a duet.

I disrobed---not as gen-tee-ly—and dared not inquire into her approval of the prevailing apparatus. I thought I caught nevertheless, a glint of satisfaction.

I sidled over to her, and stood a foot, or so, away with 'birdie' sticking straight out, twitching and chirping hysterically. I was dancing on a cloud. She however, was as calm as a robin, on a nest, on a lazy June morn. Then, unannounced, and to my great surprise and delight, reached over with one hand, and began to stroke with an unusual dexterity, ever so delicately, my delirious 'love' piece. I was, to understate the obvious, somewhat atwitter.

Up and down, back and forth, this way and that, with the most delicate of touches, and yet with distinct firmness did my love of the moment felicitously pursue. First one hand, then the other, then both, and all with an uncanny sense of decor. Faultlessly did she consummately advance toward the 'high ground,' and in no time did I reach a hyperactive state of ebullition.

She, seemingly having an uncanny sense of my frenzied state, then leaned over and began to, ever so slowly and artfully, vacuum my burgeoning, red rose-petal. Twirling her tongue around and around, then twisting her head from side to side allowing for the eagles crown to slip into each side of her silken cheeks allowing my foreskin, at each moment, to slide down and back, and with each pulsating stroke my candelabra waxed poetic.

I could endure no more; in a matter of moments I was overcome by the 'God of lust' whose might is exceeded only by his cousin 'power.'

Sweetly, Miss Higgins, somehow sensing my exact state, pulled back and snatched again into her silken hand my raging 'love' muscle. Boom!!! Boom!!! Boom!!! Thusly and quickly did birdie speak in all his glorious tumult, gorging himself fully of the 'love potion,' spurting and gushing in rapid torrents of sensuality, on, and on, and on.

My bewitching prize taken by surprise at the sudden ferocity of my flowering achievement, jerked back at the initial onslaught of the propellant juices, but was not deterred in her appointed task. Intuitively she squeezed and rubbed as I pumped, eyes blinking excitedly, and was she also caught up in the intoxicating melodrama of the rapturous, fleeting moment.

Gobs of hot, milky lava rolled down her rosy cheeks as I grasped either side of her head feverishly. Gently, while staring into the eye of cock robin did she continue until every last squirting drop was spent.

But, and with only the natural bent of the born artist, did she further 'decorate' the mantel in that she now began to squeeze and release, squeeze,

release, stroke, squeeze, release, squeeze, stroke, and then, as a finishing touch to this exquisite work of art, milked it down three, sensuous times, three exactly, as if she were the Greek goddess of love, and knew with perfect balance all the sweet mysteries of life.

Not yet through, she stopped and held 'junior' fast by the neck allowing me to relax, drain and recover, but every now and then, giving 'stretch' just the slightest of a squeeze, as if to say, 'still gotcha.' Finally, knowing the barrel was drier than a camels hump on the sun-baked Sahara, she let go and I side-stepped, lightly falling forward onto the bed making soft little noises like Aphrodite might have at the moment a giant, red-hot passion bar was eye-balled up her love-shaft.

"Well," she mindfully acknowledged, as she wiped the sticky gue from her flushed face, "you certainly had yourself a grand time."

"Yeah," I gasped breathlessly, "and quick too."

'Love-bunny' now repaired to the lavatory to 'tidy-up' as I watched enchant-edly, twin, beauteously chiseled cheeks, bountifully trailing behind.

Gratefully I used the few moments to gather myself together. Lying on my back, I stretched out with a half-a-bone waving in the soft night air, as a reminder of the previously electrifying events. I thrilled as Bobi came skipping back in smiling.

Hopping on the bed she admonished as how she was, as a result of my 'hyperactive' virility, somewhat in a quandary concerning her own needs.

"Ah, my dear honeysuckle rose," I consoled, "the embers have just begun to glow," to wit, the gleam in her eye, which had somewhat abated, returned.

For the next fifteen minutes, we, each in our fashion, reveled in the other's tangibles as we talked syrupy little nothings. Of course, the wind in the cane break began whistling again as the weather in the east became heavy with dark clouds and thunder. In other words: birdie was looking to crow once again, and Bobi, to my continuing admiration, was also looking to a further frolicking 'roll-in-the-hay.' I did not tarry; 'pursue' did not refer only to Rommel's panzers in North Africa.

Having done with the preliminaries, I now began to kiss her softly while gently rubbing her round, pink breasts enabling me to feel her hardened pointed nipples. I kissed and stroked her lovingly over her entire body eventually reaching down to her throbbing, succulent beaver, and included that in my dazzling repertoire.

She moaned blissfully as I, slowly and deliberately, pressed the now juicy folds of her heavenly, squishy vagina with the length of my tongue up and down, round and round, gradually and rhythmically, again and again. Her passion reached the point of white-heat as her legs quivered convulsively in tune with my persistently agile tongue. I clutched her clit with my lips, and pulled and tugged, forcefully but gently, her wet, surging sugar bush.

Rubbing, sucking, rolling; twirling, pressing … nimble was the way tonight as the groans of ageless love could audibly be heard.

Relentlessly I persevered dragging out each and every small tug, twirl, lick and pull; she responded in wanton frenzy: "Oh! Oh!" she moaned hungrily. "Put it in! Put it in!" she ravenously implored.

Never being one to dawdle, I pleasantly acquiesced. Rolling over on 'my Fair Lady' I grasped rooster by the neck and rubbed his white-hot, screaming head up and down the mouth of the 'love tunnel' to firm-up his thick red comb and wet his beak with her abundantly, flowing thermal juices. A mere few delightful swipes, to and fro, and-vollah! I plunged the burning love stick into the 'Valley of the Dolls.'

"Ooooah!" she ardently cried out. I gently leaned on her and wrapped my arms about her luxuriant locks as I methodically began to pump with good measure. All the lights on the love boat burned bright as the band played on, and the 'lust bug' fluttered madly about on the 'Isle of Enchantment,' and did she cling to me like a wet sock on a dank summers eve, and I to her.

Solemnly and cravenly, I maintained the path of resolution, again and again, on, up, and away. Finally, in explosive unison, we struck the climatic chord in the song of felicitation, and a fiery orchestration of mercurial turbulence spent its course.

We laid, quiet and still, two delirious souls catching a peak at heavens gate. Every few seconds I gave 'junior' a good natured pump, while she, in turn, rubbed my back and squeezed my cheeks. One hates to let go of a good thing. "Oh," she kept saying, over and over, "it was soooo good," the smoldering underside of my overheated groin attesting to the above.

"Yes," I enjoined, "it can be said I have no complaints." And indeed, in this war-weary world of wickedness and toil, that night … that night the general received a gold star with clusters.

Needless to say thereafter, we spent many an hour together, being, so to speak---of like mind. We could have been, without question, the model for Webster's 'compatibility' immensely delighted with each other's company.

What did we do? What didn't we do? A little of this, a little of that. Does it really matter? We were together; and yes, Virginia, we dood fall in love. I'll leave it there; you know the rest.

* * *

Bobi and I spent a week in Vegas one night. I don't know why … what a dump. It has to be the most over-rated watering-hole in the lower 48. An obscenity and an eyesore, have I mentioned it before? Well, it bears repeating as anything so ludicrous—to put it mildly—should go unnoticed.

For those who have never had the great misfortune to have ever passed through this mole-hole, please be advised as this is not so much a city as it is a gigantic, monstrous neon sign plunked in the middle of, and desecrating, the great American desert, the Sodom of modern times.

And, it is not the gambling or loose living as such that makes it so; hardly, that's the least of it. What it is, in fact, is the ongoing degradation, the mind-bending unreality of constant hustling while certain of our 'best' entertainers are included in the revolting practice of cleaning up a hundred-grand-per-week, at latest count, for services rendered. Put another way, one gets rewarded in amounts fit for the 'olden day' kings for the pleasure of dancing about the stage for an hour, or so. It's enough to make the likes of even Jesse James retch, he of the good, old fashioned 'stick-um-up' school of thievery. At least he had a gun. Now, a schlep will sing a little ditty, do the two step, crack a couple of sick jokes and-volah! 'A hundred grand please.' Terrific. For this we stormed Suribachi? For this? For this I wouldn't cross the Brooklyn Bridge. I shall never go back again, you'll be glad to know, Thomas Wolfe.

Bobi, and guess who, attended a Giant game, one night. Willie Mays was still with them at the time and not doing very well. Willie had seen better days. However, the night in question, some hotshot, as is their wont, tried to snag a fly-ball one-handedly, dropped it, and then commenced to play a little soccer with the horsehide, kicking it in a number of different directions, none of which led to the 'goalie' before finally snatching it up, to wit, a spectator or two, was heard to rejoin something to the effect of: "Weee, look, I think I dood find a ball." Goody.

Another time we meandered up to Bay Meadows to observe the bangtails in action. The plug in the first paid $36.60 to win, in the second $26.40. The D.D. paid $150.00 even. We did N-O-T stay for the third.

The firemen of Memphis struck the other day. Hah! Something different. The firemen did not get what they thought they should have. The firemen of

Memphis burned down Memphis the other day. The construction industry is booming in Memphis.

Recently, the mayor of one of our larger cities, was hauled in on the carpet for giving his 'assistant' a raise bringing said assistant's salary to a nicely rounded 50 thou. 'His honor,' bald-facedly defended the ungodly perversion by stating what an 'invaluable' aide she had been through-out his administration. Roughly translated, what a fantastic 'knob-polisher' she was. Now it has always amazed me, how, with all these assistant's and assistant's to the assistant's, why we need mayor's and governor's, and such, at all. Just pick up the check and shut-up, Bub.

The manufacturers, a Mom and Pop team, of that great boon to mankind DDT, sat down to a hearty meal of same for the benefit of the television cameras to dramatize the 'benign' effects of their contribution to the world. Mr. and Mrs. DDT, did in fact, survive, but it has been reported that no insects, not one of any description, has since alighted upon their insidious torsos.

Richard Nixon announced that the invasion into Cambodia was not an invasion as was inaccurately reported by the Media, but was, as any and all could plainly see, an 'incursion.' And the invasion at Normandy was a wading party, and that was only a big firecracker we dropped on Hiroshima, and all the dead in Cambodia aren't really dead, oh no … they're just playing possum.

I had a small garden once. My next-door neighbor also had a small garden. Neighbor sprayed his plants religiously. I did not. Neighbor, one evening, wished to know how come I didn't. "I'm not growing pesticides," said I, notably perturbed. Neighbor seemed puzzled, not an unusual condition, so I asked if it had ever occurred to him how it was done in bygone days before the filthy onslaught of 'progress in a can?' "As a matter of fact, no," he replied, innocently. "I suppose much of it was just lost to the pests," he added as an afterthought. (Makes you wonder who the pests are.)

"I see," I countered. "And maybe that's as it should be."

"How so?" he asked in obvious confusion.

"Well," said I, "would you rather have a garden full of aphids, or a belly full of DDT?"

"Hmnn," he mused. And that's as far as it goes, Buck.

Neighbor, for some time now, was being treated for a 'mysterious' skin rash of unknown origin. "They really don't know what it is," he said in bewilderment one day, "but I only seem to get it around spring time, and when I go on vacation it clears up. Isn't that strange?" Really; all things in their time.

I used to be an optimist. I used to be a child. Some have gotten rich writing puerile drivel about 'positive' thinking, a sure sign of bovine catalepsy. Some like to shoot blackbirds, and big-horn sheep, and mangle fresh-grown tulips. I used to be a child … once.

As can be expected—or can it—Bobi and I, decided to 'tie-the-knot.' Marriage always seemed like such a superfluous exercise, at best, but, what the hell, how often does a Roberta Higgins come along? And when she does, you do it, and that's all there is to that, Buck. Besides, what the J.P. has joined together Reno can put asunder. Now comes the good part. Bobi invited me over to dinner one evening to meet the folks. It had to be, I suppose; just another little burr in the balmy, torn drawers of life.

I picked her up at seven, and we drove to somewhere around San Rafael, knowing immediately that I had never been in T-H-I-S vicinity before. Miss Higgins, it seems, was even wealthier than I had at first suspected.

As we drove up to the house visions of Buckingham Palace kept dancing through my head. Pushing somewhere into the 1 mil range, the front contained one of those circular driveways, and enough hedges, and trees, and bushes to hide a multitude of geese.

We entered into a room large enough to hold the forty-yard dash. "Christ," I remarked in astonishment, "you need skates to get around in here."

"Yeah," she agreed, "it is kind of … spacious, isn't it?"

"Spacious? You could train a raft of hounds in here."

"You get used to it."

"And Woodstock could have played here."

"We gave it a thought," she joked, I think.

"What stopped you?"

"The lions in winter."

As we made our way to the farthest door, we were met by an agreeable looking, middle-aged woman of fifty-five, or so, wearing a dark blue dress, and a string of pearls with earrings to match. Everything looked real to me. And, for some unexplainable reason, because she really didn't resemble her, she reminded me of the late, great actress, Mary Astor. You know, she of the 'Maltese Falcon' fame? It could have been her comely manner, and graceful way of moving. Who knew?

Bobi introduced her as her Mother, one, Jane Millicent Higgins. Now I knew where Bobi acquired her class, and I liked her instantly, as she had an unassuming quality about her, in spite of her fortunate circumstances.

Extending a slim, delicate hand, she intoned how very delighted she was to meet what may soon become a happy addition to the family. I had no reason to doubt her sincerity.

"Well," she suggested after the usual preliminary small talk, "shall we go into the library and see what Mr. Higgins is about?" And without waiting for confirmation, led us thereto.

We entered into another definitely large chamber decorated in dark browns and cluttered with all manner of papers, books, folders, and similar paraphernalia. It also stank of stale, old cigars.

At the farthest end the top half of a large, hairy head of someone sitting in a leather-skinned easy chair with the front turned away, could be seen. He seemed to be casually looking out of two great windows into a back-yard, but from my vantage point looked more to be like the western half of Nairobi.

"Walter?" called Mrs. Higgins, "Bobi's here," and glancing in my direction, added, "with her young man." The chair swung around, and sitting was a rotund, greying man with a thick, rubbery face, and dark bushy eyebrows. Mr. Higgins, more than slightly resembled John L. Lewis, the former czar of the mine-workers union of a bygone era.

"Oh," he mechanically responded while rising. "So you're Bobi's fiancée." He seemed genuinely pleased until noticing my attire which can be said to be neat enough, but hardly formal enough for the particular occasion, moss green and lavender blue, the colors of my pants and sport shirt not being that designed to induce solemnity, a characteristic I somehow had no trouble whatever attributing to Mr. Higgins.

Giving me the 'once-over' with a jaundiced eye, he then extended a prodigiously, meaty hand across a messy desk and greeted, not altogether certain, "Pleased to meet you."

"Likewise," I replied mannerly.

"Well," he then added, "shall we have drinks?" and before getting a yes, no, or stuff-it, called out: William," wherein a short, thin black man wearing what short, thin black butlers usually wear during working hours, entered. I should have known, but it surprised me, nonetheless. Bobi, knowing me all to well by now, must have sensed the approaching strains of neurasthenia as she leaned toward me and whispered, "Part-time." It didn't help.

"What would you like, Mr . . . . . Mr. . . . ." the elder Higgins groped.

"Rosko, Dad," Bobi aided. "Mr. Rosko?"

"Bourbon," I uttered thinking, if I must.

"And two sherry's, and a brandy, William."

"Yes-suh, Mistah Walter."

"Yes-suh, Mistah Walter?" Christ, I thought all that woop-dee-do had gone out with Ike.

We all sat, and immediately Walter, now that his drawers were sufficiently chaffed, began grilling me. "Well now, Mr. Rosko. . . ."

"John," I corrected, since I had the feeling this conversation was going to sink into the pit of faked sincerity readily enough. "John, just what is it that you do for a living, young man?" Somehow, I sensed that whatever it was, it wasn't going to be good enough. He certainly didn't expect that I was the senior, vice-president of whatever, but neither did he expect what he did get which was a big fat "nothing."

"Nothing?" he roared agitatedly. "Nothing?"

"For the time being, Sir. I'm kind of ... in between things. But I should hasten to add, so as not to create any false impressions, that my prospects at the moment don't look any too good."

"I see. Well, Bobi didn't say much except that you were a college drop out, but I hardly expected this." Good ol' Bobi, I thought to myself. She sure smoothed things over, the little darlin. "You're not planning to go back and mooch an education off her, are you?" he queried offensively.

I sensed the conversation, and a bit quicker than I would have thought, had taken a turn for the worse. I stiffened. I didn't like his tone, and was quickly coming to dislike him, a trait these days I was, more and more, becoming acquainted with, more and more.

"Mr. Higgins," I chirped, trying to appear unruffled. "Let me put your mind at ease."

"Please."

"Yes ... well ... to begin with, I have no intention of returning to school, at any time, for any reason. Secondly: I am not getting married to mooch, as you so directly put it, off of anyone, and last, but not least, under no circumstances whatever, will I become a burden to Bobi. I love her, and I wish her life with me to be a joy, not a hardship. I'm not marrying to gain a serf."

Walter, eyeballing me like the century ago Apaches would have an unguarded wagon train, was unconvinced. "That," he quickly rebutted, "doesn't speak to the main question," which was: "What do you intend to do for a living?"

Things were getting a bit testy. Ah, life. So simple, and yet so diff-ee-cult. A sea of waves between calm shores.

"Mr. Higgins, I don't know what I'm going to do. I'm not exactly prepared to do anything. I really haven't given it much thought."

"What!" he boomed unabashedly. "Not given it much thought!"

"Dad?" Bobi interjected trying to reassure.

"Dad, hell. The man's about to take one of the biggest steps of his life … with my daughter, and he stands there without any visible means of support, and doesn't look too all-fired, get-out about it, and you say, Dad?"

Actually, he did have a point, but coming from a baboon, it takes away the shine. In any case, all I could muster under the disagreeable circumstances was a vexing, "We'll manage, Mr. Higgins."

"Sure, sure," he castigated. "On her dough and mine." He certainly was getting nasty.

"Sir," I repined, "that was uncalled for, as I do not believe anyone mentioned y-o-o-u-r bread."

"Yeah? And Hitler never mentioned Denmark, either." Uh, oh, I thought. We're not going to get a history lesson too, are we?

"I don't know about no Denmark, Mr. Higgins," I assured, "but I'm not after your lettuce. What's in your garden is yours, and I ain't planning any raiding parties."

"Then what, Mister? What?"

"What, what, Sir?"

"We're going in circles, Mister."

"Not an unexpected course. . . . ."

"And that seems to be the kind of marriage this is going to be." William gratefully, entered with our drinks. I was never so glad to see 'John Barleycorn' in all my life. It wasn't so much the heat getting to me; I've been on a hot stove before, but that I just didn't know what to tell him. Strange to say, but I had never really thought of it, me being what I was, none to concerned with such 'incidentals,' and Bobi, never asking, she being what she was, rich, and taking it all in stride. Come to think of it, this horse's ass was the first to think of it.

Nothing more was said as we each stabbed at the tray for our respective nourishment all parties welcoming the interlude.

As the interrogation resumed, Bobi, fortunately, was the first to speak. Who could get angry with Bobi?

"Dad," she tried to console. "You have the wrong impression. John is not a bum." (She sure could read minds.) Walter, on his part, gave one of those---and none to discreetly—'this chick's got to be kidding' looks.

"You see, Dad, John's right. We never really gave it much thought." And as expected, he rebutted with: "You all don't seem to have given it any. You don't think it's important? Maybe I've done a disservice by giving you what most daughters' never had, and never will."

"Let's not get maudlin, Dad." Like I said, Bobi could fling a spear, now and then, herself.

"God-damn it, Miss. The point around here somehow is escaping me." (Even the fuzzos hit upon it once in a while.) "You're going to have to face it eventually. What're you waiting for, zero bank account?"

I was so grateful Bobi had taken away the play allowing me precious time to gather my wits, although a month wouldn't have made much difference. There just wasn't much I could come back with, sad to say.

"What's the rush, Dad?" Bobi continued. "The date hasn't even been set yet."

"That's the best damned news I've heard all evening. And I don't see any ring either," he jibed irritably trying to build a case against me, although he seemed to be doing all right so far.

"I don't have one, Dad," Bobi answered coolly.

"And why not?" he rebutted equally frigid. What with all the cold weather blowing in I was beginning to feel like a naked jaybird in a March wind.

"Because I don't want one," Bobi refuted.

"You mean, H-E don't want one," he snapped nastily while motioning towards me.

"Now what would he do with one?" Bobi now was dipping the darts in a little poison. Love that Bobi. Walter stiffened, but pushed on.

"Apparently, he can't afford one," he added in the same biting tone.

"Dad, it just wasn't something I wanted, that's all. The world's not going to come to an end because I don't have one."

"Oh, c'mon now, Bobi. Everybody gets an engagement ring. It's been going on for centuries. Even paupers spring for something as long as there's a five-and-dime store around, and we got plenty of them. You trying to tell me he's not even a pauper?" I was beginning to rankle at the 'he' bit, designed no doubt, to make me feel like an indentured servant. Walter, I must say, c-o-u-l-d 'push the envelope.'

"Oh, have it your way, Dad," Bobi rejoined, despondently.

"I just don't understand the present generation," he continued in a more subdued, but nevertheless depressing tone. "They don't seem to have any responsibility. Why, hell; in my time that was the damned first thing we thought of when we decided to take the plunge." I wonder: Is it just coincidence that marriage is often spoken of in terms of 'taking a bath?' I yearned to say something but couldn't as a vapid, nauseous feeling in my gut replaced the thoughts that should have been in my head. In Walters's frame of mind whatever I did say would only have flamed the embers, anyhow. The cliché 'silence is golden' kept flashing through my mind. I dove for it.

"Well," chipped in Mrs. Higgins, "shall we go in to dinner?" And with that cheery lead-in, we all strode mechanically into the dining room, another chamber that can best be described as spacious, and uncommonly opulent.

Momentarily, after we were seated, a woman of nondescript appearance came through one of the doors and began serving chicken gumbo soup. After the soup came—you guessed it—the roast beef.

The Anglo-Saxon is curiously fond of the most unappetizing fare. Have I mentioned it before? A dollar to a donut we get bread pudding for dessert. I'll scream.

We spoke during the course of the meal, I know not of what. Mr. Higgins did most of the talking while Mrs. Higgins, darling that she was, piped in at just the right moments keeping everything on an even keel. It is one of the red-eyed shames of the world, that the Mr. Higgins's never realize what they have in the Mrs. Higgins's. Only to the manor born.

I kept wondering by what accident or quirk of fate a quality act like Bobi could ever have emerged from such a plucked goose. I have to believe that babies, after birth, are more commonly misplaced than is customarily supposed. She had about as much in common with her progenitor as I had with 'George the V.' So, life still has its little secrets. And would you believe it? We did get the pudding. I didn't scream, but I gritted my teeth.

After dinner I was ushered back into the drawing-room where, I suppose, Walter and I were supposed to have one of those 'eye-ball-to-eyeball' chats. At times, one need not be a Nostradamus to fore tell the future.

William brought more drinks—it was that kind of night—and I was decorously asked to 'make myself comfortable.' I don't know why, but Walter began to look like Judge Roy Bean, stuffy robes, stinking cigar, gavel and all.

"So," he began, "what's this all about?" Well, Jesus H. Christ. Not from square o-o-o-o-n-e? I thought we were all through this.

"A-a-a-bout?" I stuttered, obviously taken aback, somewhat.

"Come; come, now, my man. You're not really serious about this fiasco, are you? As you can well see, we're not the same kind of people as you." The 'put-down' bit was beginning to irk me. I held my mud. He continued. "We're of different worlds; you can see that, surely. Bobi's no more the girl for you than the "Queen of England."

I didn't mind him putting Bobi in the Queen's class, but I did mind him implying my being something less than 'princely.' I tried playing down this increasingly vexatious 'conversation.'

"Sir," I steadfastly rebutted, "I really don't see it that way at all. I'm marrying a woman, not her past."

No sooner had the words carelessly tumbled out did I know I had bungled. Quicker than a lust-crazed grizzly in a Yosemite springtime, he pounced. "Hah! That's where you're wrong, Mister. You sure are marrying her past, and her style of life, and everything that goes with it. Can you cope with that?"

"I haven't had any trouble till now. I never really thought it would be a problem till now."

"Well it god-damn sure can be; make no mistake about it. Can you live like we live? Do you know how?" And then, swinging two pork-laden arms about the room, he continued ponderously. "Do you see all this? Can you provide these creature comforts?"

"No, to all three questions, and, I wouldn't want to."

"What?" he asked, somewhat flustered.

"Who needs it? You planning on living forever? And even then. . . ." A definite scowl crossed his fleshy, florid face. "Don't get smart Buster," he snapped. Well now, it's that time, is it? It just had to be, I suppose.

"Mister?" I scowled in turn. "It seems we've just about crossed over the line. So, if we're going to have this palaver, then, let's have it." I, no longer in the mood for his jibs and jibes, would have my turn, and, if it came to it, then a round or two in the mud to boot. That's just the way of it sometimes. "You lay your cards on the table," I continued sorely, "and I'll do likewise, and we'll see who's holding what." Although, I am sure, if I had a full-house, he'd have four little deuces. It's that kind of life.

"That's just jim-dandy with me," he growled. Now I know what a gladiator must have felt like. I threw the first stone.

"First of all, I don't give one, good, fucking damn what you think about me, Bub." (I accentuated the "Bub" knowing it would raise a few bristles. It did; he stiffened.) "Secondly, nobody, including the parent in question, is going to kick me around like a bum on the bowery. Thunderbird has never touched this pilgrims lips. Thirdly, if we do decide to marry—and that's a damned good bet at the moment---then we'll decide it, and not her family, or her friends, or whoever. And lastly, if it appears the family of the lady in question is going to become an 'obstacle' then, I say, let them; that's their look-out, and if worse comes to worse, you all can just go and fuck yourselves."

"Just one minute. . . . ."

"Stuff it, Mister. Who needs this kind of crap anymore. Those what can't get along shouldn't associate, and that includes blood. It's as simple as that. If one wishes to manufacture a problem, it is not incumbent upon the public to buy. You're manufacturing a problem, Bub, and I ain't buying."

I thought he was coming after me right then and there. I wished he would have, conveniently standing as I was, next to an eight-pointer mounted conspicuously low. I'd have loved to have stuck a pointy horn, or two, up his well-healed arse. Instead he settled for a, "Smart-ass, aint' cha?" And then, "Okay, how much?" Now that one got me. I didn't expect that … at all. Should have, but, for some reason, it didn't seem like our little pow-wow had quite reached that 'elevated' plateau. Of mice and men. "How much?" I repeated seriously.

"That's right. How much? I know what side of the tracks you're from greaser."

"Down to that, are we? Okay, what am I bid?" I shot back briskly, deciding to ride out the crest. I was curious to see exactly what I could get … just in case. "I thought so. Ten thousand, and disappear, quietly, right now, forever; just drop out of site like you've never been."

"Ten grand?" I repeated. "Shit, you don't have a very high opinion of your daughter."

"No, I don't have a very high opinion of YOU."

"My, my, and we just met, to."

"Well?" he shot back impatiently.

"Keep your bread in your pocket Mister, or wherever it is you people keep it. This may come as a great shock to you, but I didn't come here to "ransack the premises."

"You didn't, ay?" Apparently Walter wasn't convinced.

"Twenty thousand." I said nothing.

"Thirty!" Again, no answer. Then, quite irritably, he rattled off in quick succession, "forty, fifty, a hundred. Name your motley price, god-damn it!" he boomed. "This family goes back a thousand years, and we ain't had no fuckin, greasy, dago wop in it yet!"

"Ah, hah!" I barreled out. And now the line strikes bottom. Going to have to swill around where the whale dungs, hey? Okay, but first I thought, Walter was badly in need of a history lesson, so, I obliged.

"Did you know, Mr. Higgins, that of the thousands upon thousands of wops, who fought in the second World War, not to speak of Korea and the present unmentionable headliner you know where, upwards of twenty-percent of the casualties of those named conflicts that came from my hometown, just a trifling, little burgh nestled inconspicuously somewhere in the hills of New York were 'wops?' Greazy, dago wops? Did you know that, Mr. Higgins? And did you also know that there was a greazy marine sergeant by the name of Basilone, who, if memory serves me right, was not a Scotsman from Glasgow, won the 'Medal of Honor' in a quaint little marshland called Guadalcanal, and who later mustered out permanently on a rocky, little blot in the Pacific known as Iwo Jima with his guts hanging all out like pork links on a meat hook as a result of his happening to be in the same spot, at the same time as a Japanese mortar shell, just so you and yours," and I swung my arms about the room, "can have a-a-a-l-l this.

Isn't it wonderful? Yeah, tell me about the wops, Mr. Higgins; I seem to be short on the finer points of human nature. Tell me about the superiority of the W.A.S.P. with his guns and dynamite and sado-masochistic revivalism. Tell me about his good-hearted, Christian concern in dragging the black man across an ocean in chains so he can introduce him to the 'eighth wonder of the world'—the Bible. Of course he had to pick a little cotton in the bargain; a cheap price to pay for 'salvation' wouldn't you say? And you? What are you? English? Scotch? Welsh? Or any combination there-of, with maybe a little German thrown in for good measure. Let's not forget the Nordic Superman by all means; tell me about it."

Walter, at that point must have realized somewhat, his asinine, pompous stance, or else simply refused to 'roll-in-the mud' on his turf. Whatever, he softened a bit. He didn't answer, but quietly, almost as an after thought, murmured:

"Mister, this marriage ain't for you." The noxious reprobate, mother, ala Richard M. Nixon, he didn't even have the class to apologize. No matter; dreams are not made of temporal, good wishes.

"Maybe not, pal," I rejoined straight-up, "but let it be after the fact, not before. It shouldn't be all that big a thing to anyone but Bobi and me. After all, who are we hurting? And maybe we are cutting across a few sorry notions about 'kind marrying kind' and such, but then, I think we are of a kind, her and me … and if by chance, and the 'will of the gods' worse comes to worse, there's always a little thing called divorce, maybe not the best of roads, but better than a 'sharp-stick-in-the-eye' in this most imperfect of worlds."

We both sat quietly for a moment, fatigue having caught up with our exertions. Presently, I solemnly added softly: "Mr. Higgins, this is a tough life, at best. Actually, as a very far-sighted man at one time, many moons ago noted, it could be described as mean, nasty, brutish and short, not entirely off the mark, wouldn't you say? Let's not make this any more so than need be. Fate has a few tricks of her own. She needs no help from us."

I felt like a fool lecturing the vice-president of what's-it, but what the hell, he did have it coming. So … I let all the string out. "You're a man of considerable means, if that counts for anything, and you have more than what ninety-nine-percent of the people of this world will ever have. Don't scatter it in a pit of faked superior, malicious tom-foolery. This is supposed to be a happy time for you daughter. Let her enjoy it; she's entitled. And unless she had walked in here with 'Jack-the-Ripper' you should have denied your feelings for the sake of hers cause, like I said, this is a hard world with the good times markedly short on this brief trip through this treacherous, fetid germ-laden swamp. That's all I have to say on the matter. You row your boat, and I'll row mine."

"I'm worried about it sinking."

"So am I palsy, so am I."

"Okay; okay," was all he could finally mutter, softly and despondently. It was enough that he didn't come at me with a machete. And on that somber note the dialogue ended as we traipsed in to rejoin the ladies.

I stayed another hour straining at the bit. We posed a deadly audience for a struggling comic, but, I must say, Mrs. Higgins did her best. Nice lady she. I'm hoping Bobi has most of her in her. She'd better.

On the way to the car, she, not one to miss the soft, billowy strands gliding on a summers breeze, asked what we all gabbed about, 'Dad and me,' since neither of us appeared 'any too gay.'

Not being one to lie—it being the height of puerility on such solemn occasions—so, I told her … both barrels, straight from the shoulder. Alas, it only confirmed her sad suspicions.

"Well," she declared, "I kind of half suspected it. Dad, at times, can be such a boor." I had a better word.

"Yeah," I agreed. "I guess it goes with the territory. Funny, the longer I live the more life resembles a cheap B movie from tinsel town, you being the only bright spot in a long list of dismal credits." She smiled, we kissed, and off I left for beautiful, downtown San Jose.

As I drove back down the peninsula, I wondered why lubbers like Walter seemed to have everything, financially speaking, that is, and nicelies like me nothing. But then, it's not all that mysterious, really. Given his grotesque character had he not the bread he'd be a momentous burden to the whole of society in every imaginable way. Adversity to such does not wear well, which would include, no doubt, the abuse of his mate, flogging the kids, kicking the dog, hassling his friends, neighbors, and what not, in a word—muck-it-up pretty good. I, on the other hand, with my great charm and grace, didn't need a satchel of pesos to 'make-it' and in all probability, the powers that be must have observed so. I am not entirely joshing, Virginia. Justice, in her benighted strange way, abounds. Sic.

* * *

XII

THERE IS NO PAIN

LIKE THE PAIN OF LOVE

UNLESS IT BE THE LOSS OF LOVE

AND SHOULD YOU FIND

IN THE LIGHT OF DAY

A GREATER PAIN THAN THIS TO BE

DO NOT BESEECH THE GODS TO HEED

YOUR LONGING GRIEF AND VAIL OF TEARS

FOR ALAS YOU ARE AT LAST

IN LIFE'S LONG LASTING FIRES OF HELL

WE did not set a date for the wedding, but it was assumed three or four months seemed about right. In the meanwhile, Bobi and I were 'doing it all.' I can now say, before departing from this mass of whirling debris, that I had my Innings. Happiness is love with the proper acquaintance, and the beauty of compatibility.

I saw Bobi every night, consumed by the passion and unknowable truth of the ages.

Euphoria is a trick perpetrated by the gods. Lulled into a false sense of being, one is ripe for the great swatch of the big blade. Intuitively, I knew, somehow, what Bobi and I had could never last. The flaming rocket burning bright, would consume itself in speeding flight. Nature, impervious to the harmonious welfare of mankind, has only an interest in continuity, and its means of achieving same is linear.

Two mortals meet, love, procreate, disintegrate, and then, as precise as a timeless Swiss movement, the flame becomes a flicker, and the flicker a puff of smoke.

Romance and passion is a temporary condition. Quickly it enters, and likewise its exit. Like the rodent in the sewer the species thrives on disease. Virtue is not universally noted, and, as with all things, so with us. The fire of our passion would give way to inconstant love; convenience and routine would worm its way to the forefront, and nothing short of eternal rest shall replace it.

Aye, all of life is but a transparent bubble, hollow and delicate with any force or object, a stone, a twig, a playful dog; a raindrop, a pine needle, the slightest breeze, likely to end it all of a sudden.

* * *

A few weeks after the 'grand party' at the Higgins household, my love and I, one lazy evening, were lackadaisically sitting viewing the Monday night game. (Even she was beginning to like it.) Baseball---my god, if one could only learn to appreciate the art of harmonious simplicity, paint without brushes, sculpt without chisels.

Sadly, the aficionado's now playing the game behave in a manner reminiscent of 'little Lord Fauntleroy.' The day will come when they will destroy themselves as surely as the unawares blue tail fly scampering across the hood of the trapdoor spider. Your grand children will live to see the vaunted New York Yankees reduced to a bunch of boozing barnstormers traveling this land in hectic one-night stands not to unlike the manner reminiscent of Bingo Balducci's traveling road show. All things. . . . .

As we sat watching, munching our chips and slurping our suds, the subject 'how and the how comes of civilization,' crept into the fifth inning. (Bobi could make a U-turn on Sunset and Vine quicker than a ten-dollar trollop could disrobe.) Quite innocently, the question was: 'What was it that determined the quality of a civilization?'

Dropping my chip in the dip, I rescued the crumbly morsel from the gue, where, in turn, I asked if she needed an answer immediately, or could she wait until the ninth inning, or so?

No more was said about it for three innings, but it remained in the back of my mind to resurface again. Finally, in the top of the eight, as the ball girl was painfully struck in the crotch by a swiftly bounding ball, I threw down the gauntlet, but not before gaining a certain small pleasure in the anachronistic young lady's grimacing pain. Good, I secretly assured myself. They belong on the 50 yard line at half-time at the Michigan, Ohio State game anyway, giving all the fuzzy-cheeked, wide-eyed Bucko's a scintillating, vicarious thrill eyeballing their sweet, bouncing little buns.

"Okay," I opened, "what about civilization?" My abruptness startled her.

"What about it?" she countered.

"Well," you're the one that asked?" I sputtered.

"I did at that, didn't I?" she acknowledged.

"So now what? And specifically, Miss Higgins, just what was it you had in Mind?"

"Do you think we have time?" she probed.

Glancing at the tube, I then remarked, matter-of-factly: "Oh yeah; they're changing pitchers, and by the looks of the rag arm the Mets are bringing in, it's going to be a long night … for everyone, so fire away."

"I could never understand how the richest, most powerful, most everything nation on earth, could have so many problems like mass murders, to name just one, or just plain violence, if it can be so described. How come? It should be the other way around, shouldn't it? How can we be so fantastic, and yet be so "fucked-up.""

Ah, my dear, sweet, tumble-of-love. Somehow 'fucked-up' coming from her pink, sweet soft lips sounded more like Van Cliburn at the Met. It's going to be a v-e-e-e-r-y interesting marriage, very.

I chomped on a chip. A very provocative question, I thought. Slowly, like two, blind porcupines mating, it came to me. "Well now, Miss Higgins," I drawled. "To begin with, your initial premise: How come we're so fantastic is not correct."

"No?"

"No. Any nation steeped in the atrocities previously mentioned can hardly be described in such glowing superlatives. We're boisterous, but not great.

Ever notice an American in Paris? Revolting. Acts like he saved France from Hitler all by himself. He ought to take a trip to Russia and count a few crosses.

"The Ugly American. . . . ."

"He could use a mask. "

"Hmnn, that bad?"

"Let me put it this way; you've been to the races, I know. And while there, did you ever notice a nice, big beautiful piece of horse flesh come trotting out in the post parade looking for all the world like the son of Whirlaway, dancing and prancing and what not. You say to yourself: 'My how can this lovely creature lose?' But lose he does, and with him, your 2 bucks. Well, that's the story of the 'good ol' U.S. of A. All flash and glitter, a scruffy scarecrow, clothed, but underneath---just a stick. We are, my dear, exactly what you said we are."

"Which was?

"Fucked-up."

"I said all that in one, hyphenated little word?"

"Must be the hyphen."

"Must be."

I continued. "We're attempting to build a house of cards with the highest principles of engineering and technology, but it's still a house of cards, and there's no way out."

"Why not? There's always hope."

"Not really. You see, my sweet; it's like a pennant race. Two teams may be evenly matched, but when one starts going into a slide, the momentum carries them right out of it. Then, at the end of the year, they'll all sit around and muse: 'Jesus, how the hell did we ever finish 10 games back? We were better than that.' Big Mo, sweetheart, big mo. It's a crusher, and we're caught dead in its tracks. Unfortunately, the issue to which we speak is not a game."

"But surely, at some point, it does reverse itself?"

"Oh, sure; but not before you're ten games out, which might as well be ten times ten. The point is, when a highly specialized, complex technological society begins making basic mistakes, that very technology, which heretofore was such a boon, now becomes a tool of destruction. Guns can be aimed at the cops as well as the crooks.

Let's put it another way. When I was a kid---around eight or nine---I took our 'tick-tock' apart, one of those el cheepo Big Bens. I dismantled every piece bit by bit, indeed I dood, and laid it oh so neatly on the table; I was so proud. Damdest job you ever saw, too. Only took five minutes, maybe. But that was the whole ball of wax. Two hours later it was still lying there, more or less, and three, then four, then five, and then an exceedingly 'terse' reconnoitering by Pops. Never did get it back together. In other words: We just can't get it back together, but ohhh wasn't it charming to take apart."

"I can understand that, but what, precisely, are we doing wrong?"

"Good gawd, you aaaare put-ting-me-on."

"I thought I would."

"Well, it's not so much what we're doing wrong, per se, but why? It is always—why?"

"And?"

"The and is: Attitudes, thoughts, feelings. What are we really, inside, behind closed doors? Who are we? How and why do we think and feel the way we do about things, finally? For instance: It has now become fashionable to be pro hangman. You dig it? For a while, predictably after the Chessman affair, it swung the other way; now it's swinging back again."

"Come to think of it, it is, isn't it?"

"So there it is. Where is one's soul? And I speak not so mundane as of heaven and hell. It's an intuitive thing, without being a bleeding heart. A soul would shudder at the notion of killing no matter who does it, and for what ungodly 'ethic?' Well, we don't shudder, we don't even wince, in fact, we applaud; put it on the tube, they say. Let everyone get charged up join in on the festivities.

The insanity of it all, this killing business. And you know what has become respectable it its justification? And in 'educated' circles even, mind you. Well now—and get this; you really have to be on your toes for this one or you'll drop your pearlies in the soup. 'IT IS A MATTER OF DIGNITY! HONOR! JUSTICE!' How's that for clubbing the poor ass. We show our regard for life by strapping their cold, sweaty rumps to an electric chair, and frying them like a pork chop. Haven't come very far in six-thousand years, have we? The Old Testament is rent with such nonsense, all to the everlasting credit of J.C. for having stood that idyllic, little manual of subterranean seizures upon its knotty head; thumb screw mentality at its best. And have you noticed that that is the same warped mentality that got us into Viet-Nam?"

"The same?"

"The very; it all fits, just like the prettiest of puzzles. We had to decimate a whole country to keep a handful of corrupt blackguards in power, they being useful to our purposes.

And abortion? Never. Better to starve their blighty, little asses after they get here, so's to give the lord a chance to save their suffering souls. The niggers? Send all the burr-headed, black bastards back to Africa where they belong, the smelly fuckers. Not realizing, of course, the 'smelly fuckers' carried this nation on their backs for 300 years, shining our shoes for a nickel, truckin our bags for a dime, washing our crutty dishes for 2 bits, picking our cotton for a buck-a-day, not to mention cleaning up our dainty, shitty, white-assed kids. Without their back-breaking, stoop labor, we wouldn't be a good pile of shit in the barnyard. And yes; the welfare slobs, worthless bums, all of them. Kick their malingering rears out into the street. The queers? Lousy perverts. We ought to ship them all to Devils Island, treat-um like the fucking lepers that they are. The commie's? Kill, kill every last godless, mother's son's of them. Ah yes, but doesn't it all fit. It tears your guts out; were sending rockets to the moon, and we still think it's made of green cheese. Hah! The bull's running wild in the china shop."

"Oh … all that nice finery."

"Cannibal's are squaring the universe. Give the lout a fair trial and hang-im. Stretch his gullet three ways to the wind. But, if we are to understand the problem in all its winding, twisting treachery, we must retreat back to square one, which is—the people."

"The people?"

"Begging the question? I know, but, nevertheless, the Ouija board does not lie. The people? They have cow-curd for brains, water in their veins, and crap in their guts displacing any room that might have been used for such a small article like 'pluck?' 'Grit?' 'Nerve?' 'Fortitude?' How bout 'intrepitude?' Is their such a word? There must be; it has such a nice ring to it."

"Maybe so, but I think intrepidly is as far as you can go with that one."

"No matter. You get the point."

"Yes, and very succinctly, too."

"And lest you be tempted to think merely a colorful description, but hold fast your sails; the wind is agin us."

"Hmmm."

"The average man. Now there's a bloke for ya. There is no such a thing, you know?"

"There isn't?"

"By definition, any grouping comprising more than half by 1 integer is common, pertaining to ordinary, non-exceptional, undistinguishable."

"He depresses you."

"Disgusts is more the word."

"That's snobbish."

"I can live with it."

"But apparently, not with him."

"Give the lady with the pretty curls two free tickets to the fun-house."

"Uh, huh."

"He, it is, who circles the wagons." We both paused momentarily as sickening thoughts can be fatiguing. A few deep breaths and I resolutely pressed on.

"Suppose we were to construct the human character on a scale of one to ten. There would be, inevitably, that small minority of excellence comprising the nine to ten range. Not many, to be sure, and almost totally irrelevant by its paucity. Now I realize there's a school of thought that believes otherwise, but, like most everything else, w-r-o-o-o-n-g. Then there's that small minority comprising the sub-human range of one and two. It is in that number that you'll find the Nazi's, Ku-Kluxers', Charlie Manson and the like. Not so irrelevant for evil has a geometric progression heretofore not found in the good otherwise we'd be living in the Garden of Eden. Be that as it may, we now come to the thundering herd venerably known as—ta-ra—the common man. Well, you say, so? So, yes? No?"

"No?"

"No?"

"Please to explain, Bwana."

"Okie-doke, and this is the steel trap squeezed about the lubbers what's-it: AS LONG AS EVERYTHING IS JIM-DANDY, he behaves like a five or six, fortunately for everyone concerned. He, characteristically, is living in the hollow shell of quiet desperation. But once, just once, should some small happenstance occur taxing his limited capacities, then very quickly, very quickly indeed, you will find him perceptibly sliding into the three and four range which, as you can see, is dangerously close to one and two, and woe to us all.

So, what you have actually is a supposed average class, which is not average at all, but sub-average. Now the only way to judge human nature is through its behavior when it is 'up against it' and invariably, at such times, we also find it searching for a soft spot to lie."

"So now that we know the problem, how do we fix it?"

"We don't, my darlin. It involves too much. We are paralytic zombies catatonically bumping into the four walls. Chase a rat and he'll scoot for a dark corner. We, my sweet, are hiding within our infirmity, and a soft shell cracks under the slightest pressure. Were Tom Paine alive today, he'd allow for one grievous look, and take up the kings cause."

"But getting back to capital punishment for a moment. That seems to be the least of our problems, wouldn't you think?"

"Ho! Well, on the face of it, it doesn't mean a damn thing, one way or the other, to be sure, except to the hapless dupe whose neck is stretching out the noose, and how many can we sting in a year? A few score? Hell, honey bun, there's more killing than that going on in the street in one day. In 1933, in Chicago alone, 365 unlucky inhabitants were summarily gunned down. That comes out to---you guessed it, my love—a nice, round one-a-day, just like the vitamin, although one could say a severe case of lead poisoning had run amuck … but that's not the point."

"It's not? Now I'm confused."

"The real tail swinging the dog are values, trends, concepts, emotions contributing to but surpassing that which might induce a casual 'roll-of-the-head' in the wicker basket.

Ask yourself: Why would a society institutionalize such an out-and-out fraud, such a foul, gross, sinister practice? To deter? Hah! Deter my ass. How long do we have to wait for success? We've been cooking them since Edison invented electricity."

"I didn't know Edison invented electricity. I thought it was Franklin."

"I'm getting to love you, more and more. . . . ."

"I thought you loved me tops already?"

"Tops or bottoms. I don't know where to begin."

"You're a dirty dog."

"And I'm not even 'old folks' yet."

"Getting a head start, are you?"

"I think you got me cornered."

"Let's get back to … what was it?"

"This fucked-up, pest-hole we glowingly call a democracy, a government of the people, by the people, for the people. The ass-suckin, bastards don't know a stinking dump when they're sitting right on it.

"I see. So now what?"

"Yes, well; society being the composite of the individual, for all intents and purposes, yet is not the simple addition of each of its members, it nevertheless, behaves amazingly so.

The Manson 'family' how many was it that they killed? Six? Seven? Some family they, and for what? They claimed for a higher good; they were ridding society of an unnecessary evil.

So, make a connection: Didn't we charge into Viet-Nam to halt evil in its tracks? Wasn't that the justification? The person kills seven, the society seven-hundred-thousand. We stuck Manson in a hole, but the evil mother-fuckers who continue on with this black opera are in great demand on the chicken-wing circuit, and they all someday will write their 'memoirs.' Memoirs: Hah! A big, fat 'bible of lies.' It is all hog-swill."

"We're all nuts-os's?"

"At the very least."

"So, what came first, the chicken or the egg?"

"Well, my dear, that is all bagatelle now. What is not however, is the f-a-c-t of the chicken and the egg. The one grows into the other, and again, and again, and again. The individual feeds society, and society feeds the individual. We are television, television is us, and the greening of America is found in the ongoing corruption of its institutions, and the concomitant deadening of each individual member. The cobras' kiss does not spell love, and fear and ignorance is the deadly venom of these viperous times."

"Sounds like one, big jungle to me."

"Your hearing is good. Society clamors for the head of the killer, because its own is precariously dangling on the tip of the spike. The coward's ruse is scapegoatism. The brave society faces its dilemma; it does not look for dupes to hang its mistakes on. The sane society marshals all of its resources like an army before battle, inquiring into all the possible strategies and maneuvers for the sole purpose of victory. It does not shoot at the first bird popping out of the bush.

The good society asks why? Why? A thousand times, why? For the just see the irrevocable connections between its most pernicious members and itself; between the good, the bad, and the ugly. Siamese twins must learn to live in harmony together, or perish together. Even a community of thieves respects one another. You think Manson is an exception? There is a 'little bit of Charlie' in us all."

"No doubt, according to this historical perspective."

"No doubt, and to continue, we are no more civilized than the headhunters of New Guinea. A Brooks Brothers suit and a shiny Jag does not a man make. Emily Post has not, as yet, been introduced to the Aborigine; merely an accident of circumstance. He eats with his hands, and we with silver spoons and forks. Yet, we both—those of us of the female persuasion—still squat to pee, a slight anatomical similarity we have conveniently overlooked.

And take a trip down to Wall Street on any piddling day and observe the incantations of the natives busily weaving their magic spell over the whole of the universe, and tell me they do not bear a striking resemblance to the local tribal, witch doctor casting out the evil spirits. Wall Street, the jungle; a different time, a different place. One wears a loin cloth, the other wash and wear polyester. The moneychangers are a boisterous sort, but there was but one Christ. Common is common by any other name, any other place. Our plight? It will continue."

"That's it"

"You see, love, if a culture is in the clutches of negativism, it breeds negativism. We are, and always have been, a 'thou shalt not,' civilization, a civilization of faith, and not of good works, and of all the dumb-assed, friggin devil-dodgers to follow, we had to pick that dick-head Calvin.

But, to get on with it; negativism may be a somewhat useful method of survival, but not of growth, and what ceases to grow eventually dies."

"So, we're dying?"

"Worse. We have not yet learned to live for all of our hu-zahs. We have never learned."

"And so?"

"So what we have then is a mildewed culture, snarling and ill-tempered, traits unlikely to withstand a brief squall, let alone a full-blown, tropical tempest."

"And we're approaching the tropical variety?"

"Approaching? We're dead in its eye, sweet. Would you expect a Nazi to save a Jew? Preposterous."

"You're telling me. Keep going. This trains going downhill with a full head of steam."

"Simply stated: We are living in a diseased environ and the sickness filters all through it, and touches every member, and every member is affected by it at no small price. Obviously the populous becomes hardened and insensate, bringing with it an air of callous megalomania. And the human psyche, so perceptible to manipulation, invariably also learns a surly disrespect for life, whereby its education then becomes a straight line to same. It is the way of all flesh, and the maggoty hind-quarters becomes the prime-rib on a twenty-dollar plate."

"Ugh."

"Disgusting, isn't it? So, in effect, the result is a far less salubrious colony than would otherwise be, and instead of Captain Marvel, we have Captain Nemo, and this, it is, what enables murders, violence, unspeakable acts of all description against man and beast. The hundred that might be saved by the cyanide pellet, is wiped out a thousand fold, simply by the fact of the destructive forces gripping society, of which the firing squad is merely a noisy, homicidal symptom, a knee-jerk, hypnotic reaction to frustration and impotence. What we gain one way, we lose many times over in another. And that, my darlin, is what the simpletons cannot get through their wormy skulls.

The hangman enjoys his work, make no mistake about it. And the State? By virtue of its being the State, does not, by that, give it any extra-terrestrial privileges, but even less so. It is the handmaiden, and not the maker of history."

"And it's all connected?"

"Like graft and a scum-sucking politician. Viet-Nam, bigotry, intolerance; dirty air, shylock lawyers, slimy CEO's, hypocritical 'holy-men.' They are all links on the same rusty chain. We are cannibals in a silk suit, bound at the hip to that distinguished and unsullied paragon of human excellence—the Hun."

"Not what you might call the prevailing sentiments of this fair land."

"Malevolence is eternal." I could see the color draining from my sweethearts face, and depression setting in. Let me seal this tomb of despair, I thought. This is a night for ball games and beer, and the pleasantries of merrymaking. I waited for a response so as to quickly cage this wild magpie.

"It all sounds so futile to me," she finally expressed.

"And so it is," I averred. "And the law—that mountebank in judicial robes—sits by lackadaisically playing with itself, while a dozen horny toads are clamoring for its attention. And, we all, every last one of us, nest cozily within that same dizzying travesty. It influences our religion, business, schools, industry; it's in the board room of General Motors, and the bedroom of General Smith; in local 101 of the Amalgamated Meat cutters of America, and 202 of the Grand Order of the Moose; on the back bench, and the park bench; on main street, and the boulevard; in the cities and in the country; it hangs in the air like volcanic ash, and is everywhere ungodly prevalent. It is, love, our world, and it is this community of disease that kills, flaunting the face of evil and mendacity. What we have on our hands, my sweet, is the plague, and killing a few rats will not dispel it."

"But we're sure having a go at it."

"We cannot see the fleas for the hair, so the dog scratches and becomes mangy. He will N-O-T win any blue ribbons."

"We certainly aren't in very good shape, are we?"

"Shape? And what about religion?

"Uh, oh. Haven't we dipped that cat's claw in the brine already?"

"Uh, oh? I suppose, but let's swish it around once more. These pukes got a lot of balls parading that pig-shit across the landscape. You can do whatever you please darlin, but don't forget to press the collection plate. God must be in a real quandary. Two-thousand years ago he sent his son to be crucified to save all our scumby asses. He saved neither his, nor ours.

I don't know; I guess I'm just nuts, but somehow that doesn't seem like a very imaginative, not to mention humane way to do it."

"I can't argue with that."

"So now what's he gonna do? Send a daughter. How bout, Nephew? Shit, they must really be scratching their nuts up there, and I don't think they have the crabs. And how about this one? Free Enterprise. Oooo-eeee. Throw the word 'free' in there, and it practically takes on the aura of holiness. And this from a country that bought and sold slaves for 250 years, used and abused them, and then retooled them.

Free enterprise? Sure, for you, Bobi, but not for me. What the hell; when was the last time you looked at a price-tag?"

"I never have."

"Indeed. Yet I have to count every stinking penny dirtying my pockets."

"You should do your laundry more often."

"You're funny, a real riot."

"Or wash your pennies."

"And you're getting more hilarious by the moment."

"I try."

"Moving right along. You see those little old ladies at Ralph's, fingering those old-fashioned, crutty change purses with skinny, crooked fingers for a dirty, wrinkled buck and a few pennies to pay for a can of dog food, AND they don't even have a dog. You get it?"

"I'm hep."

"And there's two little words you never hear; never, never, never, and never will—two."

"Two?"

"Two. Can you guess?"

"I think you're putting me on the spot. I haven't the vaguest."

I persisted, knowing I did have her on the spot, but I dragged it out since it would make the impression I thought it should. Lord knows, we drag enough dead, old cats through the mud, why not a nice cleaned up and brushed one.

"Bobi," I cajoled, "give me the two little words you never hear, but should."

"Here we go again. I-don't-know-Admiral."

"Admiral? You should have been my C.O."

"Should have."

"Those two little words; it's not ringing a bell, is it?"

"I'm deaf."

"Okay, guess I'm gonna have to "drop the hammer.""

"Just point to the spot. I'm deaf, not immobile." I really did love the girl. "Okay, here it is, but you're gonna feel like a fool when I tell you."

"Want'a bet?

"Pull up the draw bridge, here it comes: I-n-d-u-s-t-r-i-a-l D-e-m-o-c-r-a-c-y!!!"

"Ah, hah! I don't feel like a fool, but a little misused and abused."

"I'll settle for that."

"My, but aren't we generous. I'll admit, you could have put that one on any test and noooobody would have got it. Not at Harvard or Princeton, or Cal Tech, noooo-body."

"Sickening, ain't it? How come? You can turn on that stupid, friggin tube any time day or night, and catch all manner of dog-shit, and why not, dogs are running it, but never, and I mean never, ever, by anyone, black, white, young, old, smart, stupid, male, female, Indian, Chinese, or Eskimo, no-one, and I mean no-one, will ever mention those two little words, not even in passing. How come, jelly bun?"

"Conspiracy?"

"I would think so except we're too stupid to conspire on that lofty a level."

"How bout lame?"

"You pays your buck, and picks you poison."

"I dood."

"You think there just might be a bit more to it?"

"Like what?"

"Like what if some klutz of a CEO wanted to up his expense account, or put up his slutty mistress in a penthouse, or merge, or expand, or raise prices, or dirty-up some stream with their crutty waste, what about it? What if he couldn't spit without getting the workers okay? And when the company's going in the toilet, do you think he could run down that 'you guys got to take a cut' crappola, while he's giving himself a hefty raise, among other things? And at what point do you think the workers would say, "Okay, El-Shmucko, let's see the books, and just the one set, if you please.""

"It'll nev-ah hop-pen," she chimed in, in a sing-song voice, and then added, "You know, John; to be serious for a moment. . . . ."

"For a moment!" I objected. "What the hell have we been doing here, planting geraniums?"

"Petunias? But you're right. You never hear those words. It never occurred to me before. After all, you can't get through the day without hearing 'democracy' 10, 20, a 100 times, but never with the word industrial in front of it, now that you mention it."

"And you never will."

"I think you're right, obviously."

"Obviously."

"Well, is that it?"

"Not quite."

"But the game?"

"That one can wait; this one's in the ninth inning and we're 10 runs behind."

"Okay, batter up."

"Thank you, and let me take a few more cuts before I shally back to the dugout to lick my wounds."

"And burn your bats."

"Like I said: You're' a riot."

"Be careful with that word these days."

"No lie. Anyhow, this thing we're so proud of, this political system, this so-called democracy, it's all a sham."

"It is?"

"Of course. If you had asked God, 'God, discounting an out-and-out tyranny, construct the worst possible system you can, the very worst' this would be it."

"It would?"

"Think about it."

"I am, and that's not what they're peddling in civics classes."

"Of that you can be sure."

"All right, but you're gonna have to give me a hint on this one."

"I gave you a hint on the last one."

"Well, last one, first one; it's all the same when you don't know what's going on."

"Oh, don't give me that, sister. You know damn well what's going on."

"Sister? I must say, I'm certainly glad I'm NOT your sister."

"And me be that as it may. . . . ."

"Be that."

"As I was saying, we vote, right?"

"Right."

"Big deal. Or is it? How would you like to be wheeled in the operating room for brain surgery, knowing that the guy who is about to do a little carving on your noggin, was selected by 'the people?' Shocking, isn't it? Yet, that's what we do with our public 'servants,' easily, easily, every bit as serious a matter as brain surgery, wouldn't you think, given that what they do, or not, effects all of us, and not just the one. Or how'd you like to be up for murder 1, and your hot-shot, legal-beagle happens to have been selected by 'the people.' Wouldn't that inspire confidence in your chances."

"Well how else can it be done?"

"Hell, Bobi. How do they do it in the military? It's the one thing they got right, and nobody noticed."

"Meaning?"

"You go to West Point, or Annapolis, graduate, then work your way up the ladder on merit and experience, not some stupid election by a bunch of doe-doe's, what don't know the difference between a foxhole and a suck hole."

"I see we're back to "you KNOW that's not going to happen."

"Of course. So we go to step two."

"That being?"

"Everybody has to vote. Everybody over the age of 18 who's not senile or a convict, and you get a week to do it, and not one day like we have now. I always wondered, what's the big rush, especially since what we end up with isn't worth a bag of dog-shit to a starving, old soul anyway. And no one is excused unless he's practically dead, and if he don't, he gets slapped with a $500 fine. It's your duty, just like the draft. Garbage in, garbage out."

"Does Ben Franklin know you're talking like this?"

"I'm not worried about that dead ass. It's the live ass waving the flag and totin the bible, who'd just love to stick my bloomin carcass in the can because I A-M talking like this. And he of course, would NE-VER think of violating the first amendment. Uh, huh. And I'm going to replace Willie Mays in centerfield."

"Ooooh ... I really don't think so."

"Ooooh ... and you've been right a number of times tonight, my dear."

"It's not that hard if you think you're going to replace Willie Mays."

"You think so, huh? Well I'll replace Willie before that other fuckhead defends the first amendment even if by some wild crookery he might stumble upon what it means. More likely, he'll confuse it with the second; they know all about the second. 'Oh! Please! Please! Don't take my little pistollero away.' Why those mangy mother's, they must be swillin' hog spit; they'd rather have a gun than an education. Doesn't that say it all?"

"Probably so; and now what?"

"Now we take all the green out of the system, all of it, every stinking, corrupt red cent, and no campaign is to last longer than 3 months, and none of those idiotic TV. commercials designed to make your brain soft and your eyes cross. By the time you get in the voting booth, you don't know if you're in there to vote, shit, or make a phone call, and that's just the way the vile fuckers want it."

"I do believe you're on to something."

"And all the sadder for it."

"All the more."

"And every Sunday the papers have to publish for 3 months up to the election, each candidates stand on the issues. Every Sunday, and if you can't read, let somebody read it to you. Additionally, at least 3 debates, and then maybe, just maybe, we might be able to elevate a campaign somewhat higher than the belly of a whale resting peacefully on the bottom of the Pacific ocean. And 50% of the congress and the state houses have to be female, by law. What kind of crap is this? Here we are in the twentieth century, fought a revolution to get rid of the king, and all we can stick up there are dirty, old white men? And those piss-ant broads; this is what they should be demonstrating for, and not trying to get in VMI or PMI, or have their crooked-kneed kid wasting her time trying to get on the baseball team."

"You sure do get excited about things, don't you?"

"Ah, Bobi. I'd like to be President for one week, just one little week. This country would never be the same again I'll have you know, Mrs. Smith."

"You're telling me."

"And for the better, if I may be so bold, much, much, much, for the better."

"Much."

"You're being funny again."

"Againnnn?"

"If you don't mind, I'm gonna have to ignore your snide, little jibes."

"I don't mind."

"Where was I? You're making me lose my train-of-thought."

"I have a feeling you'll get it back."

"Don't make me start to wonder about you. We're almost married. I can't back out now. How would it look?"

"Nowwww you're worried about public opinion." (You see, Virginia, when a Bobi' comes along you just marry her, and don't even look back.)

"It's back," I announced, tongue in cheek.

"Thank god," she also announced, lovingly sarcastic.

"If I may continue … now … still with the congress, 20% should be Afro-American, that being about the percentage in the general population. It could be more; if that's the way it works out, but no less. And no more than 1% lawyers. Now it's close to 95 percent. Cripes, how the hell am I represented by those bloodsucking leeches? I have about as much in common with them as I have with a Tutsi tribesman. And this one is absolutely essential, absolutely, at all costs. Actually, it's all essential, but let me make the point."

"You're doing all right so far." I wasn't sure if Bobi was getting ready to 'throw another spear,' but I was taking no chances. She reminded me of Bob Feller; once she got warmed up, she sure could take the sting out of your bats. I quickly continued. "Everybody with an income below $20,000 gets 2 votes."

"W-h-a-a-a-t?"

"W-h-a-a-a-t? I speak pretty clear English."

"That's not how I meant it. And that also will never happen."

"What the hell, Bobi, none of this is gonna happen, but I can dream, can't I?"

"And that's just about what all this is, so dream on."

"Might as well, huh, sweetie-pie?"

"Might as well, cause there ain't none of this e-e-e-v-e-r gonna happen."

"You just got to keep saying that, aint'cha?"

"I don't see nobody else around here."

"But allow me my little fantasies; I have so few."

"Indulge."

"I shall. Between $21,000 and $50,000, one-and-one-half votes. Between $51,000 and $100,000, one vote, between $100,000 and 500,000 one-half vote and 500,000 on up a quarter vote. My dear, I guarantee the end of lobby rot and bribery, and extortion, and all the rest of that grand malarkey of which we have all become so familiar these oh so many years." I waited for a response. Bobi remained quiet.

"Well?" I obstreperously nudged.

"Well? Well? You can "well" till the cows come home. This is all talk."

"This is all talk. This is all talk," I mocked. "Of course. If the bastards can do it, so can I. At least mine ain't all lies."

"Small consolation."

"Don't be so sure, cupcake. But one more, little thing."

"Phew. There's more?"

"The cream on the cake. Anyone convicted of a felony while in the commission of his public office, will, upon conviction, receive 30 years in the slammer, 30, automatic, and no parole, never, for any reason. A misdemeanor, 10 years, and you lose your pension, and the same goes for those crooked, cock-eyed moguls. Thirty years, and they can share the same cell, preferably the one Al Brown adorned at Alcatraz, or Devils Island, then you won't even have to support them. Let them do like Papillion—grow a garden, and once a week we'll deliver a few other goodies to them.

"Such a pleasant thought, but never to be."

"Yeah, all the slime-balls occupying the same hotel."

"Only in America."

"To be sure, and not in this century, and probably also, the next; so sad. And tearfully so, because we have it within our grasp to be a truly great nation, but instead, remain a mouse in a lion's mane, and a jackal at heart." I swigged down my suds, and the game ended—both of them.

Tomorrow starts another day, Buck, and another game. Some games end, and with a winner. Some games never end, and one side is always behind.

As time passed, our love, to our great joy and fascination, looked to be developing into a permanent condition. And why not? After one has been around the flag pole a few times, what is there left that can make a difference? A little compassion? Understanding? Empathy? So, where are we then? In the Stone Age, sweetheart, in the Stone Age. The missile has replaced the club, and the jet, the foot. We call the cave 'home' and rim it with fences, hedges, blacktop and marigolds. A rose, is a rose; stone age, sweetheart, Stone Age.

* * *

One bright and sunny, sleepy afternoon, as I tranquilly laid watching the shadowy cobwebs drifting to and fro under a patchwork, greying ceiling, Rita, unannounced danced into the 'den of iniquity.'

"Well, what the hell!" I exclaimed upon noticing.

"Is that all you have to say?" she responded, in a huff.

"Well what would you like, Woody Herman and the thundering herd?"

"Woody who?"

"Christ, am I that old?"

"You're getting there."

"As we all are."

"Uh, huh. Well, are you just going to lie there, or are you going to greet a gal properly?"

Smiling whimsically to match her mischievous one, I rose and placed my arms about her sun-tanned neck, and kissed her warmly.

"Well, now; that's more like it," she pleasantly admitted

"And what the hell are you doing here?"

"And what have you been doing with YOUR-self?" she asked as she sat on my bunk ignoring my inquiry. "Anything exciting?"

"Oh, you know; a little of this, a little of that," I drawled matter-of-factly.

"Just a little?" she interrogated with an upturned brow.

"When you do it right. . . . ."

"Working?"

"Does it look it?"

"I don't know why I asked."

"Neither do I. And you?"

"I'm going to college."

"What! No shit: Good God, good God, almighty! Well, that's great, just fucking great."

"A girl's got to do something."

"I guess, well, hell; damn it all, kiddo, I'm really happy for you. What are you taking?" I asked, genuinely interested.

"Psychology," she replied as her face lit-up proudly.

"Well ain't that something, that's really something," I declared lustily, not letting on my dislike for the dippy abstraction. "How do you like it?" I asked honestly.

"I like it a lot. It's interesting."

"I'll bet, but then, your background. You're one-up on all those other yahoo's."

"You're not going to give me that: 'A good hooker is a good psychologist' bit, are you?"

"No, but I'm glad you're getting out of the bedroom and into the classroom."

"I don't know as I'd put it that way. A gal never really gets 'out-of-the-bedroom.' The trick is to stay out of the kitchen." My, my, but how times have changed. My granny---bless her heart---the kitchen was her favorite chamber commanding the attention of most of her waking hours.

"By the way: What place of learning do you happen to be so studiously attending?"

"L.A.C.C., for two years, then I think I'll transfer to Cal State, or U.C.L.A., if I can get in."

"Why? They prejudiced against 'working' girls?"

"They're prejudiced against dumb working girls"

"Hah! Don't you believe it. The football team can't recite the alphabet."

"Then I have to get on the football team?"

"Or under it."

"You're a real Palooka."

"I liked 'Alley Oop' myself."

"Either way."

"Then, that's it? You're staying down there for good?"

"Looks like it."

"Be careful. The god-damn place is going to slide right into the fucking ocean one of these days."

"Wud'ya mean?"

"What-do-I-mean? There's a crack down there spread wider than Lana Turners cheeks.

"Hah! You're a bright one, you are. And where the hell do you think you're standing ... on the North Pole?"

"Comes this far, does it?"

"Let me put it this way: This moat, of which you happen to be restfully residing in at the present time, could be sitting right smack on top of it."

"It dood? That close, huh?"

"That's r-i-i-i-g-h-t."

"Damn and I thought I was safe, temporarily."

"Yeah, sure; There A-R-R-R-E no safe places."

"N-O-W she tells me."

A clanking noise was heard to come from the foyer as Rick came bounding in swinging his little, black pail. Rita gave an uncertain look. I introduced them wherein she turned to me and asserted judiciously, "Looks like this one kissed the Star-Kist can." Rita caught on quick.

"Yeah, but it seems this one kissed aaaall the cans."

"How can you stand it?"

"It is a fright. I hold my nose a lot." And at that, Rick piped in with: "I got something you can hold." And I replied with: "As you can readily see, we are in no danger of being over-run by the Mensa society."

"Apparently not," Rita shot back.

"But don't forget; if I go any lower I'll strike oil." At that last retort, Rick gratefully upped and repaired to the bath works. Rita and I talked 'old times.'

Midway through the seventieth century, another maidenly voice was heard straining through the soft, afternoon breeze.

"Hello? Hello? Anybody home?" The voice was vaguely familiar. "Come on down!" I mimicked one of the more revolting game shows which unabashedly parade daily across the American television scene making a continuing mockery of the memory of Edison and Faraday.

When I saw who it was, you could have knocked me over with a feather duster, for it was none other than sweet, sweet, dear Melissa of 'far-away-and-long-ago' desert fame.

"Jesus!" she exclaimed upon entering the 'den of nocturnal delight.' "You sure are a hard one to find. Who the hell do you think you are, Howard Hughes?"

"Not anyone so esoteric; and how in fucking, Christ's name, did you find me? This ain't exactly the 'top-of-the-mark,' you know?"

"It's the top of something all right, but you don't get any 'marks' for it. And I don't have time for a book."

I'll say one thing for Melissa; she W-A-S built. Her only deficiency, if it can be so stated, was, actually, an addition. Her derriere, for her size, was quite bountiful, quite. But, being so magnificently perched, as it was, its generous beneficence only added to her charm. To put it bluntly: She had one, big, beautiful, celestial carnal bun-de-jo. Melissa, most certainly, had to be the inspiration for the now popular phrase 'sit-on-it.' I swear you could balance a 'jigger of scotch' on that rear among other things.

"Okay," I announced, "so now what?"

"Ho! Ho!" piped Rita with a definite twinkle in her eye. "So now anything."

"What are you doing here, anyway?" I asked, trying not to seem disappointed, which I surely wasn't.

"What a question," she rightly complained. "It seems perfectly obvious, doesn't it?" she countered while giving the 'rustic' surroundings the quick 'once over.' "You don't think I'm sightseeing, do you? Unless, of course, one is a fan of ancient ruins."

"Cute. Want to try for "ecstatic?"

Rick reentered, wearing only a pair of faded jeans, and a towel draped around his neck, appeared somewhat startled at the new addition. He was not however, 'displeased.'

"Oh, and who might you be?" he asked Melissa while sauntering over to his bunk. I could see for all the world he was trying to act casual, succeeding to only a slight degree; but then, Melissa could've turned Cary Grant into a simpering wimp with merely a wink.

"This wonderful piece of female pulchritude, my fine fish smelling friend is, Melissa. Melissa, this is Charlie "you know what.""

"Really? Charlie 'you know what' what?"

"Close enough."

"I never met a celebrity before."

"You're safe. You ain't meeting one now."

"Actually, I kind of gathered that."

"Can I get in on this?" Rick inquired.

"Only if you dunk yourself in a barrel of cologne first," I advised.

"Look who's talking. Sometimes YOU come in here smelling like a squirrel."

"You sure got a lot of balls, you fucker you."

"Now, now, boys; let's not fight," Rita piped in. "I got a better idea."

"I can only imagine," I retorted. Rita, catching on to that last remark, nuzzled close to me and whispered: "Hey, I'm getting a funny feeling. I've never been in a room with a 'john' before, and him dressing before we even had a chance to do the "two-step?"

"Yeah. I get your drift. So?"

"So?"

"So what are we standing around for? My sexual proclivities aren't any less now than they were six-months ago."

"Lucky for the female gender, hey?"

"That's what I always liked about you, Rita … always so agreeable."

"What the hell; why be difficult?"

"My very sentiments, and would you excuse me while I break the good news to Rick? I do believe it will "make his day."

"But of course," she quickly agreed, and thereupon waltzed over and whispered—what I can only imagine, in Melissa's ear.

I, now having gotten my cue, walked over and asked Rick if he were in a 'performing' mood. Sitting there tugging on a pair of argyle socks, he never said a word, but his bulb glowed.

Directly, I then sauntered over to Melissa and explained as how I was always so crazy about her, and how much I missed her, and how I was prepared to show it 'right then and there.'

She mumbled something about 'how come I never came to see her,' whereby I portended a slight case of 'deafness in the afternoon.'

Rita meanwhile was beginning to disrobe. Subsequently, Melissa and I disrobed in our corner of 'god's little acre.' Ah, tis moments like these that weaken the faith.

We all jumped in the sack as thoughts of sugar plums danced through our heads.

Now, being the naturally athletic type, I, in due course, assumed the upper position—to put it delicately—and so joyously ensconced, dutifully began 'caging the wild bird.' Good heavens. Were it so sweet for all time.

Ambidextrously, I glanced over toward Rick and Rita. Apparently all was not well in the Van Winninger camp, as there seemed to be an inordinate amount of muffling and scuffling in yonder direction, and I thought I heard Rita complain once---as only a hooker can, something to the effect of: "Just put the god-damn thing in, will ya, chump?" No mind. Would it we all should be so blessed. As the world turns.

Hark, is that yet another familiar voice I hear ringing out in the hushed, languid mid-day air?

An "Anybody home?" sliced through the dreamy afternoon, and a deathly chill zinged down my spine. And then, "Oh! Oh! Oh, no!" Damn, too late. With my butt held so high like a pig in his sty, my bethroed, Dear Miss Higgins, came casually swinging by, before I had a chance, to even say, 'hi.'

As quick as a flash I jumped from my fun, ready and willing to face all the guns. Standing there all naked and blue, I turned to see that my loved one had flown.

I dressed, oh so fast, with hurry and a scurry, and raced to the door to see my luck had run too.

I listened for sounds to tell me 'what's what' and came forth they sure did, as I heard a 'putt, putt.'

I went back to my roost to sit like a goose, for now it was certain there never was such a goof.

That evening, wondering how I was ever going to face my loved one again, I dolled myself up and prepared to do just that. As I traipsed up the walk, a gradual numbness began to take hold. Unsteadily, I rang the bell, and momentarily a voice was heard to call out: "Yes, who's there?"

"It's me," I answered shakily.

"Go away," was the unwelcomed and expected response, and in a decidedly disagreeable tone. It was the first time ever, Bobi gave any indication of even the slightest dislike for me. It was an instantaneous, shattering experience, and one I could well do without.

I rang again, and again she called out, this time a bit more sternly: "G-o-o, a-w-a-y."

"You might as well let me in," I advised, "because I'm not leaving till I have my say." I tried to sound bold, but was certain more than a little of my apprehension had shown through.

I waited; no-answer. Shortly, however, the buzzer sounded, and, pushing open the door nervously, I felt like James Bond entering the secret water works of the maniacal Dr. Fu.

Slowly, I jelly-legged climbed the one flight of stairs, all the while wracking my brain for impossible explanations. The task at hand was indeed, momentous: How to explain, yet remain reasonably literate, seeming, as it was, bouncing around a caboose with a wagon load of voluminous and whopping lies.

As I entered, Bobi was rigidly standing in the middle of the room all red-eyed and explosive looking with her arms folded across her chest. A human time bomb in skirts.

"Okay," she announced testily, "say it, and scram, Buster." The 'Buster' instantly deflated me, and I knew I was 'scuttled' before leaving port.

Rubbing my forehead, I gazed down at the floor and stalled for time like one readying to be shot. It was one of the few times I wished I drank, as I could have used a stiff belt, or two, standing before this overheated figure of discontent. Up to now I thought she was supposed to be the calm one, and said so. "Well, if I'm not, I'm entitled, don't you think?" she shot back with nary a trace of deference.

"Absolutely… uh … yes, of course," I stuttered searching for just the slightest opening of agreement. "But if you would just calm down a bit, you might see that I have an … an explanation."

"You wan'ta bet?"

I began, but stopped abruptly and asked if she would please sit as she was making me as jumpy as a one-legged mongoose in cobra country, standing there all stiff and straight like 'Mother Superior.' She quickly obliged, more, it seemed, to hasten the increasingly, distasteful proceedings, than to please me. "These two girls' . . ." I began again.

"I only saw you," she snapped, "and only those parts not usually so unceremoniously exhibited." As I have said before, Bobi, when she was of a mind, had the snap of a rock-lobster. She, now, was of a mind.

"Well, just for the record," I continued undaunted, "there were two young ladies. The one with Rick was a very good friend of mine whom I had known for quite some time."

She raised a brow. "A friend of y-o-u-r-s?" she quipped, "and she was with Rick? My, my; how quaint."

It was my turn to glare; I did. "Please let me get on with this, it's not easy, you know."

"I-T'S N-O-T S-U-P-P-O-S-E-D T-O B-E."

Her hawkishness was a hair-shirt, but I resolved to retain sufficient control to complete this sordid ordeal.

"The other young lady I had met before I knew you," I informed.

"And how many times did you M-E-E-T her, before you knew me? And I'll thank you to stop referring to them as 'young ladies' if you don't mind. They were a couple of chippies looking for a quick 'roll-in-the-hay' and apparently, they found the barn." Ignoring her latest brick-bat, I persisted in what I now could see was a fruitless endeavor. But what had I to lose? Mechanically, I continued. "She lives in Los Granos, and she came up just to see me."

"Well isn't that special. It's a cinch she didn't come up to see the 49'rs."

"She said she missed me."

"Hah! No doubt; and of course, she preferred you naked."

"Come on, huh? Gimme a break."

"I'll give you a break; and I'll bet it was all just for 'old time's sake' too, huh?"

"Not exactly, but like you said, she sure didn't come up to see the 49'rs."

"Maybe not, but it didn't stop you from doing a little 'prospecting' though, did it?"

The arrows were coming from all directions. I was, however, determined to see this Chaplinesque charade to the end.

"I felt like an idiot. We were all just kind of standing around. . . . ."

"But not for long." (This was definitely not going well.)

"I knew what they came for."

"P-u-u—l-e-a-s-e, we've been through all that; to see you, and she certainly did that, didn't she, the little darlin?"

"I didn't mean it that way. It's just that a girl gets lonesome too, once in a while, you know?"

"Yeah, and you're good ol' 'Johnny-on-the-spot.' Why don't you just 'cut bait' and call it a day, huh? What kind of a fool do you take me for, anyway?"

"Bobi, if anybody can understand this, you can, and that's why I'm even bothering. Anybody else and I wouldn't even waste my time.

"Well, it's the only thing you got right so far; don't waste your time." I ignored that last, and continued. "I also happen to love you, and that has more than a little something to so with it." At that she stiffened like a Christmas herring in the freezer department. "You've got your nerve ... love ... love; you can mention love now!"

"Well what the hell do you think I'm doing here, planting potatoes?" It was my turn to be offended.

"You'd have better luck," she snapped. "I damned well am beginning to think you really are out for my bread."

"Oh, Christ; anything but that old horse, please."

"It has been known to happen." I now, thoroughly felt like the cardboard ass on a homemade dart board. What the hell, I thought; I might as well play out the string. I never did hit the numbers, maybe I can hit this. I pulled out all the big guns.

"You see Bobi, Melissa is a kind of a lonely sort, and that little, hokey dump-of-a-town, ain't exactly 'the strip' on Saturday night."

"Sooo?"

"Well, she's a kind of a warm-blooded type and with her 'old man' out to sea, and all. . . . ."

"Oh, a cheater too, ay?"

"Well I felt sorry for her. . . . ."

"You 'felt' a little more than sorry." Obviously her anger wasn't interfering with her mind. I pushed on.

"I know what it is to be lonely, Bobi."

"Tell the truth, and shame the devil."

"Yes, well; it can be devastating, and I just couldn't refuse her in that condition."

"You should have … t-h-i-s … t-i-m-e."

"Well what the hell are friends for if you can't depend on them when you really need them? I did it for her, I really did." It seems I was overplaying my hand because she quickly shot me one of those, 'Okay, Bub; you'd just better stop right there' looks, so I did. I thought it best to hold back my 'hole' card— for now.

"It didn't happen because I desired her."

"Of course not. You just, almost against your will, 'forced' yourself, friend that you are. You really are something, you know that?"

"What I'm trying to say is it wasn't because there was something lacking in our relationship or anything like that. I just felt sorry for her, that's all. And although she's not my type, that don't keep me from a little sympathy."

"Oh, you're really 'kicking-the-dog' now, aren't you?"

"I'm no saint, Bobi."

"I'm not looking for one."

"But sometimes the pain in this stinking world gets to me, and I have to … to … dispense an aspirin."

"Hah; now you're a pharmacist too, hey? I thought you were an engineer."

"I'm trying, Bobi, I'm trying." I paused momentarily, looking for a mellowing reaction, and though still wearing that icy glare, she seemed, somehow now, more bewildered than furious. Could it be that this cock-a-mammy story was going to work? What the hell, what if it was all a big crock? The basics were there. I just kind of dazzled them with my footwork. I gained heart.

"You know, sweetheart? Yesterday, at Ralph's, I saw a little tike, no more than two, sitting in the cart while her mother pushed, oh so merrily. Nothing odd, you say, and so would I. But she seemed unusually still for a little girl, and as they came closer, I saw that the little cherub was blind. Yeah, blind. How do you like that? Two-years-old and blind. Probably from birth, but what matter, and probably for all of her life, a great matter. Blind. Why? Two-years-old. Jesus, what godless kind of fucking dump is this? The fuckheads want to justify something? Justify that, and then we'll cart them all off in a basket."

"How long do I have to sit through this? I'm depressed enough as it is."

"I know, and I'm not exactly 'walking through tulips' either, but bear with me. So, now having lost my appetite, I shoved the half-filled cart to one side, and beat a hasty retreat. Suffice to say, I felt like … like strangling this whole god-damned, bloody, fucking world. So you want to know about Melissa?"

"Not really."

"Well, she's blind too, in a way."

"And you were going to teach her a little Braille?" I ignored her latest stone.

"She doesn't know who she is, what she is, or where she's going from one minute to the next."

"And now you're a traffic cop, too; you were going to show her?"

"You really know how to stick in the knife."

"Be grateful I'm not holding one."

"I get that feeling."

"Among others, apparently."

"Anyway, she's bumping into the damn furniture. She's lonely, and confused, and frustrated, and who isn't in this fucked-up, malformed, motley gathering of half-breed troglodytes? So I did the only thing I could---I laid a kindly hand on her shoulder to let her know she wasn't alone."

"You should have stopped there." The arrows were coming from all directions.

"Well, that's it. It may not be the softest of beds, but the sheets are clean."

"It's going to take more than clean sheets to warm this bed again; I don't think it can ever be the same between us, John, I just don't," she added despondently.

"Don't say that," I quickly admonished. "Let's not skin the cat before we catch him, after all, nobody got shot, or maimed, or raped; no blood flowed. Don't make anymore of this than it is."

"Easy for you to say."

"I've said easier things."

"I can't help it. I guess I'm not so liberal after all."

"I'll settle for hasty."

"I just don't like the idea of you jumping every chick while. . . ."

"Hold it, please! Who said I am? What happened this afternoon is something that wouldn't happen again in a hundred years, two hundred. It's a shot-in-the-dark, and I couldn't even hit the wall."

"What couldn't happen again? You snatching a little candy, or me catching you?"

"That wasn't necessary. And what the hell were you doing there anyway? This damned day of all days. Three-hundred-and-sixty-five friggin days in the year, and you had to pick T-H-I-S one to go visiting.

"And don't you ever close the damn doors down there?"

"Nobody's been in that hole in years, and what the hell was so special about today?"

"Don't blame me for when you cracked out of the shell."

"Damn. That's right. Christ, what a time to have a birthday."

"Don't blame him, either. And to think I used a 'sick' day to make a special trip to get you something you so richly deserve." The sarcasm throughout this whole, unreal colloquy never left her.

Retreating into the bedroom, she returned in a matter of seconds with a small package which could only have contained a hunk of jewelry of sorts.

"Here," she abruptly announced handing it to me. "I wouldn't want you to go without this."

Snatching at it brusquely, I quickly jammed it in my pocket, visibly annoyed at the obtuse intrusion.

"Well, now; isn't that grand. I go through all the trouble and you stuff if in your pants like a bad debt." Irritably, I retrieved it and hurriedly tore off the paper. Opening to see a black, onyx ring enveloping a glassy growth of considerable heft, I unwittingly complained to the effect, "Very impressive, but you know I don't care for jewelry."

"Shove it, then," she shot back forcefully.

Wishing to be over with this side attraction, I again disdainfully crammed it back into my pocket thanking her curtly. "Don't mention it," she snarled sharply.

We both stared for a brief moment, and then she reported directly: "John, I don't think we should see each other for a while. I think it would be good for both of us, no matter how you look at it."

It was true. Bobi wasn't as liberal as she thought. In her inimitably, classy way, she was telling me to 'get lost.' I, sweethearts, was summarily being dumped. My pride wasn't all that shattered, but I did love the girl—in my fashion—and, if anything, I wasn't going to meekly slouch back to the dugout before I 'had my cuts.'

"Okay Bobi," I feebly protested, "If that's the way you want it, then that's it." She shrugged. "But you just remember one thing, and I've told you before, and I meant it before, and I'll tell you again: I wouldn't do anything in this world to hurt you, anything, no matter what my bumbling transgressions. I love you, and I don't know what else there is, and I'm not a 'butterfly' and you wouldn't be worrying from one day to the next whose drawers I was trying to jimmy, and that's about as old fashioned as you can get."

"It's not your fashion I'm concerned about. It's those 'transgressions' that has my sonar beepin."

"Bobi, give it time."

"Oh, I plan to, yes indeed."

"Just keep an open mind." Now I was beginning to sound like the myriad of 'motivational engineers' which the good ol' U.S. of A. has so unconscionably produced this last generation, and on whose behalf it can gratefully be said, 'all things must end.'

Bobi, no doubt noticing my sudden descent into the maelstrom, could only respond feebly: "Uh, huh." I tried recouping my losses. "We are what we are Bobi," I posited. I don't know why I said that, unless I was on the last paragraph of the last page of sensibility. And Bobi, for her part, did not respond, thankfully, but obviously her thoughts were not broaching any pleasantries.

Knowing there was no more to be said, I hoofed it to the door, opened it, and before leaving, added, "If you want to get rid of me tell me straight, tell me you've had it with me, and that's it, and I'm beginning to bore you, because otherwise it's going to be 'Banzai' all the way baby."

"And just what is t-h-a-t supposed to mean?"

"Just what it says. This ain't over, not by a long shot, and if I have to, like a half-crazed, glory-hungry Prussian, charge into machine gun fire to get you, then charge I will, so take your time and think r-e-e-a-l hard about it, cause like Mac Arthur, I shall return."

She did not answer, only glared, and meekly I made my way down the stairs. I heard the door slam behind me. It sounded final, and maybe it was.

On the way back to the pit, I cursed all the saints, and near saints, the four heavens and the catholic church who, had they not always been 'four-square' for more and more little catholic babies—all for the honor and glory of the Christian army in the war against Satan—I might have missed this boat altogether.

I did not see Bobi for 2 days; on the third, she called. I, morosely sitting in the pantry watching the bubbling sun slowly slinking into the red-eyed, western sky and dreaming of better times, the pestering little 'ring, a-ding, a-ding' was a definite intrusion sounding more like a civil war cannon. Reaching over, I picked up the receiver and blurted into the mouthpiece a dismal "hello." The voice on the other end simply said, "It's me." The 'me' I knew only too well. It was not the sound of a voice bearing good tidings, and how right my instincts were I was soon to find.

"You said last time," it went on to say, "that if I didn't love you that would be the end of it."

Like a marooned, shipwrecked, sea-dog, I waited helplessly knowing my future, up to now bereft of even the tiniest of those shimmering, rocky nuggets we all so fondly refer to as G-O-L-D!! was dim, at best. I listened for the other shoe to drop. It did, with a 'thud.'

"Well," she continued, "I don't." I was not surprised, but I W-A-S shocked. Not wanting to believe what I was hearing, I did not believe what I was hearing, and said so.

"Why not!" she screeched. Her distress was clearing the lines. "I'm not in the habit," she assured, "of telling people I don't love them. It's not something I do every day, you know, like brushing my teeth."

Now what does a body go for? I settled for, "Look, Bobi, two days isn't exactly a lifetime. I think you might be a bit overwrought."

"Is that what you call it?"

"And besides, you just can't turn it 'on and off' like a faucet."

"Well, god-damn you, I am!" and abruptly slammed down the receiver. She seemed to be on the verge of displaying her extensive 'waterworks,' and apparently didn't care for an audience.

Now I was in a pickle. To do, or not to do. If it were true, and I believed it, and stayed away, it was over, everything was over, in which case I might just as well have gone and taken up residence in a cave, because what little use I may have been up to now, would now be less than a one-legged centipede. on the other hand, if I did not believe, but it were true, I risked creating one of those unsightly B movie scenes and with it, a complete ass of myself, not to speak of a shattering one. If I did believe, but it was not true, and stayed away on that false assumption, then the effect would be the same as step one. Lastly, and under the distressing circumstances seemed to be the only prudent course to follow, was, not to believe, but also to stay away—for the time being, anyway. The plan then, was too merely 'bide my time' take the 'wait and see' approach, and if, such was the case, love would win out. Not, under any circumstances, did I consider the matter closed. I was ready, as the saying goes, to 'suck-it-up.'

This can be a very long and dolorous life. To have to spend it without the one or two things one truly needs, can indeed approximate the intolerable. I, for one, can do without almost anything not having to do with self-preservation. My loved-one was not one of them. Someone once said, I suspect in a frivolous mood that every man should make a complete fool of himself at least once in his life over a woman. Well, Buck, I can't say if the unwitting sage meant it that way, but once is all a body can take.

I am not now, nor have I ever been, suicide prone. But more and more these days, does the thought creep in and out of this weary head … more and more.

* * *

XIII

Sail on with me this river of death

With eyes so wide, but strength you need

Round and round with dizzying speed

To hope, to dream, perchance to be,

No time to think, no longer wail

The lily has begun to fade

The amaranth does also pale.

The stones so sharp, the sand is coarse

My bloodied feet run out to sea.

The waves don't lie; they tell me stop!

Pushing me back, and back, and back.

Black rolling clouds descending low

Fall away through darkened skies

My ship! My ship! This ship has sailed.

THE days drifted, the nights languished. Two, four, six, eight. Two weeks approached, and I was beginning to feel like a hawk in a cage. Even in the best of times the flower withers. Could it be she really didn't love me? Could it? Had my luck run so cold? In the boiling cauldron of witches brew, the poison juices unceasingly seep out into the slinking, grey slag of mortality.

I thought of Bobi incessantly in those two deathly weeks of private hell. Not eating or sleeping. I know, you've heard it all before, but then, you heard the kazoo before too, but what's New Year's Eve without it?

I had never experienced wobbly kneed worry before. I've had my cares, I've had my woes; I have not been an orphan to pain and adversity. But worry, constant, 'rock-in-the-gut' bone-wrenching grief?—never. This bitter, agonizing, twenty-four-hour anxiety? What black-horned devil picked my number out of the hat?

I lost 5 pounds, a somewhat difficult dance considering I was already a fighting trim 141. I knew it couldn't continue. I decided to confront the issue head-on that very night, for if I waited much longer I would soon be merely a shadow of my charming, former self. The sun, I vowed, would not rise another day without this matter being resolved, one way or the other. And if, by chance, worst came to worst, well then, so be it. They still sell guns, don't they? Anyhow, there's something to be said for decisive action. If Hamlet wasn't a coward, he was tip-toeing all around it.

That afternoon, my task became a bit easier. A welcome, but unexpected al-ly—Adrienne—paid me a visit.

As soon as I laid eyes upon her, I knew something besides sheep-dip was in the wind since she had never been in 'the pit' before.

After the usual greetings and salutations we got down to business.

"Well," she observed smartly, "you don't look any better than Bobi. This might be easier than I thought."

"Come again?" I quizzed.

"I said," she repeated, but this time more emphatically, "you-don't-look-so-hot."

"I don't feel so hot," I asserted in keeping with the 'festive' mood.

"Neither does your ex-fiancée."

"Oh, really?" I feigned surprise. "How come? Somebody keeps mentioning my name to her?"

"Close enough," she rejoined straight-away.

I asked her to take a seat as I reheated Colombia's finest. "Shall we get down to tasks?" she now uttered more seriously. I threw up my hands: "By all means," I quickly agreed eager to see what track this train was rolling on. "Let's get to it."

"Okay, we'll start with why I'm here at all."

"You heard there was gold in "them thar hills?"

"Not quite."

"Me then?" I joked pitiably. "You came to see me?"

"Look Rosko? You could say 'I like you' but I'm not here on account of your magnetic attraction."

"Always so close, and yet so far."

"Whatever. You see, I'm exceptionally fond of Bobi, as you very well know."

"Very well."

"She's the nicest person I've ever known, hands down, and nobody else even comes close, so it follows then, that I'd like to see her get the best, so to speak, and what is happening to her right now, can hardly be described as anything remotely resembling that pinnacle of ecstasy."

"Well I'm not exactly standing naked in a limpid pool, surrounded by a bevy of over-heated, gyrating, tantalizing Turkish belly-dancers."

"You're not the subject of this conversation, just yet."

"Not?"

"Not. But I do like you too, pretty much. I haven't known you all that long, but you seem to be a 'cut-above' in a world overpopulated by heels."

"I think that was a compliment."

"Somewhat. In any event, Bobi's word is good enough for me."

"I like you too. So now what?"

"So now, I think you ought to know your girl is going through hell."

"Haven't you heard? It's a prairie down there. Room for a multitude."

"This ain't no joke."

"I ain't laughing."

"And how about you? How are you taking it?"

"Like Nixon in 62."

"That bad, huh?"

"And he only lost an election."

"He came back from the grave."

"So did Dracula."

"Well?"

"Well? You're not suggesting I have to be Nixon to overcome this?"

"Sad to say, but. . . . ."

"Sad to say, but can I be Dracula instead?"

"Be anything you like, but it'd better be what she likes."

"I thought I was."

"Yeah, well; with one little discrepancy."

"Yeah, one small step. . . . ."

"If it were only. . . . ."

"Oooooh?"

"She told me what happened."

"Did she now?"

"Oh, don't sweat it. She told me the same way you'd tell your best buddy, that's all."

"Well that's a relief," I answered sardonically. "Let's hope she doesn't have too many 'best' buddies."

"Actually, I thought it was kind of … funny? shall we say?"

"Yeah, hilarious. I should have been engaged to you."

"Oh, don't get me wrong. It was funny precisely because you WEREN'T engaged to me."

"Ain't that the goat's horns. Not me, the other guy."

"I think if I was me, I probably would have stabbed you right then and there, with a letter opener, or something."

"Nice touch. Are you sure you don't write screen plays for Warner Brother's?"

"Don't I wish."

"I tried to tell her it didn't mean a wagon-load of rat-shit."

"Somehow I don't think that'd get it."

"It didn't."

"I'm not surprised, but it is kind of tough when they catch you with the 'smoking gun' in your hand, if you'll pardon the expression."

"Well you sure are hitting all the 'high-notes' today."

"Purely a coincidence."

"Uh, huh. You know she called to tell me her love had 'taken leave.' That's why I've been staying away. It could be true; who knows? But I had decided to go up tonight to see for myself."

"Take it from me; that 'I don't love you anymore' bit is a lot of bunk. She's wound up tighter than a Stradivarius."

"You don't say?"

"I do say, and if you take that little trip up there tonight she'll fall apart like, like . . . .?"

"A bamboo shack in a cyclone?"

"Or a fig leaf in a hurricane."

"We sure have been getting rotten weather lately."

"And, you know? That's just what she needs right now—a purge, get it all out of her system."

"Like cheap booze after a long night out on the town."

"You said it. Anyway, I think I've got her a little softened up, if you're interested?"

"Interested? I'm ready to climb the walls like a starving lizard after a fat, juicy roach. And what, may I ask, have you been softening her with?"

"You know. The usual stuff. 'She was being foolish.' 'Why let a little thing mess up a good thing?' 'Guys like you don't come along like a bus every 20 minutes.' 'Good guys are hard to find.' Nothing all that profound, but effective."

"We hope. And?"

"And, like I said, if you're careful . . . . ."

"Careful? Hah! Imagine a lust-crazed, cock-eyed, one-legged, male black widow spider warily approaching the female, black-widow spider."

"She's ready to spring."

"Hopefully, not at me."

"We pays the price, and takes our chances."

"And hope the odds are a mite better than the double O on a crooked roulette wheel."

"It i-i-s a gamble."

"She's really strung-out, is she?"

"Strung-out? Honey, there's enough string there to make a pair of jammys for big-foot."

"Kind of a double-edged sword, isn't it?"

"How so?"

"This love shit. You're a mess with it, and without it. It's like food. You can get too much, or not enough." And when you get it just right, you're gonna die anyway.

"Well that's one way to look at it."

"If we care to look at all."

"It do get ticklish."

"It do."

"Anyhow, the rest is up to you. But let me give one t-i-i-n-y bit of advice."

"Which is?"

"You'd better not make one false move, not one, or one wrong word, and brother, you really c-a-a-a-n kiss it goodbye."

"My dear, dear friend, Adi. I'm going up there with a dictionary."

"You'd better."

We talked a while longer, not about the 'problem' but just talk. I liked Adi.

I liked her very much, and when she left, I hugged her warmly. She reciprocated. We had formed a bond it doesn't take long, Buck, when sincerity is the go-between.

Adi informed me of my not being welcome, so I had to tell her exactly what time I'd be there, and she'd make a point of just kind of 'casually' be standing by the buzzer when it rang. I said 7, and it was on.

I arrived at 7 precisely, rang, and immediately the gates opened. Adi must have been kissing that button.

Slowly and shakily, I walked up the one flight of stairs, and jelly-legged strolled over to the open door where Adi, who must have been waiting as nervously as I, whispered that Bobi was in the bedroom mechanically combing her hair, unaware of my arrival. The expectation of subsequent uncertain events made me as fidgety as a crippled hare in Coyote County. I was not good at this sort of thing, not good at all. As a matter of fact, I was an abject coward right to the bone.

"Hey, Babe's, look who's here?" Adi called out. She was a cool one.

Bobi lackadaisically strolled in carrying the hair-brush. As soon as our eyes met, I realized instantly—for better or worse— we had to be together.

She, completely startled, dropped the brush, and, with lips slightly parted, began to tremble perceptibly. For just the briefest of moments, it seemed like all a great mistake. But, mustering the courage of ages, I took a few halting steps, stopped, started again, and upon reaching her, gratified she had not tried to emasculate me with the hair-brush, which she seemed to be waving like a deadly weapon, gained hope while saying honestly: "I'm sorry," and again, "I'm sorry," and again, "I'm sorry." My mind was a pail of mush. I just didn't know what else to say.

She didn't respond, but merely stared catatonically. I tried again, somewhat more coherently. "I'm not an idiot, Bobi. I … I know you're about the last person to deserve all this, and it's all me, all of it; I know it; it's not one of those fifty-fifty, or sixty-forty, or whatever. I know it. You did absolutely nothing, nothing. That's why I feel like such a god-damned reprobate. I'm such a fuck-up, but I'd do anything to take it all back, anything … anything. There's got to be a way out of all this.

Bobi, I, I … for the first time in my life, I'm down, really down; I'm going nutzo."

She seemed to be trying to say something, but didn't, or couldn't, and instead became thoroughly unglued. My lands, I never figured her for all that passion, although I should have.

She stood, ashen-faced and wide-eyed, and burst violently into tears. Quickly I reached out to her as she let out all the pent-up despair of two weeks on my five-ninety-five, wash and wear, no iron polyester, fun-in-the-sun, 'California dreamin' shirt. As she cried, I held her tightly, and whispered softly, "Okay, okay. I understand. I'm sorry. It's all right. It'll be all right."

In a minute she gained control a bit, and seemed embarrassed for acting like such a 'silly little, school girl,' and apologized. "No apologies necessary," I quickly assured, "not on your part, anyway. These last couple of weeks hasn't exactly been a 'walk-in-the-park.' It's been pure hell, and, well, just hell, and there isn't any other word to describe it."

I took her by the hand, and led her to the sofa. We sat facing each other, and giving her my hanky, she patted dry her wet, streaming tears. She looked relieved; my heart jumped.

"Bobi," I began again my 'soliloquy-of-the-damned,' this can't go on like this. I'm dying, wasting away, bit by bit. I love you; you've become as much a part of me as my right arm, and if I knew of another way to say it, I would. You've cut me to the quick." She didn't answer, but when she did, I knew it was going to be the whole ball of wax.

"You did something to me from the very first time I ever laid eyes on you; something happened to me, and, I don't know, I'm not even sure it's normal, but there it is, and it's no small potatoes.

This is heavy stuff, Bobi, heavy, heavy, heavy, and I don't think we can just fluff it off because we've hit a bump in the road."

"It was more than a bump."

"It was whatever you say it was; I accept it, I'm a cad; I'm a rat; I'm an imbecile, put any name you want on it, stamp it, kick it, mail it, but I am very, very sorry, and I guarantee you it will never happen again, and I love you more than, than … you name it, and I'm dying a slow death honey, a slow, slow, slow, agonizing death, and you've just got to be able to overlook this, this disgusting, low-life transgression this one time, you've just got to."

Out of breath, and out of words, I hesitated for a moment as I looked for some sort of softening on her part as she continued to remain silent, just staring. I couldn't tell if she were ready to kiss me, or kill me; I felt myself starting to become anxious again, as if I already wasn't. Out of sheer frustration, I pleaded:

"Please say something. I can't take anymore of this; I'm getting that 'queasy' feeling." A concerned look crossed her face as she replied softly: "It's really been that rough?"

"Rough? Rough? You're being kind. I wouldn't wish this on the most fiendish of devils. I don't know, honey, but it can't end like this, it just can't."

"Well I never expected you. . ." I cut her off abruptly.

"Expected me? Well it's true. You think the male gender's superior? Shit, just look at the mess he's got this world in, and he's had 6000 years to get it right. And look at me; what am I, Gandhi? Einstein? I'm just a crutty, smaltsy, wise assed shmuck, that's all, and it seems I didn't know you as well as I thought. You are awful, awful, emotional. I just felt it pouring out of you like water over a busted dam. You must have stirrings under those skirts the psyches haven't even begun to touch, and you've got me backed into a corner. But one thing's for sure: I'm not ever going to meet anyone like you again, and I know it, and the thought of trying to get through this friggin snake-pit without you is just a little too much to bear. As a matter of fact, it will be downright impossible.

"I had no idea I … it's just that; I really got to you, huh?"

"Bobi, you may be a little more than I can handle, I don't know, but like I said, I don't have a life without you, none, and this coming from a guy who says he don't need a god-damned thing in this stinking world.

I don't know what you've got, Bobi, but it's killing me," and with our faces no more than a foot apart I added truthfully, "I love you sweetheart, and I'm beginning to sound like a parrot, I know, but there's nothing else for me, this is it, just you, that's all, and the world can shake its naked, dirty ass in a mud hole."

"My, I don't know what to say except, "me too." And with those 'two little words' I was reborn.

Putting both arms around her, I kissed her flush on her sugary, red sensuous lips, and then hugged her, and kissed her, and hugged her, and kissed her, and she seemed to hold me just as tight. I was making-up for two weeks of starvation. I pulled away, and looking straight into her misty green eyes, declared soberly, "Sweetheart, it'll work."

Well," she answered with a faint smile, "it better, because it looks like it's going to be me you and me, after all."

"You gave me quite a start, you know. I was kind of half believing that maybe you weren't joshing about all that "I don't love you anymore" hokey doke."

"You hurt me, John. You hurt me real bad." The Battle of Stalingrad flashed through my mind. Hurt? I guess it's all a matter of perspective.

"I know," I agreed, still thinking of battered and frozen bodies in the snows of Russia, "I know." Life, I thought, can easily become a trail of silliness.

Getting back to the matter at hand, I added, morosely: "I'll make it up to you somehow, believe me, for the rest of my life, I'll make it up to you." Some half-wit fool in 1930's tinsel town could have written that last line, and probably did.

"Oh, oh, no you don't," she quickly rebutted. "You're not putting me in that box."

"What'ya mean?" I asked, somewhat bewildered.

"We're not going down that "I owe you kind of jive" road. That's no basis for a marriage. We just got over one hurdle; let's not throw up another so soon, hey? Love will do just nicely, thank you."

Like I've said many times, Buck; Bobi was no dumbo. "Yeah, I can dig it, I agreed. "It's just that, well, having hurt you so much and all. . . . ."

"Granted."

"The thing is, some folks deserve, and other's don't. You? You didn't deserve this, you just didn't, and it's going to take me awhile to, well, you know—adjust."

"I'm sure; after all, it's not every day a body gets caught with their. . . ."

"Okay; okay."

"Well, Adi said I should learn to joke about it."

"I know." Uh, oh. Those were not the 'two little words' she expected to hear, so neither was the flustered response unexpected.

"You do?"

"Yes, but. . . ."

"Well! So that's why you're here?"

"No, no, damn it. I was coming anyway, for sure. You ought to know that. She just dropped by this afternoon, being beside herself, and all, she had to find out the score, and if I had any feeling at all for you, I'd better get my ass over here pretty quick, because she wasn't going to stand around while the person she loved was going to pot right before her eyes, and that's the truth."

"Well I'll be; she really said that?"

"Yes, she really said that. It seems you have a way of getting to a body, as I've come to learn with some apprehension."

"Apparently."

"You should feel real proud of yourself," I kidded, I think.

"I really get to ya, huh?" To wit, I could only give one of those uncertain, raised eyebrow looks. "I feel like a damned ass," I continued. "You weren't supposed to know anything about this."

"Obviously, a conspiracy."

"What the hell else could she do? And don't put the drop on her for it, as I have more than a sneaking suspicion you'd have done the same, had the shoe been on the other foot, and you wouldn't have hesitated a hot second. I know she wasn't too thrilled about cutting in like that, and I also know she felt worse about you. She really did feel bad. So? What the hell was she supposed to do … the fandango?"

"Oh, I'm not mad; actually I'm kind of flattered. You really were coming, anyway?"

"This very night. She just kind of gave me a little push since I was kind of losing heart."

"You've had a rough time too, huh, she asked, again?"

"You have no idea, or do you? One or two more weeks of this, and the bells would have been tolling for me. You're quite an exceptional young lady, as you're probably aware. So, we do what we must." A look of quiet concern, and joy, came over her. "We shall," she agreed solemnly, "we shall."

"And do you think someday," I added quixotically, "we might be telling our grandchildren of this little escapade?"

"You really don't know when you're standing on a nail, do ya?" she admonished.

Ah, my dearest Virginia. T'was a sweet and glorious night that night. Play it again, Sam.

It should be noted, that, as time passed, my love and I became inseparable, enjoying each others company as we did.

We spoke on every subject known to man or beast, and while we did not always agree, we never fought.

We took a turn on the town, now and then, mostly just to get out and catch a slight bit of musicale if one were about. As for sex, well, the cigar burned bright. It is not always so, to be sure, in love, or not. Somehow we managed to keep it fresh. The secret must be guilt-free relaxation. It was that all right. The bedroom, for us, was an extension of our personalities. We grew, we had no fear, and we had no shame. We did experiment some, slight variations upon the three basic themes, and mainly as a challenge to our wicked imaginations. Actually, we delighted each other so, just lying there, side by side, usually did the trick. And so it goes. . . . .

IXV

Barrels of wine and golden ale

Dionysian delights swirl about

Jump, scream, hail the king

Slay the deer in humid woods

Games, tricks, the magic of life

Painted face and tawdry garb

It is the court jester who shows the way.

Freedom, love, the good and true

But cowards breathe, and hero's fall.

Alas, why more? The sight is cruel

Dry fields strewn with the bloodied

and maimed.

The dusty ground home for the broken

I sha'nt return upon my shield

But cast it thence and dare to contest

The awful truth of thee and thou

* * *

LOVE is, at its relentless best, faultless compatibility, Gestalt psychology run wild, an arrow shot at a vital organ precariously floating in a sea of rolling turbulence encasing the unfathomable depths of enchantment. Yet the rocky shores of time, silent and majestic, cannot withstand the persistent thundering of the heaving, battering waves.

Sitting aimlessly one evening, watching the night life carousing in the back yard, I thought of Bobi, who had left that afternoon for a teacher's convention in Honolulu. She had wanted me to accompany her but visions of grass skirts, Hawaiian lullaby's, tourists and large drunken crowds making noises partially resembling the living, was a bit more than I could bear for four deadly days, so, I passed.

As I sat there thinking of my loved one, the phone rang, and I listlessly rose to answer. A voice I thought I had recognized as Adi's mouthed something incoherent, or else there was a bad connection. She tried again, this time more distinctly: "John? Is this you, John?" I did not like the tone of her voice.

"Yes, it's me," I replied, waiting for the next shoe to drop. It did, like a horse on a fly.

"Bobi's dead," it blurted.

"What?" I questioned, unbelievingly.

"Bobi's dead," she repeated. "Dead; the plane went down in the ocean. There were no survivors. I can't talk anymore," she hastily remarked, and hung up.

She need not have explained why she couldn't continue. It seems she was given the distressing task of informing me of the shocking event, an event which left me standing there with the receiver in my hand, quietly observing my whole body slowly traversing into a state of shock. I stiffened, and my stomach tensed; beads of perspiration formed on my brow, and I began to tremble uncontrollably. Blacking out temporarily, I recovered to find myself dazedly staggering in circles, zombie-like.

I made my way to my bunk, and flopped down like a sack of wet rags. Consumed by cold shivers, the same thought kept occurring and reoccurring: 'This can't be happening,' 'this can't be happening,' 'this can't be happening,' and grief, bone wrenching, gut clutching, grief—the second time now in but a few mere weeks—closed in upon my tormented, pitiable soul.

Moment by moment it built, as in stages, and when the initial shock abated, it took hold of me once again, and shook me, much like a dog violently shaking a rag doll. And over, and over, and over, the inevitable question: Why? Why? Why? A harmless, gentle soul like Bobi, young, bright, beautiful, good. Why? What sense? What purpose? And me? What great pleasures of life had I that this unspeakable tragedy was visited upon me to even the score? The keeper of the scales must be mad, mad. It's all a bad dream. I wondered will I awake momentarily in a shivering cold sweat from this macabre nightmare? No, no dream, reality, madness.

Is there a difference? Is all of life the illusion of sanity and the imagery of good? That is the madness, the thoughts of holiness and joy, perfection and beauty in this crypt of excrement. There are too many demons in the world, too many saintless, merciless gods.

No good to think, but it salved my grief, then added to it. My stomach churned, I twisted, and I turned. I slipped into semi consciousness; I awoke almost instantly. My anguish would not allow even a moment's respite. No good to lie. I rose, torpidly ambled outdoors, and gazed helplessly at the still, beclouded sky in the forlorn hope that some small miracle might fall from its bloated belly. The only thing that fell was my hope.

I returned, sat, rose again, walked again, sat again. Impossible to sit; no good to lie. What am I to do? Where am I to turn? To what can I turn? Drink? Drugs? Debauchery? Oh great god of misery and torment, shoot the poisoned dart of comforting diminution.

Back to earth was I quickly pulled. 'Not in this life, not in this life,' a hardened, muffled voice, softly whispered.

* * *

We later learned that the 727 went down some 100 miles northeast of Honolulu in what they claimed was one of the worst storms in years.

Very little of anything was recovered, including the black box, but sixteen bodies, or parts of sixteen bodies, were. Bobi's was one of them.

At the wake I came nearly at closing time, and sat alone in the back. There were quite a few gathered, but I only recognized Mr. and Mrs. Higgins, and Adi.

As I seemed not to be making a move to approach the coffin, Adi came around to inquire "into my intentions."

"I'm not sure," I informed honestly, wherein she puzzledly asked "precisely what did I mean by that?"

"I think I'll just sit here for a while," I replied.

Not buying it for a moment, she persisted concernedly, "John," she said, "You've got to go up there."

"I don't think I can, Adi," I curtly answered.

"What a-r-e you saying?" she asked unbelievingly.

"I'm saying I can't do it." I liked Adi; she was the 'ace of diamonds' in a deck full of jokers, but I wished she would go away.

"John, you've got to go up there, and say goodbye, you've got to. She's waiting; you're the only thing that mattered to her, and she'll never rest if you don't. You've got to do this one, last thing for her."

"I know; I know, but I'm not good at this kind of stuff. . . . ."

"Who is?"

"I'm choking inside. I, I, if I see her. . . . ."

"Come on; you have to; I'll help you."

"Help me? No; I'll do it alone, or not at all."

"Okay, but do it, John; don't let me think bad of you, and you'll never be able to live with yourself." And with those 'comforting' words bouncing around my head, she rose and went over to speak to a friend.

Living with myself was the least of my concerns at the moment. It seemed 'just living' was going to be the problem.

I continued to sit, and Adi, every so often, would glance in my direction. She must have been wondering, as was I, if I ever were going to make a move.

Presently, I slowly stood up, and mechanically made my way to the casket.

Upon reaching it, I felt myself becoming light-headed as I glanced down and saw my betrothed lying peacefully as if asleep.

Standing there, just looking down at her, it occurred to me how she really looked to be not much different from the living state. Whoever made her up did a magnificent job. Even in death the buck rules. I can just imagine the conversation that took place between Mr. Higgins and the funeral director. Specials for the special. Well, I had to admit, she deserved every bit of it.

I stood frozen, just staring down. Adi must have been watching me like a hawk guarding the nest, as I saw her through the corner of one eye, she starting to walk towards me. As she came abreast, I motioned that everything was all right, and she turned and went back to her seat.

Finally, I leaned over and kissed Bobi softly, one last time. I gazed at her for a few seconds more, then rubbed her cheek with the back of my hand, and then her forehead. Whispering, "I love you, sweetheart," I then stepped back, turned, and rubbery-legged walked out. The last chapter in this sordid journey had seemed to close.

* * *

Mr. Higgins was a pathetic sight at the funeral. He slouched in the pew and kept whimpering pitifully liked a whipped dog. I would have guessed. Mrs. Higgins? Well, true to the sterling character I thought I had recognized when first we met, she sat straight and quiet, only now and then dabbing at red, puffy eyes with a white, lace hanky. I caught a glimpse of her face, once or twice; grief lay upon her brow like stale dough in a forgotten cake pan. The deep lines and crevices were telling. Only a matter of time now, I thought, for the quickened pace of creaky, old age to silently creep in like a thief in the night, and steal what's left of a once-so-pretty a face.

They laid Bobi to rest on the top of a small knoll. She would have liked that, and as she was slowly being lowered, Adi seemed to be approaching hysteria.

Well, well, well, now; kum see, kum sah. Quickly I reached about her shoulders, and squeezed tightly. The human touch, in the midst of this funereal aura, seemed to do wonders, for both of us.

I remained after everyone had left, standing at the foot of the grave, just staring down. What else had I to do? It seemed so unreal, like a short subject before the main feature, neither of mind or substance. Somehow I just couldn't grasp the fact of Bobi being dead. My best deserted me now, as I stood alone in a foreign, hostile land. I hoped for the inevitable 'bullet in the back of the head.' What came instead was a resurgent dose of sorrow, nature being so keenly 'aware' of our innermost needs. (Sic)

As I stood there wallowing in my grief, all I could think of was death, and how it had a way of surprising us with its sudden manner of introduction. Life, a whirlwind speeding headlong into the flash of time, and then, 'bang' do we crash into the steel brickyard of evanescence. Death. Death. Death. How could anything be so alive one moment, and extinct the next? No time to adjust. Horror, bit by bit, crept into my hollow, creaking soul.

I stayed; I am not sure how long. One does not usually keep track of the flies in the barn. It was, however, an effort to leave, having the feeling that once I did, it would indeed be the end. In truth, I never did leave.

Slowly I traipsed back down the hill, and with each agonizing step, I became sicker and sicker. As I reached the entrance to the bone yard, I was suddenly overcome by piercing cramps and crumpled in a heap. An elderly woman, who happened to be passing, inquired into the exact nature of my 'condition.' "Nothing serious" I assured, "just an old war wound."

Presently, I was able to continue, and did so slowly some two blocks when it finally dawned on me that I had left the car back at the grave. Is this what it's going to be like henceforth, I thought to myself?

Trying not to think, I returned, daring not to look in the direction of my love's final resting place, retrieved the muscle bound hunk-of-junk, and drove straight-a-way to the pit.

Fate was kind. No one was there to interfere with my torment. It, like anything of worth, is nothing, if not entirely of itself. It must surely be the only thing left untouched by the smooth, cold, dead hand of plastic.

I lay on my cot and wept. I writhed in agony. Good god, good god, what does it mean, what does it all mean.

Two weeks past, I think, but what matter; I was not keeping track these days. It could just have well have been two years. Sleeping badly, eating little, walking much. I grew a beard, messy and dirty, lost much weight, and cared not a wit. The dead leave the living to die.

A month passed, I continued as I had been. Six weeks, more of the same. It seemed now that Bobi had been gone a thousand years. The agony endured. It should have begun to abate by now, I know, but it hadn't. Seems I had a particularly virulent case. I sensed that, in time, as with all things, it would run its course. I knew, but it didn't help. I also knew that it damn sure was taking its bloody time about it. Knowing does not always help. Knowledge, at best, is but a dirty band aid in the wild woods of life.

* * *

It's been six-months now, and I tell you truthfully, I don't know how I did it. But something's amiss; I remain in the throes of depression. Tis not the normal way of things; tis not the way of life. I have always prided myself for being able to live as close to the natural as possible, and now this? This is not the way of it. I am now of the mind that, the sudden and grievous shock, might have unhinged me permanently.

It cannot continue. There is no reason, no purpose for all of it. I am not Stanley searching for Livingstone. My character doesn't need to be molded and built for some great mission in this most ludicrous of lives.

Life? I am nobody, doing nothing, going nowhere. This perambulation, some 70 odd years, and pfftt. Why is this happening? Why can't I get on with it? Why can't I enjoy a taco like everyone else? Without meaning, life is a blind, fat frog in a dry lagoon. Not a shred of purpose can I find in all this. Not through this entire maze, this entanglement of emotional barbed-wire, can I find one bit, one little shred-of-a-clue to lead me to the light at the end of the tunnel. More and more, these days, do I think of the 'little black box,' more and more. . . . .

* * *

Well, it's been 10 ghastly months now, 9 bloated pregnant, and one extra for good measure, and that fine edge has begun to dull some, although that habitual feeling of ensuing panic remains, and the constant gnawing in the pit of my stomach with it. A general feeling of ennui has now become a permanent fixture of my personality I can now see.

One conquers nothing, one merely adjusts, accommodates himself even to the worst of situations. And is it a sign of strength, or weakness? Does it matter? Survival is temporary. Evolution proceeds at snails pace; the machinery of history wobbles and creaks, and I but a small dent in a rung in the ladder ever descending into the pit of oblivion.

Extraordinary, how one can become so attached to another, or an idea, or a belief for that matter, as though there is a compulsive urge to attach to something in the hope that that something will lead to the lifeline of immortality.

Isolation is not becoming to the human form and solitary confinement a crudely carved cellmate. It has been refined to include bread and water, darkness and filth. We learn so well, it seems, the finer points of acrimony, and like octopi, we ravenously gather in every delicate morsel of hate within our seemingly limitless grasp.

Love? Love is an accident of circumstance not included in the equation; a statistical aberration produced in one of the mad gods frivolous flights into the land of shadows and dreams.

So ... we believe what we like and usually that which is most comforting. The brain is not a thinking machine, but merely a nest of neurotic constructions, a breeding ground of incivility, and life but a bundle of electrical impulses, nestling snugly in the bosom of creation, a lumpen mass of rock-hard, knotty, raw nerve endings, and god a defunct chiropractor.

It is all a cruel hoax. Couldn't he have been instead, the local hooker who showers daily, smells sweetly, has a penchant for jumping every Tom she comes upon, and takes cut-rates and credit-cards. The world will never be a precious place until sex is elevated to the level of professional football complete with preseason, league games, playoffs, and that grand finality of all blessed obscenities—the Super Bowl—wherein the winner gets six-months in the Bahamas with a bevy of beauties, and the loser six-days in Pittsburgh with Tijuana Tonya.

* * *

I think I've just about had it, Buck. I never was one to engage in the futility of 'beating a dead horse,' so I bought a gun today. It's not hard, you know. Were it all things so easily done.

First time in many a moon I've had one of the bleak, little destroyers in hand, and mindful of reptiles, it's cold and elemental function, equally deadly.

I took one of those rat and roach infested rooms downtown per three-fifty, one dank and rainy afternoon, and stared at the blunt, steely tool lying, seemingly impotent, on a rickety old, dirty wooden table, with visions of a drug-laden Poe, stumbling through the dirty streets of Baltimore on a dark, wet autumns eve.

Sitting there calmly and dispassionately, the same thought kept occurring and reoccurring: When there is no point, there is no point. The light at the end of the tunnel is the flash of an explosion; reach for it, and you become dust, a memory, a flitting, petulant thought in the mind's eye of antiquity.

I did not wish for my last act in this fretful life to be wholly spontaneous since I was somewhat aware of my predicament. I was, to speak of, greatly despondent, but not mentally unhinged, a distinction worth noting, and it is certain many have survived in like condition, but not me. I resolved therefore, by all that is holy, to make one, last, conscious rational decision, seemingly independent of all outer machinations.

Suicide may seem an extravagant means to attain freedom; it may be, but do not be jinxed into thinking it can be attained in any case. It cannot. It is the 'joker in the deck.'

Why then, am I using my skull for target practice? It is one mistake, assuming that it is, that cannot be retracted. But then, so what, and what matter? What is one life? Any life? Not so much as a spit-in-the-dark. Sacred? Hah! An alluring sentiment appealing to those who believe that the earth is the center of the universe. Cynical? Faithlessness? Cowardice perhaps? Gibberish; all subjective, lazy minded nonsense. The forces that are are, minus scruples, feelings, conscience, and to the extent I am a part, I am also. As for philosophies, there are none save one---the unyielding continuity in the faith of illusion. Inhuman, you say? Admittedly, but six-thousand years of violence, war and genocide, all committed with the enthusiasm of a sex-starved sheik lost in a harem with a gallon of Spanish fly, is not the record of the 'Good Shepherd' leading his flock to the promised land.

The world is the mirror of immorality. It is all rot: The law, constitutions, government, education, religion, science, progress, all rot, every stinking bit of it, and if we had any conscience at all, any courage to speak of, we would scrap it, every stinking bloody shred, every piece, every nail, junk it, every last damnable bit of it, and with only the purple taint of Eden hanging over our cursed heads, start anew. Of course, i-t—w-i-l-l—n-o-t—h-a-p-p-e-n; it will n-e-v-e-r happen. The tail wags the dog.

The trail is winding and narrow; the trees overhang. The night is black, and the wind howls. Wolf-packs abound, and their pursuit of warm, fresh blood is tireless.

Fear, like the California smog, prevails, while mankind drags its prostrate past noisily through the ages, the distracting clamor its bony skeleton banging on the churchyard door.

Where are our heroes'? Our saints? What shows are the weekend gladiators and perfidious salesmen of fright masquerading as 'ministers of the soul,' the great comforters directing the dolorous to the hallowed halls of salvation. Vaudeville isn't dead; it has merely changed its makeup.

So this is the 20th. Century? The era of scholarship and discovery. Hah! This couldn't make a bad day in the thirteenth. You can't tell the kings from the pawns. The king is dead, the king is dead.

Rousseau was right. How many 'evil' babies have you seen lately? It is the system, ultimately. It can't be anything else. Is there a-n-y-t-h-i-n-g without an environment? But what is the system? Who is the system? He racing 200 miles per at Indy? Mr. Macho felling the great, white rhino? A seven-foot freak slamming a ball through a hoop? He 'making' money? Selling? Learning? Politicking? My god; we sit, we stare, we take the test; we pass, smugly, we think we know. Madness. We persist in viewing life through a glass darkly and, like the court jester, we are in it, but not of it.

We don't live, we joust. We dream, but never awaken, quaking at the edge of the cliff, anxious in our trembling, forward steps to take the plunge.

Apprehensively we watch the relentless, careening waves crashing below, and, like the mortician, are doomed to lives of restrained waiting. For all of the new dawns procrustean urge to shed its inhibited skins, we now find them resplendently replaced with plain, old-fashioned dishonesty, the sneaky killer crawling about in the dark for any victim happening by.

So the clapper has come full circle. The music man is peddling a false note. The twins of human deficiency—mendacity and ignominy—are ever born anew, and adversity, holding up the ugly head of fear, spreads its skinny, hairless legs beckoning, and we rush to dive in. For all our supposed mastery of the animal kingdom, we live, nevertheless, as treeless apes, apeing the apes in the trees. Truly, we have become a nation of sheep.

I dozed off languishing in the chair staring out the window in what couldn't have been more than fifteen or twenty minutes. When I awoke, I knew for certain, the sun would never set again upon this weary head. No longer was it, should I, or shouldn't I? Is it right? Why am I? No, none of that. Now it was simply—when, Buck?

I rose, and in complete control of my faculties, walked slowly over to the small table, picked up the profane, silent angel of death, turned, and deliberately stepped toward the window. Outside resembled a Burmese Monsoon. Nice weather for a killing, I thought, in keeping with the mood.

As I stood watching the torrent, all the little devils, the host of imbecilities, the legion of inanities, the lumpen drivel of it all welled up within me. I could resist no longer. I had to have my 'piece of cake' one last, sparkling tribute to the ages, one last contemptuous act of defiance.

I raised the window, and realized for the first time, that I was on the third floor. Hah! Even now the trivial gains the seat of ascendancy. I recall once, of one, who, when having decided upon this same pallid exercise in futility, haggled with the proprietor over the price of the musket. No matter; life, whatever, all twaddle. Much ado about nothing.

It poured mightily; I leaned into it and shouted: "Fuck you America! Fuck you!" I waited; no answer. Just like the despicable, bloody cowards. I repeated: "Fuck you, America! Fuck you! Fuck your gods! Mother! Church! Country! Apple pie! Your dirty little meanness, your holy Joe's; fuck you all, you perverted, degenerate cocksuckers! F-u-c-k y-o-o-o-o!"

Enough of this. Why give the slimy, belly-walkers the satisfaction. I walked back towards the bed, and fidgeting about seeming to lose my nerve, I stalled for time.

What a farce. What time? It was up to me; I'm king here. I make my own time. I noticed a fat, red roach perched on the far wall, its antennae wagging and scoping the foul, musty air. He seemed to be STARING AT ME! Forever stare, do the creepers of the night shade. I'll fix his germ-laden carcass. You're coming with me suc-kah. This very day will you observe first hand the likeness of cockroach heaven, or wherever you filthy, putrid mis-cell-an-ii go.

I looked for something with which to bash his gross, crunchy head. A rolled-up newspaper, a book, a shoe, anything but my pet pistollero. That was to be reserved but for me only.

Over by the bed stood a small night stand. I pulled out the one drawer, and there it was, a torn, moth-eaten, Gideon bible. Momentarily, it shall be put to better use than it had ever been.

I picked it up, and walked over to the brazen mite, still hanging, still staring. Maybe he was blind, I thought. They're usually not so 'accommodating.' No matter; he will not need to include Braille in his uses. "Hello, you disgusting, red devil," I greeted. "Goodbye, you scab on the world's back," and "Bam!" was he irreverently slammed into the eye of eternity.

I stood there eyeballing the loathsome splotch on the mucky wall. Now what?

"Now what? Get on with it, Buster. You're not going to back out now, not after that fulsome display by the window a bit ago of misplaced nobility."

"But what if?"

"What if? What if bananas. You've had your rounds, and now you're down-for-the-count. Stay down. This world is more than willing to throw in the towel on you anyway."

"But maybe there's something … something decent waiting for me.

"Cap that jar, Bozo. Decent was buried months ago. You're going to pick NOW to turn into a wimp?"

"But."

"But what? Get on with it."

"Maybe I should leave a note."

"Note? Note? To whom? And what are you gonna do? Run down to the corner for a pencil and paper? This is beginning to turn into a charade."

"But I just thought. . . . ."

"Thought, hell; you just climbed that hill."

"Maybe I should sit."

"Sit? I would call this crawl."

"But it seems less, less … violent if I sit."

"Now? Now you're concerned with violence? A snapper-up of piddling trifles; tis not the time to sit about and tell sad tales of the death of kings.

"Hah! Listen to him."

"Screw up your courage to the sticking place. You're just a pound of flesh; hardly the noblest Roman of them all."

"But just as high in my own heart."

"Lord what fools these mortals be."

"Nevertheless."

"Life is as tedious as a twice-told tale."

"Uh, huh, and vexing the dull ear of a drowsy man."

"Courage, man. The hurt cannot be so much."

"Twill serve."

"The devil can cite scripture for his purpose."

"Aye and who better?"

"Tarry no more, but snatch-up the bare bodkin and your quietus do make."

"Everyone can master a grief but he that has it."

"You think too much."

"There was never yet philosopher that could endure the toothache patiently."

"Tis a matter for the tooth-puller."

"I have seen better days.

"Let's hope no more."

"How sweet a thing to look into misfortune through another's eyes.

"Don't fret; the hole will be the same."

"Oh, God, that men should put an enemy in their mouths, to steal away their brains."

"And make rather bear those ills we have, than fly to others that we know not of."

"There's a divinity that shapes our ends."

"And all our yesterdays have lighted fools; shuffle off this mortal coil. The roach had sterner stuff."

"And didn't even flinch."

"Then set it right."

"But then he never knew."

"That dreaded something after death comes to lads and gals alike."

"The time is out-of-joint."

"The time is well enough."

"This tale, weary, stale and flat, has misused this day."

"Aye, every inch a king, you be."

"Told by an idiot full of sound and fury."

"As you like it."

I walked back towards the window. It's over; it's over. With a trembling hand I raised the pistol pointing it to my right temple. Slooowly I squeezed the trigger. Click. Nothing. The Malignant bazoom misfired. I aimed again, but this time out the window. Bang! Again. Bang! Yep, sure enough, it misfired.

Good Lord! Of a sudden did it hit me unlike the leaden pellet. What were the odds of a brand new, well-oiled pompom misfiring? Astronomical perhaps, but it did.

I became giddy and light-headed, for now I knew, after all these years of frettin and sweatin, and woes and blows, I knew. To me it was given, the microscopic glimpse into the universal test-tube. There W-A-S meaning after all too all this seeming haplessness.

Well, Buck; so frivolity is forever and education where you find it. But there must have been a better way, surely, and quicker too.

Still in a somewhat excitable state, as you can imagine, I merrily tossed the steely 'merchant of death' on the bed, and unsteadily---but jubilantly—made my way out.

It was still raining torrentially but what did I care. Wash away washerman, wash away the sins of the world. What difference now. Rain, shine, hot or cold. Could anything ever douse my passion, shackle my thirst for the golden quest? I had it all, and, with feet as light as a pheasants plume, I gingerly stepped off the slippery curb, joyful in my newly found prize.

* * *

I never saw it coming. All I heard, somewhere in the back of my mind, was a skidding, a shriek, and a "Hey! Look out!" The next I knew I was lying in the street, half conscious, with strange faces hovering over me. "Take it easy, buddy; the ambulance will be here any minute. You'll be all right," and: "get a blanket, somebody." The softened hand of kindness, the quaking voice of care, all now so infinitesimal, so very, very … far away.

I stared, they stared. The rain spattered my face. A few feet away, its front hugging the curb it had jumped, stood a black-and-white van with the words 'Ace Laundry' blazoned across its tinny side.

A laundry truck, a damned laundry truck. Meaning? Hah! S-h-i-i-i-t. A stinking, damned, lousy, mother-fucking laundry truck. And, with that last and loving sentiment dutifully stamped upon my wettened brow, I closed my eyes … and died.

* * *

EPILOGUE

A GATHERING OF EAGLES

WELL, I'm dead now. Ah, yes, Virginia; it comes to us all. But no matter. Let me tell you a bit about heaven and hell. (And it might interest you to know, you are all wrong again, as usual.)

For one, it's not referred to in such glorious terms. Up here it's just 'up' and you-know-what, is 'down.' Up and down, up and down, that's all. We call it Otis.

My first day here-a-bouts, I had to take a number. Yeah, a number; how's that for clubbing the ox? Felt like I was standing in the cold-cut line at the A&P.

When called in, I was confronted by a coarse, grizzled old gent, sporting a shaggy, grey beard seemingly harboring all of the world's mites, who went by the name of 'Peter,' he of the fishes and thrice crowing cocks.

Number two had been looking over my record, and recognizing no acts of terrorism, and was neither a politician, priest, judge; lawyer, general, TV. technician, auto mechanic or corporate executive, was duly informed of my entitlement of choice of residence: "Up" or "down."

Now having just recently arrived, and seeing very little of 'up' and none of 'down,' I therefore inquired into the speed with which I was expected to decide.

"Take all the time you need," was the matter-of-fact reply. "We gots nothing b-u-u-t time up here, Bub."

However, in view of the notions usually associated with visions of heaven, and such, I wasted no time in silly conversation. I chose 'up.' No big deal. And bye-the-bye: You all can lay off the prayer beads, baptisms and candles, and such, since it all counts for about as much as a filthy maggot earnestly worming his way up a dead horse's ass, and of no interest to anyone including the horse.

It was all kind of exciting, at first, meeting up with old acquaintances, and all, Caligula, Savonarola, Machiavelli; Louie XVI, the Borgia's, Robespierre, Marc Antony, Cortez. I felt like I was in a 'school for cabals.' You'd be surprised to learn how many of their ilk was really very ordinary, very. It gave credence to my long held belief that most 'great' men were great creatures of circumstance, to wit: Everybody has to be someplace sometime.

As a matter-of-fact, now that I've been able to witness the phenomenon first hand, the prime ingredient in this stale, half-baked cake seems to be a decided lack of character, rather than an abundance of it. On the other hand, they most all seemed to have one defect in common—they crave fame and power, their appetite in this regard being insatiable, and upon further investigation it turns out that this dipsomania is the result of a decidedly, sickly, swollen ego, combined with a voluminous sense of insecurity, alongside a glaringly, irrational sense of self importance, all of which goes hand-in-hand, of course. A veritable 'montage of miscellania.'

One uneventful morn---we have them too---a comical looking chap with a long, silky white beard, struck-up a conversation. He squirreled about until finally inquiring into my general likeness of things, and if everything was 'Jim dandy.' I politely intoned, "fine," excepting I would appreciate someone getting that damned, gaudy, red paint off the walls in my room, and replacing it with something a little less bold like … lavender blue, maybe? He said he'd 'look into it,' and thereupon vanished in thin air. Spirits can do that, you know. I can do it. It ain't no big thing, though, not when every blockhead can do it, and to no apparent advantage. The Tokyo express would do just as well.

Ol' Pete reappeared and I asked him who 'old folks' was. "Oh," was the casual reply, "that was him."

"Him? Who him?" said I, wonderingly.

"Yeah, him; the Lawd."

"The hell, you say?"

"I do "

"Well I'll be damned."

"Careful. Wishes have a way of happening up here."

"He don't look like much."

"You cain't go by that. Appearances can be deceiving."

"Apparently."

"Anyhow, that's what he looks like today. Yesterday he was a crocodile, and the day before, a giraffe. The Lawd, he a fun guy. He lok tu play games."

"I kind-of gathered that from my brief respite down under."

"But don't let his unassuming and genial manner fool ya, ya know? He can be a woe powerful dude when he's a mind to."

"That little twit?"

"Oh, yeah; that little twit. Why this very minute he knows everythin we're sayin … and thinkin. He knows everythin about everythin."

"And he ain't mad? Us speaking of him like this, I mean?"

"Whats-du-yuse-meen—US? Sides, he da Lawd; he nevah git mad. Cep one tahm, and ther wust hell to pays, den."

"I can imagine; and when was that?"

"Time Lusufuh try to muscle him. Yuse remembuh Lusufuh?"

"Of course. Really ticked him off, did he?"

"Madder dan a barrel fulla pissed-on wildcats."

"That's mad."

"Tells me bouts it."

"Well, hell; with all his juice, and all, why didn't he just cut off his balls, or something?"

"Well he did … or sumpin. Sides, he da Lawd. He lok foh tings tu jist kient of take dere natule kaus."

"Say? Are you black, today? You keep talking, more and more, like a Georgia, field-hand of a by-gone day."

"No; we cula-blynt up heah."

"Then, what?"

"We all gots to talk lok sumpin."

"You ain't puttin me on?"

"Ah's dunt hasta. Ah's big stuff round heah."

"Somehow I get the feelin you wasn't talking like this when that boat was sinking."

"Yuse got dat raht."

"Getting back to 'da Lawd.' Uh, huh. Now you got me doin it."

"Catchy, ain't it?"

"You sure you're Peter?"

"Ah's not da punkin-eater."

"Gettin back to 'the La . . .' the Lord; you say he's a natural kind of guy. Likes for things to happen step-by-step, so to speak."

"Yaa-suh."

"But wouldn't this whole shmear have been a whole lot simpler, not to speak of kinder, if he had created the universe such that perfection in all things, big and small, was the order of-the-day?"

"Cud haf, but purfikshun ent tu intrestin."

"Ain't, huh? But crippled children, yellow fever and napalm, is?"

"He da Lawd."

"Sho nuf. And I don't think I'm going to like it much up here. Same folks up here as whence I came.

"What did you expect … unicorns and sea-nymphs?"

"Now you speak the King's English."

"Ah's kin du enathin ah's loks."

"To be sure, and is oft the case, the leadership resembles a one-eyed, shaggy, three-legged jackal."

"Da Lawd, he not gonn tu lok dat wun, litta bit. No, suh."

"He ain't, huh?"

"No, suh, not wun litta bit."

"So, what's he going to do, send me to hell?"

* * *

"Hah!" You say? Well, he did. Damned if he didn't. And that, my sweets, is power. Pfftt, a minute here, and pfftt, no more. The speed of light is not so bright. Oh, what the hell; it's where you find it. Anyhow, I was coming down here eventually. The atmosphere up there was a bit stifling for my simple ways. Not a bad break, really. Ees no so bad down here. Beats me why they call it hell. Seems to be a measure of double-speak about here, also.

No sooner did I arrive when guess who comes over? Prance, I should say, all nice and frilly, and smelling like he'd been dipped in French cologne---Oscar Wilde. Yeah, good ol' Oscar. Nice head, too. Made it known as how he was glad to be dead, what with all them 'born-agin' Christer's running loose like a pack of wild dogs. It's the Victorian Age all over again, and worse. "We should know better," I asserted. "Or maybe not."

"Do tell," he replied, in turn. "The air veritably stinks with their stygian morality."

Oscar showed me to my room. (I think he was trying to 'hit on me,' and had to, very politely, make it known as how my sexual proclivities pointed most definitely in other directions.)

"Straight-as-an-arrow, huh?" he ruefully commented.

"Well," I admitted, "let's just say, imaginatively conventional."

"There's no such thing," he sarcastically noted.

Come to think of it, I had to agree, and said so. "You're right," then added, "but in any case, it's the female gender that "lights my cigar."

It wasn't much to speak of—the room. A small bed, a table, and a hot-plate. The hot-plate, I gathered, was mere decoration, and we have, I am told, the finest cafeteria in all of creation. And why not? If not here, then where?

Oscar drifted back to the 'born-gainers.' Wanted to know how serious it was. "Aw, hell," I reassured, "if it wasn't that, then another crusade against the 'bubbly.' He seemed relieved and off he spirited.

As I was searching for a closet, forgetting of course, what need had a spirit for clothes, Goethe, in a puff of smoke, upt and appeared. And as you can plainly see by now, the clientele down here was definitely a 'cut above' the norm.

He introduced himself, and in keeping with his civil manner, asked if everything was "all right."

"Fine," I replied, "so far." Said if ever I needed anything, to just bang on the pipe, and, "quick-as-a-flash," someone would "see to it," and then before one even had a chance to say 'Jack Sprat,' was gone. It then occurred to me, that he, having been the creator of 'Faust,' it was no great surprise his now having to live out the deal.

Having now nothing to do, I made my way for that highly regarded cafeteria. Exactly where I was going though, I cannot say, for hell gathers in a stupendous range. But walk I did until realizing eternities dimensions, I stopped outside one of the simple, bedecked dwellings, and requested assistance.

"Entre," was the quick reply, and in so doing saw before me a wispy, silken-haired old chap, reclining on his bunk, and sucking on a briar pipe whilst reading a copy of "Gulliver's Travels." I knew instantly—he not having been long departed himself—that it was the esteemed 20th century mathematician and gad-about, Lord Russell.

"Good day, Sir," I greeted friendly. "And could you be so kind as to point me in the general direction of your highly touted restorante?"

He slowly pulled the pipe from his mouth, and replied casually, "The restorante?"

"The cafeteria."

"Ah, yes; I should have known. Straight down this corridor some 200 yards, make a left and straight on. It's but a short, jolly jaunt."

"Thank you, sir," I responded, and turned to leave, but did not. Instead, I asked, although knowing, if the gentleman, to whom I was speaking, was indeed, the esteemed Lord Russell.

Admitting same, he however, questioned the honored title, noting as how it counted for less than a deranged Tory in Lenin's attic in his present place of domicile. And, he added sapiently, "that's as it should be."

"Ah, yes indeed," I rejoined in agreement. "And it has been a pleasure meeting you, my friend. I have always been an admirer, in truth." He nodded warmly, "and I look forward sometime, to a more extended conversation."

"Young man," he instructed, "there will be time-a-plenty for tittle-tattle and whatever else. As you may or may not have noticed, 'Big Ben' is nowhere to be seen. I do miss a certain modicum of artful decoration in this vaporous realm of perpetuity."

"There does seem to be a lack of boundaries here."

"Neither can the eye see, nor the mind leap so far."

"It never ends, does it?"

"Never" seems so elfin a word to describe such immensity."

"Shakespeare was right then. . . . ."

"And now."

"That's not how I meant it.

"I know how you meant it; it suffices."

"Yes … well … by the way? I have not, as yet, seen any fair damsels about. Might I be so unfortunate as to inhabit a province devoid of the enchanting maidens? They, for all their contrary ways, have always been a great source of comfort to this poor soul. Tis truly a gruesome thought to think I should have to languish eternally in hell, a distraught celibate."

"You can put your mind at ease, young man. Your hell is behind you. They are all about and easily obtained."

"Do tell. You have made my day, kind sir.

"You have not seen them because they are doing the cooking."

"Cooking! Cooking!" I exclaimed in obvious befuddlement.

"But of course. Did you think it was done with wands? Tis not heaven, you know. Some mild effort is still a lively presence in the "belly of darkness."

"But the young ladies … do they not object?"

"Object? Hah! They love it."

"Do they now. . . ."

"Of course. This is hell, ladie. None of that bloody liberation, and what not, down here. Just fire and brimstone," and with a twinkle in his eye, added mischievously, "and fun and games."

"Am I really in hell? But this is heaven."

"It is all in the mind's eye, and you needn't concern yourself with any of the frilly, earthly contrivances either. All that was just so much sport to accommodate the capricious moods of the gods while romping about blighty earth, their backyard sandbox, their little, bitty playpen where short spurts of time are consumed in wayward flightiness. We, of the ghostly presence, are the eternal creation. Our existence is one of unbridled, total bliss, with some minor exceptions, of course; all to be expected."

"To be sure. And how might I go about engaging in ... uh ... er, the companionship of the delightful chickadees?" Spreading his spindly arms like a big bird about to alight from his roost, amusedly replied: "You have only to ask."

"That's it?" I blurted, breathlessly.

"That's it."

"And one will be given?" By now my heightened state of elation gave way only to my fevered impatience.

"Merely denote height, weight, race, and, or, national origin."

"I do believe I'm in heaven."

"Just as well." And noticing my gaped-mouthed amazement added: "It appears you need convincing, unless you catch flies." I blinked excitedly.

"Very well," and in a second, appearing at the foot of the bed stood the most ungodly, radiant, marble-skinned oriental lass I had ever seen in A-N-Y world. It could be said she was angelic perfection in all matters pertinent, but then, why not? Michelangelo himself could not have carved a more elegant figure.

"You called, Bertie?"

Good Lord. This exquisite creature from the blue lagoon even spoke. I was expecting a mere machine, the particularly beauteous often being nothing more, but this? Good god, I hope this isn't all a dream, for upon awakening I will be v-e-e-e-r-y despondent.

"Yes," his lordship replied, but tis only a test. New chap on the block; you understand."

"Certainly."

"You may return to your duties."

"Very well. I am yours at your beckoning." And with those beatific, heartening words, whisked herself away.

"I don't believe it," I responded incredulously, still in an exhilarating, state of shock. "Fond pleasures are not so easily come by."

"And so they aren't, but take them when you can."

"I shall; I shall," I promptly assured. "And there really ain't no women's lib?"

"You keep forgetting what you are, and where you are."

"I am having some difficulty … all these treasures … so fast. I still owe on my social security."

"It is all very social, and very secure, and no lib, lab, lob or blobs. Everything that pertained yonder does not here. No hates, or anger, or frustrations, or envy, or jealousies. We have no egos, therefore what need have we for liberation? Liberation from what? Here it's just "hug-um-and-fuck-um." (Salty old dog.)

"And no one demonstrates? Or pickets? Or writes letters? Or strikes? Or … Or. . . ."

"Nothing, nothing, nothing, my man; the thing in itself minus all the earthly lunacy."

"You'll get no argument from me on that score. Were it so delightful from whence I came."

"Were it."

"Well, thank you so much, your Lordship, for this … uh, 'rules seminar.' I think I've got the hang of it now. Can't wait to see what kind of restaurant you all have down here, if that little 'to-do' just now is any indication of the normal way of things." He gave a friendly wave, and off I scooted.

No sooner had I gone 10 feet, when an uncontrollable sexual craving came upon me. Unbelievingly I had only to wish, and it shall be given? Mealtime could wait; what I had in mind was far more appetizing.

Steadying myself, I wished for an Island type. You know, one of them wiggly Tahitian's what act like they're afflicted with the St. Vitas dance? I was always fond of the athletically exotic, and presently, one just upped and appeared.

But let me not wander about trifling details. You can well imagine by now, what had 'lit my fire.' A brownish beauty, without a blemish or fault of any kind and wearing a mini sarong, popped right up. My 'ghost-of-a-dickie-bird' didn't stand a chance. With the face and a smile to tear at the heart of the sternest of beasts, she asked so sweetly: "You called, Master?"

"Master! Master!" It was all too much. I was ready to shoot my bolt strait-away.

"Yes," I responded meekly. The habits of quivering humanity dying slowly, I stood jelly-legged, gawking witlessly.

"Well?" she asked without a trace of irritation.

"Well, what." I shot back getting simpler by the moment.

"Do you not want me?" she now asked incredulously.

"Want you? Yes, by all means, but please to allow me to catch my breath. All these 'goodies' of a sudden; I can't, uh, well, I'm not yet, how shall I say— acclimated?"

"Oh, you cherry?"

"Well now, my little chickadee; I'm a tike more acclimated than that."

"Okay. You take time; I wait."

"O-k-a-a-a-y?" I panted, all but beside myself. My time had come, and gathering myself, I announced breathlessly: "I'm ready," and waited feverishly for the next move.

We stood staring at one another. So maybe we did play a lively tune on time, but somehow I envisioned something other than spending forever in one spot, throbbing with a massive bone pointing in the eye of eternity.

"We do it here?" I asked presently, not knowing what to expect next from this lust encrusted angel of the ages.

"If here is good," she answered tutorially.

"Here is definitely good," I sheepishly intoned.

"Then?" she unabashedly enunciated, waiting for something on my part other than a pallid imitation of the 'statue of David.' Sooner or later I was going to have to 'get hep' to the new, uninhibited ways down here. I decided to take destiny 'in my own hands.'

"Okay, if here it must," I boldly announced, "then here it will be."

"You will like," was the pleasant rejoinder.

"R-E-A-L-L-Y," I mumbled. Deftly I moved forward, and my pretty playmate of the moment, observing my willingness, did likewise. Her sarong floated effortlessly away as we clinched lustily, and I can now say, at long last, thanking whoever, I was pixilated. And you know, Virginia? Dying so young wasn't so bad.

Thanking the young lady----what else could I do, offer her the penthouse suite at the Waldorf Astoria—I continued on with a gleam in my eye.

Shortly, I came upon the dining room, and a large sign, purportedly being the menu, hung over the entrance, and read, simply: "Anything you want." Indeed. How appropriate I thought, after that dazzling tête-à-tête, just a moment ago.

Well now; the second momentous decision of my short but frolicsome afterlife—what to imbibe.

I chose Lobster Calvados only because the thought of a scorching lobster tail, soaking in a tub of apple brandy, was more than in keeping with the empyrean ambiance, and no sooner had I wished when of a sudden 'volah!' did a sizable, hefty morsel appear right in front of me on a buffet style line.

I took one of those tinny, military trays—old habits die hard—placed it lovingly on same, along with a small basket of warm, French bread, (I don't know why … bread … with lobster?), a side of crepes, also because I had never had any in the previous life, although it didn't seem to go with lobster, and about 3 ounces of a feathery-light, golden chardonnay, shimmering in glassware of the finest Italian crystal. If not here, where; if not now, when.

I meandered over to a smooth, dark-stained, hardwood table made for four, and sat. Across from me also sat, an elderly gentleman, who I am certain, I did not recognize. "Good evening," I bubbly greeted, my jocularity no doubt betraying my novitiate.

"I suppose," was the curt reply.

"Food here's not bad," I stated, just trying to be friendly.

"Well that you think so, because it's not going to get any better."

"Hmnn," I thought to myself. Not a very sociable sort, considering. "Can I get seconds?" I then asked like a shave tail boot, hoping to get something more than a, 'uh, huh.' What I did get wasn't exactly anything I'd rush to put in my diary before the ink in my bic dried.

"And thirds, and fourths, and fifths. You can spend the rest of forever here with your mouth permanently stuck open if you like," he responded mechanically.

His enthusiasm was in no danger of being overrun by the gelded horse of quiet solitude. I persisted, but only out of curiosity since I wondered whether the 'ebullient' condition to which my newly found companion seemed to be afflicted, was the 'marvelously common' in these particular surroundings. I did not wish to spend endless time in such an 'overheated state of exhilaration.' (Sic)

"Oh," I answered as shortly as I could. "I don't think that'll be necessary."

"Nothing here, my good man, is necessary, he informed, "Only permanent."

"To be sure."

"Just arrived, have you?"

"Does it show?"

"Like a hounds tooth on a moonless night."

'Pilgrim' was enjoying a meal of borscht and beans, and chocolate mousse. An odd triumvirate, I thought. This joker had to be American, but I couldn't quite place him. Someone from another age perhaps, gathering from the clothes he was wearing, or trying to wear I should say, success in the matter seeming to be safely tucked away under lock-and-key, as he gave the appearance of having dressed in haste, in a dark closet.

"How do you like it down here?" I asked, looking for a 'terrific' or a 'faaan-tas-tic' but instead got a not unexpected tepid 'can't complain,' which, all things considered, ain't exactly a slice of cold watermelon on a hot summers eve.

"My, but you seem to be somewhat of a lugubrious sort, if I may say so," I injected, matter-of-factly.

"Soldier, if you've been here over 100 years, you might also be in danger of sliding into a disagreeable state of melancholia yourself." And at that, I could only muster a perfunctory, "I see."

"Let's hope so ... if not now, then. . . .?"

I gathered the forlorn soul wished not to be disturbed, so I ate quietly minding my own, it usually being good policy in a strange habitat.

He finished his meal in silence, and just like that, disappeared. A moment here, a moment gone.

I dawdled. Seated at the next table was an extraordinarily, elegant figure of a woman wearing a high-collared dress that reached to her ankles. Amusing, I thought, but no doubt fashionable for her time, whenever that may have been. With her sat a tall, dark, dashing, thirtyish gentleman, wearing, I believe, a military uniform of some sort, but could've been the postman for all I knew. All these different ages coming to the fore, at the same time, in the same place; I needed a scorecard.

I leaned over pardoning myself, and asked, if by chance they knew who I had been dining with just a short while ago. The gentleman, I was told, was Henry Thoreau.

"T-H-E-E, Henry Thoreau?" I questioned.

"One and the same," she replied.

"Well I'll be," I muttered. "I thought I'd never see the day."

"An admirer?" inquired the comely young madam.

"You might say, in a world not all that admirable, although I had no idea he was such a ... a mournful soul."

"You mean, grouch?"

"That too."

"That too. It seems he expected things to be---how shall I say---more 'heavenly' down here?"

"But why? This I-S hell."

"It seems he bit off more than he can chew. He doesn't like it anywhere."

"Ah, hah! Isn't it the way. Neither heaven nor hell can satisfy the dissatisfied. And mightn't I inquire as to your lineage?" I asked willing to change the subject. At that, she stiffened, and proudly answered, "Russian."

"Of coarse; and your name?" And again, she proudly enunciated: "Anna Karenina."

"Anna Karenina!!" I blurted out in astonishment.

"Why yes; is something the matter?" she countered noticeably perturbed. "Could it be my ill-gotten reputation is still an object of scorn?"

"No, nothing of the sort, at least, not to my knowledge," I hastily assured.

"Well then?"

"But," and leaning ever so close, whispered, "there is no such person."

"I b-e-g y-o-u-r p-a-r-d-o-n," the gentleman seated beside her corrected. "There most certainly is, I can assure you." It was now apparent; he could have been none other than, 'Vronsky.'

"Okay," I agreed. "If there is, there is."

"You see," Anna clarified, "all things having been created, by god or man, are created. Nothing is fiction; all is imagination, and imagination is life. There is no matter, but the matter of imagination. Correction—the extension of imagination. It is eternally mellifluous in its varied configuration, and there is nothing else. I am as real as a squiggly zygote of two overheated Marxists in a downtown, Petersburg hotel."

"Yes, N-O-W, but you had to die before y-o-o-o-u-r life began."

"W-e-e-l-l?"

"Oh, of course."

"But, to be more specific, I was born on the tip of Count Tolstoy's pen, and he, on the tip of God's"

"A mystical marvel, indeed."

"Not all that mystical, but marvelous."

In this environment, or lack of one, when one wishes to terminate a repartee, one merely terminates oneself, and that is precisely what Anna and the Count did—terminate. As I've said, there's no real trick to it. It's like opening a door, simpler even. Like the dear lady intimated: "It's all in the mind. . . .

Having finished my meal, I sat back restfully sipping on my barely touched chardonnay, when of a sudden, sexual fantasies seized upon me once again.

But, no longer being a novice, I put in my order, post haste, and instantly a thirtyish, buxom brunette luxuriously bedecked in gleaming pearls and black lace, appeared before me. Standing there by the table so sweetly, my head cleared itself of all extraneous thought. Like Anna and Vronsky, they just … disappeared.

There's a thing about sex; it's in the doing, as most things, not the telling. Suffice to say, I never did do it in a dining room before, on a mahogany table, doggy fashion. The dogs should have it so good.

After 'dinner' I moseyed over to the rec hall, a room some two-thousand square-feet where folks were casually sitting around playing parlor games (cards, checkers, monopoly, scrabble). It's not heaven.

Off to one side another, smaller, dimly lit room housed a television. Needless to say, I was curious to see the program lineup, since NBC down here was just a plucked peacock sitting in a pot surrounded by skinned apples and carrots.

I walked in and sat off to one side. I did not recognize the show, or its players. Presently, I asked the spirit next to me what it was we were all so dutifully watching. "A night uptown," he informed. "And," said I, in return, "exactly what is uptown?" He gestured upward, and snorted: "Uh, you know?"

"Oh," I acknowledged. "But why should you all be so enamored with, 'you-know-what?' You all just left there."

"We're not; that's what they give us." G-o-o-d l-o-r-d; here too?

I watched a few minutes more, but soon tired. And not caring to live according to the whims of the Madison Avenue syndrome, I left. I refused to be dictated to in hell.

Back in the playpen, I inconspicuously took a seat behind two elderly gents having at it in a tranquil game of chess. The smaller of the two was fighting a losing battle, and knew it. Enveloped in a pale of gloom, slowly and methodically, he rose, let out a piercing yelp, hysterically flung the board and all its little pieces high in the air, kicked the table, banged the chairs, and, in general, behaved rather poorly.

"What was that?" I inquired of the nearest spectator, a shabbily dressed peasant-looking sort.

"That? Just the usual," he matter-of-factly informed.

"Usual what?" I pressed.

"Usually General Bonaparte looo-sing. He can't stand to see his itty-bitty, king get trapped. As yet, we haven't been able to tell whether it's his lingering ambitions to royalty, or military spade that's getting the rub. In any case, the show begins after the "hostilities."

"No doubt," I agreed, surveying the 'war-torn' battlefield. And, you may find this somewhat incredulous, but I was looking for sex again. I do believe I was orgasmically addicted. Oh, but what a lovely way to go through hell. And mightn't I remind you that not a little of the gusto of this wondrously, filthy diversion, and all its attending electrifying emotions, revolve not only in the fact itself, but also in the realization that no one, but no one hereabouts, has anything but the highest regard for the comforting gambollery. No guilt, no shame; no cops, courts, judges, laws or imbecilities to interfere with the delirious 'cock in the barnyard.' Just unsullied felicitation, over and again, voluminously cradled in pungent lust. Indeed, might this be heaven after all? Is there a difference?

And what is heaven, anyway? The absence of all mental, emotional, and physical manacles of any sort; the omission of success or failure, reputations, contrived civilities and affectation; suppressed ids and shabby egos. No past and no future to fetter my employment. I am free! Free! Free at last!

Bring on the gash, the furry, succulent beavers, the frilly, little bunny tails. Let me licentiously swim in this honey-sweetened pool of over-sexed water-sprites, this freshened, mountain hatchery deliciously overstocked with magnificently formed, beauteous sea-maiden's … t-h-a-n-k y-o-u.

* * *

In the ever likely event you might be somewhat confused concerning the ordinary work-a-day proprieties in the province of perdition, aside from the asides, let me clarify forthwith before meandering on in this amorphous cloud cryptically resting in the realm of dark shadows, dead dreams and ashes.

Well, it can be anything you like it to be. The sea is vast, the fish plentiful, and no day the same if spice is your game.

Always one to try anything at least once now was my chance to 'run' the gamut. I reveled in my predicament. I would rise at five. Early, you say? Hell, Buck; I disliked sleeping at all down here. What difficulty in waking when the day is one big, irreverent carnival? Remember now, a spirit never tires, and is in no material discomfort of any kind, as there is no substance to tire, sleep merely being a method of breaking the continuity, and giving all a sense of time and place in a domain of ceaseless time and no place.

This may seem all very confusing at first, I know, for you may ask, how can one experience sex if one is lacking in the necessary apparatus? But sex I-S but a matter of the mind, as is everything. And eating? Dam, Buck; there ain't no food down here. It's all mime. Are we not all puppets dangling from a string? The difference between life and death—no strings; in other words, down here the puppet dangles of his own. Existence without disposition, or supposition. Life without environment. A place nowhere, a tenancy mathematically incalculable. That is the super life, everything and nothing, everywhere and nowhere. A hastily woven basket of quantum equations, drifting in a sea of absolutist contradictions straddling a parallel universe. String theory minus the string.

I put on the coffee, showered and shaved, all in the 'blink of an eye.' While it bubbled, I would usually do some stretching exercises, nothing strenuous, mind you, just a little something to keep the lower back limber, it being the locus of all motion. Then, resting comfortably in my old granny rocker, I would lazily teeter by the window, and observe the new day dawning while sipping on the morning's refreshment.

Having now been sufficiently aroused, a sexual performance would naturally follow, after which slight conversation with the lady in question would of nature occur, me being the amiable sort.

At the hour of nine, a few innings of hardball out on the dirt and grass, followed by a quick-dip at the water-works, and a nap.

At twelve I embark for the dining room, and a lunch of grilled ham and cheese, endive salad, a tall glass of skim, (ice cold), and a cut of Dutch, apple pie. Back to my place of domicile, for yet another bout of revelry and heavy breathing, followed by nine holes of golf, and, you guessed it, Buck: spin the bottle with six enchanting virgins in heat, then off to the rec room for a slow, easy game of chess, literate conversation with the partner of my choice, and calming relaxation, and as you can plainly see, easy is, as easy does. Tis the beast in us that makes it otherwise.

One quiet, lazy day, while dully watching my dawdling king getting himself blindly and unceremoniously ambuscaded, I glanced off to one side as I waited indignantly for my opponent to make his next move—conceivably his last—and noticed a quiet, forlorn figure, sitting dejectedly in a corner sporting an old, Nazi uniform.

I could not quite make him out, as his head was partially turned to one side, so I nudged one of the spectators, an elderly, Czech Jew who'd been prematurely terminated at Dachau, and asked hesitantly who the 'sad sack' was while motioning in said direction. Straight forward enough he certified none too cheerily: "Yeah, that's him, the unspeakable dickhead."

At that horrifyingly precise moment---like a gallon of two-dollar cologne---it hit me clean in the smacker, shattering all pretense to pretense. Truly, was I in hell, sharing as it were, the same lodgings as Herr Schicklegruber, the 'beast of Bavaria.' LUC--KY.

Gradually, my feelings traversed from shock, to fright, depression, and anger. Presently I lost interest in the exact where-a-bouts of my hapless king, the realization of my occupying the same sitting-room as Herr Adolf, having duly unhinged me.

No longer knowing what to expect, I felt as one might have if set in the midst of a dozen cholera carriers. I regained enough composure however, to curiously continue the questioning. "What, might I ask," I inquired of the same embittered neighbor, "does the filthy beggar do all day? And is he still the same 'Adolf,' we all once 'knew and loved' so well?"

"Yes." replied my foreign friend, "he is one and the same, and he sits there as you see him now, quite down in his cups, but every now and then will hysterically jump up and bellow excitably: "Today Chermany, tomorrow, da vorld."

"No?"

"Yes."

"It's hell, ain't it?"

"It not Baden-Baden."

"Or even Philadelphia."

"And his mind, it's quite gone, you know."

"Wasn't it always? And could it not have happened much longer ago?"

"Much, but you are quite right, it really always was."

"Maybe so, but I think it was his soul that encased all the little, red devils."

"A more exact sentiment was never uttered. And to think such a malty, squirrely sap could have done so much, to so many, for so long."

"I'd rather not, and how is it that he ever came to be here?" In my confused and irritable state, I was no longer making sense of any kind, the mind so easily willing to descend into the sappy bog of torpidity.

"Well," my friend responded in obvious surprise, "where did you expect him to be, in a summer home on the Black Sea? He is where he belongs."

"But he doesn't look like he's suffering too much to me."

"How would Y-O-U like to be him?"

"Good point."

"Sides, to one such as he, it is pain enough not to have a command and bark his infernal orders. He is a leader without followers. He agonizes, worry none about that. He will ride through eternity on the horse of impotency."

Maybe so, I thought, but it seemed a cheap price to pay for the holocaust, and a world war. I wondered: Would it not have been better to have him, in a blaze of light, realize the gross immensity of his evil-doing, and let him live into forever with that filthy peccadillo tearing at his mean, dirty little soul. Shit, there ain't no justice down here either … or there … or anywhere. It's all just a sick, silly joke; IT NEVER ENDS.

My king, now having gotten himself duped in good fashion, I resigned and retired to my den for sport of a different kind. So far I had bedded down with a Turkish belly-dancer, an Indian, a Polynesian, an Afro, A Latino; oh, what the hell, Buck, they were all dolls.

Upon 'boxing' the compass, I napped once again, rising at 6 for another delightful sitting of 'chopsticks in the round,' then back to the rec room for more 'fun and games' followed by a little tele. (Mightn't I have mentioned it before? This is hell.) However, on this particular occasion, the Canadian national curling classic was inexplicably beaming from Quebec.

I could see through the din that there were only four of us, three of whom seemed to be asleep. It's hard to tell down here. W-e-e-l-l-l?

Have you ever done a bit of curling? Great game. Not so popular in the lower 48' what with that fatuous football, and all, but it fascinates the bee-jeebers out of me. Probably because of my ancestral tree; you know—bocce ball?

Somebody, or other, from the Edmonton team, made an unconscious shot hooking his rock around another to knock out his opponents, and thereby—as oft stated—snatched victory from the jaws of defeat. The hopeless will always exact its fair share of fascination.

The match over, I switched to the first episode of 'Search for the Nile' far and away the most engrossing show I had ever seen on the big bubble, up to that time, but since then, the tube has been graced with such sterling productions such as 'I Claudius,' 'The Jewel in the crown,' and, 'Sydney Riley, Ace of Spies.'

Why is it that America cannot produce a "Masterpiece Theatre?" And why is it the more fortune we have the bigger the slop pile?

The 'search' told of the relationship between Speke and Burton in their compulsive quest for the origin of the Nile back in the 1850's. Of course, when I first saw it, it was in the 'Land of Nod' as public television fare, and unusual in that they were usually showing you dying cockroaches, a skinny lion dragging a half-alive bug-eyed, terrified impala through the bush, Jane Goodall cavorting with Baboons, or a block-busted, herniated Diva straining for the elusive high-C in Madame Butterfly. This time, this time I got lucky.

Equally astonishing lolling about the putrefying, electronic landscape, a trifling, dipsy morsel of frivolity where the leader is a quaint, docile frog, and the main character a pig perpetually in heat. An exquisite little-bit-of-fluff in the midst of a monumental accumulation of debris, but hardly high drama.

There can be no doubt had television been invented during the time of Caesar, it would have lasted just long enough to axe it to death. Somehow, the thought of a Roman dully sitting about watching 'Sissy and Bobby' slap-doodling, or that trio of pinheads on 'Three's company' racing to see who can screw-up the dumbest face, an exercise where all three seem, eminently equipped, just doesn't get it. "Sorry," you say, Buck? Me too, slugger. But sorry don't feed the cat.

Having sufficiently gorged myself in video land, I strolled back into the yard to observe---as you very well know is my wont from time-to-time—the night life, and sitting there reposefully under the 'yum-yum' tree listening to the little birdie go 'tweet tweet' was a stern, hearty-looking devil sporting a toga and sandals.

"Well, I'll be damned," I said to myself, Julius Caesar, had to be. Yes Virginia, wrong again, but I did have the right time, more or less. Marcus Aurelius was the wanderer in space.

After having introduced himself and dispensing with the usual greetings and salutations, the man, true to his Roman heritage, got right to it.

"So," he began, "I see the 'American Empire' is going the "way of all flesh." Mildly startled at his frankness, I hesitated but for a moment, and quickly acknowledging my new found friend as a man of keen perception, recovered sufficiently from my stupefaction to announce forthwith: "Yes, you could say they're going right in the crapper."

"Crapper?" he repeated in befuddlement.

"Uh, well, down the tubes?"

"Tubes?"

"Shambles?"

"Ah, shambles. Yes, yes. You agree, then?"

"But of course. It is perfectly obvious to all, I should think, except the Christians who actually believe in the damn sick system the way they believe in the 'second coming of Christ' the reactionaries, who, in all probability are one and the same with the lethargic faithful, and who don't give one, good dam as long as they can cash in their bonds at nine-and-five-eights, and senile optimists, said bagatelle unfortunately gracing about 95% of a quickly disintegrating landscape."

"The imperfect and mediocre are boundless. They would do well down here."

"And they just may get the chance."

"But then, it was the same in my time. Nations, down through the ages have always wondered at the fall of the Roman Empire. It should never have been a matter of such astonishment. It had to happen; merely a question of time."

"Probably so, but what really did happen?"

"Until humankind is made perfect, all civilizations will, at some point, cease and desist."

"Must it always be so?"

"Invariably, if one believes in the continuity of the celestial."

"How's that?"

"The law of the universe is change. It portends therefore, that first, all things cannot succeed always, and second, any one thing cannot succeed indefinitely. Life and matter, being what they are, innumerable variations are continually introduced insuring the ongoing complexities of alteration. It can be said that, at some point, the change will be in the negative, or, opposite growth, and eventually death. And civilizations, as with all things, are included in the "passing parade.""

"No doubt. And how do you see the American predicament?"

"I see it not as an exception, but quite the rule. It could in large measure, be used as the definitive, text book case."

"SO?"

"SO. In this progression of organized catalepsy, America, at every step of the way, is exhibiting all of the mongrelized traits of stunted growth and disintegration; however, the dissolution is proceeding at a must faster pace than would be supposed due to the galloping times. The electronic age is vastly shortening its life. What took 100 years in Roman times, takes but 10 in yours."

"It is quite probable then, that we could die, and not know it.

"Worse. No one will bereave you. You could rot where you lay, your head-stone a flock of buzzards picking at your dried-out bones, your eulogy the busy silence of ants crawling across your rotting carcass."

"Good, god; and we think we're great."

"Everybody thinks they're great. Carthage thought it was great. You couldn't find it today with a brigade of Archeologists, and a thousand sharpened spades.

You have too many deficiencies, and had it not been for technology and circumstance, you'd have been dust long-ago. Viet-Nam, a country half your populous thought was an Asiatic disorder, beat you in the ground. Your place truly, is with England and France, the remnants of a dying species. The only difference being, they know it, and so are now busily preparing for a quiet and decent burial.

"So, what exactly is our problem, then—will?"

"Will? Yes and no. You have the will, as all nations do, to some degree, but not for excellence. Will needs time to cultivate, and you are an impatient lot. You are too busy selling soap and cologne, beer and brassieres. It is surprising though. . . ."

"What?"

"For certain, I would have thought, by now, that someone would have built a gold-plated commode."

"Spoken like a true Roman, but I think someone has."

"You also seem to have a death-wish.

"Really?"

"I would think so. There are workings contributing to your demise we can never know, but then again, there are other stirrings not so mysterious, and remain the same at all times, affairs a mere two-thousand years can never change. It has happened before, it is happening again, and, and yet you persist."

"Precisely?"

"The matter at hand. When a nation or an individual bequeaths to arbitrary values the seat of preeminence, then all is lost and hope fly's through the window like a sparrow in flight."

"Arbitrary, you say?"

"What else? All this frenetic activity to acquire goods and comfort is a stranger to veracity. Of what import is opulence? None. Does one become brighter, stronger, more sensible or courageous by it? For all of your wealth and refinement are you a better people today than you were two-hundred years ago?

On the contrary; you are barren and have been rendered useless, blustering about the world stage like a bull in a china shop. You have all the subtlety of a 300 pound, drunken sailor in a bawdy house. Your potential exceeds, to an obscene degree, your accomplishments, and that potential, vis-à-vis accomplishment, is the yardstick by which all civilizations are measured. By those criteria, the cannibals of New Guinea are the only great people of the age, for his meager achievements are in step with his limited potential. But you? You are an eternal fraud; you revel in perfidy; you gloat in mediocrity."

"But doesn't capacity count for something? After all, one has to b-e something to develop into something."

"Capacity is a function of circumstance. The capacity of the fish is an accident of his ancestral stem. The carp cannot climb a tree, now can he throw the discus. It counts for as much as a raindrop in a hurricane, a toothless flea on a dead dog. Of what good is a Beethoven sonata to the deaf, or an eye for beauty to a blind man? It is all a sham. You excitedly scurry about decorating your houses without, while mice harvest within. You are a well-educated immensely stupid people.

"And I can't even say 'pooh-pooh' to that."

"You have developed sophistry and deception to a fine art."

"Yes, the lights are too bright; I cannot see the naked lady."

"America has no respect for the truth, for the timelessness of the ages. It behaves as if the world were only two-hundred, years old."

"Aye and how is it noted?"

"The signs are all about. You insecticide your most precious treasure—the land—a cursed act and a desecration. Indiscriminately you pervade the world with all manner of poisonous chemicals, trees, bushes, the air, crops, people, the oceans. Nothing is safe from your cursed, deathly hand because you do not care."

"Somehow I get the feeling that if I rose in 'outraged' defense, it would only serve to prove your case."

"Each of you habitates a world unto itself and it has become remote and barren."

"Here, here."

"Truly, you put the cart before the horse. I believe, in your 'lingo' it is known as "ass backwards."

"And we do have 'the fat' for that. But then, we, everyone one of us knows that materialism is a horny toad, a funhouse with crooked mirrors, and yet. . . . ."

"Yet notice the blatant workings of 1984."

"1984?"

"Surprised, are you?"

"Now that you mention it, no, but. . . . ."

"But stridently, America, the champion of the free and the oppressed, the, progenitor of Washington, Franklin, Lincoln and Twain, the land of hope, bellowed: "Peace!" "Peace!" while your most exalted leaders, with the deranged exhortation, 'more is less' begged like common street-urchins for missiles you all admitted were obsolete, so as to incredulously parade the redundant rockets under understandably suspicious Russian noses, which, it can be said, rivals that of a thief attempting to holdup a bank with an empty pistol, when all parties concerned have advance knowledge of its impotency. And, as yet, no one has debunked the specious psychology of expressing a fervent desire to disarm while at that very moment increasing same.

"To arm is to disarm."

"And it behooves me to consider the mindless train of thought, which attempted to blackmail a nation of six-hundred million people which had mercilessly pummeled Napoleon's legions, pushed the vaunted Wermacht all the way back to Berlin, squashed Czarism like a bug, and controls, at last count, one-sixth of the worlds population.

You were not fighting an isolated, momentary aberration such as Fascism, a deranged burst of spiritual debilitation advanced by a tremulous period in history. You were fighting the contradiction of Christianity and imperialism, and a movement seeded in your disordered, negligent past; the Red was consumed in his own tyranny. The Russian bear spent itself to death; your turn will come, and before, a small coterie of blackguards picked their man, now a sham election is held, and that same man is anointed with all the supercilious fanfare thereof. They learned well from the west.

And didn't Y-O-U just have an election where your apparent winner was displaced by 3 old, dull, white renegade hacks, one half-witted Tom, and a sappy, innocuous, phlegmatic old ninny?" Flustered, I could only stutter: "Uh, huh; I guess."

"And also, on the night in question, didn't the aforementioned doodle, fly into an apoplectic fit upon hearing your Mr. Gore may have won Florida---which he certainly did—and thereby the election, wherein she proceeded, somewhat indelicately, to practically blow herself right out of her drawers?"

"I say, but you all do keep on top of things down here."

Not paying one wit to my affirmation, he continued: "Democracy? Democracy? If you'd have stayed a bit longer up top, you'd have come upon the esteemed Socrates, of far-away-and-long-ago, who when every time he hears the word 'America' chokes down yet one more, long gulp of hemlock."

"Hmmm, that's not very pleasant."

"Democracy? Why you don't even have a Republic; what you have is what you have: Government of the few, by the few, for the few, and, you have no shame. You are as corrupt as a Latin American dictator, more even. It is part of your law; you call it 'contributions' as if somehow legalizing bribery mitigates the stench. At least a venal, corrupt dictator doesn't pretend to be anything but, but you … and that same court, mentioned but a moment ago, gave it all its legal blessing by ruling that to curtail such larceny would be an abridgment of 'free' speech.' Supreme Court, is it? Supreme crooks; they belong in chains."

"Not exactly a popular sentiment."

"A common court, for a common people."

"Is there no end to it?

"You can take a pig to proceedings, and have him duly acclaimed forthwith, a horse, and you can feed him hay, and put a saddle on him, but he will not run in the Kentucky Derby." (Now he tells me; and to think of all the pigs I bet on.)

"As long as you persist in wallowing in shallow, crass patriotism and short-sighted, arrogant self-righteousness, your success will take more than good wishes, jittery sabre-rattling, and references to an uncertain deity. The world continues to spin, and what was once in the east, soon becomes west, and vice-versa. You are dissimilar, and yet you are alike; your god is their god."

"Which is?"

"A sick debilitating lust for power, originating in a wretched, voluminous strand of insecurities, comprising a high place in a ghastly, squalid corner of the human soul, unmercifully corrupting, and bull doggedly propelling itself on, and on, into the eternal grey slag of nothingness. You will lose because you are a vapid imitation of the Roman, and where he fell on his spear, you will fall on your head. You are not the stuff of great tragedies, or even small heroes', and your broken dreams shall lay fallow in shallow graves housing half-alive, red, raw flesh, squirming under the dark shroud of incubus looming ominously overhead."

"Good merciful Christ, perdition is indeed upon us."

"And mores' the reason in your blindness to it. And yet, Rome, for all its greatness, suffered from the same malady as you."

"There's more?"

"There is the seed, for the son is father of the man. Vision! Rome lacked vision! and squandered its greatest asset—energy, while its raison d'être was conquering, and built upon that formidable rock. The Roman was, first and foremost, a stoic, and a believer in effort. When it gained the 'good' life, it lost its own by allowing a rag-tag band of itinerant beggars, peddling an errant, petticoat philosophy of decay and negation, to defeat it without so much as spending one, solitary, quivering arrow in its defense."

"Not one?"

"Not one. It became a circus replete with gladiators and hungry lions. Instead of crushing them, which would have been a matter of no great import, they played with them, and laughed, and ridiculed, and in the end, where it was thought to conveniently absorb them, were absorbed themselves.

Stinkingly unwashed, unkempt and cootie-laden, their armies of beads, and crosses, and homilies, first infested, then surrounded, then overran, and finally consumed their weary, jaded souls. One does not fight filthy, diseased rats by ignoring them. Rome should have perished in a momentous battle consistent with its greatness, but instead, left quietly, unnoticed, with a crawl and a whimper.

And what were we left with? A thousand years of darkness and gloom, a world cravenly slinking about in the shadowy, murky bog of morbidity, pushed and pulled every step of the way by the undying sickness of the slimy, foul hand of evil, abetted and led by the tyranny of Christendom and monarchical backwardness. One could not paint a more putrescent portrait, and all part of the natural order of things."

"It would seem then, that it had to be, given the inevitable march of historical decree."

"Yes," he somberly admitted, "history makes puppets of us all … and there are no exceptions."

"But y-o-u certainly seem to have struck the bulls eye squarely now."

"It is no great trick to orate like a wizened, old king with hindsight."

"Nevertheless, and we shall succumb also?"

"The infirmity remains."

"That being?"

"The species, as yet, is not of gladiatorial caliber. It cannot sustain strength;

courage and intelligence is a rare commodity spasmodically created. The spirit quakes before hardship. Even in times of crisis, nations, like individuals, inevitably search for the easy life. It is a sign of your paucity that you equate the good with the easy, and not a matter of wonder that, at one time, your most popular electronic spectacle was aptly named, 'Good Times.' And what are those 'Good Times?' The easy life, forgetting that nothing of worth is soft and easy. To live is to struggle; perfection is born in strife without which the trek to stagnation and death being swift and sure. That is why Rome conquered; war demanded the supreme effort, and in that effort a new man was born. When Rome 'laid down the spear' Rome perished like a blighty tulip in the scorching, noonday sun."

"But the end of war is killing, and. . . . ."

"Ho! Not so. The end of war is conquest---killing merely being the inevitable means to that end---and in conquest, solidification, in solidification, unity, in unity, harmony, and in harmony---art—the art of the ages impregnated, surrounded and escalated by the vastness of this momentous, omniscient universe, and that, Mr. America, is the end all of life, not happiness, or progress, or comfort, or sport, and games and revelry. They are all mere diversions, sharp, gritty stones ensconced in the darkened, narrow path to enlightenment. Art it is and art it shall always be.

But then, war to a Roman was an art. We fought with spears, you, with bombs. We gave birth to new life, you destroy it. We looked our adversary in the eye, and touched his flesh. You roll over him with tanks, obliterate him from the air, and detonate him with giant, cannon shells fired from miles away. To a Roman, war was the 'art of madness', to you, just plain madness. To us, it was a part of life, the natural order of things. To you, life blasted into little bits and pieces. We destroyed the enemy; you decimate him and everything in his wake, the land, the air, and the seas. We destroyed him, you destroy the world. After our wars, not a moment was needed to rebuild. You? Generations.

You beat Hitler not knowing Hitler sits in your churches, and congress, and courts and corporations. Your shortsightedness is staggering in its dimensions. England, the land of 'Richard the lion-hearted' Queen Elizabeth, Shakespeare, and Wellington, is now the land of rock, ribbon-cutters and horse shows. France? The land of Charlemagne, Moliere, Voltaire and Napoleon, now the land of dead kings and fallen hopes, a strike-a-day effete intellectuals, and milksop communism."

We both sat quietly for a moment, letting the sad truth dwell.

"Well," I gloomily interjected, "it certainly looked good for a little while though, didn't it?"

"How so?"

"The founding Father's, I mean. Exemplary men, wouldn't you say?"

"Oh, quite so, admittedly. But unusual circumstances, I would think."

"Unusual?"

"They were a majestic band of like-minded men endowed with a universal sense of purpose, separated from their adversary by a great body of water."

"How fortunate."

"Great successes usually are."

"But lately, I have come to feel it was all a monstrous travesty."

"Travesty? I do not recall your 'cause célèbre' having ever been so expressed before?"

"I don't believe it has, but our Mr. Thoreau said it best when he enunciated in blessed perspicacity, "I can do very well without tea, thank you.""

"There was, I believe, however, a small matter of 'freedom' to be considered, if I am not mistaken."

"Freedom? Of course, the last refuge of a scoundrel, or was it patriotism, or religion, no matter, same, same. And far be it from such a novice as myself, to correct such an esteemed personage as yourself, who's exploits and reputation have withstood the corrosive sands of time, but might I submit that it seemed to be more a sluggish, mundane matter of 'high taxes' than such a lofty perch as freedom."

"But what do you think freedom is? Some convoluted abstraction setting straight the misguided ways of men?"

"Not me," I quickly expounded, not wanting to seem completely unhinged.

"It is nothing but the shiny, gold coin, jiggling about in one's knickers. Remember: History—with an eye toward whitewash—is written by the victor's for the coming generations to wallow in, and on the fourth-of-july, you couldn't shoot off one, wet firecracker for "high taxes.""

"It seems we've come to the same station from opposite ends."

"It does not however, detract from the Fathers' magnificence. They were men of their time, who reached above their mortal constriction, and for that alone, are to be forever celebrated."

"But, I must say again: I too, can do without tea."

"Young man, drink what you like, but that war was to be fought, for tea, or for fun."

He did have a way, this serio-roman. "We are not," I agreed in a manner, "likely to see their kind again."

"Yes, it is all now—but for the memory—gone with the wind."

"And, a sad, sad, thought, indeed," I mused, "especially nowadays when a dullard can rake in millions hawking hula-hoops, pet rocks, ghost dogs, and cabbage-patch dolls."

"My, my," he dolefully murmured. "My, my; Rome is dead, long live Rome." And on that mournful note, vanished as he appeared. And yet, I thought to myself, like dog-shit floating down the Mississippi, this too, shall pass.

* * *

As I made my way back to the whatever, wherever, I couldn't help reflecting upon the conversation recently concluded. America; America; America; what about America. Even here, even here confusion abounds?

America, the revolution; a war of, by, and for the few. Rich white men here, fighting rich white men there. Do you think we could have done it differently Thomas Paine? Thoreau W-A-S right. We could just as easily have drunk coffee.

A few short naps later we bungle into the war of 1812, then a tearing up of the Native American way of life, then another to steal the southwest from the Mexicans. Funny, how easily history can become so twisted. "Remember the Alamo!!!" Sure, for Mexico; it did belong to them, didn't it? Then that monumental exercise in stupidity—the Civil War—brought to us by a manic depressive in a stove pipe hat, and a bearing bending dangerously close to a Greek tragedy including all the elements necessary for a thorough going bloodbath on behalf of an historical view euphemistically known as 'manifest destiny' a small matter handed down from that great comrade and defender of the common man and "protector" of the Indian and his distinctively singular way of life, one—Andrew Jackson.

Why? Why? Why must we always seize upon the worst in our stars, the dark side of the moon; can't this 'ship of state' ever steer on a true course? Must it always veer upon the rocks and shoals? Must it?

And so, Lincoln, who sided with the hypocritical North against the rapacious South, dragged the Nation into a conflict that would have, nor could it, no satisfactory conclusion on any account. And, at one point in this feverish, melancholic blood bath, answered to the rejoinder that "God was on our side," to wit: "We'd better be on his" at which point someone should have had the clarity of mind to ask whether God gave a dam, one way or the other.

Without any doubt, along with Adams, Jefferson and Madison, our most intelligent, literate and versed President, (we haven't had many so it isn't all that hard to note one when we get one) yet, the South by leaving (it could never have survived on its own) was handing him a gold plated solution on a silver platter. Who would W-A-N-T to keep anyone around that believed in slavery? Even then. Let them drown in their own scum-filled, dirty pond. And if you were going to go to war, at least have the sense to do it to end such a soul killing malignancy as slavery an exercise in evil as ever existed, the long-standing version of a holocaust. Do it for that. But, by his own admission his paramount objective, so stated, was to "Save the Union, and not either to save or destroy slavery." This I submit, Buck, is patent nonsense bordering on lunacy. Since ancient times, the list of countries that threw over slavery without warring is endless; might I mention but a few? In the sixth century B.C., Cyrus the Great; in 1117, Iceland; in the sixteenth century, Japan; 1778, Scotland; 1823 Chile; 1831, Bolivia; 1847, Sweden; 1848, Denmark; and in the cradle of Democracy—Greece, 1822, and including in the twentieth century, Iraq and Saudi Arabia among a host of other Arabic Nations. Lincoln, great? There's a long, long line ahead of you, brother.

So, after a million casualties, slavery still, the south still; nothing changed. And we told them, "Play nice now; take your gun and horsey and go home." Terrific; a million casualties and no consequences. How about a little occupation and putting the black man in charge of certain small incidentals such as Governor maybe, or mayor, or sheriff, and handing over an acre or two, and letting whitey pick a little cotton and tobacco for a change. Hah!!! Sure. Don't hold your breath.

And then we get to the "Robber Barons." They weren't called robbers because of there charitable tendencies I can assure you Mrs. McGillicudy. And, if I am not mistaken, also, right about this time, we had just about "finished off" the American Indian, after having broken every treaty even before the ink was dry. There are two known reptiles in this universe that display forked tongues. One of them is the snake.

Continuing on this merry journey, we also had time to kick around labor, immigrants, the general all around dispossessed or anyone else who brazenly attempted to participate in "The American Dream."

Then we come to the Spanish American War. Getting familiar? How is it that a nation who is so committed to peace, and love, and freedom, and all of the sterling Christian virtues, always seems to be involved in some filthily, squalid bloody war somewhere? Then World War One, (it just goes on and on, doesn't it?) Then the depression, and if FDR had had the horse sense to have listened to Frances Perkins a little more often, we wouldn't have started to slide back in it in 38'.

And then we come to "government created jobs," World War Two. That's right, government created jobs. But you say "government can't create jobs." Really? It can create guns, and tanks, and planes, and missiles, but it can't create washing machines, and stoves, and refrigerators, and cell phones, and solar panels, and wind mills, and electric cars, and all sorts of green jobs, or whatever other color you wish to dump in the hopper. Uh, huh. It just gets so tiresome, the tiresome. When are we going to get this thing right?

But it shall be duly noted that America's participation in that swinish, blood letting, was the one, special, bright star in our milky way, (but yet another war, Buck) and not a stretch on any account to infer that we, along with the Russians, saved the world from not only a fate worse than death, slavery under the heel of the Hun, but from an evil unsurpassed in this galaxy, that cursed bestiality—Nazism. For just one, brief shining moment, we were everything we could be … but, alas, not to last; all to soon do we sink back into our accustomed state of the average; the common; the very ordinary at best, wherein we are beset upon by Mr. Truman, the Missouri haberdasher. He was a better hat blocker than he was a President, and I never could understand why he dropped the second bomb. Why two? Didn't he think he got their attention with the first one? Didn't he think they heard it? They must have heard it on Mars. But then the story was going around that he wanted to scare Stalin. Scare Stalin? That psyche job from the Asiatic steppes? Textbook paranoia. Well I guess he did; he must have been scared right smack out of his woolly, red Russian jammys, because he immediately went out and stole the secrets to the aforementioned firecracker. What A-R-E these guys thinking. And by recognizing Israel, against the advice of Marshall, we can now thank him for the mess in Palestine after cowering to the worst kind of lobbying seen to that time, to put it mildly, a mess, which, at any moment can rise to tinderbox, and hold your breath world.

A hot-headed, none too bright ninny, he had the self confidence of the woefully impervious, a deadly combination, all in all. Unfortunately 'the buck' did stop with him.

Next comes Korea, another war from which we slide right down into the military, industrial complex, and Ike, who was not a bad President; he did get us out of one war, and refused to be horn swaggled into another, (Suez) but did nevertheless, have the audacity to warn us of a disease he had so much to do with cultivating, (in between golf outings,) while lackadaisically standing about with his finger up his itchy, round robin hole, and which has since blossomed into the political, corporate complex. Uh, huh, again; Democracy. Democracy? There's a plutocracy brazenly sitting at the kitchen table and instead of kicking its rear right out into the trash where it belongs, we invite it to have coffee and sweet rolls, and don't be surprised when it invites itself to dinner and drinks later.

Now we get to Mr. Kennedy, our first 'siss, boom, bah,' President, replete with pom poms, and cheerleaders. At the time, the idle rich had two, and only two, ambitions in this world: to be President of G.M, or President of the world. Mr. Kennedy, choosing the latter as the prize with the greater possibilities, rolled into the White House with much fanfare ado, and with a load of hot coals perpetually sagging his royal Bostonian drawers, proceeded to do just that—act like he were king of the world, meaning, he developed a penchant for trying to assassinate certain other foreign leaders who disagreed with his world vision, (and being successful on at least one occasion,) and so it should come as no surprise that he would eventually catch an assassins bullet himself.

We now herald in the sixties where the black man said, "enough already," and we said 'not before we kill off a few more of you black mothers first.' And then Viet-Nam, and 'guns and butter,' (I said it never ends,) and the 'best and the brightest' McNamara, Rusk, Rostow, Bundy. But we should have been suspicious of a President who referred to certain members of his family as "birds." But how come no one ever referred to him as Lyndy bird?

From there we slide right into "the creature from the black lagoon," Richard Nixon, and if the truth be known, our second certifiably "non compes mentis" President, (Jackson claims the honor for being number one in that unpleasant department, or if not, could have, at least, been at the head of the line in anger management classes.)

Tricky Dick, a man who went into the laundry business, although unfortunately for him, he should have used soap instead of the back doors of Mexican banks, and friend of that giant of "high finance" one, Bebe Rebozo.

Paralyzed to stop that nutso war in Viet-Nam, he started his own little skirmish here, blasting away at a bunch of hairy, unkempt college kids who whatever else you could say about them, did have that stinking, dirty little war pegged. But then, Mr. Nixon, being not only of unsound mind, was equally challenged in the ethics department. He deserved Watergate, every damned bit of it if, for no other reason than giving us Kissinger, Agnew, Colson, Mitchell, Haldeman, Erlichman, Magruder, Segretti, Liddy, a rogues gallery for the ages, ta,ra—ta,ra—ta,ra. Requiescat in Pace.

So now we get to Mr. Ford, who's entrance into the white house must have exceeded anything he ever dreamed of while getting bounced around on the line at Michigan.

The accidental President, who elevated the status of the Veto to heights only previously known to Mssrs. Hillary and Tensing, and who never really wanted the job until he actually got it, became accustomed to all the perks, privileges and gratuities thereof, and so decided he'd like to keep it. However, as so often happens to best laid plans, a tiny glitch developed throwing a sizable tool of some heft—the monkey wrench—into what at first seemed a set of perfectly well oiled gears.

Mr. Ford, having learned more football than history at Michigan, was belaboring under the mistaken opinion that Poland did not reside behind the iron curtain, an assumption somewhat more tolerable within the province of someone selling shoes at Tom McCann, but not for a duck looking to renew his lease at 1600 Pennsylvania Avenue, and so officially and without fanfare, by an electorate who from the very beginning, thought it to be participating in the 'Great Experiment' democracy, testament to the power and depravity of the rich at all times, who now control just about everything except the demons in their own souls, was brazenly dumped upon the ash heap of ex President's, an expanse he would soon find much to this liking. However, it should be noted in all fairness, that compared to what the Republican's are trotting out these days, it would not be a stretch to have considered Mr. Ford a leading candidate for Dean of the history department at Harvard University.

Having never been much of a President, he seemed to resist breaking the mold, and so was not much afterwards, either. Relocating to Rancho Mirage, he should have shown the same determination in perfecting his political game while in the White House, as he showed with his golf game in the California sun. He will be remembered with the likes of such luminaries as Fillmore, Pierce, Buchanan, Hayes, and Coolidge. We are what we are. Not a bad guy really, but neither was Harpo Marx, and neither should ever have been allowed on, near, or around the White House grounds without a ticket.

Moving right along, we now come upon the man from Georgia and the unluckiest guy to ever cross Pennsylvania Avenue in a top hat, not to speak of a round peg in a square hole. A classic case of the wrong man, in the wrong place, at the wrong time. He meant well, for the most part, but so did "wrong way Corrigan." Ambition is not always so well served. He also, wasn't much of a President, but then, said condition is an ever present malady in our continuing saga. From peanuts to cherry blossoms, from the farm to the city, from success to failure. He has, however, 'gained the high ground'—after the fact. Welcome home, Jimmy.

And now we come to Mr. Reagan. Ah, yes; Mr. Reagan who made Mencken's' remark, "someday we will succeed in putting an idiot in the white house" prophetic. Mr. Reagan, the October surprise, Voodoo economics, union buster, arms dealer, environmentalist extraordinaire, income redistribution (from bottom to top,) deregulation and the flourishing of an insidious oligarchy, and the beginnings of our financial ruin, and why anyone would want to get involved with a bunch of goon gangsters like the Contras, is more than a mystery. And why stick your nose in Nicaragua of all places; not exactly a hotly contested "sphere of influence" or maybe he was just nuts about bananas.

The "great communicator" who couldn't string two sentences together without the aid of a slew of three by five cards, and had Nancy check with the 'tea leaf reader' up in the 'city by the bay' before deciding whether to have marmalade or blueberry jam with their breakfast toast. One should take care to not start off the day by pooh, poohing the gods. The master of the idiot witticism: "If you've seen one tree, you've seen them all," this from an inveterate "outdoorsman," and, "the deficit is big enough to take care of itself," and "welfare queens," (clever) and author of the thoughtlessly insane, flippant remark, "We bomb Russia in five minutes," a caricature of a President who resided in the White House, but lived in La, La, land.

Friend of the rich and the privileged. He, who spent the Russians into financial ruin, they being dumb enough to take the bait after having nibbled on that stinking fish for thirty-five years, were now suckered into swallowing the whole cadaver. We would do some swallowing ourselves, in due time.

The man from fairy land who once remarked to Tip O'Neill: "I really only came here to lower the tax on my pals Frank, and Bob, and Bing," et al. Nice guy; Frank, and Bob, and Bing? They really needed his help.

If he wasn't an idiot he sure gave an academy award performance by it. And lest we forget, it was the beginning— again—of Fascism in America. It could, and is, happening here. The Christian right? Not Christian, and never right. The "tea party?" Just the latest foray into the deep and tangled woods with the Prince of Darkness. Thank you, Mr. Dummo. Let me leave you with just one word about "Bonzo"—BITBURG.

Now off we go to Mr. Bush and the little mouse April Glaspy who told Saddam, "nah; do what you like. The Presidents' an all around, good guy; won't touch a hair on your scabby, Sunni ass." He'd have done well to have 'brushed up' on Mr. Bush's time at the CIA, a record of surreptitious villainy as ever been recorded, and should have, at least, been somewhat aware of our relations with the Native American.

Read my lips. Unfortunately, lip reading was not among Saddam's rapidly diminishing talents, and so off we went to Iraq 1. It would be left to the simple minded, parrot faced son to repeat us into a more deadly version of Iraq 2, and a descent into the soul gripping, black hole of mendacity.

If you get a chance, Virginia, read about the Kennedys. For all their faults, they do understand the concept of service, and duty, and responsibility. Read about the Kennedys, then read about the Bushys. I will say no more.

Now we come to Mr. Clinton, our first "black" President. Poor blacks; just can't catch a break, can they? Stupid, friggin Republicans; they had there man in the white house, and kept trying to kick him out. UN-BELIEVABLE. Mr. Clinton, who every time that moral degenerate Newt Gingrich sneezed, he couldn't wait to rush right over and rub his back and kiss his ass. And welcome to Nafta. Bright guy. Bright crook would be more to it.

Mr. Clinton, who brought in every thief not occupying a cell in Leavenworth. We can start with Mr. Summers, and Robert Rubin, and the Bobsy twins Phil and Wendy Gramm, and the end of Glass Steagall and the beginning of government of, by, and for the banks, and who, with the help of his newly found playmates treacherously stabbed Brooksly Born in the back. All these 'nice guys,' then how come we're standing in such a deep hole? We'd have done better to have put Hillary in there, at least she had something in her pants besides an in-built, fire-breathing sexual tool, giddily accepting death killing overtime in a super-human attempt to scale the empyrean heights, climbed by a previously over-heated resident of the big white house.

And now we sink to Mr. Bush, the second, and sink I-S the word, you can be sure, Virginia.

Yes, H.L., we did it again, twice in twenty years—another idiot in the white house. Imagine, in one lifetime; Nixon twice; Reagan twice; Bush twice. It appears the Gods have it in for us, although he was installed the first time by a thoroughly corrupt Supreme Court—or at least five of them anyway—giving lie to another easily held foolish belief "separation of powers." Supreme Court; that most august body what ruled that a corporation is a person, and limiting political bribery is a violation of the first amendment. Does anybody reee-ally think they care about the Constitution? Anybody?

But this time, not being satisfied by mere corruption, he brought a criminal organization with him, and who started a little ol' war just by himself so's he could go down in history as a war time President. Well he certainly got his wish, didn't he? His crimes are so extant we need not beat that dead horse again. Suffice to say, he belongs in a cell in Leavenworth also, and not in a mansion in Dallas. But, I must say, you have to hand it to Laura; he wasn't dragging her feathery, Texas rear back to that one stick, cow town in tumbleweed junction, fifteen hundred acres of dust, sagebrush and gopher holes. Once a big ol' pig farm; the attraction must have been magnetic.

Yes, Virginia, even in America justice is blind, especially in America, although it wouldn't seem so to hear it told by the literati these days. Remember now, we couldn't wait to stick Sacco and Vanzetti in the chair … for robbing a payroll, and killing two guards? Nooo; for being Anarchists. Are things beginning to clear up a might? Are the darkened shades beginning to unfurl?

And now for the coup de grace—Mr. Obama, fired up and ready to go; hope and changie. Don't you wish. Everybody fell for the sweet talk all wrapped up with the flowery phrases. You know what they say: fool me once? A slow train like John McCain spotted him as all talk.

Mr. Obama, a classic case of what can happen when a tall, stringy galoot in a Brooks Brothers suit becomes more successful than he has a right to, another case of ambition surpassing talent, the Peter Principle in action—again. One listens, but can't help coming away with the impression that h-e i-s all words and vapor, more form than substance, like listening to a brass band; sounds nice, but it's not making you any smarter, and these days we need much more smarts than brass, and who'd do well to pay heed to the admonition: I come here to comfort the afflicted, and afflict the comfortable.

Mr. Obama, What we get when our bright star meets up with an empty nut sack, a guy who likes playing at, instead of being, a President; he of the bi-partisan, half-a-loaf mentality; "give them what they want before they ask for it" school. Fortunate he wasn't around in December of 41'. He'd have immediately given California to the Japanese, and we shall live to see the day when a new designation 'the cave-in,' will be included in Webster's: What is it when the party of the first part asks for an egg, and the party of the second part gives the whole chicken? And is it any wonder you got half a health plan, half a stimulus plan, half a bank plan, half an energy plan, half a tax plan. You have only to imagine what wonders will be forthcoming.

Forty million blacks in America and we had to pick a half-baked community organizer from Chicago, an admirable vocation; he should have stayed there.

Whatever in this godless world makes the eminently unqualified think they should be President? Why must we all pay for the inadequacies of the few? Half, half, half; half this, half that. Half black, half white, half assed.

It is said a society needs three things to be a Nation—Culture, Law, and an Economy. Well as for the first, don't put it on any recording to Mars; I wouldn't spread it around that we're braggingly proud of such excretion as what passes for modern music. Music; pleasant to the ear, calming to the mind, soothing to the soul. I'd rather have the crabs.

Motion pictures; written, produced, acted and directed by pimply faced juveniles what think filthiness in thought, speech and behavior is a sign of avant garde, literary talent, and who's idea of a great script are twenty-seven indiscriminate car crashes, an unglamorous motley crew of skinny, naked, bulimic looking twits parading across the screen with no apparent connection to even a modestly, thoughtful script, and no less than a couple dozen, or so, bleeding disfigured, bludgeoned torsos, flung in all different directions for dramatic effect, and we wonder why our children have become violently, brutal little freaks with a morbid love of guns and other more powerful and exotic killing implements. We wonder.

Commercial television; sandbox for the ignorant, uneducated, immature, irrelevant and ill informed. Right-wing talk radio; a world of clowns, buffoons, charlatans, mental defectives, and moral degenerates. Televangelism; the debilitating, sickly twin of the just previously mentioned; the WWF, Nascar, the NFL and sports in general, which has become just another dirty little business run by rich, dirty little men who buy sports teams like you'd buy a bicycle, and all of which can be seen to be tethered at the hip.

As for the law, well let's see now, there's one for the rich, one for the poor; one for the corporation, one for the public, and if you should happen to get yourself busted, it soon turns into a spin-off of "let's make a deal" and DNA is uncovering flies in the barn faster than a truckload of DDT can snuff them out. Yes, Virginia; everything's for sale.

The economy? Of course; free enterprise; free for him, enterprise for you. Tax breaks for the rich, sixty-hour work weeks for you; socialism for the rich, capitalism for the poor, and you can sell a tank easier than you can sell a washing machine, and we're all just so proud of it, we export it every chance we get, by hook or by crook; it's euphemistically called "Globalization." It used to be called Imperialism. Like the Titanic, this ship is headed for an iceberg, and, like the Titanic—it-will-not-miss-it.

And there you have it, Buck. From the founders to the flounderers, from Grant to Westmoreland, from Teddy to Ronny, from Murrow to Hannity, from Eleanor to Sarah, from the Bronte sisters to the Pigeon sisters—Susan and Olympia, the two klucks up in Maine.

America; not very pretty, is it? And not what you get in the history books either, but then, I never did learn to white-wash a barn, but there it is. It never ends. IT—NEVER—ENDS.

* * *

The days came, the days went. I made my acquaintances; I 'did my thing.' Heaven and hell, howsoever, it was all getting to be a bloody bore. Had I not already been, I would have wished to be dead.

But was I? It came to be, ever so slowly but surely, a grievous lot to languish in everlasting boredom, to pick my way through each timeless day, with no thought of the morrow, or sense of the past. Not even the momentary lapses into sexual ecstasy, for which I was unspeakably grateful, could countermand the slowly creeping ennui.

The problem was, simply: life, consciousness, another time, another place, but all the same in the end. There was no escape from the incessant erosion of sameness. Something different, always the same.

Aye, and now I know: hell, it was, and will forever be. This infernal continuance of thought and being, seemingly changing, but never so, nauseating in its enormity, fatiguing, irksome, dull, insipid, and downright fatuous. To dream the dream of dreams: death, death, death. A beauteous thought, exquisite and never to be. Death, resonating; the mightiest fear in the temporal life, the grandest delight in the after. But the after is forever, and death is never.

Life, to live on, and on, and on, it is too much; sweet Jesus of Nazareth, where art thou now? I need not grace, nor salvation, nor the pontifical blessings of the pompous. I need the soft, sweet, incendiary hand of extinction. Is it too much to ask, this, my final prayer? I ask not for fame, and riches, and everlasting glory, or perpetual feasting, or power, or omniscience and all its encumbrances. I ask only for eternal rest. The spirit also tires. A dagger through the heart, if you please.

Alas, it was not to be. The chilling, steely blade for which I so yearned, bestowed a rubber tip.

How long I remained in the land of the forsaken I know not, for one takes small note of things everlasting.

Time is a depthless ocean, and, my condition, pleased to say, subsided in due course. Grief, and all notions and particulars thereof, abated. How alike all things everywhere.

Eventually, it was brought to my attention, that one, even here, can request small favors of the great white father, he gorging in every mythical opportunity to exercise his providential right.

Quick as a flash, like dapper and dancer, I flew to the roost, and waited my turn. He, of the magical powers, soon chose my number, and, with much fanfare ado, a sizable angelic escort floating effortlessly on gossamer wings while tooting 'hail to the chief' on golden flutes led me into the great imperial vault.

Immediately therein, trumpets blared, flags waved, and drums rolled. I was surprised not to see the hokey, Dallas cowgirl's somewhere in the arena swinging their fluffy, bouncy, over used tails in tune with the usual, attendant, raucous, juvenile ditty of the moment, of which there are many and seemingly endless variations.

"Y-a-a-a-y-s?" the almighty one asked with the greatest austerity. Awed, for the moment, I did not readily respond.

Scrutinizing the landscape for burning bushes and grey puffs of smoke, I saw none. What? No chimes? Symbols? Clanging bells? Was that the extent of it, that glaring display of ostentation at the entrance? What a comedown; his most exalted eminence merely a Babbitt in princes' raiment, slovenly chamber of commerce tastes. Let me rid myself of this yoke.

Boldly did I step forward enunciating my request. "Would it be possible, your highness," I asked warily, "to return to earth once again?"

Taken aback, he asked, in turn, "Earth? Earth?" wondering, no doubt, what new form of madness was upon us, and why anyone, (in whatever frame of mind) would want to return to the land of 'night and fog' once more.

Nevertheless, he assented without question. "And would it also be possible to return as a rich, white, Episcopalian Republican?" I now asked breathlessly, becoming giddy at the prospects of my chances. I wasn't stupid; if I was going to go back, it would have to be in a crib in Palm Springs. I felt like one of those half-witted professor's, joyously stupefacted at the news that the federal government, in all its mundane wisdom, had just granted the furry-faced clod, a grant of substantial proportions to study the mating call of the Canada goose, to determine its effects on the sex habits of the Alaska King Crab.

"Anything you like," was the heartening reply. This was too good to be true. I was tempted to ask for more, but for what? What more could one ask? The white slavery ring out of Vegas, a 500 station televangelist empire from Dusty Trails, Oklahoma, ten-percent of the NASDAQ? Why be greedy; I had enough. Better than a hot-hand at a crap-shoot, I decided to take my gains and run.

Forthwith was I shipped back to the land of 'est and pests.'

However, it seems the great and mighty one has also in his voluminous bag of tricks, a fiendish sense of humor, or an errant sense of direction, for, as per request, he did indeed grant my wish for another life, and yes, I was a rich Republican in good standing with the party, and yes, also, a card carrying Episcopalian, and indeed was as pure and white as the driven snow, but not in S-I-B-E-R-I-A!! A GOLDWATER REPUBLICAN IN Siberia!!!

And so, my friends, unceremoniously was I dumped into the land of the white fluff.

Ah, it is all such a cruel hoax, from birth, to death, and beyond, and back. And if that were not enough, I WAS WEARING A SKIRT!! Either I was a chick, or a transvestite, neither of which appealed to my sense of decorum, or previous inclinations.

Good heavens. Now I'll have to start from scratch all over again, for what did I know about being a 'Betty.' I can't even cross my legs without slipping on the floor. Candy, to me, was a bountiful, butted chickadee, broad was my favorite, derogatory word, and here I was swaddled in a straw hut, in a babushka, in 30 below weather.

So, and if, one day, you Greengo's, in a paroxysm of Christian virtue and moral probity, should decide to invade this frost-bitten terminus, this land of the long, dark winter, please!! Please!! Don't shoot. It may be one of you.

Finni . . . . .?